RAND TURNED TO THE LOVELY LASS, PERUSING HER SLOWLY FROM HEAD TO TOE.

"You look all grown up to me."

"Do I?" Miriel asked coyly.

"Oh, aye," he murmured with a lazy grin. "You feel like a woman." He raised her hand and rubbed it gently against his cheek. "And you definitely taste like a woman." He lowered his gaze to her mouth, then dipped his head until his breath caressed her jaw. "Even if you spy on people like a naughty child."

He nipped at her lips once, twice, then engaged her fully. Miriel eagerly responded, opening her mouth for him, tilting her head, spreading her fingers across his chest. Encouraged by her enthusiasm, Rand wrapped an arm around her shoulders and pulled her closer...

The next thing he knew, the earth was yanked out from under him, and he was laid out flat on his back.

REVIEWS FOR SARAH MCKERRIGAN'S *LADY DANGER*

"Four stars! Will heat the room and melt any woman's heart. You couldn't ask for much more."
—*RomanceReaderAtHeart.com*

"A fine historical tale."
—Harriet Klausner, *Midwest Book Review*

more . . .

P9-DCC-436

"Entrancing…a fantastic medieval read."
—*MyShelf.com*

"A delight…A good story, well told."
—*RomanceReviewsMag.com*

"A very engaging story…McKerrigan is a writer to keep an eye on."
—*TheRomanceReader.com*

"Well-researched and with interesting characters, *Lady Danger* is a very enjoyable read."
—*RomRevToday.com*

"An adventure…very entertaining and well worth the read."
—*RoundTableReviews.com*

"Captivating! Passionate! Powerful! McKerrigan writes of a Scotland she knows and loves."
—*Noveltalk.com*

"Terrific! Bursting with action and sensuality…*Lady Danger* [is] a keeper that will definitely be reread."
—*JoyfullyReviewed.com*

For Kay...

**KNIGHT'S
PRIZE**

May all of your
adventures have
happy endings!

Sarah
McKerrigan

10/10/09

Also by Sarah McKerrigan

Lady Danger
Captive Heart

ATTENTION: CORPORATIONS AND ORGANIZATIONS:
Most WARNER books are available at quantity discounts
with bulk purchase for educational, business, or sales
promotional use. For information, please call or write:

Special Markets Department, Warner Books, Inc.,
237 Park Avenue, New York, NY 10169
Telephone: 1-800-222-6747 Fax: 1-800-477-5925

KNIGHT'S PRIZE

SARAH McKERRIGAN

WARNER

FOREVER

NEW YORK   BOSTON

This book is a work of fiction. Names, characters, places, and incidents are the product of the author's imagination or are used fictitiously. Any resemblance to actual events, locales, or persons, living or dead, is coincidental.

If you purchase this book without a cover you should be aware that this book may have been stolen property and reported as "unsold and destroyed" to the publisher. In such case neither the author nor the publisher has received any payment for this "stripped book."

Copyright © 2007 by Glynnis Campbell
All rights reserved. Except as permitted under the U.S. Copyright Act of 1976, no part of this publication may be reproduced, distributed, or transmitted in any form or by any means, or stored in a database or retrieval system, without the prior written permission of the publisher.

Warner Forever is an imprint of Warner Books, Inc.

Warner Forever is a trademark of Time Warner Inc. or an affiliated company. Used under license by Hachette Book Group USA, which is not affiliated with Time Warner Inc.

Cover design by Diane Luger
Cover illustration by Craig White
Book design by Giorgetta Bell McRee

Warner Forever
Hachette Book Group USA
237 Park Avenue
New York, NY 10169
Visit our Web site at www.HachetteBookGroupUSA.com.

Printed in the United States of America

First Printing: April 2007

10 9 8 7 6 5 4 3 2 1

For
my son Dylan . . .
who shares with me a love of swords,
the Super Bowl,
the guilty pleasure of action movies,
and who convinced me that what romance novels
really needed were great fight choreography
and 'splosions.

Special thanks to
Melanie, Helen, and Lori,
who kept my chin up.

Acknowledgments

A heartfelt thanks to . . .
"America," Kathy Baker, Brynna Campbell,
Dick Campbell, Richard Campbell, Carol Carter,
Lucele Coutts, Lynette Gubler, Karen Kay,
Heath Ledger, Natalie Portman, Lauren Royal,
Betty and Earl Talken, Shirley Talken;
my elite sales force—"Sarah's Champions":
Ana Isabel Arconada, Terra Codack,
Mariah Kathleen Crawford, Joelle Deveza, Diane Dunn,
Marguerite Hembree, Etta Miller, Lois J. Miller,
Heather M. Riley, Sandra M. Schaeffer,
Leslie Thompson, Jodi Villanueva;
and everyone who plays "Savage."

You can become one of "Sarah's Champions" at
www.sarahmckerrigan.com.

Chapter 1

Autumn
1136

H<small>E IS COMING.</small>"

Miriel's eyes widened, and she stumbled out of her last *taijiquan* posture. She glanced anxiously about the chamber. "Who?"

She was always on guard now. Since the Knights of Cameliard had insinuated themselves into the household of Rivenloch Castle, she never knew when a Norman warrior might barge into her bedchamber.

"The Night," Sung Li replied mysteriously, continuing with the measured *taijiquan* poses, moving with a youthful grace that belied the wrinkled face and long snowy braid, shifting slowly from left foot to right, then arcing like a bow being drawn.

But Miriel's tranquillity of a moment before was irreparably shattered. "*What* knight?" she hissed.

Sung Li spoke serenely. "The Night that comes to swallow The Shadow."

Miriel scowled, her tense shoulders relaxing. So Sung

Li was only being intentionally obtuse again. The old servant's prophecies were usually accurate, but sometimes Miriel's wise and wizened companion seemed impossibly inscrutable. And inevitably chose the most unfortunate times to deliver the darkest omens.

Shivering out her rattled nerves, Miriel resumed her exercises, shadowing Sung Li in their daily ritual. Beyond and below the open shutters of the keep, the first slender spears of sunlight pierced through the Scots woods.

But now that Sung Li had cast a stone into her pool of calm, rippling her meditative poise, Miriel's movements grew awkward.

What did that mean—the night that comes to swallow the shadow? A cloudy evening? A harsh winter? Another invasion by the English? Or could it mean something more . . . personal?

Lost in thought, Miriel wobbled and wavered and lost her balance, coming down hard on one bare foot.

"Curse it all!" She crossed her arms, blowing a stray tendril of dark hair out of her eyes. "How can I concentrate when you deliver such ominous tidings?"

Sung Li broke from the pose long enough to turn an amused, smug look upon her. "A true Master would not be distracted, not even by—"

"A dragon breathing its fiery breath upon his head," Miriel finished in a mutter. "I know. But you could have saved it for later."

Sung Li finished the last extended movement, bowed respectfully toward the sun, then faced Miriel with a solemn expression. "Later is too late. The Night is coming *soon.*"

A slip of a breeze drifted through the window just then,

bringing in the crisp October air. But the preternatural chill that shuddered Miriel's bones had naught to do with the season. Night was coming soon? 'Twas scarcely dawn.

Their gazes met, and Miriel thought she'd never seen her *xiansheng,* her teacher, look so grave. 'Twas as if those ancient black eyes bored into her soul, seeking out her weaknesses, weighing her worth.

Sung Li at last took hold of Miriel's forearm in a surprisingly firm grip. "You must be strong. And brave. And clever."

Miriel slowly nodded. She didn't always understand Sung Li, who spoke often in riddles, but there was no question the warning was serious.

Then Sung Li released her abruptly and, as if naught had happened, resumed the role of Miriel's maidservant, donning a roughspun kirtle over the loose hemp garments worn for *taijiquan,* pulling on stockings and slippers, then selecting a deep azure surcoat for Miriel from the great pine chest at the foot of the bed.

Miriel frowned, slithering into the soft wool gown while Sung Li dutifully turned away. They'd kept many secrets, the two of them, since the day five years ago, when Miriel had deigned to purchase, along with *nunchakus* and a pair of *sais* from the Orient, a Chinese servant from a traveling merchant.

Sung Li had *insisted* on being purchased. 'Twas Destiny, the curious peasant had sagely proclaimed. And at thirteen summers old, Miriel wasn't about to argue with Destiny.

Her father, Lord Gellir, had not approved, nor had her older sisters, Deirdre and Helena. For a long while, the denizens of Rivenloch turned disparaging Scots glares upon the wee foreigner with the strange eyes and impertinent tongue.

But they'd grown accustomed to Sung Li now, and no one questioned the presence of the crone of a maidservant who clung as tightly to Miriel as a duckling to its mother.

Of course, if they'd known that the wee old woman was in sooth a wee old man, if they'd known that he devoted most of his hours with Miriel teaching her the fine art of Chinese warfare, and if they'd suspected that under his tutelage, Miriel had blossomed from a timid child into a fierce combatant to rival her warrior sisters, they might have taken exception.

But as Sung Li was fond of saying, The greatest weapon is the one no one knows you possess. Certainly no one suspected meek, innocent, docile Miriel of possessing the skills to kill a man.

"Hmph." Sung Li was staring out the window, his narrow white brows furrowed.

"Hmph, what?" Miriel fastened the silver girdle at her hips and wiggled her feet into her leather slippers.

"A knight arrives."

Miriel tensed instantly. "The Night that comes to swallow The Shadow?"

Knees bent, arms raised, she was ready to fight this very moment, whether against a human foe or the dark forces of nature.

Sung Li turned on her with an annoyed scowl, then shook his head. "You are like a child today, starting at your own shadow." He left the window and began tidying the chamber, clucking his tongue. "It is only a common knight."

Miriel lowered her hands and fired a scathing glare at

the old man, a glare wasted on his back. A child. She was weary of being called a child. By Sung Li. By her father. By her sisters. She was *not* a child. She was a woman full grown.

With a sniff of disdain, she moved to the window to peer out for herself. There *was* a knight on horseback cresting the rise above Rivenloch. He was in full battle dress, chain mail and surcoat, a wise choice, since a stranger alone could make fast foes in the wilds of Scotland. As he rode down the hill toward the castle, the silver helm beneath his arm caught the light of dawn, glinting like fire.

She couldn't make out the crest upon his brown tabard or see him clearly, not with the shaggy mane of chestnut hair that obscured his face and reached almost to his shoulders.

"Who do you suppose—" She looked around to Sung Li, but the elusive servant was already gone, probably on his way to filch the best bread from the kitchen for his mistress's breakfast before any of those ravenous Normans could take it.

Miriel returned to the window. Mayhap the knight was a guest arriving early for Helena's wedding. He paused then, halfway down the rise, to scan his surroundings. As his gaze swept across the castle, Miriel felt an uncharacteristic shiver of trepidation skitter up her spine. She ducked reflexively behind a shutter, out of sight.

After a moment, scolding herself for her cowardice, she peered out again. The knight had changed course. He now reined his mount into the dense forest that surrounded Rivenloch.

Miriel frowned. 'Twas most irregular. Why would a strange knight travel all the way to the remote keep of

Rivenloch, only to swerve at the last moment into the woods?

By the Saints, she intended to find out. With Deirdre and Helena distracted by their Norman lovers, someone had to keep an eye on the castle defenses.

Her sisters believed that Miriel had sealed up the secret exit from the castle, the one at the back of her workroom beneath the keep, after Rivenloch's soldiers had made use of the tunnel to defeat the attacking English army last spring.

But Miriel had done no such thing. That passageway was too useful to close off. After all, 'twas the only way Miriel could leave the keep without being under the constant scrutiny of her overprotective siblings.

So she'd hung a tapestry over the entrance, pushed her desk against the opening, and piled up books of accounts to obscure the passage. 'Twas little trouble to move them out of the way whenever she needed to escape.

As she did now.

'Twas yet early morn. Later, Helena would need her to help with wedding preparations. But Miriel could spy upon the stranger in the woods for a bit and steal back to the castle before anyone was the wiser.

She smiled grimly to herself. 'Twas clandestine adventures like these that relieved her of both the boredom of managing the castle accounts and the oppression of playing the helpless little sister of the Warrior Maids of Rivenloch.

Rand la Nuit sensed he was no longer alone in the forest. 'Twasn't that the intruder made a sound or exuded a scent or even cast a shadow. But years of training as a mercenary had honed Rand's senses to a keen edge. By the faint prickling at the back of his neck, he felt sure he was being watched.

He casually eased one hand over the pommel of his sword and moved to the far side of his horse, placing the beast between him and where he guessed the intruder to be. Then, hunkering down as if to check the horse's girth, he peered beneath the beast's belly, scouring the bushes for some trace of a trespasser.

Aside from a few wraiths of steam chased from the wet oak trunks by the warm glare of the rising sun, the misty copse was silent. Branches of lush cedar drooped in slumber. Thick ferns stood like quiet sentinels. Not a beetle stirred the leaf fall.

He frowned. Mayhap 'twas an owl late to bed. Or mayhap some lost spirit haunted the Borders woods. Or, he thought, patting his horse's flank and rising again, mayhap 'twas his imagination, and he was only growing weary of the hunt, like an old hound whose sense of smell was failing.

Still, he'd always trusted his instincts. Just because he couldn't locate the threat at this moment didn't mean it wasn't there. He'd have to keep one eye on his surroundings and one hand on his blade as he searched the woods.

He didn't know exactly what he was looking for yet. All he'd been told when the Lord of Morbroch hired him was that the outlaw he sought was a man who worked alone, an elusive thief who roamed the forests of Rivenloch.

The task had seemed simple enough at first. In Rand's experience, robbers were seldom clever. 'Twould be an easy matter to locate the fellow's hideaway, take him by force, and convey him to Morbroch for judgment.

But when Rand learned how much the lord and several of his neighboring barons were willing to pay him to catch the thief who had lightened their purses, he began to wonder if 'twas not so simple an undertaking after all.

Apparently, the denizens of Rivenloch didn't mind their local outlaw. To them, he was but the subject of fireside tales and jongleur's songs. Even knowing the scoundrel had relieved numerous traveling noblemen of a vast quantity of silver, they refused to expend any effort to capture the man. Nor did they welcome the interference of outsiders.

Thus Rand would have to work in secret beneath the noses of one of the most formidable forces in Britain, the Knights of Cameliard. The Norman knights had come last spring to take command of the Scots castle, and already they'd routed a huge force of rogue English lords who'd tried to lay siege to the keep. If they wished, they could easily prevent one paltry mercenary from capturing their outlaw.

So Rand would have to be clever.

He needed three things: a believable pretext for coming to Rivenloch, a reason to linger there, and access to the intimate workings of the keep. The Lord of Morbroch had offered him a deception that provided him with all three.

Of course, if he could catch the robber at once, there would be no need for deception.

He scanned the path again for signs of inhabitation—footprints, discarded bones from a meal, remnants of a fire. The sooner he could find some clue as to the thief's whereabouts, the sooner he could quit this place and collect his reward. But all he sensed as his gaze ranged the woods was that eerie feeling that he was being watched.

He'd been searching for some time when his ear caught a new sound intruding upon the silence of the forest. Footsteps.

'Twas not the stealthy passage of a thief he heard, but the purposeful approach of a pair of men.

He'd expected as much. Rivenloch's guards had likely spotted him as he'd approached the castle, and now they'd come to investigate the stranger lurking in their woods. They'd find him in another few moments.

He needed to act quickly. He stepped to the side of the path and casually began to whistle. Hefting his chain mail, he unlaced his braies. Then he swiftly yanked them down to relieve himself upon a bush.

A sudden loud gasp sounded from the branches high above him, his heart bolted, his whistle suddenly turned to air, and he almost missed the bush.

God's eyes! Someone *was* there. Nearly on top of him.

And, he realized in wonder, by the sound of the gasp, that someone was distinctly female.

But the shrubbery along the path was already parting to make way for the approaching men. There was no time to confront the naughty spy hiding in the tree.

"Wicked lass," he softly chided, casting an amused grin up toward the concealing foliage.

Then, shaking his head, he resumed whistling and returned unabashedly to his task. The way he looked at it, if the sight of a man pissing offended the maid, she deserved as much for her mischief.

Miriel was appalled. Not by the man's rude display, though 'twas most audacious and disconcerting. But by the way she'd gasped.

For years she'd ranged these woods, as silent as mist, as invisible as air. Thanks to Sung Li's guidance, she knew how to make herself imperceptible, even to the keen-eyed owls that inhabited the trees. She could flit from branch to branch as nimbly as a squirrel and blend seamlessly into the foliage.

How the stranger had startled such a loud gasp from her, she didn't know. True, she'd never seen *that* part of a man before, but 'twas not so much different than she'd imagined.

Worse, she'd almost caught her breath again when he'd peered up in her direction with that smug grin. Not because he'd discovered her presence, but because his handsome face—that strong jaw, those curving lips, the unruly hair, the perplexed furrow between his brows, and those dark, sparkling eyes—literally took her breath away.

"Good morn!" Sir Rauve's booming voice almost toppled her out of her perch. She watched as the giant black-bearded Knight of Cameliard, dogged by young Sir Kenneth, tromped forward, one cautious hand on the hilt of his sheathed sword.

"Good morn!" the stranger called back cheerfully. His voice was rich and warm, like honey mead. "And pardon me," he apologized, making a show of hauling up his trews. "Just taking care of a bit of business."

Sir Rauve nodded, wasting no time and mincing no words. "And what type of business do you have at Rivenloch, sir?"

The man grinned companionably. By the Saints, Miriel thought, his smile was absolutely stunning, wide and bright, complete with endearing dimples. "That depends on who is asking."

Rauve drew himself up to his impressive height. "Sir

Rauve of Rivenloch, Knight of Cameliard, defender of this keep."

"Sir Rauve." The stranger put his hand forth in greeting. "I am Sir Rand of Morbroch."

Morbroch. Miriel knew that name.

When Sir Rauve only eyed him with suspicion, he added hopefully, "You might remember me from the tournament last month?"

Miriel frowned. The Lord of Morbroch had attended the tournament at Rivenloch with a half dozen knights. She recognized the crest on the man's tabard now, a boar's head on a ground of sable. But she didn't recall Sir Rand. And his was a face she wouldn't have easily forgotten.

At Rauve's lack of response, Sir Rand withdrew his hand and lowered his eyes with a sigh. "Then again, perchance not. I was knocked witless in the melee. Didn't recover for two days."

Miriel caught her lip beneath her teeth. That might be true. Someone was always getting knocked witless in a melee.

But Rauve was not convinced. "You've not answered my question."

"Why am I here?" Rand's brows wrinkled in charming discomfiture as he scratched at his temple. "'Tis a matter of some... delicacy. I'd rather not say."

Rauve crossed his beefy arms over his chest. "And I'd rather not let you pass."

"I see." Rand took a deep breath and let it out in a bracing rush.

In that instant, Miriel saw his hand drift subtly yet purposefully toward the hilt of his sword. By the wink of danger in his eyes, she suddenly feared he was about to do something rash, like single-handedly challenge Rauve and Kenneth to battle.

But at the last moment, he hooked his thumb harmlessly into his leather sword belt and flashed them a sheepish grin. "If you must know then, sir...I've come...courting."

Miriel raised a brow. Courting? Then why had he been foraging through the leaves as if he were tracking prey?

"Courting?" Young Kenneth made a moue of displeasure, as if he'd said he'd come to swallow live eels.

Rauve only grunted.

"Aye." Sir Rand let out a long, lovesick sigh that would curdle honey. "You see, I fear one of Rivenloch's bright angels has stolen my heart."

Miriel scowled. If there was one thing she despised, 'twas sappy proclamations of love. Especially when they were full of deceit. As this one was. Rand might have said the words, but she could tell by the amused glimmer in his eyes that he meant none of them.

But, of course, the guards didn't know the difference. Men could never smell deception the way a woman could.

"One of Rivenloch's angels?" Rauve growled, jutting out his bearded chin. "Well, it had better not be Lucy."

Both Miriel's brows shot up. Lucy? This was a surprise. Was the bearish Sir Rauve admitting a fondness for saucy Lucy Campbell?

Kenneth issued his own warning. "And if you've come for Lady Helena, 'tis too late. She's to wed in two days."

"Fear not," Rand said with a lighthearted chuckle. "'Tis neither, good sirs."

When the varlet pressed a hand to his chest as if to still

the beating of his beguiled heart, Miriel couldn't resist rolling her eyes. Who was this alleged ladylove then? The widow Margaret Duncan? Joan Atwater? Young Katie Simms?

"I fear my hapless heart has been claimed," he gushed, "by none other than the youngest daughter of Rivenloch…"

Miriel almost choked on her surprise.

Her?

He'd come for *her*?

How could that be? God's blood, she didn't even know the man.

Apparently, he didn't know *her* either. He finished on a dramatic sigh of pure adoration. "Lady Mirabel."

Chapter 2

As soon as he breathed the name, Rand sensed something was wrong. The long silence was telling.

"You mean Miriel?" the younger knight asked.

Rand blinked, his composure thrown. Satan's ballocks! How could he have gotten the wench's name wrong? "Aye, Miriel." He furrowed his brows in confusion. "Is that not what I said?" He smiled in chagrin. "I fear I'm a bit nervous."

"As you should be," Rauve said. "You *have* heard of the Warrior Maids of Rivenloch?"

"Warrior Maids?" Disquiet tingled at the base of his skull. Who the hell were the Warrior Maids? He was beginning to suspect there were details about this mission that Morbroch had omitted, details that were going to make his generous reward seem like a pittance by the time he was done. "Oh, aye, certainly," he bluffed. "Who has not?"

The younger knight's eyes twinkled. "I'll give him two hours," he said to Rauve.

"With Helena's warm welcome?" Rauve shook his head. "One hour."

Rand glanced from one man to the other. What the Devil were they talking about?

"Come along then," Rauve said. "If you hurry, you can be on the road back to Morbroch before noon."

"Back? But I've only..."

The guards exchanged knowing smirks before they turned to go, and Rand fought the urge to knock their insolent heads together. He supposed 'twas his own fault. He'd chosen to play the lovesick lad. Now he'd become the butt of their jest.

"I hope you're good with a blade," the young knight called over his shoulder, grinning.

Rand smiled back grimly. Good with a blade? He could have drawn his sword and run the lad through before that mocking grin left his face. But experience had taught him 'twas wise to keep one's best weapons hidden until they were necessary.

He wondered how soon his blade *would* be needed. Already this undertaking was proving troublesome. He'd hoped to spend a few days at Rivenloch, courting the lady for appearance's sake, a few more hunting the thief, and have his prey well in hand by the end of the week so he could return to collect the rest of his pay.

What he *didn't* want were complications. Already, the idea of leading an innocent maid down the path of courtship when he had no intention of wedding her left a sour taste in his mouth. Not to mention the fact that he'd be spending a great deal of time with a lass about whom he knew naught.

Morbroch had assured him that the damsel was comely

and sweet and, most important, malleable, that she'd easily play into his deception. But now he wasn't sure he entirely trusted Morbroch.

Retrieving his mount's reins, he clucked to urge the animal forward.

As far as he knew, Miriam might be a sharp-tongued shrew. Or a pouting child. Or an old crone with rotting teeth and shriveled breasts. He shuddered inwardly.

He'd gone a good five yards when he suddenly remembered the wench in the tree. He turned back, scanning the heavy-laden cedar branches overhead, still unable to see anyone amid the thick green. But he could sense her presence.

He grinned. "Farewell, imp," he called softly, blowing her a kiss. Then he turned to face whatever fate awaited him at Rivenloch Castle.

The moment he'd called her Mirabel, Miriel's eyes had flattened with displeasure. If the knave was going to pretend infatuation, he could at least have the decency to get her name right.

Yet despite her irritation, another part of her was intrigued. Numerous men in the past year had expressed an interest in Miriel, but none had dared request to court her. Between Sung Li guarding her like a mother hen and her sisters greeting any suitors with a blade, men tended to keep their distance. Only Pagan Cameliard had gone so far as to offer marriage, albeit a marriage of political convenience, and even that had been usurped by Deirdre, who was now happily wed to him and plump with his babe.

Her sisters would doubtless have this prospect slinking

back to Morbroch with his tail betwixt his legs quicker than she could say, pleased to meet you.

She couldn't let that happen. Sir Rand had been up to some mischief here in the woods, and she needed to know his true intentions.

Still, 'twas a shame, she thought as she leaned her cheek against the soft moss covering the cedar, watching the three men below converse. He *was* rather handsome. His shoulders were broad, his hips narrow, and he looked nearly as tall as Rauve. Between his brilliant smile, his perplexed brows, and his adorable dimples, he was surely the most attractive man she'd ever seen. His eyes sparkled like dark topaz. His voice was at once soothing and arousing. And his tousled chestnut hair seemed to beg for the untangling touch of her fingers.

How terrible would it be, she mused with a guilty blush, to play along with his overtures, to overlook the likelihood that he had ulterior motives, and let him court her anyway? Let him put his broad hands upon her waist… Let him press gentle kisses upon her mouth and whisper endearments in her ear… Let him unsheathe that dagger in his trews again and…

In the next moment, she was wrenched back to her senses. The men were leaving. But as they turned down the path, and the horse's tail flipped in farewell, Rand paused, angling his head to look directly up at her. Of course, he couldn't quite see her through the thick cedar boughs. But the impact of his gaze made a queer shiver go through her. And when he blew her a kiss, she almost felt the warmth of his breath upon her lips.

The instant they were out of sight, she clambered down and raced back through the woods the way she'd come.

Mayhap Sir Rand of Morbroch *was* a knave and a varlet and a cad. Mayhap he was entirely unfit and unqualified as a suitor. But 'twas not for her sisters to decide. Or her father. Or her *xiansheng*.

Besides, the man was definitely up to some mischief. If it meant she had to pretend to be receptive to his advances to discover the nature of that mischief, then by the Saints, she'd do it. For the good of Rivenloch.

When she finally burst from the passageway into her workroom, her heart pounding from the thrill of the chase, she was so distracted, she nearly crashed into her servant.

"Oh!" She started guiltily. "Sung Li."

"Breakfast." He thrust a platter of bread and cheese at her.

"I'll eat it later." She tried to skirt around the old man, but he subtly blocked her way.

"You must eat now, keep up your strength."

Miriel pursed her lips. Why did everyone think they could issue commands to her, even her servant? "I have no time, Sung Li."

One of his white brows arched up in silent accusation. "Yet you have time to take a walk in the woods."

Miriel scowled in exasperation. "Fine." She snatched up the cheese, bit off a hunk, then shoved a chunk of bread into her mouth, so large she could barely talk. "Satisfied?"

Sung Li's eyes narrowed to slits. "You are a foolish, foolish child."

With a growl of anger, she pushed past Sung Li and opened the door of the workroom.

"Once and for all," she declared, her words muffled by the wad of bread, "I am not a child!"

Then she slammed the door behind her.

* * *

Rand stood in the middle of Rivenloch's enormous practice field with his arms crossed self-consciously over his chest. He'd drawn the glances of many a wench in his two dozen years, but none to match the scrutiny to which he was now subjected.

So this was Helena, Muriel's sister. She was a comely lass, with her emerald eyes, wild tresses, and generous breasts. Were it not for the armor and the menacing sword buckled about her hips, not to mention the bridegroom she had waiting somewhere, she might have been dangerously tempting.

At the moment, however, all he could think about was the fact she was circling him like a stable master shopping for a horse, narrowing her eyes at his chest, staring at his legs, nodding in satisfaction, clucking her tongue in disfavor. He half expected her to pry open his mouth and take a good look at his teeth.

"So you've come to court Miriel?" she asked, stopping in front of him and crossing her arms in challenge.

Miriel. Not Muriel. Or Miriam. Or Mirabel. By the Saints, he *had* to remember the lass's name. "Aye, with your leave."

Since Lord Gellir's wits had grown feeble, Miriel's suitors were apparently required to seek the approval of the two older sisters.

"And do you think you can protect her?"

"Protect her?"

"Can you fight?"

He stifled a smile. He'd been a mercenary for six years. Of course he could fight. "If need be."

Then in one fluid movement, she drew her sword and faced him. "Prove it."

His arms fell out of their fold. Surely she wasn't serious. He furrowed his brow. Mayhap, he thought, 'twas a trick.

"Let's see what you've got," she urged.

He glanced toward the spectators. Sir Rauve and his companion were there, a couple of other knights, a wee lad sucking his thumb, and a trio of maidservants. None of them looked surprised by Helena's challenge.

"My lady, I don't think—"

"Come on, fight me." She poked his chest with the point of her sword.

He retreated a step. God's blood! She *was* serious.

"With all due respect, my lady, I cannot—"

"Cannot what? Protect Miriel? Then you may not court her."

"Of course I can protect her, but—"

"Then prove it." Reaching across with her left hand, she tugged his sword from its sheath. "Show me." She handed him the weapon, hilt first.

He took the sword, but refused to wield it. "My lady, 'tis not a matter of—"

Her sword slashed toward him so swiftly that 'twas all he could do to block the blow with his own blade. Reeling in astonishment, he almost missed deflecting her second strike as well. He stepped back, but she followed, her weapon swinging with such unexpected speed that he could scarcely keep it from biting him.

This couldn't be happening, he marveled. He couldn't be sparring with a lady. 'Twas unseemly. And undignified. And unchivalrous.

Naturally he could have beat her soundly. He was far more powerful than she and surely far more experienced, no matter how quickly she moved. But he dared not unleash the full measure of his strength.

"My lady, I beg you, stop!"

She jabbed him in the shoulder. "What? No ballocks?" she taunted.

"God's breath! I will not fight with a woman."

"And what if that woman means to kill you?"

Her eyes glinted like green fire, and he wondered if she *did* mean to kill him. Perchance that was what Rauve meant when he predicted Rand wouldn't last an hour.

Still, when he'd earned his spurs, he'd sworn to do no harm to a lady. He might be a half-Scots bastard and a lowly mercenary, but he proudly upheld the vows of knighthood.

So, praying he was making the right choice, he cast his sword to the ground in surrender.

"Helena!" came a scream from outside the lists.

He glanced away from Helena's eyes, which had taken on a wicked gleam, and looked toward the source of the outburst. A lovely little lass was rushing across the sward, her unwieldy blue skirts gathered in her fists, her unbound hair streaming out behind her like a dark pennon. Her face was beautiful, as delicate and pale as an apple blossom, but her pretty features were twisted with worry.

"Don't kill him!" she cried, skidding to a stop beside the others at the wattle fence.

Helena called back over her shoulder. "I wasn't going to kill him." One corner of her lip curved up. "I was only going to maim him."

Miriel wasn't about to let Helena slice one hair from Rand's head. "Nay!" She hoisted up her skirts and began scrambling over the wattle fence.

"My lady," Sir Rauve protested, seizing her shoulder, "'tis best you stay out of it."

His patronizing tone tested Miriel's good nature. Nonetheless, she managed to smile sweetly at his restraining fist as she bit out, "Unhand me, you great oaf."

His black eyes widened in surprise, and he let her go at once.

As she rushed across the field, 'twas all Miriel could do to keep her temper in check. Curse it all! She'd had enough of being treated like a helpless babe. It had been *she* who'd saved Rivenloch from the English, after all. It had been *her* secret passageway. Her weapons. And her genius. Even if no one knew it. She was not an infant to be coddled and swaddled in a smothering mantle. Especially not by a sister only a few years older than she.

Helena was going to ruin everything.

As Miriel drew near, her sister sighed, her gaze softening in condescension. "Silly lass, I was only going to teach him a lesson."

Mayhap 'twas the years of being silent when Miriel wanted to scream. Or pretending she was helpless when she could easily overcome men twice her size. Or standing in the long shadow of her illustrious sisters. Whatever the reason, against all Sung Li's training in self-control, counter to everything she knew about the importance of serenity, contrary to her usual complacent behavior, when Miriel felt the blood simmer in her veins, she acted on pure impulse.

With a great heave of rage, she shoved Helena away.

Surprise made Helena stagger backward, but her warrior instincts were strong. Out of habit, she swept the point of her sword to Miriel's throat, eliciting a huge gasp from the onlookers at the fence, who'd never seen anyone brandish a weapon at meek Miriel.

Equally stunning was the speed with which a second blade knocked Helena's aside.

'Twas Rand's dagger that did the deed, and both Miriel and Helena swiveled their heads toward him in awe.

The exchange happened so fast, Miriel hardly knew what to say. And poor Rand, his brow creased with confusion and distaste and amazement, stood suffering in indecision, his fingers clenching reflexively around the dagger handle.

Helena's wonder quickly turned to disgust. She silently fumed, her pride doubtless stinging from the fact that Rand had gained the upper hand. Her humiliation was made complete when Rauve called out from the fence, "Do you require assistance, my lady?"

"Nay!" she snapped. Then she muttered to Miriel, "Now see what you've done? Why did you come between us?"

Miriel's jaw dropped. That Helena would so readily lay the blame at Miriel's feet only made her more determined to defy her sister once and for all. "Because, you overbearing, meddlesome wench," she snarled, "this is not your affair. 'Tis mine."

The shock on Helena's face was priceless.

Before she could lose her nerve, Miriel turned to Rand, who looked as bewildered as a fox cornered by a pair of mad hens. Tossing her hair over her shoulder, she reached forward, snagged him by the tabard, and hauled him toward her. Then she planted a kiss hard on his mouth.

Chapter 3

MIRIEL INTENDED TO LAY claim to Rand before Helena could gainsay her.

She didn't anticipate becoming waylaid.

But she'd never kissed a man before. Once she pressed her lips against Rand's, a wave of amazing sensations that completely distracted her from her purpose began to wash over her.

A man's mouth was much warmer and softer than she'd imagined, and he tasted faintly, pleasantly of honey. His ragged sigh of pleasure sent a sultry shiver along her flesh.

Curiosity compelled her to tilt her head, deepening the kiss, and as she did, a strange, delightful warmth flooded her body.

"Here now!" someone scolded.

But Miriel was too engaged to pay heed. She felt as if she quenched an unknown, eternal thirst. She drank more and more, happily drowning in the dizzying wake.

"Stop that!" came the irksome protest again.

Rand, unresponsive at first, now returned the kiss, slanting his mouth over hers, and suddenly the current swirled to sweep her away completely. The real world diminished around her as she swam in a languorous pool of feeling.

Gone were the spectators at the fence.

Gone was Helena.

Gone were the tiltyard and the keep and all of Rivenloch.

The only thing left was this kiss.

He parted his mouth as if to taste her, grazing her bottom lip with his tongue and sending a lightning strike of desire through her loins that turned her knees to custard. 'Twas as if her very soul gasped, and the heat fortified her passions even as it melted her bones. She clutched Rand's tabard tighter, no longer to keep him near but to keep herself aright.

Sweet Mary, this was divine. She never wanted this moment to end.

Rand knew, when the dagger fell from his limp fingers, he'd gone too far. He was fast losing control. This was no way to gain the trust of the people of Rivenloch, by ravishing one of their maidens. Especially when he'd claimed to be here to court Lady Meryl... Marion... Mirabel.

But Lord, this wench's kiss was sweet. And wet. And hot. And arousing.

It took all his strength of will to pull back, to break contact. When he did, the hungry glaze over her smoky blue eyes and the inviting curve of her open mouth made him long to assail her again.

But the sharp length of steel that suddenly intruded to separate them brought him back to his senses.

"By Lucifer's ballocks, cease!" Helena commanded for the third time, narrowing suspicious eyes to glance back and forth between them, finally focusing on the lass. "What do you think you're doing? Do you know this man?"

The lass, still swooning from the effect of their kiss, didn't answer at first.

Helena thumped her on the shoulder. "Do you *know* this man?"

The maid blinked the mist from her eyes and raised her chin in defiance. "Aye," she boldly lied.

"How?"

"I met him…" Her voice was rough with desire, soft and ragged. "I met him at the tournament."

Rand was stunned speechless. He'd never seen the maid before in his life. And she didn't have a face he'd easily forget.

"He told me he'd come back for me," she continued, "and as you can see, he has."

A faint breeze could have knocked him over at that moment, and perchance taken Helena as well. Helena stood with her mouth agape as the damsel looped an arm possessively through his and tugged him away.

"Shall we, Rand?"

If Rand's brains hadn't been scrambled by that soul-searing kiss, he might have figured things out before they were halfway across the field. When the truth finally dawned on him, he stopped so abruptly in his tracks that the lass collided with him. "You."

She glanced up at him, her face deceptively sweet, her gaze deceptively wide.

A glimmer of recognition crept into his eyes. "You're the wicked lass from the woods."

She raised innocent brows. "I don't know what you mean."

Wicked *and* deceitful. He chuckled, then bent low to whisper, "How else would you know my name?"

"Why, sir," she murmured back, "I cared for you when you were injured at the tournament. Do you not remember?"

Her expression was perfectly guileless, but of course, she was lying. He'd never come to the tournament.

He fought back a grin. If she could bluff, so could he. "My brain *was* very scrambled," he admitted.

They resumed walking toward the gate, and he smiled, wondering if the little imp made a habit of spying from the trees. Perchance she singled out eligible bachelors so she could pounce on them before any other damsel had an opportunity.

Not that he minded. The lass was beautiful and charming, even if she was a conniving sprite. Indeed, if the woman he'd come to court proved as hostile as her sister Helena, Rand would gladly suffer the attentions of this sprite instead for a few days. He might even take his time hunting for the outlaw if it meant earning more of the damsel's unbridled kisses.

But as they passed the small audience gathered at the fence, Rand began to feel uneasy. Their looks weren't just curious glances, but gape-mouthed, wide-eyed, gasping stares of disbelief.

And suddenly a mortifying possibility wound its way into his thoughts.

This was no ordinary lass. Not by the way she'd stood up to the lady of the castle. And not by the attention she was getting now.

Almost afraid to ask, he tentatively cleared his throat. "Forsooth, my lady, I fear my fall in the melee left my wits quite addled. Will you remind me again of your name?"

Her forgiving smile didn't quite mask the irritation in her eyes. "Of course," she said sweetly. "'Tis Mirabel."

Rand grimaced. He'd walked straight into the little vixen's trap. "Lady Miriel?" he ventured.

"You *do* remember."

He sighed. "'Tis coming back to me now."

"Is it? Well, I hope you won't forget it again if you're to court me."

"By my spurs, I will not," he vowed. Nor would he forget that earthshaking kiss. And now, since she'd given him leave to woo her, he looked forward to many more. Indeed, this mission might turn out far less unpleasant than he'd expected.

Miriel's heart was pounding. Not from the heady thrill of standing up to Helena. Not because she'd shocked the castle folk by walking past with a strange man upon her arm. Nay, her blood pumped through her veins with alarming fervor from the stranger's kiss.

Lord, what had she been thinking? She *hadn't* been thinking. Like impulsive Helena, she'd acted with no regard for the consequences of her actions. If she'd known how weak-kneed and flutter-hearted one kiss would leave her, she'd have never done it.

Of course, she didn't intend to let him court her for long. Sir Rand was a completely unsuitable suitor. The knave's proclamations of love were as suspect as his account of the tournament. She *would* send him away.

In a day or two.

After she discovered what he'd been doing in the forest.

By then, mayhap she'd have tired of his kisses anyway.

She hoped so. Sweet Mary, even now the gentle caress of his mouth lingered on her lips, making her yearn for more.

"Allow me," he murmured.

Oh, aye, she'd allow him, she thought dreamily.

But he only meant to open the gate of the practice field for her. With a polite bow, he pushed the hinged wattle aside.

As they passed the stables, Miriel was half-tempted to lead him inside. There in the sweet straw they might find a quiet, dark corner in which to resume their kissing and, thus, her questioning.

But as luck would have it, they'd already been spotted by more obstructionists. Striding purposefully toward them across the courtyard was Deirdre, accompanied by her husband, Pagan, and Colin, Helena's betrothed.

"Hold there!" Pagan barked.

Deirdre gave him a sharp elbow, and he softened his tone. "If you please, Lady Miriel," he amended.

Miriel had no choice but to wait while the three of them ambled up, their curiosity as apparent as Deirdre's thickening belly.

"Who is this?" Pagan demanded, narrowing his gray-green eyes to study Rand as if he were a strange and unwelcome bug.

Rand had much better manners. He extended his hand and gave a slight nod. "My lord, I am Sir Rand of Morbroch."

"Morbroch?" Pagan grunted with his usual eloquence. "Morbroch who attended the tournament?"

Rand nodded again.

"Hmph. I don't remember you from the games."

Colin chimed in, "He wasn't in the joust." His green eyes twinkled cheerily. "I remember all the contenders in the joust."

Deirdre squinted pensively while she nibbled on a crust of pandemain. "'Twasn't the archery either."

"Nay," Colin agreed, arching a proud black brow to add, "My Helena won the archery."

Pagan scowled and placed a threatening hand atop the pommel of his sheathed sword. "By what right do you lay a hand on Lady Miriel?"

Miriel felt Rand tense beside her, and her ire rose. Pagan had served as lord of the castle less than a year, and yet he'd quickly adopted an imperious attitude.

She smiled as sweetly as she could manage under the circumstances and gave Rand's arm a doting squeeze, as if he were a favorite cousin.

"Do none of you remember Rand?" She glanced at them expectantly. "Well, I suppose that's no surprise."

Then she gazed fondly into Rand's exquisite eyes and explained to him, "You see, Lord Pagan *was* terribly distracted, it being his first tournament at Rivenloch. Sir Colin? He was half-blind with his affection for my sister, Helena. And Deirdre... well..." She confided in a whisper, "She *is* with child." Then she tapped her forehead, indicating that Deirdre's condition might have addled her brain.

"What?" Deirdre squeaked.

Before her sister could whip out a weapon and challenge her for the insult, Miriel ran a finger affectionately along Rand's sleeve. "But *I* couldn't possibly forget Sir

Rand. He was injured in the first melee, you see, knocked witless. I took care of him in the Morbroch pavilion. We became... friends."

To her satisfaction, Rand followed her lead. "Great friends," he said, giving her a wink. "Forsooth, I believe this lovely damsel saved my life."

Pagan wasn't swayed in the least by their touching story. "Why have you come back?"

Rand hesitated only a heartbeat. "Miriel, my sweet, did you not tell them?"

She smiled weakly. By the Rood! What was he up to?

Clucking his tongue, he covered her hand on his arm with his own. "My timid little angel." Then he told the others, "Lady Miriel asked that I return to court her."

"What?" Pagan blurted.

Miriel held her breath.

Colin began shaking his head in bemusement.

Deirdre stared pointedly at Miriel, as if to divine the truth from her.

Before anyone could speak, Miriel filled the silence. "That's right. I wished him to return. In fact," she added, her courage bolstered by virtue of having an accomplice, "I insisted he return. Now if you don't mind, the poor man has traveled all morn and hasn't had a morsel to eat." Tugging him in the direction of the keep, she shook her head. "Some Rivenloch hospitality we've shown. God's wounds! Helena greeted him with a sword."

Colin frowned. "You've met Helena?" At Rand's nod, Colin briefly scanned him from head to toe. "And you have no scars to show for it?"

Rand looked horrified. "I would not fight her, I assure you."

To Rand's surprise, Colin chuckled. "Then, good fellow, you've chosen the right Rivenloch sister to court."

Pagan was not so amused. "No one's given him permission to court her."

Anger simmered inside Miriel again. She needed no one's permission. Who did Pagan think he was?

Fortunately, Deirdre intervened before Miriel's ire could come to a full boil. "I don't see any harm in it," she said, resting a calming hand atop Pagan's formidable forearm. "He comes from a respectable household. They're acquainted. And Miriel's old enough. After all," she reminded him pointedly, "she was nearly betrothed this summer to a man she didn't love."

That man had been Pagan himself. He grunted at the pointed reference.

Deirdre gave her a conspiratorial smile. "'Tis only fair she be allowed to make her own choice in this."

Pagan muttered something under his breath about headstrong Scotswomen.

"Besides," Deirdre added, "Sung Li will doubtless be nigh to keep them out of trouble."

As if her words had conjured the servant, Sung Li appeared in the midst of the courtyard, his arms laden with a platter of food.

Miriel sighed. She'd won her way. Rand had permission to court her. But with Sung Li present, her opportunity to learn what Rand was up to by charming it out of him had disappeared.

Rand wondered how many more surprises awaited him at Rivenloch. First he'd been challenged to battle by a warrior maid. Then the delectable Lady Miriel, who lied almost as smoothly as he did, had stolen a kiss. Now, unless he was mistaken, the ancient maidservant who scurried forward to deliver breakfast to them was a curiosity from the Orient.

The shriveled, old, white-braided woman offered him pandemain loaves and soft ruayn cheese with a nod. "You must be hungry from your long journey."

How she guessed he'd had a long journey, Rand didn't know. But he *was* hungry, and the fragrant steam of fresh-baked bread made his mouth water.

"We'll break our fast in the garden," Miriel decided, clearly as anxious as he was to be away from her meddling kin.

"When you've finished, Sir Rand," Lord Pagan said, "come to the lists. You may as well make yourself useful. I assume you can handle a blade?"

Rand knew better than to boast, especially when he was talking to one of the famed Knights of Cameliard. "I manage."

Pagan's skepticism was evident, and he exchanged a glance with Deirdre that said as much.

Rand smiled to himself. If they knew how skilled he was at swordplay, they'd likely *insist* he wed Lady Miriel. She could ask for no better protector.

The garden turned out to be a walled square adjacent to the practice yard. Though 'twas bleak and bare at this time of year, the odd little maidservant seemed determined to take Rand on a tour of every inch.

"I am certain you did not see the garden," she said, adding pointedly, "the *last* time you came to visit."

He and Miriel exchanged careful glances. Was the old woman alert to their deception?

"Besides," the maidservant told him, "if you learn what grows in the garden, on the morrow I can send you to fetch what I need for the wedding."

"Sung Li!" Miriel scolded. "He's not a kitchen lad."

"Oh, aye," the servant said. "He is your, what is it, *friend*?"

As if to prove their relationship, Miriel looped her arm through his. "Rand is my suitor."

The impertinent maid only huffed once in disapproval, then led them down the garden path. "These are pasternak and rafens."

"Ah," he said, feigning interest, gulping down a warm morsel of bread.

"And these are roses," the old woman continued, adding with heavy sarcasm, "which you, of course, will be cutting to give to your... ladylove."

"Sung Li," Miriel warned.

They didn't look at all like roses. At the moment, they were naught but bundles of sticks with their heads chopped off. "Indeed? My love, would you like a bunch of these thorny stems for your hair?"

Miriel's lips twitched with amusement, and she raised a defiant chin to Sung Li. "Perchance I would."

The maidservant growled in displeasure, then resumed her tour.

"Colewarts!" Rand called out as they passed the familiar white mounds that grew in every winter garden and graced every supper table in Scotland.

"Every child knows colewarts," the maid sneered. "They are common."

"Aye, most common, unlike my fair Miriel," he cooed, half to amuse the woman on his arm, half to annoy the maidservant. Still, 'twas not a lie. Lady Miriel was a rare sight, with her pale-as-cream skin, her crystal blue eyes, her dark, shining tresses, and that cherry-sweet mouth...

"Wolfsbane."

"Wolfsbane?" he murmured distractedly, capturing Miriel's gaze with his own. She bit her lip to keep from laughing, and he lowered his eyes to that succulent lip, making his desire to kiss her evident.

Sung Li added with sarcastic hospitality, "Perchance you would like to try some."

"Mm," he said, still gazing at Miriel's tempting mouth. "Maybe later."

"Hmph." The old woman pointed to a row of strange plants with leaves like paddles. "You do not know what *that* is."

Feigning interest, he gave her his most earnest frown. "Nay." But while Sung Li explained that they were *kailaan*, an honorable vegetable from her homeland, Rand glanced over at his beguiling companion. Her eyes had gone soft and dreamy, and he felt a swift tightening in his braies as a jolt of desire raced through him.

"And what about these?" Sung Li demanded smugly, nodding to a bed of plants resembling large green roses.

Growing weary of Sung Li's game, Rand rolled his eyes, making Miriel giggle.

Sung Li whipped around, planted her fists on her hips, and snapped, "*You zhi!*"

Rand furrowed his brow, trying to appear serious. "*You zhi,*" he repeated.

Miriel giggled again, this time freely. 'Twas a delightful sound, and her teeth shone as white as pearls. "Sung Li just called you a child."

Rand arched a brow of disbelief at the impertinent maid, who nodded in curt agreement.

"A child?" Simple mercenary he might be, and a bastard by birth, but he was a proper knight. No servant had the right to insult him.

"You are *both* children," Sung Li decided.

The impudent maid was asking for a beating.

But before he could chastise her, Miriel barked, "Sung Li!"

The maid threw her hands up in frustration. "I am done with you. You do not listen to me today, Miriel. Tell me when you have grown up."

With an imperial swish of her skirts, the tiny maid brushed past them and out the gate.

Rand couldn't be more glad to see the old crone go. 'Twas obvious that Lady Miriel desired him, and the wanton wench was probably accustomed to getting what she wanted. He was only too happy to oblige. Particularly because it served his purposes so well.

After the gate slammed shut, he turned to the lovely lass, perusing her slowly from head to toe. "You look all grown up to me."

"Do I?" she asked coyly.

"Oh, aye," he murmured, with a lazy grin. "You feel like a woman." He raised her hand and rubbed it gently against his cheek. "You smell like a woman." He bent close and inhaled the flowery fragrance of her hair. "And you definitely taste like a woman." He lowered his gaze to her mouth and hungrily licked his lips, then dipped his head until his breath caressed her jaw. "Even if you spy on people like a naughty child."

He nipped at her lips once, twice, then engaged her

fully, sinking into the kiss as she made a soft moan of pleasure. Releasing her fingers, he cupped her face in his hands, reveling in the silky texture of her skin, the soft sweep of her hair, the delicate shell of her ear.

His loins pulsed as she eagerly responded, opening her mouth for him, tilting her head, spreading her fingers across his chest. She was definitely a woman who knew what she wanted, and she knew how to get it. Encouraged by her enthusiasm, he wrapped an arm around her shoulders and pulled her closer, delving tenderly between her teeth with his tongue.

He slid his palm along her spine until his hand rested at her waist. But he hungered for more. Pressing the bulge in his braies against her belly, he slipped his hand down farther to urge her close, cupping the sweet curve of her buttocks.

The next thing he knew, the earth was yanked out from under him. He was laid out flat on his back. And beside him was the patch of—what was it? Ah, yes, *kailaan.*

Chapter 4

"Wʜᴀᴛ ᴛʜᴇ...?"

Miriel looked down at him with a mixture of satisfaction and horror. She hadn't wanted to do that. Forsooth, her heart was still racing with the thrill of kissing Sir Rand. But she couldn't allow him such liberties, for if she did, she feared she might forget all about her real motives for courting him.

"Sweet Mary!" she exclaimed in faux surprise. "Did you trip over the roses?"

Of course he hadn't tripped over the roses. He'd tripped over the foot she'd swept behind his heel.

He blinked and sat up, utterly perplexed.

Before he could think too much on what had happened, she reached down to help him up. "Perchance you fainted from hunger. Would you like another piece of pandemain? Sung Li left the platter."

"I'm not hungry," he said as he struggled to his feet, studying the ground, trying to ascertain what had tripped him.

"You're not?" She brushed the dirt from his shoulder, then said carefully, "You seemed hungry in the forest."

He looked keenly at her. "Indeed? What makes you say that?"

She gulped. When Rand smiled, he was irresistibly handsome. His dimpled cheeks were boyish, and his eyes twinkled like stars. But now, pinning her with a dark, questioning stare, he seemed possibly dangerous.

She forced a nonchalant shrug. "Isn't that what you were doing in the woods? Hunting for something to eat?"

His eyes narrowed slightly, and she got the feeling he was trying to read her thoughts. Then he lightened his grip on her hand and let amusement creep into his gaze. "You know perfectly well what I was doing in the woods, sweetheart."

Miriel blushed at the memory. She hadn't meant *that*.

"And anytime you'd like to take another peek at what's in my braies..."

She nervously withdrew her hand. "Sir, we've only begun to court," she chided. "You move too swiftly. I am a maiden, after all. Mayhap later, when we are better acquainted—"

"Better acquainted?" He plucked up a tendril of her hair and wound it around his finger. "Why, my lady, I'd have thought, looking after me night and day in Morbroch's pavilion, you'd be very well acquainted with my every aspect."

Lord, the deceit dripped off his tongue as smoothly as honey from a comb. She'd never looked after him. She'd invented that. And he knew it. Forsooth, she was beginning to wonder if the scheming varlet had ever come to Rivenloch at all.

He raised the lock of her hair and kissed it. "At any rate, forgive me, my lady, if I frightened you. I'll try to temper my passions in the future." He stroked her cheek with the back of one finger. "Though 'tis devilishly hard." Then he leaned forward to whisper in her ear. "Devilishly. Hard."

There was no mistaking his meaning. God's blood, he *was* a knave. She should have cracked him across his handsome face for such vulgarity. But 'twould not serve her purposes. If she meant to wheedle information from him, she had to play his game. So she gave him a deceptively timid smile.

"Fear not, dear heart." He gave her a benign kiss on the brow. "I'll take my leave now before your ill-tempered maid reports that we are unaccompanied. Your kin do not seem the understanding kind, and since I've been summoned to the tiltyard..." He sighed. "'Twill seem an eternity till we meet again."

With a sly grin and a cursory but suggestive appraisal of her from head to toe, he saluted and strode out the garden gate. Miriel was gratified to note that the varlet's tabard bore an incriminating stain where he'd landed bottom first in the mud.

No sooner had Rand gone than she started plotting. She had to find out what mischief he intended. Where were his things? She'd seen a pack of supplies on his horse. Something in that pack might give her a clue as to his business. What had happened to it?

'Twas likely still with the horse.

Scattering the remaining pandemain for the birds, Miriel stole from the garden and made her way toward the stables. Peeping inconspicuously around the corner of the kennel toward the practice field, she glimpsed Rand crossing swords with Pagan. Deirdre and Helena leaned against the fence, looking on. Out of curiosity, she watched him for a moment.

He wasn't very good.

Not that it mattered. 'Twasn't as if he was going to be her husband. But she could see that his clumsiness aggravated Pagan, and her sisters were murmuring together in concern.

She supposed she shouldn't have judged them so harshly. They could sometimes be unbearably smothering, but 'twas only because they cared for her. 'Twas her own fault in a way for pretending to be so helpless all these years. Yet what else could she do? 'Twas that very perceived vulnerability that enabled her secretly to control the workings of Rivenloch, to gain access to rumors leaked by careless servants, and to run surveillance on suspicious strangers like Sir Rand without attracting attention.

She was in charge of the castle accounts, but not even her sisters appreciated just what that entailed. She managed all the goods and services, doled out and collected payments, monitored the supplies of grain and cloth, ale and arms, meat and firewood. And she made certain the accounts were always balanced, not an easy feat, particularly with her father's penchant for wagering. The fact that she made it look easy fooled everyone into believing she was essentially powerless.

Which was why, when she casually ambled by the stable lad and into the stables with a timid smile, he only bobbed his head and let her pass, not even curious as to her business.

Once she found Rand's mare, her nonchalance vanished. 'Twas a spirited creature, and she had to calm the beast several times with soothing murmurs and gentle pats to the neck before she could access the rest of the stall.

His things were in the far corner—the pack, a thick wool blanket, his saddle. She dragged the heavy satchel through the straw into the sunlight, crouching to take a look inside.

Most of the pack's contents were common enough, not incriminating in the least. There were spare clothes, an iron cooking pot, a spoon, a firestone, a wooden cup, a few knives, rope, things any traveler would carry on the road. Farther down were strips of linen and a bundle of herbs, probably for medicinal purposes. Rummaging deeper, she found a small purse full of silver and a pair of worn leather gloves. Then her fingers alit upon a heavy metal chain.

She tugged it out of the satchel and held it up to the light. She frowned. There, clanking before her eyes, was a rather sinister pair of iron shackles.

The chiding cluck of a tongue behind her startled her, making her shove the shackles quickly back into the pack.

"Find something useful?" She glanced up to see Sir Rand looming over her, his arms crossed over his chest, a smirk on his face.

God's blood! How had he managed to steal up on her like that?

"I… I…" she floundered. "Why aren't you sparring with Pagan?"

He shrugged. "His patience wore thin." He arched a brow. "Why are you rifling through my things?"

"I wasn't rifling." She gulped. 'Twas exactly what she was doing. "I was..." Inspiration hit. "I was just wondering," she said softly, dipping her eyes and running an idle fingertip around the opening of the satchel, "if you might have... brought me something."

The doubtful squint of his eyes said he wasn't convinced by her excuse, but he gave her the benefit of the doubt anyway. "You mean a token of my affection? A lover's gift of some kind?"

She sucked her lower lip beneath her teeth, a shy gesture that always brought out the protectiveness in men.

But he only chuckled, then hunkered down beside her, stuffing his things back into the pack. "Greedy lass."

Miriel pretended embarrassment, but as he closed the top of the satchel and propped it against the stable wall, she couldn't help but feel a shiver of unease. Why would he carry such a grim item as a pair of shackles?

He rubbed his chin. "A while ago, I heard one of the maids say something about a fair."

"A fair? Oh, aye, in the town. In a fortnight." She narrowed her gaze, trying to discern what he was plotting.

"I promise I'll buy you something there, my sweet." He caught her chin affectionately between his thumb and finger. "A gift fit for the loveliest damsel in all Scotland."

Her smile quavered uncertainly. Never mind his engaging grin. The man carried shackles in his pack. What the bloody hell was he up to?

He cocked his head and squinted one eye. "Unless, of course, you've stolen the silver from my satchel."

She gasped, pretending great offense. "What? You think I would steal another's coin?" Yet even as she reacted in hurt, she felt a warm glow flush her cheeks. She *had* been rummaging through his belongings, after all. He had every right to be suspicious.

Aye, Rand thought, the pretty little damsel was definitely a thief. She'd probably stolen dozens of hearts with that innocent smile and those wide blue eyes that could summon tears at the slightest provocation.

Rand wasn't fooled for a moment. He knew her kind well. She was the kind of woman who used her affections for barter, trading adoring glances and kisses for silk ribbons and precious jewels, bleeding one lover dry of resources, then moving on to the next. She was the sort of wench he could love and leave without remorse. Which was perfect for his plans.

Still, the lass was a bit too curious for his comfort.

"I'm jesting," he assured her with a wink, holding out his hand for hers.

She placed her hand tentatively in his palm, and he stood, helping her to her feet. He dusted the straw from her skirts, taking secret pleasure in swatting her on the backside as he did so, eliciting a gasp from her.

He feigned innocence, unhanding her, then bent to retrieve his pack. "Will you show me where I'm to put my things?" he asked, then added slyly, "Somewhere they'll be... safe."

The maid blushed again, though whether from shame or anger, he couldn't tell. "Of course."

He shouldered the satchel and followed Miriel to the keep.

Pagan had given Rand permission to bed down with the other knights in the great hall, though after Rand's poor display of swordsmanship, the disappointed lord would have likely preferred that he sleep with the hounds. Now, admiring the gentle sway of Miriel's hips as she walked across the courtyard before him, Rand wished he'd arranged to share a pallet with the tantalizing damsel.

In time, he promised himself. Though Miriel was definitely a woman of passion, she was also a tease. She was the sort of wench to throw herself at him like a wanton in one moment, only to plead her virginity the next.

When he bedded her, 'twould be on her terms. And he *would* bed her. There were few who could resist Rand when he put his charm to work. In another day, maybe two, he thought with a lusty grin, he'd have Lady Miriel wrinkling his sheets and cooing his name in the most dulcet tones.

Entering the great hall of Rivenloch, Rand was impressed. Myriad bright banners and silver shields graced the walls. Fresh rushes imparted a sweet scent to the chamber, and tallow candles set in sconces gave the hall a warm, welcoming glow. Servants scurried to and fro, tending to the fire on the hearth, scrubbing soot from the plaster walls, carrying buckets and baskets and bundles across the hall, climbing up the tower stairs, descending to the storerooms below.

"Preparations for the wedding feast," Miriel explained, as they passed a pair of maids polishing the oak trestle tables with rags and a pot of beeswax.

Rand nodded. The ceremony in two days might prove fortuitous indeed. What thief could resist lightening the purses of departing wedding guests, who were likely to be suffering from the groggy aftereffects of their merrymaking? If Rand kept a close watch on the woods the morn after the feast, he was sure to catch the robber.

"You can keep your things here," Miriel told him,

opening a large oak chest along the wall that was filled with several similar satchels.

As Rand dropped his belongings inside, a young lad approached and bobbed his head. "My lady, the wine's arrived from the monastery, but Cook says it's short."

"Short? How short?"

The lad screwed up his face, trying to remember. "Twoscore?"

Miriel gasped. "Twoscore? Are you sure? 'Tis only half what I asked for."

"Aye, twoscore short."

While Miriel chewed at her lip, considering what to do, another servant came up, an old woman with a face like a dried apple.

"That God-cursed spice monger," she groused. "He's wantin' more coin for his goods now."

Miriel furrowed her brows. "Well, he can't *have* more coin."

"That's what I told him."

"And?"

"He says it cost him more this time, on account of his ship was attacked by miscreants."

"That's not *my* concern."

The wrinkled old woman shrugged, and Miriel clenched her teeth in frustration.

Then a couple approached, a stout woman looking smug as she hauled up a stick of a man who worried his doffed hat in his hands.

"Go ahead," the woman said, "tell the lady what ye've done."

"Beggin' yer pardon, m'lady," he said, "but one of the hounds got loose and... and..."

The woman crossed her arms over her generous chest. "Pissed all over the table linens, he did."

"He didn't mean to," the man argued. "Besides, what were they doin', hangin' up on the bushes?"

"They were airin', ye big dolt."

Miriel held up her hand for silence, then turned to Rand. "I'm sorry."

"You have your hands full."

"I'm in charge of the castle accounts," she explained. "I'm likely to be quite busy over the next two days with the wedding preparations."

"Anything I can do to help?"

"Not really. Unless you'd like to interrogate the hounds."

He grinned at her dry wit. "'Tis such lovely weather, my love, I think I'll take a stroll about the countryside, get to know your magnificent Rivenloch." Taking a few things from his satchel, he nodded to the others, excusing himself from their company, but not before hearing the stout woman echo in wonder, "My love?"

Rand smiled to himself. He couldn't believe his good fortune. Not only had he managed to secure an excuse for being at Rivenloch, an excuse that was young and desirable and lovely to look upon, but it seemed the lass was too preoccupied to pay him much mind, which meant he had the freedom to track the outlaw at his leisure.

He wasted no time. Armed with his sword, a pair of daggers, and the shackles, and taking along his silver in order to remove temptation from that overcurious Miriel, he set out to explore the forest on foot.

The woods of Rivenloch were beautiful in a fey, wild way. Moss covered the stones and the trunks of the sycamores and cedars, muffling the sounds of his footfalls as he searched along the leafy path. Beside him, fern fronds bowed under the weight of dragonflies, and overhead, rust-colored squirrels leaped from branch to branch with cheeks full of acorns. Toadstools clustered like baldpated old men at the foot of ancient oaks. The mist had all but vanished, and here and there, where shafts of sunlight shot to the ground, a lizard or a mouse might pause in its scurrying to soak up the precious warm rays.

'Twas the kind of place one could imagine inhabited by all sorts of magical woodland creatures—mischievous sprites and enchanted elves. Forsooth, Rand almost believed, by the exaggerated accounts of the outlaw he sought, citing the man as nigh invisible, as fast as lightning, as quiet as death, that The Shadow was such a creature.

Rand shook his head. 'Twas little wonder the lords continued to be terrorized by the robber when they endowed him with such impossible talents and such an ominous name. The Shadow indeed. No doubt he was a mere mortal of desperate means who answered to Wat or Hob or some other humble appellation.

Thus far, however, Rand had been unable to find even a trace of his passing in a few hours of hunting. No crumbs or coney carcasses lay discarded by the path. None of the moss on the rocks was flattened by the weight of a robber's arse. No scent of smoke lingered on the air. No branches had been bent into a shelter. No human dung littered the leaves. Naught existed to indicate anyone took refuge in the wood at all.

He was examining a broken stick on the path when he felt that telltale prickling on the back of his neck again, the prickling that told him he wasn't alone.

Carefully, so as not to raise suspicion, he picked up a dead tree limb by the side of the trail and began stripping off the side branches, humming as he did so. When he was finished, he stabbed it into the ground a few times, testing its strength for use as a walking stick. But all the while his senses were highly alert and finely tuned, listening for the slightest breath of sound, looking for the merest flicker of light.

Behind him. He was certain the intruder was behind him.

Whistling softly, he proceeded down the path at a jaunty pace, letting his purse dangle and bounce from his belt, sending up a merry clank of coins sure to tempt any robber.

He knew the thief must be following him, though he was making too much noise himself to hear any pursuit. Rounding a spot where the path curved and disappeared momentarily, he let a piece of silver drop to the ground and moved on, as if oblivious to his loss.

But instead of continuing down the trail, he ducked behind a screen of bushes and hefted up the walking stick, waiting to waylay the unwitting outlaw.

The instant he saw the flash of blue cloth, he sprang forward. But to his horror, the scoundrel he collided with was neither Wat nor Hob. 'Twas Lady Miriel.

What happened next, he wasn't sure. In one moment, he was lunging toward her, trying in vain to slow his momentum. In the next, he seemed propelled forward with even greater force, past her and into the holly bushes opposite, as if the walking stick had taken on a life of its own and catapulted him there.

"Oh! Rand!"

After a moment of stunned disbelief, he managed to disentangle himself from the shrubbery, wincing as the sharp leaves scraped his cheek. What the bloody hell had just happened?

Miriel stood before him, her trembling hands clasped at her breast, all innocence, but for the sliver of a silver coin visible between her fingers. "Are you all right?"

꩜

Chapter 5

Miriel didn't know why she'd bent down to pick up that dropped coin. Perchance 'twas simply instinct bred from long years of watching every farthing of the household accounts. But now she suspected it had been a trap. Rand, sensing someone was following him, had dropped the coin intentionally, meaning to waylay whoever retrieved it.

The fool was fortunate he'd lost no more than his balance. Startling her like that, he might have suffered far worse than just a few holly scratches. If she hadn't caught herself at the last instant, she might have broken his arm or sent him into temporary oblivion with a sharp blow to the chin.

Not that he didn't deserve it. Her instincts had proved correct. The varlet *was* up to something.

She'd been following him for a while now. Solving the troubles at the castle hadn't taken long. She'd sent a lad to another monastery for more wine. She'd employed tears to convince the spice merchant to lower his price. And she'd suggested the master of the kennel launder the linens himself.

Then she'd crept out to spy upon Sir Rand. Sure enough, he was searching the forest with all the thoroughness of a hunter tracking boar.

What the Devil was he after?

"Rand?" she asked in feigned concern.

"I'm fine." His brow creased in perplexity. "Are you?"

She nodded.

"What...?" he wondered, scrutinizing the trail to see what he'd fallen over.

"The ground is very slick," she improvised. "Between the moss and the mud, 'tis a wonder one can walk at all."

"Hm." He used the walking stick to lever himself to his feet, then cast it aside, shaking his head hard to clear it of cobwebs and restore his decorum. "What are you doing here, my lady?"

"I was... looking for you," she hedged. "I feared you might have gotten lost."

He raised a brow in amusement. "Lost?"

"Oh." As if suddenly remembering, she held out the coin. "And I think you may have dropped this."

"Indeed?" He patted his purse, checking to see if there was a hole in it. "Nay, I do not think 'tis mine."

Her eyes flattened. He was lying. It *had* to be his. Silver coins didn't simply spring up like mushrooms on the woodland path. "Who else could it belong to?"

He reached out, but instead of taking the silver, he enfolded her hand in his, closing her fingers around the coin and giving her a wink. "If you found it, 'tis yours, my lady."

"I won't take silver that doesn't belong to me."

"Ah. A woman of high moral value."

It had naught to do with moral value. It had to do with the compulsion she had for balance, a compulsion fostered by her training in Chinese warfare. "'Tis only that I cannot abide unbalanced accounts."

"You must be quite good at managing a household then."

She tried not to be flattered. To succumb to flattery made one weak. But 'twas gratifying to be recognized for talents no one else seemed to notice. She lowered her gaze to hide the secret pleasure in her eyes.

"Wait."

She glanced up again.

His brows came together as he opened her hand, then lifted it up to study the silver more closely. "Hm." He angled her hand this way and that. "Mm." He flipped the coin over in her palm, examining both sides. "Mm-hm."

"What?"

He stared soberly into her eyes and confided, "I think this is no ordinary coin."

"What do you mean?"

He shook his head. "'Tis not like any I've seen before."

She frowned and studied the coin herself. It looked perfectly ordinary to her. "But—"

"Forsooth, I don't think 'tis a coin of this realm at all." He closed her fingers around the silver once more, glanced about to ensure there were no ears to hear, then whispered solemnly, "'Tis faerie silver."

For a moment, he looked as serious as the grave.

A hundred thoughts rushed through her mind. The man

was crazed. Or addled. They were alone out here. And he kept shackles in his pack.

Then a gleam of mischief slowly crept into his eyes, and she realized the varlet was jesting with her.

She shouldn't respond to him. Such trickery was childish. And manipulative. And wicked. But despite her best efforts, a glimmer of amusement gradually found its way into her own gaze.

"Indeed? Faerie silver?" she echoed.

"Oh, aye," he assured her, his expression quite stern. "They must have left it on the path... to help guide you to me."

Miriel stifled a smile. He was a gifted teller of tales, this knave, almost as gifted as she was. "Forsooth?"

"Mm." Though he furrowed his brow, there were crinkles of restrained delight at the corners of his eyes. "Pity, though, you found me so soon," he said on a sigh. "Otherwise, they might have left a whole *trail* of silver."

She arched a brow. "That much?"

"Oh, aye."

"Well, we cannot leave the faeries' accounts unbalanced." With a wicked gleam in her eyes, she snapped up the coin in her fist and prepared to toss it into the bushes.

"Nay!" He seized her arm.

She smirked. No man liked to part with silver.

Rather than abandon his pretense, he quickly improvised. "'Twas coin spent... for a *service.*" Then he faced her with a brilliant smile of victory. "Very well spent if it led you to me." He raised her hand, giving the back of it a chivalrous kiss.

Lord, he was good. His banter was almost as charming as 'twas suspect.

Tucking the coin into her purse, she wove her fingers companionably through Rand's.

"So," she asked as casually as possible, swinging their clasped hands leisurely back and forth as they ambled along the path, "what have you been up to?"

He shrugged. "Walking, exploring, soaking up the beauty of Rivenloch." The way his gaze drifted over her face, there was little doubt of what beauty he spoke.

She looked away and ran an idle finger along a moss-covered oak branch. "You'd been absent so long, I thought mayhap you'd gone trout fishing or cattle raiding or hunting... for something." Her gaze slid sideways, gauging his reaction.

He studied her for a moment before answering, as if he wondered how much she'd seen. "Forsooth, I *have* been hunting."

She blinked, stopping on the path, admittedly startled by his candor. "Indeed?"

"Aye." He gave her a sheepish grin. "I've been hunting for flowers." He lowered his gaze and dug a toe into the dirt. "I'd hoped to offer you some small token of my love. But alas, I found not a blossom."

Miriel raised her brows. Flowers?

He took her fingers in his and ruefully shook his head. "Yet here I am, gone so long I've made you fret." He lifted her hand to his lips and kissed her fingertips in apology. "Forced you to search for me..." He kissed her knuckles. "All alone in the wood..." He kissed the back of her hand. "Where all manner of dangerous creatures roam."

She smirked and withdrew her hand. She'd wandered this forest from the time she was a wee lass. Dangerous creatures indeed.

"Savage beasts," he confided, his eyes twinkling darkly, "that might spring out to devour you." He inclined his head so that he whispered into her hair, and his breath blew warm upon her brow. "Ravage your tender body. Feast upon your sweet flesh." He growled.

The knave was insufferable. Miriel rolled her eyes and slapped him away. But he seemed undaunted. And the way he was looking at her now, his dark eyes smoky and sparkling, like stars peeking through clouds, made her fickle heart flutter.

Still, she refused to be charmed. "I'm not afraid of beasts."

"Ah, but you should be, my lady," he warned her in dramatic tones. "They're wild and unpredictable. You never know when one will... attack." Before she could brace herself, he lunged forward all at once to nip playfully at the side of her neck.

She sucked in her breath and pulled away, but not before a shiver of unwelcome lust coursed through her. She countered breathlessly, "Then beasts should beware, for a lady has teeth as well."

His grin turned wolfish. "That may be. But unlike the beast's," he said, lowering his eyes to her mouth, "your teeth, my lady, are sheathed in the softest of lips."

She didn't mean to become distracted. But the sultry warmth of his gaze, the gentle rasp of his voice, and the sensual memory of his kiss sent a disturbing ripple through the still pond of her thoughts. Suddenly, solving the mystery of his clandestine activities seemed not so urgent.

Her gaze drifted to his mouth. Would it be so wicked to taste his lips again? They'd be sweet and supple and moist. His arms would drift around her, pulling her close, and she'd feel his broad chest pressed intimately against her breasts. His hands would roam over her back, stirring her flesh and perchance wandering up to tangle in the cloud of her hair. 'Twould not be an unpleasant thing.

Besides, she reasoned, did she not have to keep up a pretense of courting him? What would be more convincing than allowing him to kiss her now and then?

He cupped her cheek and stroked her bottom lip with his thumb. Then he lowered his head to murmur against her hair. "Forsooth, my lady, one kiss from you would tame the wildest of beasts." Tilting her head back, he leaned forward to place a single, featherlight kiss upon her mouth.

'Twas as if an angel touched her. Or a spirit. Or mayhap one of Rand's wee faeries. Indeed, if her eyes hadn't been open a peep, she might have believed she'd imagined the kiss, so insubstantial was it.

'Twas not at all what she remembered. She remembered the heart-racing, blood-searing, breath-stealing sensation he'd elicited in her before.

He started to back away, and she leaned forward. He withdrew his hand, and she snagged her fingers in the front of his tabard. And when his lips parted in surprise, she advanced to claim them.

"My la—"

She cut off his words with her kiss, and this time there was no question that he was a man of substance. His mouth felt firm and real beneath hers. His skin was vibrant, almost as if lightning flowed through his body. When she let her fingers rove, climbing up the wide expanse of his chest to settle upon the warm flesh of his neck, she felt his pulse beating strong and true.

Most convincing, when he at last succumbed, sighing into her mouth and hauling her up against him, she felt the unmistakable manifestation of lust pressing against her belly.

Rand was more than willing to oblige the wanton lass. After all, he'd claimed to come with courtship in mind.

If she wanted adoring glances, he'd melt her with his gaze.

If she yearned for honeyed words, he'd seduce her with flowery verses.

If she hungered for sweet kisses, he'd let her feast upon him until she was sated.

Of course, he could go no further, not yet. If he succumbed to her will too soon, she might tire of him before his work was done.

But, God, he wanted her.

Why she summoned forth such powerful desire in him, he didn't know. 'Twas not as if he hadn't bedded his share of damsels, some of them certainly as willing and as fair as this Scots maid. 'Twas not even that it had been that many days since he'd engaged a woman in his bed. A mercenary with silver in his purse never suffered long for want of an agreeable companion.

But something about this lass in particular both delighted him and drove him mad with lust.

Perchance 'twas that their lies had pushed them into intimacy far quicker than was natural. Or mayhap 'twas simply that they were cubs of the same litter. Whatever 'twas, their fellowship of deception was rapidly taking on a life of its own. One mere kiss from her left him trembling like an untried lad.

When her hand wandered mischievously from his neck, down his chest, to the back of his waist, then descended his hip to squeeze his buttock, he finally woke to his own perilous lack of control, to the awareness that he was becoming distracted from his mission.

He broke away with unaccustomed violence, holding her at arm's length, scarcely able to catch his breath, trying to force his lust to subside.

Her expression was so bewildered, so bereft, so ravaged with need, that he almost drew her back into his arms again.

But 'twould be a mistake. 'Twas too soon for more than kisses.

"My love," he gasped, "you sorely tax my restraint."

"Must you restrain?" she breathed, her eyes glazed with desire.

"Aye."

"Why?"

"Oh, lady," he said, half-groaning, half-chuckling, "if you have to ask, then I must not be the man I think I am."

Her gaze lowered then, taking in the blatant evidence of his need. "Oh." Her cheeks flamed at once, and she retreated another step.

"Fear not, my lady," he bid her. "I am not quite so wild a beast as that." He blew out a hard breath. "Yet."

He had made his point. The fire in her eyes cooled, and she began looking anywhere but at him, crossing her arms defensively over her bosom.

"Mayhap we should return to the keep," he suggested,

adjusting his braies, "before that vigilant maid of yours comes to see if I've ravaged you."

Miriel nodded in agreement, looking flustered and quite eager to quit the forest. She brushed past him, then paused, fishing in her purse for the silver coin. She turned and pressed it into his palm.

He favored her with a one-sided grin. "Sweetheart, my kisses are not for purchase." He clasped her hand and turned it over, leaving the coin in her palm.

A troubled wrinkle creased her brow.

He stifled a chuckle. He rather liked leaving Lady Miriel out of balance. She was delightful, this naughty little spy who could match him in a battle of wits, set him aflame with her kisses, and keep an entire household in order, down to the penny.

Forsooth, he found himself almost wishing he could extend his stay at Rivenloch, to better acquaint himself with the intriguing lass.

Their discourse was suddenly interrupted by the heavy footfalls of an intruder tromping through the forest toward them. Miriel quickly tucked the coin back into her purse.

"Miriel? Miriel!" 'Twas her meddlesome maid, thankfully late to arrive. "Miriel!"

How such a small woman could make so much noise, Rand didn't know.

"I'm here, Sung Li!" A note of slight irritation colored Miriel's voice.

When the old crone came shuffling angrily through the leaves, she narrowed her already narrow eyes at Rand in accusation, then elbowed her way past him to address her charge.

"You should not be wandering about," she said, planting her fists on her hips, then adding pointedly, "where there are wild beasts."

"That's what I told her," Rand chimed in, giving Miriel a sly wink.

He could almost see the hackles rise on the old woman's back. "You come now," she said, grabbing Miriel's forearm.

To her credit, Miriel pulled her arm away. "Sung Li, I'll come when I'm ready."

For a long moment, there was a standoff between the two, Sung Li with her squinting scowl and Miriel with her superior glower. Finally, Miriel decided, "All right. I'm ready."

Sung Li crossed smug arms over her flat chest. "I am glad you could tear yourself away. Meanwhile, the keep is drowning in wine."

"What do you mean?"

"Your half-wit kitchen boy does not know how to count."

Miriel frowned. "What's he done?"

"He brought more bottles of wine."

"That's fine. I told him to."

"*Eighty* more bottles?"

"Bloody hell."

Miriel rushed past Rand in a blur of blue skirts. If owing him one piece of silver troubled her, he could only imagine her distress at having a surplus of twoscore bottles of wine for the wedding.

He trailed after them, done with searching the forest for the moment. Clearly no one had camped in recent days, at least in this part of the woods, which was where Lord

Morbroch said they'd all been robbed. 'Twas possible the outlaw lived in the outlying forest and only ventured close for his thieving, which meant that Rand would have to widen his search over the next few days.

But for now, it might serve him better to learn more about The Shadow from the folk who knew him best, the denizens of Rivenloch.

᠀

Chapter 6

As she hurried back to the keep, Miriel's heart raced with . . . was it panic or excitement? She couldn't tell. But she found herself alternately annoyed with and grateful for Sung Li's interruption. Sweet Jesu, she'd never felt so warm and giddy and wanton, enfolded in Rand's arms, at least not without the benefit of a great deal of ale. But neither had she felt so vulnerable. His embrace left her curiously powerful and weak at the same time. Her body sang with strength, yet it seemed her knees would collapse beneath her.

'Twas a wonderful sensation. And yet terrifying.

In warfare, self-control was everything. So Sung Li had taught her. Discipline of one's emotions was essential. Mastery of one's body was key.

Miriel had worked for years, learning to shut out pain and fatigue and doubt, increasing her physical and mental strength, focusing her body to perfect obedience and her mind to a point as sharp and effective as a sword.

How could something as simple as a kiss so effortlessly destroy her concentration? How could a single smile from a stranger, a wink, a nod, shatter her serenity? How could the touch of his hand so radically disturb the balance of her *chi*?

Aye, she decided, 'twas good Sung Li had come when he did. Miriel needed time away from Rand, time to meditate, to realign her senses.

She knew what she had to do. Just as she'd done with pain and fatigue and doubt, she needed to inure herself to Rand's influence. As Sung Li often said, One does not conquer fear by running from it but by embracing it.

She would embrace Rand then. Often. And thoroughly. Until she ultimately conquered him.

By the time they reached the keep, Miriel was already feeling more in control. After a quick midday repast, Rand set off for the tiltyard to try his sword against the Rivenloch knights again, and absent his unsettling presence, as Miriel began issuing gentle orders in the great hall, her sense of calm and quiet authority returned.

By nightfall, Miriel had collected herself and was actually looking forward to Rand's company at supper. Then he appeared with Sir Rauve, chuckling companionably, his face freshly washed, his hair slightly damp and dark, his broad chest draped in a brown surcoat that perfectly matched his laughing eyes, and 'twas all she could do to keep her heart on a steady course.

'Twas ridiculous how naturally her body responded to his presence. After all, she'd only just met the man. Yet it took all her strength of will not to skip up from the bench at the high table and rush into his arms, as if to announce, he's mine. 'Twas disgusting, really, and yet she could no more curb her feelings than she could stop rain from falling.

When he spotted her, his face lit up with a wide smile. He came up to take her hand and pressed a kiss to the back of her knuckles. "I've missed you, my sweet."

His words affected her more than she cared to admit, more than she'd let him know, certainly. She quickly withdrew her hand. "Pah! No doubt Pagan and Colin kept you so busy in the tiltyard, you had no time to miss me."

He grinned and slid in beside her. "They did keep me busy. But every time I drew my sword, 'twas to battle in your honor, my lady."

"Indeed?" Pagan grunted from down the table. "Then you'd better keep a close watch on your honor, Miriel."

"Pagan!" Deirdre scolded.

"He's not very good," Pagan replied with a shrug.

Colin came up in back of them and clapped Rand on the shoulder. "He'll improve. Remember how the Rivenloch knights were when we arrived?"

Helena, close behind her bridegroom, swatted him hard enough on the buttocks to make him yelp. "The Rivenloch knights were quite capable when you arrived, Norman."

"Come, you two," Deirdre said with a chuckle. "A lover's quarrel, so soon? You aren't even wed yet."

When Miriel's father arrived, Pagan and Rand stood to help him to his place between them. Miriel hoped Lord Gellir wouldn't object to Rand. Sometimes in his feeble state of mind, he was troubled by the sight of unfamiliar faces at his table.

"Who's to wed?" Lord Gellir asked, looking in confusion at the diners around him.

Pagan answered in a loud, slow voice. "Colin and Helena are to be wed in two days, my lord."

"And he can't fight?"

"Colin can fight," Pagan replied. "'Tis Miriel's new suitor who can't fight."

Deirdre protested again. "Pagan!"

"Well, he can't."

Lord Gellir turned slowly to look at Rand. "Who's this?"

Rand smiled and offered his hand. "I'm Sir Rand of Morbroch, my lord."

"You can't fight?"

Miriel had heard about enough. "What does it matter?" she said impatiently, unfolding her napkin onto her lap. "Why is everyone so interested in whether he can or cannot fight? Fighting isn't everything. I'm sure—"

"What?" Lord Gellir roared.

Miriel flinched.

Deirdre intervened, reaching past Pagan to lay a calming hand upon Lord Gellir's forearm. "Father, 'tis Miriel," she explained. "You know Miriel doesn't approve of fighting."

"Miriel?" he mumbled.

"Aye," she assured him. "And this is Sir Rand, Miriel's . . . friend."

Miriel didn't realize she'd been holding her breath. But as Lord Gellir relaxed, she let out a sigh of relief. The last thing she wanted to do was offend her father. Lord Gellir was of Viking stock, born and bred a warrior, and though his days of glory were long gone, he'd never lost his warrior spirit. To question the importance he attached to battle was to question his very existence.

Thankfully, in his present state of mind, Lord Gellir usually forgot within a moment or two whatever he'd been discussing. But he could be so unpredictable at times. She only prayed he wouldn't ask Sir Rand any embarrassing questions.

"What business do you have with my daughter?"

Like *that*.

Miriel smiled tightly. "I met him at the tournament, Father. Remember the tournament?"

He grunted. "I thought you said he couldn't fight."

"He ... He ..."

Rand saved her. "I was knocked from my horse in the melee, my lord. I never got the chance to fight in the tournament."

Pagan muttered under his breath, "Thank God for that."

Deirdre elbowed him.

Rand must have heard the insult, but he was too polite to respond to it. Instead, he took Miriel's hand gently in his and smiled at her father. "'Twas your daughter who saved me."

"Deirdre or Helena?" Lord Gellir asked.

"Miriel, my lord."

"Miriel? Miriel can't fight." Lord Gellir shook his head in disgust as the servants began serving up supper, ladling mutton pottage into the trenchers. "Nobody can fight anymore."

Miriel felt her cheeks go pink. "I wasn't fighting, Father. I was ..." Bloody hell, was she about to lie to her father? Aye, but what choice did she have? They'd concocted this tale together, she and Rand, and they had to stick by it. "I was treating his wounds."

"An angel of mercy she was, my lord," Rand added,

patting her hand. "She watched over me, mopped my brow, brought me food and drink..."

Colin smirked. "I thought you were knocked unconscious."

"He was," Miriel quickly interjected.

"She assured me she watched over me," Rand amended.

"And changed his bandages," she added.

"Forsooth?" Helena asked slyly. "And where were you wounded, Sir Rand?"

"His arm," Miriel replied.

"My leg," Rand answered simultaneously.

"His arm *and* leg," Miriel said. "'Twas a very... very grave injury."

"Indeed," Deirdre said, frowning in mock concern.

There was a long and painful silence.

Then Colin burst out laughing, and the others snickered into their trenchers. He raised his flagon toward Rand. "I might have been knocked witless for two days as well, had I such a pretty nurse."

Helena gave Colin a chiding swat on the shoulder.

Rand lifted his flagon in return, grinning.

Miriel was mortified. "You think Rand—You think I—"

Rand set his drink down and enclosed her hand between his two. "Sweetheart, we may as well confess."

"Confess?" This was not going well. Not well at all.

"'Tis true I may not have been as witless as all that," he admitted. "After all, a man would have to be witless to choose getting pummeled in the lists when he might suffer instead under the healing hands of a beautiful maid. Am I not right?"

Miriel felt her face turn to flame. Nobody would believe his story now. Everyone knew Miriel was not the sort of damsel to linger in strange pavilions with strange men.

But to her surprise, most of the men at the table laughed and raised their flagons in salute. Not even her sisters stepped in to defend her.

Miriel lowered her head to drown her ire in a flagon of wine. There'd be no convincing them now she hadn't dallied with Sir Rand at the tournament. Particularly when she'd so blatantly stolen a kiss from him this morn in front of witnesses.

Suddenly, she lost her appetite. 'Twas one thing to live in a deception of her own making. 'Twas quite another to get caught up in someone else's deceit, particularly when that someone else cared not a whit for her reputation and proved damnably creative in his storytelling.

Fortunately, the interest in Miriel's nursing skills and Rand's fighting talents waned quickly. Soon the conversation turned to ordinary things—Helena's upcoming wedding, the abundance of salmon in the loch this year, the need for repairs to the chapel, the raiding of two of Lachanburn's cows.

Then, just as Miriel was becoming lulled into a sense of safety by the soothing drone of normal Rivenloch chatter, Lord Gellir decided to engage Rand in one of his favorite conversations.

"Anyone told you about our local outlaw?"

So unexpected was the propitious turn of conversation that Rand nearly choked on his bite of mutton. He managed to swallow without incident, nonchalantly washing the bite down with a swig of wine.

"Nay," he replied, frowning with what he hoped looked like casual curiosity. "Outlaw, you say?"

But Miriel, the well-meaning but meddlesome wench, leaned forward to interrupt. "Father, I'm sure he wouldn't be interested." She explained to Rand, "'Tis mostly a lot of wild rumor and speculation, grown all out of proportion."

Rand gave her a tight smile. He wondered how rude 'twould be to gently clamp his hand over her mouth so Lord Gellir would continue.

"Although," Pagan said, jabbing the air with his eating knife to make his point, "I still say 'twas The Shadow who destroyed the English trebuchet."

Suddenly the room was filled with overlapping threads of argument, too tangled to unravel. Everyone seemed to have an opinion on the matter.

"I saw him once," Colin put in. "In the crofter's cottage where Helena held me hostage."

Rand blinked. Had he heard Colin correctly? Helena held him hostage? God's blood, these Rivenloch women were intrepid indeed.

Feigning only the mildest interest, Rand nonetheless carefully tuned his ears to every word.

Helena added, "He left one of his knives."

"His knives?" Rand asked.

She nodded. "Slim daggers, all black. He leaves them after he robs his victims."

"Not always," Miriel murmured.

"Not always," Deirdre agreed. "But there's no mistaking his work."

Rand poked offhandedly at a piece of mutton. "Indeed? And why is that?"

The old man took up Rand's invitation, as if he'd been patiently waiting for someone to ask him to relate a treasured, oft-told tale. "The Shadow," he began, his bright blue eyes lighting up like sapphires in the sun, "is as swift as lightning. Nimble as flame. Nigh invisible."

"Nigh invisible," Miriel muttered, "and yet so many claim to have seen him." She rolled her eyes.

Lord Gellir continued, waving his long, bony arms to add emphasis to the story. "He dresses all in black. From the top of his head to the tip of his toes. Black as night, but for one narrow slit where his gleaming eyes peer out like the Devil's."

He made the sign of the Cross then, and everyone mimicked the gesture, everyone but Miriel, who seemed to be horribly embarrassed by her father's dramatic rendition.

So far Lord Gellir was only describing what Rand had already ascertained. The outlaw, known only as The Shadow, was quick, agile, and apparently obsessed with black garb. But like Miriel, Rand didn't believe the man possessed any attributes of a demonic or mystical sort.

"He can flip like an acrobat," Lord Gellir said, "land on his feet, and, before his victim can so much as blink his eyes, cut his purse... or his throat."

Miriel sighed in disgust. "He's never cut anyone's throat, Father." She frowned at Rand, trying to convince him. "He *hasn't*. He's actually quite harmless."

"No one knows where he dwells," Lord Gellir intoned. "He appears out of nowhere, does his bold mischief, then vanishes into the woods... like a shadow."

"Has no one been able to catch him?" Rand asked. "Has no one tried?"

Helena and Deirdre exchanged a swift glance then, one so subtle Rand almost missed it, a look of sisterly communication only they could decipher.

Then Deirdre shrugged. "Miriel's right. For the most part, he does no harm."

"Forsooth," Helena added, "he's never bothered any Rivenloch folk, not really."

Deirdre chuckled. "Besides, what would poor Father have left to go on and on about if we arrested his favorite outlaw?"

Rand wished the old man *would* go on and on, but it seemed his addled mind had already drifted elsewhere. He was currently absorbed in picking a crumb of bread out of his long, white beard.

"No one could catch him anyway," Colin said. "He might be small, but he's wily as a fox."

"Slippery as an eel," Pagan agreed.

Helena chimed in, "Faster than a—"

"But surely someone must have tried." Rand attempted to keep his tone flippant, but he didn't want to drop the subject. "No one can be that—" As he raised his hands for emphasis, his finger caught the base of his empty flagon, and he knocked the vessel off the table.

It should have hit the floor. But Miriel's hand whipped out and caught it an instant before it did. For a heartbeat, their eyes met, his amazed, hers guilty. Then she let the flagon drop.

It clattered with damning delay on the rush-covered flagstones.

Chapter 7

"Oh!" MIRIEL EXCLAIMED. "Clumsy me."

Bloody hell, she thought. How could she have been so careless—not in dropping the flagon, but in catching it? Rand had seen her. And he must know what she'd done was nigh impossible. Gently bred, meek, mild maidens didn't snap up falling tableware in the wink of an eye.

Sung Li, who had been watching the high table from his place among the servants with increasing interest and annoyance, as he always did when the conversation turned to the overblown legend of The Shadow, stared hard at Miriel.

"Lucy!" Miriel called out. "Will you bring more wine and get Sir Rand another flagon?"

She bent to retrieve his dropped vessel, but as she handed the empty flagon to Lucy, her gaze met Rand's again, and there was no question in her mind. He'd seen everything. A suspicious furrow creased his brow, and his eyes glittered with speculation.

Now she'd have to think up a good explanation.

Or...

She could get him drunk.

If she got him drunk enough, mayhap he'd forget everything—the humiliating conversation about his lack of fighting skills, her father's foolish tales of The Shadow, his brief encounter with Miriel's fleet fingers.

Indeed, getting men drunk was an offensive strategy Helena oft employed. If it worked, if Miriel could make a blur of Rand's memory, they could begin anew on the morrow. And this time, she'd remember to keep her talents to herself, to play the helpless, docile damsel who couldn't catch a caged dove with a broken wing.

"Leave the bottle," she bade Lucy when the maidservant returned with the wine and flagon.

Rand lifted a brow.

"We have plenty now," she explained, pouring him a brimming cup. "Besides, you've yet to be treated to true Rivenloch hospitality."

He gave her a wry glance, then picked up the bottle and poured a measure into her flagon as well. " 'Tisn't hospitable to make a man drink alone."

She smiled weakly as he lifted his drink to toast her. This was not part of her plan. But she supposed 'twould have been rude to decline.

A half hour and five toasts later, she wished she *had* declined. Even Deirdre noticed the pronounced list in her bearing.

"Miri," she whispered, "I think you've had enough to drink."

Miriel frowned. "I'll decide when I've had enough to drink," she whispered back.

"Don't act like a petulant child," Deirdre hissed.

"*You're* acting like a child," she hissed back.

Deirdre only rolled her eyes, but Miriel sensed that her sister might be right. The problem with this tactic, she realized as she teetered a bit too close to Rand, rapping her flagon against his with a loud clunk, was that she wasn't Helena. Helena could drink men into the rushes. Miriel had felt dizzy after her second cup.

But he was keeping up with her, cup for cup. Soon his brain would get as muddled as hers. Then she was sure he'd forget all about…

What was it he was supposed to forget?

She couldn't recall, which suddenly seemed terribly amusing. She chuckled, while the hum of carefree conversation continued around her. Rand laughed at someone's jest, and the blend of that delightful sound and the sweet wine flowing down her throat caused a fuzzy, buzzing feeling to wash over her like warm rain. Everything seemed so pleasant. The great hall was bright and cheery. The food was tasty and plentiful. Everyone was perfectly content. She didn't know what she'd been so worried about.

She giggled happily, then clapped a hand over her mouth. Holy Rood, had that burp come out of her?

Rand grinned at her, and she grinned back. Lord, she thought, looking askance at him and running a finger lazily around the rim of her flagon, he was a handsome man. His eyes looked like polished topaz. The dimples in his cheeks were adorable. And his mouth…

Sweet Mary, she wanted to kiss him.

She was going to tell him so.

She leaned close to whisper in his ear, balancing herself

with a hand atop his leg. The sudden flare of his nostrils told her 'twas more than his leg she touched.

She should have snatched her hand back at once. But the wine must have slowed her reflexes. And ruined her judgment.

His loins felt warm and yielding beneath her palm, and her lips curved up as she remembered how dark and mysterious, forbidden and beautiful he'd looked to her when he'd unlaced his trews in the forest. Nay, she didn't want to unhand him just yet.

Rand felt pure lust shudder his bones. Surely Miriel hadn't meant to touch him there. 'Twas only a slip of her hand. But the naughty lass didn't seem in a hurry to remove that hand.

Not that he wanted her to. There was naught quite as thrilling as the brazen touch of a desirable woman. Her palm cradled his rapidly swelling loins with gentle coaxing as she seduced him with her sultry gaze.

Still, 'twas neither the time nor place for such play, not with a dozen pairs of watchful eyes studying Rand's every move.

'Twas his own fault, he supposed. It had been his idea to get her drunk in the hopes of loosening her tongue. There was something unnatural and highly suspicious about the way Miriel had snatched that flagon in mid-air, and he intended to find out how she'd acquired such reflexes.

But Miriel was a wee lass, and a half dozen cups of wine were apparently enough to do more than loosen her tongue. Indeed, it seemed to have transformed the mild-mannered maid into a wild and wanton she-beast.

Not that he minded. Especially when she gazed at him, as she did now, with fiery longing.

But her father need only glance down, and her sisters need only glimpse Miriel's expression, to determine what was afoot.

With great reluctance, he caught her stray hand and moved it, gently but firmly, back to her own lap. As soon as he did, her brow furrowed with bewilderment, and her lower lip began to tremble.

Her wide blue eyes filled with tears, and her delicate chin started quivering. He feared at any moment she might burst into loud sobs. Deirdre frowned, noticing her sister's distress. Even at a distance, Sung Li's accusing stare burned into Rand.

He had to do something.

He lifted her hand again to press it fondly against his cheek. "Miriel, my love," he said in concern, "you look weary. Would you like me to escort you to your chamber now?"

She blinked at him as if he'd spoken to her in another language, then gushed hopefully, "My chamber?"

Of course, that brought the table to silence. Several sets of expectant eyes suddenly glared at him. And the gleam of desire that flared anew in Miriel's eyes didn't help. Her family no doubt imagined he'd offered to ravish her.

"Miriel?" Deirdre asked.

Miriel wasn't going to help matters, not with her lusty gaze. He'd have to clarify his intentions himself.

"After all," he told her, loudly enough for everyone to hear, including that prying Sung Li, "you have a busy day on the morrow. You need your sleep."

"Sleep?" Miriel complained. "But I don't—"

Quickly, sure she was about to say something incriminating, Rand helped her up from the table.

Before he could make his escape, Deirdre caught his sleeve and muttered between her teeth, "You'll guide her up the stairs, no more. Leave her at the door, else you'll feel the prick of my blade this night."

He pretended great affront. "Of course."

Nonetheless, Helena, in sisterly accord, pinned him with her own threatening glare of warning.

Then he bade everyone a hasty farewell and whisked Miriel away on his arm.

'Twas no easy feat. She shuffled and swayed, tripping over her skirts. Whatever remarkable reflexes she'd employed earlier to catch his flagon in midair were gone.

He smiled and shook his head. He'd have to remember not to encourage her to imbibe so freely again. At least not in the company of others.

They awkwardly climbed the stone stairs. Miriel alternated between leaning heavily on him and bracing herself against the wall, giggling every few steps.

"Wait," she gasped, pushing him against the inner wall. "There's somethin'... I wanna tell you."

He grinned. As drunk as she was, she was still adorable. And alluring. And incorrigible.

She frowned, concentrating, trying to remember what she wanted to say. Then it came to her. She patted his chest and looked up into his eyes with serious intent. "I wanna kishoo."

The corner of his lip drifted up in amusement. Kishoo?

He caught her chin and ran his thumb lightly over her bottom lip. "If I give you a kiss, will you tell me a story?"

"A story?" Her eyelids dipped, whether from the effects of the wine or the touch of his fingers, he wasn't sure.

"Aye, a story of Rivenloch." He cradled the fine curve of her jaw. "Something adventurous." He let his fingers drift up to caress the smooth skin beneath her ear, sending a visible shiver through her. "I know. Tell me a story about... The Shadow."

Her eyes widened. "Why... why d'you wanna hear about him?"

He shrugged. "Between my time in the tiltyard and at supper, I've already heard all the glorious exploits of Lord Pagan and Sir Colin."

She smirked.

"Will you tell me a story, my love?" he murmured, toying with the soft curls at the back of her neck.

Her brow creased in a tiny frown, as if she battled against the pleasure of his touch. "All right. But first I wanna kishoo."

He was more than happy to oblige. He might have assured Deirdre he'd only guide Miriel to her door, but he'd made no promise concerning what they might do on the way there. Slipping one hand around her narrow waist, he pulled her up close, against his chest and his belt and the beast in his trews, which was growing bolder by the moment.

She gasped, and he caught the gasp in his mouth, swooping down upon her with purposeful desire. He'd thought to give her a brief-yet-powerful kiss, one that would disarm her quickly, so that she could get on with her tale.

'Twas not to be. Once he tasted the wine-sweet nectar of her lips, the liquid honey of her tongue, the naive yet worldly ambrosia of her naked desire, he was lost.

Lust set fire to them both, igniting their blood as swiftly as summer wheat struck by lightning.

She slanted her mouth to delve more deeply, sighing his name between kisses, pressing closer until he could feel the yielding rounds of her breasts, the smooth curve of her ribs, the tempting angle of her hips.

Never had he burned so brightly, so fast. Never had he so quickly lost control.

He knew he should cease. There was plenty of time for dalliance later. He was wasting precious time that could be better spent gathering information.

But he couldn't stop himself. He felt as if he'd slipped off a precipice, and there was naught he could do to halt this interminable slide. His desire raged like an avalanche. She clung to him as if for her life, weaving desperate fingers through his hair. She panted thirstily as she drank from the font of his passion, and he sipped from her in turn, growing rapidly dizzy from the intoxication of her kiss.

So caught up was he in the pleasurable whorl of sensations and emotions that he didn't notice they were no longer alone.

"So!"

The sound startled him so severely that he wrenched backward, banging his head on the wall. He had his dagger halfway out of its sheath before he noticed 'twas only Sung Li.

"Bloody hell," he muttered, resheathing the dagger and rubbing at his bruised skull. Lord, that cursed maidservant must have traveled on ghost feet, so quiet was she.

Miriel wasn't frightened. She was furious. "Sung Li!" she scolded.

The old woman ignored her to address Rand. "Is this what honor means to the knights of Morbroch?"

He couldn't help but color at her remark.

"'Tisn't his fault, Sung Li," Miriel said, weaving a bit on the step. "'Twas my idea."

Sung Li pursed her withered lips. "You *have* no ideas. You are drunk."

Miriel's exaggerated gasp only lent truth to her words.

"You're right," Rand agreed, reaching out a hand to steady Miriel. "I should not have taken advantage of her weakness."

"Weakness?" Miriel challenged. "I'm not weak!"

"Miriel!" Sung Li snapped.

Before Rand could apologize, forsooth, before he could even think, Miriel did something to crumple the back of his knee, and somehow his heels went out from under him. The next thing he knew, he was sitting flat on his arse on the hard stone step, groaning in pain and wondering how he'd gotten there.

"Oh," Miriel said, clapping her hand to her cheek. "I prob'ly shouldna done that."

Sung Li scowled and crossed her arms over her chest.

"Sorry," Miriel told him. Then she assured the maid in a loud whisper, "'S'okay. He won't remember anything. He's drunk." She bent down toward him and gave him a sloppy wink. "You're drunk." She staggered up the rest of the stairs then, waving. "G'night."

When she was out of sight, Sung Li stared at him as if weighing the consequences of beating him to a bloody pulp on the spot. And as strange as it seemed, even though the tiny woman's head barely reached his as she stood one step below and he sat on the stair, Rand began to wonder if she might be capable of doing just that.

These were peerless women, the women of Rivenloch.

They were strong-boned and strong-willed. And they engaged in curious mating rituals—challenging men to duels, holding bridegrooms hostage... leaving decrepit maidservants to rough up prospective suitors.

"'Twill not happen again, Sung Li," Rand assured her.

Her black eyes focused suddenly in on him, like a knife thrown into his heart. "Oh, aye. It *will*." The shining intensity of her gaze made him uneasy. 'Twas as if she probed his very soul. "There is an ember between you," she intoned. "But this ember, it does not make fire." She lifted her snowy brows. "It makes *huo yao*."

Rand frowned. Her words were likely just old womanish nonsense. But he was intrigued.

"*Huo yao*," she repeated, scowling as she searched for a suitable translation. "Fire... metals. Fire minerals."

"Firestone? Flint?" he tried.

She shook her head impatiently. "You have no word. But it is more powerful than fire. You should beware. Watch," she advised pointedly, "that you do not get burned."

He nodded. He understood now. 'Twas just Sung Li's version of the same warning he'd received from Miriel's siblings. Numerous times. Miriel must be the most precious gem in Rivenloch's crown, for they all rushed to protect her.

From hurt.

From harm.

From him.

No wonder the poor lass resorted to trapping men in the forest before they had to undergo inspection by her family.

Sung Li swept past him then, ascending the stairs with almost silent grace. Rand remained on the step for a while, kneading his banged buttock. 'Twas pathetic. He had yet to engage The Shadow, but between the trials of the tilt-yard and the rigors of courting, already he was thoroughly battered and bruised.

'Twould not be so, he decided, if he weren't so utterly distracted by that slip of a maid with the chestnut tresses and the twinkling blue eyes. He didn't know what she'd done to sweep him off his feet, but he was sure it wouldn't have happened if he'd been paying attention to something other than her flushed cheeks, her rosy lips, her heaving bosom…

God's wounds, he decided, wincing as he pushed himself up to stand, the pain was worth it. Miriel was not only beautiful. Not only desirable. She was unique. With no other woman had he felt such—what was it Sung Li had called it? *Huo yao.*

It almost made him wish he *could* court her. Of course, 'twas a ridiculous notion. She was a proper lady, the daughter of a lord. And he was little more than a vaga-bond with a bastard's name and a borrowed title. He wandered the land, taking work where he found it, making as many enemies as he made friends. He was unfit to be any woman's bridegroom, noble or not.

But that didn't keep him from dreaming now and again of settling down, of leaving behind his mercenary ways and finding a sweet young lass to warm his bed and bear his children, to stoke the fires of his hearth and his heart, and, aye, he thought with a grin, to knock him on his backside every once in a while when he needed it.

Chapter 8

Wbeneath the coverlet. "Quiet."

Everything hurt this morn. Her head. Her eyes. Even her teeth. And Sung Li had seen fit to yank open the shutters to blinding sunlight when Miriel had just closed her eyes for the night.

"What will you say?" Sung Li nagged, pulling the coverlet down despite Miriel's protests.

"I don't know," she whined. "What difference does it make? He probably won't remember anyway. 'Twas only one cup." Mayhap now Sung Li would leave her alone, let her go back to sleep.

"Cup? Cup? What cup?"

Lord, Sung Li sounded like a chicken, a chicken with a very loud, insistent cluck.

"The flagon he dropped. The one I caught."

Sung Li shook her hard by the shoulder, rattling her already sore joints. "Wake up."

Miriel finally whimpered in surrender. "What?"

"And what you did on the stairs?"

"What stairs?" Miriel pressed her fingertips against her pulsing temples.

"You do not remember?"

Miriel scowled against the encroaching sunlight. She did remember something. Something on the stairs. Something pleasant.

Oh, aye, she'd been kissing Rand.

Her lips curved up with the memory. He'd tasted wonderful—like honey, nay, like wine. His arms had enclosed her as warmly as a soft lamb's wool cloak. And she'd felt the thick dagger of his manhood pressing against . . .

"This is what you will say," Sung Li commanded.

Miriel sighed.

Sung Li continued, "It is only a silly trick my sisters taught me."

Miriel frowned. Something else *had* happened on the stairs, and now 'twas starting to come back to her. Dear God, 'twas not possible, was it? Surely she'd not been that drunk. But as her memory began to return with increasing clarity, she realized that, aye, she'd been that drunk. Rand had accused her of being weak, and she'd knocked the poor man on his arse. "Oh."

"Oh." Sung Li shook his head in disgust. "Is that all you say? Oh?"

"I'm sorry, *xiansheng*."

She *was* sorry. In her drunkenness, she'd done the very worst thing. She'd endangered Sung Li. Now she understood what he was telling her, what he was asking her to do. She nodded, practicing the lie. " 'Tis only a silly trick I learned from my sisters."

Sung Li grunted, as minimally satisfied as he ever was with her performance. "Now get up. We do *taijiquan*."

Miriel groaned.

As it turned out, Miriel didn't need her rehearsed lie after all. She didn't see Rand all morn. Preparations for Helena's wedding kept her bustling about the great hall and everyone else out of her way. Fortunately, Sung Li had brewed her an herbal infusion to relieve most of her ills, so she was able to function with reasonable efficiency.

She supervised the servants as they first polished and swept, then decorated the hall with cedar boughs and holly berries and sprigs of purple heather. She made certain there were plenty of candles, as well as linens and cups for guests. And she kept a written account of all the provender leaving the buttery and storerooms to make sure none found its way into private quarters.

'Twas late morn when Rand finally made his appearance at the entrance of the great hall. Miriel's heart seized suddenly at the sight of his boyish smile and merry brown eyes. A wave of sensual memory assailed her at once. She could instantly imagine the taste of his lips, the texture of his hair, the smell of his skin.

She bit her lip and willed her heart to steady its beating. She needed to get her responses under control. 'Twas a matter of grave importance. She had played with fire last night, allowing herself to act on impulse, and she'd been lucky to escape unscathed.

She might not be so lucky in the future.

She had to inure herself to Rand's presence. No matter how sparkly his eyes were or how endearing his dimples.

Besides, she told herself, fixing a sconce with a wobbly candle, 'twas the day before her sister's wedding. There was no time for idle chatter. Or long, adoring glances. Or hungry, steaming, passionate kisses.

Apparently, she had no cause to worry. Rand seemed determined to stay out of her way. He hovered at the outskirts of all the activity, lending a helping hand here, a strong back there, a word of caution or praise where 'twas required.

His charm was truly astonishing. In only a day, the clever knave had managed to weave himself neatly into the human tapestry of Rivenloch, like an earnest suitor.

Or a wily fox.

Which made him very dangerous indeed to the trusting folk of Rivenloch, folk like the maid who currently giggled as Rand bowed to her with exaggerated gallantry.

Miriel narrowed her eyes and clapped the dust from her hands. 'Twas time to intervene. She couldn't afford to have lovesick, loose-lipped servants falling at his feet. There was no telling what secrets they might divulge.

But just then the guards introduced the arrival of the first overnight guests for the wedding, and Miriel became embroiled in welcoming them. She made certain their horses were stabled, ordered refreshments for them, and invited them to make themselves comfortable by the hearth. Such duties always fell to Miriel, since she was the most congenial of the sisters.

'Twas nigh an hour before she spotted Rand again in the great hall, and when she saw with whom he was conversing, a sudden pang, sharp and unpleasant, tweaked her breast.

Lucy Campbell.

Lucy was trouble. She was too buxom for her own good, and she seemed to have difficulty keeping her twin assets inside her kirtle. She had a saucy smile and sly eyes she used to great advantage, and her rosy cheeks and unruly tresses always made her look as if she'd just come from swiving. Most of the time she had.

Even worse, Lucy Campbell was an incurable gossip. She found it as hard to keep her lips together as her legs. Rand need only give her a wink, and she'd tell him anything he wanted to know.

Lucy stood at the entrance of the buttery now, coyly tucking a stray tendril of hair behind her ear, while Sir Rand leaned against the wall beside her, smiling and chatting.

The sight made Miriel's ears burn.

It couldn't be jealousy, she told herself. After all, Rand didn't belong to her, not really. Their courtship was a farce, wasn't it?

But something about their open flirtation set Miriel's blood to simmering.

It must be anger. Lucy was her servant. Helena's wedding was on the morrow. And the lazy wench was wasting precious time, wagging her tongue and fluttering her lashes at Miriel's... at Sir Rand.

Besides, she thought, making her way across the hall, wasn't Lucy supposed to be courting Sir Rauve?

"Lucy!" she snapped, startling the maid. "Have you started the cheese yet?"

"Aye, my lady."

"Aye?" She doubted it. Lucy seldom did anything the first time she was asked.

"Aye."

Miriel frowned. "What about the dovecote? Has it been cleaned?"

"I did it yesterday, my lady."

Miriel blinked in surprise. What was wrong with Lucy? She wasn't giving Miriel her usual brash replies. And it appeared the lass had finally learned to tie the upper laces on her surcoat. "The mead. Did you—"

"The mead's been brought up."

"Oh." She glanced at Rand, who seemed taken aback by the harsh tone she was taking with Lucy. "Then what were you doing in the buttery?"

Lucy's face was the picture of innocence. "Just hanging the bacon up like you said, my lady."

"Hm. Well. Good." But Miriel still felt as irritable as a cat in the north wind. She nabbed Lucy by the elbow and steered her away from Rand, out of his hearing. "So now you've decided to dawdle away the day," she whispered, "flirting with the guests?"

"I wasn't dawdling," Lucy hissed back, "and I wasn't flirting. 'Twas him who started talking to me. What else was I supposed to do? Besides," she said, her eyes taking on a dreamy cast, "you needn't fret. I have my own man now. I won't be stealing yours."

Miriel felt a blush warm her cheeks. "What were you talking about then?"

She shrugged. "Naught. He was just asking about Rivenloch. The castle. The castle folk."

"Did he ask you anything about me?"

"Nay."

Miriel couldn't help but be displeased. Blessed Mary, she'd known Rand less than two days, and already she'd spied upon him twice and rummaged through his pack. Where was *his* natural curiosity?

"Was there something else?" Lucy asked.

Miriel shook her head. Then she reconsidered. "Aye. There is. Take a cup of ale to Sir Rauve. He's been working hard in the tiltyard."

"Aye, my lady." The way Lucy's eyes lit up as she rushed off, one would have thought Miriel had asked her to sit at the king's table.

Mayhap one day Miriel would find a man who made her eyes glow like that, the way Helena's did when she looked upon her bridegroom, the way Deirdre's did when she talked about her husband.

Sir Rand certainly didn't make Miriel's gaze go soft. Nay, he elicited completely different emotions in her. Suspicion. Amusement. Irritation. And inexplicable desire.

Shivering with the memory of his kisses, she turned to see where her welcome, yet unwelcome, suitor had gone. There he was, emerging from the cellar stairs. And he wasn't alone. Not one, but *two* giggling maidservants accompanied him as he carried a sack of oats over his shoulder, merrily proceeding across the hall and out the door.

She felt the hackles rise along her neck. What was the bloody knave up to? Was his goal to flirt with every maid in Rivenloch by sundown?

She didn't care. Truly she didn't. And she'd say those words over and over in her mind until she believed them.

Her only interest in Sir Rand was to learn what his business was at the keep. She intended to find out what he'd been talking about with the women of Rivenloch. Once she discovered that, and why he'd come to the castle, she'd discard him like a stale trencher.

Chapter 9

BY THE TIME THE COCK CROWED on the wedding morn, and the rising sun started to paint the frosty sod with silver, Rand found himself pacing the damp courtyard in front of the chapel in finery he'd borrowed from Sir Colin, as lost in his thoughts as the bridegroom himself.

Where was Miriel? Nearly all the rest of the castle folk had gathered already for the ceremony. She should be here.

The front gates opened, and Rand stopped, gazing toward the motley cluster of guests spilling through the entrance. They were Rivenloch's neighbors. Perchance he'd obtain useful information from them regarding The Shadow.

He figured he'd spoken to just about everyone in the keep yesterday. Between offering his aid in the great hall in the morn and lending a hand in the kennel, dovecote, stables, mews, and armory in the afternoon, he'd managed to exchange at least a few words with each of the several dozen Scots and Norman servants of the household and several of the nobles as well.

All the servants agreed that The Shadow was small, wore black, and was as quick as lightning, though few had actually laid eyes on him. No one had been seriously hurt by the outlaw. Mayhap that also helped to explain their reluctance to pursue him. If The Shadow had never harmed or stolen coin from any of *them*, why should they begrudge the thief his livelihood?

Indeed, if Rand hadn't heard the witness of several lords, he might have suspected The Shadow was but a legend, like George and the Dragon, or Beowulf. The robber seemed to possess powers no mortal man could claim. Rand had heard little to illuminate the true character of the outlaw he sought.

Until he'd spoken alone late last eve with Lord Gellir. The old man had been reminiscing by the fire, and Rand had asked him if he'd ever seen The Shadow himself. The lord's eyes had lit up with mischief, and he'd given Rand a sly grin.

"I believe we've *all* seen The Shadow," he said enigmatically. "The outlaw walks among us, oh, aye, right under our noses." Then he snickered into his beard as if at some private jest.

Unfortunately, 'twas all Rand could pry out of the old man. After that, Lord Gellir's mind started to wander, and soon he'd drifted off to sleep.

But with that one statement, he'd given Rand the impression that not only was The Shadow in league with the folk of Rivenloch. He might indeed *be* one of them. Someone small and agile and swift. The idea left Rand tossing half the night, considering the possibilities. But the one that kept coming back to haunt him, no matter how absurd, and no matter how he tried to banish it from his thoughts, was that he was quite familiar with someone at Rivenloch who was small and agile and swift.

Now, sighing for the hundredth time, he scratched the back of his neck and resumed his pacing. 'Twas a preposterous idea, and yet...

"Good morn," came a sudden voice immediately behind him.

Rand almost leaped out of his braies. How Miriel had managed to sneak up on him, he didn't know. But when he turned to give her a stern scolding, words failed him, and his suspicions about her scattered like chaff in the breeze.

She looked as lovely as a rose. She was attired in a surcoat of deep red, cut low across her shoulders to expose her creamy skin. A small ruby hung from a silver chain about her neck, dangling above her bosom as if to taunt him. Part of her shining hair was caught up in a fantastic labyrinth of tiny braids, while the rest spilled down her back in enticing curls. But her most beautiful aspect was the mischievous twinkle in her dancing blue eyes.

Miriel grinned smugly, taking wicked delight in having startled Rand, doubly delighted she'd taken extra care with her appearance this morn, for she'd obviously left the gaping varlet off balance.

Her own troubled *chi* she'd restored this morn with meditation and *taijiquan*. She felt prepared now to face the handsome knave with a clear head and a steady heart. She wasn't about to let Sir Rand of Morbroch ruffle her calm.

"My lady, you look..." he began.

She arched a brow. Was he going to gush out some commonplace, insincere, overly honeyed compliment now? 'Twas what a man pretending to be a suitor would do. And by his heated gaze as he perused her, he might even half mean what he said.

"You look... well rested," he decided.

Her brow creased in disappointment. "Well rested?" she echoed. Was that the best he could manage? Mayhap she wasn't as fair as Deirdre or as voluptuous as Helena, but she'd spent nigh an hour on her tresses alone.

Then she spied the spark of devilry in his eyes. The lout was baiting her intentionally.

He grinned and leaned toward her, whispering, "You look breathtaking."

Despite her best efforts, her pulse quickened as if she believed him, and she found herself giving in to the smile she couldn't control.

Curse the varlet. He might not be as duplicitous as she was, but he was damned good at it. Sweet Mary, 'twas going to be a long and challenging day.

Helena's wedding passed in a hazy blur. Miriel couldn't remember afterward anything that was said. Mayhap 'twas because Rand hovered so close to her during the ceremony, distracting her with his masculine warmth and the subtle spicy scent of his skin.

Or perchance 'twas the fact that as they stood together in the crush of witnesses while Helena and Colin recited their vows, Rand made clandestine love to her hand, twining his fingers through hers, stroking the back with his thumb, tracing delicate patterns on her palm, until she thought she might swoon with desire.

There wasn't a blessed thing she could do to stop him, not without attracting the undue attention of her protective sisters.

She couldn't snap at him. She couldn't slap his hand away. And she definitely couldn't give him an upward chop to the chin, followed by a foot sweep that would lay him flat on the floor of the chapel.

Somehow Miriel made it through the ceremony without fainting and without resorting to violence. But the wedding feast proved an even greater challenge. From the moment Rand and she sat together at the high table, he began playing to the hilt his role as her devoted suitor.

"Allow me, my lady," he cooed, feeding her a sweetmeat from his fingers.

She smiled sweetly and accepted the bite, but not without a warning nip of her teeth.

He sucked in a startled breath, drawing a sharp frown from Deirdre.

"Sweetheart," he chided affectionately, "take care you do not bite the hand that feeds you."

Now Helena was staring at them as well. Miriel forced a smile to her lips. "'Twas but a love nip, I assure you."

"Mm."

Helena rolled her eyes as Rand clasped Miriel's hand in his, pressing a fond kiss to her knuckles. Miriel had no choice but to allow him the trespass as his thumb brushed slowly to and fro over the tops of her fingers, simultaneously arousing and distressing her.

With his free hand, he picked a bottle up from the table. "More wine, darling?"

She longed to guzzle the entire bottle. Mayhap that would settle her rapidly fraying nerves. But Deirdre was keeping a watchful eye. So instead, she gave him a playful swat. "Are you trying to get me drunk, my love?"

He nuzzled her hair. "Only on my affections, sweetheart."

Now Deirdre rolled her eyes, and Miriel had to bite her tongue to keep from gagging on the cloying syrup of his words.

He released her hand and set the bottle down. For one moment, Miriel had a reprieve from his assault. Then he casually wound the end of one of her tiny braids betwixt his thumb and fingers. Slowly but surely he began to reel her closer.

Miriel clenched her teeth. She might need to keep up appearances, but she wasn't about to be hauled in like a salmon. With a twinkle in her eyes that was more mischievous than fond, she coiled her own finger in a curl at the nape of his neck, gradually tightening it until he winced in pain.

When he sent her a bewildered glance, she withdrew her hand, pretending innocence.

He let go of her braid as well, and for a moment, she imagined she'd made her point, that he'd gotten her message. Until he began casually to stroke the top of her shoulder where the red fabric met her bare flesh, back and forth, back and forth.

Miriel's hand tightened upon her eating dagger. She raised it slowly from the table.

Rand's fingers suddenly froze on her shoulder as he eyed the blade. "My love," he said conversationally, despite a tense smile, "allow me."

He placed his hand over hers on the dagger. For a moment they fought for control of the weapon.

"Miri?" Helena's brow furrowed with concern, and the entire table fell silent. Bloody hell. If Helena suspected Miriel was in the slightest distress, she'd jump up from the bench, draw her sword, and fight Rand atop the tables.

So with a silent sigh of defeat, Miriel relaxed her grip on the dagger and let Rand take it from her.

"One slice or two?" he asked innocently, the dagger poised over the meat in their shared trencher.

"One," she replied, adding between clenched teeth, "my love."

Reassured, Helena and Deirdre and everyone else returned to their supper, blissfully unaware that while they made merry around her, Rand was secretly waging war upon Miriel's senses.

'Twas when he slipped his hand beneath her tresses and began stroking her gently at the base of her skull, sending tingles of pleasure shivering along her spine, that she knew she was in trouble.

Through weighted lids, she spied Sung Li at one of the lower tables. He was scowling at her. She blinked, trying to clear her thoughts. Her *xiansheng* had once told her that the wise warrior knew when to retreat.

Perchance now was the time. If she removed herself physically from Rand's presence, mayhap she could gather her wits again.

"I...I'm going to check on the mead," she said, her voice more ragged than she expected.

"Hurry back," he replied with a wink.

Rand had to admit he was rather enjoying this game of cat and mouse. Miriel was a wickedly clever lass, but she'd cornered herself into a far more intimate relationship with him than she'd intended. Which didn't trouble Rand in the least, though it apparently set Miriel's teeth on edge.

He leaned back to watch her walk away from the table. She strode briskly, as if fleeing a snarling dog, her hips twitching, her skirts snapping behind her like a red sail. He grinned. A mischievous, quick-witted imp she might be, but the lovely lass with the feminine curves was no skulking outlaw. He'd been a fool to imagine it.

Meanwhile, he needed to find out who the real villain was. Since Miriel had excused herself, 'twas a good opportunity to make conversation with some of Rivenloch's guests.

Unfortunately, no matter how skilled Rand was at eliciting information, he quickly discovered one could get no blood from a stone.

He listened halfheartedly while one of the Lachanburn men retold his encounter with The Shadow.

"... black as coal ... fleet as a fox ... leaving a wake as chilling as the North Sea ..."

Another Lachanburn lad volunteered, "No bigger than a child."

And a third chimed in, "But the cleverest acrobat you've ever seen."

Rand nodded. He was getting nowhere. They all told the same tale. Mayhap he'd have more luck with the women.

The ladies of Mochrie were delighted to make his acquaintance, forsooth so visibly delighted that Miriel's sisters began firing accusatory glares Rand's way. Deirdre and Helena might not deem him a suitable suitor for their little sister, but they certainly didn't approve of his flirting with other maids while he claimed to be courting Miriel.

He flashed them a sheepish smile. He could hardly be blamed for the Mochries' friendliness. 'Twas not his fault if women were enchanted by his dimples.

"The Shadow?" one of the Mochrie maids asked, fluttering her lashes. "I've not seen him with my own eyes. But I've heard—"

"He's not of this world," another lass intoned mysteriously, laying a hand upon Rand's sleeve.

The first maid nodded in accord.

The woman beside her shivered. "He must be terribly dangerous."

"Terribly," agreed a fourth maid, pressing her hand against her breast. "I'd be so frightened to meet him in the wood."

"Indeed," said the first. "We're only gentle maids after all." She bit her lip in a helpless gesture.

The second woman slipped her fingers along Rand's sleeve, as if measuring the muscle beneath. "I wager *you'd* not be frightened, Sir Rand."

The others cooed in agreement, and Rand's smile became taut as he felt the knot of adoring females close about him.

From the corner of his eye, he spied rescue. Miriel was emerging from the cellar. Eager to extricate himself from the bevy of clucking admirers, he waved his hand toward her in greeting.

She glanced up, but when she saw him in the midst of the fawning Mochrie maids, her eyes narrowed, and she turned up her nose, ignoring him completely to visit with other guests.

The naughty imp! Surely she could see he was trapped. One of the Mochrie women clung to his sleeve, another had seized his hand, and they were all chattering away at once, winding words around him like silk ribbons.

"My ladies," he said, gently withdrawing his hand, when he could finally slip a word in, "I must take my leave now."

A flurry of protests went up, and 'twas another long while before he could make himself heard. Eventually he managed to tug loose of their clutches, but only by vowing to accompany them through the woods on the morrow.

Which was fortuitous indeed, for he'd been seeking an excuse to travel through the forest in the hopes of encountering The Shadow.

Beaming with success, he passed by the hounds, giving one of them a scratch behind the ears, as he watched Miriel making her dutiful rounds about the hall.

She checked to make sure no one's cup was empty and ruffled one of the scruffy red heads of the Lachanburn children. She squeezed the hand of a withered old woman and pushed a teetering trencher back from the edge of the table. She scooped up a wee child who'd tripped and banged her knee, then turned to straighten a garland hanging on the wall.

How he could have suspected her of being The Shadow, he didn't know. Miriel was domestic and nurturing by nature. And irresistible, he decided, letting his gaze rove down her lovely backside.

Harboring thoughts of sweet revenge for her earlier ambush, he sauntered across the hall and sneaked up behind her, then caught her about the waist. But instead of a feminine gasp of pleased surprise, he immediately earned a sharp jab of her elbow to his ribs that bent him in half and left him gasping.

"Oh!" she exclaimed. "I'm sorry. Are you all right?"

For a moment, he couldn't speak. The blow had knocked the breath from him. Lord, the wench had sharp elbows, and he wasn't sure she sounded all that sorry. There'd be a black bruise there on the morrow, certainly, even if the lass hadn't actually cracked one of his ribs.

"I... slipped," she said.

If that was a slip, he'd hate to feel what she'd do if she *meant* to hurt him.

"Nay, 'tis my fault," he wheezed. "I shouldn't have startled you. I'd forgotten how quick you are."

"What do you mean?"

"Your reflexes."

"Mine?" she squeaked. "I don't know what you're talking about. Sung Li says I'm... clumsy."

"Clumsy?" He caught his breath while he massaged away the bruise. The pain eased in a moment, and he was able to straighten. "You didn't seem so clumsy the other night when you caught my flagon in midair." He leaned close to murmur, "Nor when you kissed me later on the stairs."

She stiffened, blurting out, "'Tis but a silly trick my sisters taught me."

He grinned. "The catch? Or the kiss?"

Her cheeks pinkened. By the Saints, was there anything prettier than a maiden's blush? "Neither. Both."

He chuckled. Glancing about the hall to make sure no guardian's gaze was pinned on him, he reached up to smooth a stray tendril of hair back from her brow. "Then I must speak with your sisters, my love. They may have some very interesting information to share."

She ducked her head away, rejecting his placating

gesture. "I thought you *had* talked to them." Her words were innocent enough, but there was a subtle edge to her voice as she added, "Haven't you spoken to nigh *all* the ladies of Rivenloch, and Lachanburn, and Mochrie in the last two days?"

"Why, my love," he said in soft surprise, "are you jealous?"

Her eyes went all dewy and soft, yet Rand spied a gleam of devilry in her gaze, a spark other men might not notice. She lowered her attention to his chest, walking her fingers coyly up his surcoat. "'Tis just that I'd rather you spoke to *me.*"

He almost laughed aloud, but instead dipped his eyelids in sultry approval, edging closer to murmur, "And what would you have me say?"

Her tongue slipped out the tiniest bit to lick her bottom lip, making him suddenly long to do the same. Then she gave him a subtle shrug. "What did you say to *them?*"

"Who?" His mind was already losing focus as he began to feel the full force of her allure.

"All those women."

He gazed down at her tempting mouth, so pink, so wet, so inviting, and gave her a knavish smile, "I told them I could not wait to run my fingers through your hair, to press my lips to yours, to wrap my arms around your—"

She gave him a scolding cuff on the arm. "You did not." She thrust out her lip in a charming pout. "I'd wager you didn't speak of me at all."

Forsooth, she was right. He hadn't inquired about her. What was there to ask? He already knew she was beautiful, sweet-natured, intelligent, delightful, and a bit wicked. He didn't need to know more. Besides, he was on the trail of a dangerous outlaw, not a desirable imp of a wench.

But for a man to admit he could think of anything other than his ladylove when he was supposed to be courting her was a mistake of the worst kind.

"Of course I spoke of you, my love," he lied. "I'm hungry to know everything about you. What your childhood was like. Where you like to wander. What you like for breakfast. Your favorite color."

Her eyes narrowed slyly. "What *is* my favorite color?"

Without missing a beat, he trapped her gaze in his own and replied, "I'm hoping 'tis brown."

"Brown?"

"Aye," he told her, lifting the corner of his mouth in a wry grin, "the color of my eyes."

Miriel resisted the urge to groan. Instead, she forced a honey-sweet smile to her face and cooed, " 'Tis my favorite color *now.*"

Curse the varlet, he was destroying her *chi* again, and along with it, her judgment. She couldn't tell, even staring directly into his eyes, whether he was telling her the truth or not. Surely he wasn't serious, and yet the adoration in his gaze seemed real. Was he genuinely lovestruck or just diabolically clever? 'Twas difficult to discern.

But if anyone could eventually ferret out the truth, 'twas Miriel. She'd find out what he was up to even if she had to flirt shamelessly to do it.

"What about you?" she asked, coyly lowering her lashes.

"Me?"

"What's your favorite color?" He'd say blue, of course, the color of *her* eyes.

Instead, the varlet let his gaze drift suggestively down to her lips. "Rose red."

Her heart fluttered at the uninvited memory of his kiss, and to her disgust, she felt a blush heat her cheeks.

Bloody hell. This was proving more difficult than she'd anticipated.

She forced a nonchalant shrug. "The Mochrie maids have lips of rose red. Perchance that's the reason you've been consorting with them."

"Are their lips rose red?" he asked, arching a brow. "I couldn't tell. They never stopped flapping them long enough."

Miriel bit back a smile. The Mochrie women *were* notoriously chatty. She asked casually, "And what were they flapping on about now?"

Glancing quickly about for witnesses, he caught her chin between his thumb and finger, tipping her head up to gaze lustily into her eyes. "Naught nearly as engaging as the conversations *we* have, my love."

She gently tugged out of his grip. This was not going well. The varlet was turning her every inquiry into a flirtation.

"Well, whatever they said must have been fascinating indeed," she countered. "It seemed you could hardly tear yourself away."

He grinned and gave her nose a patronizing swipe of his fingertip. "I'm beside you now, my jealous little darling. 'Tis all that matters."

She clenched her teeth against the urge to bite his finger. Curse the wily fox. He was stealing his way out of her trap again. She forced her tight mouth into an innocuous smile. "But what could you have possibly asked them to spur them to such lengthy discourse, my love?" She added for good measure, "Why, *I* can hardly get the Mochrie maids to put two words together." 'Twas a blatant lie. The Mochrie women would wag their tongues at the drop of a pin. But Rand wouldn't know that.

"Ah," he said. "What subject do women most like to speak on?"

Miriel waited for his answer with bated breath while she made silent guesses. Secret love affairs? Hidden wealth? Castle defenses?

He chuckled. "Themselves, of course."

Miriel did not find him amusing. And she didn't believe him for an instant. "Indeed?" she asked lightly. "And these maids, the ones who told you all about themselves, what were their names?"

He blinked.

She figured as much.

While he continued to stall, she flashed him a deceptively sweet smile, kissed her own fingertip, then pressed it against his damningly silent mouth.

Clucking her tongue, she swept away, back to her spot among her sisters at the high table. Despite her smug departure, she was far more troubled than she dared let on. Rand of Morbroch was proving a challenging opponent.

Miriel recognized his evasive tactics, for she'd used them herself. Over the years, to protect her own secrets, she'd learned to dodge in and out of probing interrogation by her sisters or her father through deflection, distraction, and maintaining a calm demeanor. The skills required were not unlike those used in effective combat, the fighting principles Sung Li had taught her.

But she'd never been faced with anyone who understood

and employed the tactics against *her.* 'Twas maddening, as frustrating as wrestling a mud-slick piglet. The two of them seemed cut from the same cloth, and after thrusting and dodging as expertly with words as any warrior with a sword—simpering, mincing, pouting, flirting, fawning— Miriel was completely fatigued and no nearer to uncovering his secrets.

Worse, she began to fear that Sir Rand of Morbroch was better at this game of deception than she was.

❧

Chapter 10

Dawn found most of the household still abed, exhausted from the revelry of the night before. Not Rand. He was on a mission. Today might be the day he at last came face-to-face with The Shadow.

By the fire, he wolfed down a breakfast of buttered oatcakes and watered ale, glancing about the hall at the remains of last eve's celebration—broken cups, wilted flowers, snoring hounds with full bellies, melted candles, discarded bones, and here and there an intrepid mouse searching for food among the rushes.

It appeared Miriel would have a lot of accounting to do. A smile blossomed on Rand's face, albeit a weary one, as her beautiful, mischievous, irresistible image materialized in his thoughts.

His ladylove was proving an admirable adversary. 'Twas difficult enough, juggling the real pursuit of a criminal with the feigned pursuit of a lover. But when lust and jealousy rose up to complicate matters, and when relentless

Miriel kept probing closer and closer to the truth, Rand found himself in a position of dissembling faster than a priest caught in a brothel.

Not that he minded a little harmless lying. 'Twas part of his work. He refused to feel guilty about it. Besides, Miriel wasn't exactly without sin herself. Lies slipped off her tongue as easily as water from a swan's back.

He'd known women like Miriel before. As adoring as they seemed, once they'd won him to their affections, they'd let him go without shedding a tear. For them, the conquest was everything.

He understood. His own livelihood was based on the hunt. There was naught more thrilling than circling around and closing in on one's prey, outwitting and ultimately capturing that quarry.

Meanwhile he'd have to suffer through a seduction that left his mouth dry, his heart pounding, and his ballocks aching with unrequited desire.

At least this morn he'd get a respite from Miriel's charms. According to the scowling Sung Li, who must have risen with the chickens, the lass was still lying abed, and nay, she did not wish to be disturbed.

The Mochrie maids, on the other hand, were only too eager to meet their escort. They descended the stairs in a flurry of chatter, making Rand wonder if they ceased talking when they slept. His presence in the great hall pleased them almost as much as it displeased Sung Li, who immediately scurried back up to Miriel's chamber, probably to report to her mistress what a philandering scoundrel he was.

Rand couldn't stop the old woman's tongue-wagging, but with luck, he might apprehend The Shadow today.

Once that task was accomplished, Rand could drop his false pretenses, give Miriel what they both wanted, or at least a reasonable taste of it, then wish her a fond farewell and be on his merry way back to Morbroch to collect his reward.

There was a good chance he could achieve his goal this morn. If, as he suspected, the robber was knowledgeable about the wedding guests, aware of their comings and goings, he'd know the Mochries were an easy target. They'd won considerable silver last night, gambling with Lord Gellir, and there were only two men-at-arms in their party, so they'd not put up much of a fight. What thief could resist such tempting prey?

There were a dozen of them altogether—five maids, two men, three children, an old woman, and himself. As they set off through the forest, the men took the fore and rear of the line, with Rand in the middle, which greatly pleased the infatuated maids. But after a quarter of an hour of listening to unceasing prattle and jangling giggles, he almost wished he'd taken up a different post. He could hardly hear himself think, much less listen for intruders.

He nonetheless kept his gaze roving through the trees, alert to any shifting shadow or telltale turn of a leaf. Twice he was fooled by startled quail bursting from the underbrush. Once he thought he saw a suspicious flicker in the branches, but it turned out to be a reflection off one of the women's medallions.

As time wore on, he began to doubt that he'd meet the robber. Perchance he'd chosen the wrong clan. Mayhap The Shadow preferred to attack travelers who were fewer in number. Perchance Rand should have followed the Lachanburns instead.

Then, just as they passed through a sunlit glade, he heard the man at the head of the line draw in a sharp breath. Rand's hand went instantly to his sword.

When the man stopped walking, the line compacted, each traveler colliding with the one in front, trapping Rand in the midst.

Rand was not a man to draw hasty conclusions. Anything could have frozen the man in his tracks. A wild boar. An English scout. A silver coin on the path.

But before he could even poke his head around to see what lay before them, a whisper of fearful awe traveled back like a fleet breath of chill wind.

" 'Tis The Shadow."

"Shadow."

"The Shadow."

By the time Rand extricated himself from the crowd of bodies and drew his sword, the Mochrie man at the fore was already lying, belly down, on the ground.

Rand's nostrils flared. God's blood! Was he dead?

Nay, the fallen man's fingers scrabbled weakly in the mulch. He was only stunned.

And standing over him, a purse already cut and clutched in his gloved fist, was the outlaw known as The Shadow.

True to legend, he was attired all in black, from his supple leather gloves to his soft leather boots. His legs and arms were swathed in layers of black cloth, which continued around his head, leaving one narrow slit for air and two more for his eyes. Over it all, he wore a kind of close-fitting, sashed surcoat, a deceptively made garment that might conceal a multitude of weapons.

But Rand wasn't daunted. Though The Shadow bore

a startling resemblance to the Devil, 'twas clear he was a mortal, and a rather small-framed mortal at that.

"Halt!" Rand barked, raising his sword.

The thief glanced up long enough for Rand to glimpse a dark gleam in his shrouded eyes. Then the man sprang with sudden, inexplicable agility, leaping and swinging through the branches to land beside the man at the rear of the line.

Rand wheeled about. The thief *was* fast. But Rand was surely faster. This time he wouldn't wait for the knave to make a move. He charged forward, brandishing his blade.

Before he took two steps, The Shadow had waylaid the second Mochrie man as well, twirling him halfway round to force his arm up behind him, then cutting his purse and catching it before it dropped to the ground.

While Rand watched in amazement, the robber shoved the man headfirst into a tree trunk, knocking him out, tucking both purses into whatever pockets his strange garb contained. Then he faced Rand, cocking his head as if to ask if Rand was certain he wished to challenge him.

Rand was no coward. The man might be fast, but he was small. His only weapon was a slim dagger against Rand's broadsword. In this instance, brute force would prevail.

"Stand aside!" he commanded the women and children. 'Twas said that The Shadow had never mortally injured anyone, but Rand didn't want to take any risks.

At his order, the Mochries dutifully scattered to the sides of the path.

The Shadow gave a slight nod then, almost a mocking salute, and Rand got the impression that beneath the layers of black cloth, the man was grinning.

Rand intended to smite that grin off the outlaw's face. With a grim scowl, he took a step forward.

If he'd blinked, he would have missed the swift kick that The Shadow aimed toward his sword arm. Even so, he was barely able to retract his hand fast enough to keep hold of his weapon as he felt the close brush of The Shadow's boot upon his fingers.

There was no time to be amazed. In the next instant, The Shadow advanced with a forward punch that fell short of Rand's jaw only because he reflexively jerked his head back.

The next succession of blows Rand was unable to avoid. Like a quintain spinning loose from its mooring, The Shadow's foot came around and caught him in the ribs. Rand was folded forward by the impact, directly into a fist that clipped him on the chin. Then the outlaw used both hands to shove him backward.

Somehow Rand managed to stay on his feet, though he had to retreat to shake off the rapid attack and collect himself.

Meanwhile, The Shadow stood waiting like an insolent lad, his arms crossed over his chest in smug challenge.

Rand flipped the sword over in his grip. With a roar that usually sent men scurrying, he swung the flat of the blade forward with enough force to knock the outlaw cold.

But the agile thief dropped to the ground as the sword whistled past, and Rand was almost spun around backward as his blade sailed through empty air.

Rand slashed diagonally downward then, once, twice, but The Shadow leaped nimbly aside both times.

Now Rand's determination was aroused. This was absurd. Rand was an experienced warrior. And the thief was not much bigger than a child. Rand had the advantage of power and size and reach. Surely he could bring the outlaw to his knees.

With a sharp exhalation, he began circling the robber, brandishing the blade before him, calculating the best angle of attack.

In transparent mockery, the thief whipped out his much smaller black knife and began aping Rand's stealthy steps.

Behind him, Rand heard one of the maids giggle at the performance, which only fed his growing irritation with the varlet.

Then he saw his opportunity. The Shadow's attention shifted slightly as one of the maids whispered to another. Rand thrust suddenly forward, intending to give him a harmless but incapacitating slice along the ribs.

Not only did the thief dodge the strike, but he simultaneously sent his own weapon spinning through the air toward Rand's head, not close enough to do him injury, but close enough to distract him.

As Rand reared his head back, startled by the flash of the silver blade, something happened. He wasn't sure what.

But in the next confusing moments, he was struck in several places, the sword was knocked from his grip, and he was bowled over as readily as a set of kayles, to collide with the hard ground.

Rand lay flat on his back, stunned, his lungs robbed of air, staring up at branches that hung over him like concerned bystanders.

How the bloody hell had it happened? How could it be that some wee fellow in black rags, armed with a tiny knife and clambering through the trees like a monkey, had not only eluded capture, but felled him?

Him. Rand la Nuit. Seasoned warrior. Esteemed swordsman. Respected champion. And one of the most reputable mercenaries in all of Scotland.

For a moment all he could do was lie there, breathless, while The Shadow swung up to perch in the branch of a nearby tree, wagging his scolding finger. While he watched, the thief tossed some small, round object onto Rand's chest, then, in a flash, leaped down to scamper off into the woods.

After what seemed an eternity, Rand was finally able to drag in a hefty breath of air. He coughed once, twice, dislodging whatever The Shadow had thrown at him. Then he rose onto his elbows.

"Are you all right?" one of the Mochrie maids asked. There was definitely diminished admiration in her voice. She apparently was as disappointed as he was.

He nodded graciously. But inside he was fuming. The brazen thief had humiliated him. Outwitted him. Outmaneuvered him. Made him into an absolute fool.

Worse, it seemed the Mochrie women were more than just unimpressed with Rand's defense of them.

"Did you see him?" one of them asked eagerly.

"Aye, barely," another replied. "He moved as quickly as ... as ..."

"As lightning."

"Nay," another said dreamily, "as swift as ... shadow."

The other maids murmured in soft agreement.

"I wonder what he looks like beneath that mask."

"Blond," one of them guessed.

"Nay, black-haired, to match his garb."

"I'd wager he's as ugly as sin. Why else would he cover his face?"

"To hide his identity, addlepate."

"Do you think we know him?" one of them asked, wide-eyed.

"Nay. No one I know can fight like that."

"I think he wears a mask," one of them cooed, "because he wishes to remain a man of mystery."

"Aye, mystery."

"Forsooth, I'd wager he's as handsome as the Devil."

The maids tittered behind their hands.

"He reminded me of—"

"Ladies!" Rand had heard enough.

The empty-headed wenches had no idea how close they'd come to harm. If the thief had taken it into his head to hurt or maim or kill them, Rand had no doubt he would have succeeded.

Now, to listen to them glorifying the villain as if he were to be admired . . .

He shook his head and pushed up to his feet, wincing at his injuries.

"Are you unharmed?" he asked them pointedly.

They nodded.

One overbold lass languidly volunteered, "I don't think The Shadow would ever hurt a woman."

Rand's disgust almost equaled his fury. They were half-wits indeed if they believed an outlaw followed a code of honor. Satan's ballocks! Even the mercenaries he knew bent the principles of chivalry.

The Shadow was certainly capable. And that both alarmed and enraged Rand. He knew now that The Shadow was a serious threat. The outlaw might have only stolen a bit of silver and entertained the ladies with his antics today. But there was no telling what he might do when he grew bored with cutting purses. 'Twas a short distance to go from cutting purses to cutting throats.

Aye, he decided as the Mochrie men-at-arms, still groggy but recovering, gathered their wits and their weapons, he definitely intended to catch this villain.

'Twas not a matter of reward now.

'Twas a matter of honor.

"Look!" one of the maids cried. "There's his dagger!"

Rand scowled as the damsels rushed over to examine the slim black knife protruding from the trunk of an oak. Unbelievably, they began to quarrel over the thing, as if 'twere some champion's favor. Rand could only roll his eyes.

One of the Mochrie men clapped a consoling hand on Rand's shoulder. "At least you got to fight him." He shook his head. "The man moves faster than a monk out of a whorehouse."

The second man joined them. "Aye, you're lucky he didn't get to *your* coin."

Rand frowned, patting his purse. 'Twas true. The Shadow hadn't stolen from him. But was it because Rand had defended himself so well, or had the thief simply not wanted to bother with his coin?

"Do you need a few shillings to get you home?" Rand asked.

The first man shook his head. "Nay. 'Twas only our winnings anyway."

"Winnings?"

"Aye," the second man told him, "coin won wagering last night."

The men thanked Rand for his offer and for his admirable attempt with his sword, but already Rand's brain was reeling over what they'd said. He stared off into the forest where the outlaw had disappeared.

The Shadow must be connected somehow to Rivenloch. Someone at the wedding supper last night, someone who'd been wagering at the table, someone unhappy with his diminishing purse, must have found a way to recover his losses. Could The Shadow be a hireling of sorts, an agent of retribution for one of Rivenloch's denizens?

'Twas difficult to imagine. The Cameliard knights were highly regarded in chivalrous circles, renowned for their honor and loyalty. And the Rivenloch men he'd spoken to seemed too fiercely proud to resort to such underhanded tactics.

But then Rand had seen the worst of men. Traveling in the environs he did, he came into contact with villains of the roughest sort, men who could grin and clap you on the shoulder while shoving a knife into your back. He'd seen once kind and peaceful men, tormented by some act of violence against their loved ones, ask for the kind of vengeance only the Devil should exact.

Rand drew the line at cold-blooded murder. He refused to be a hired assassin. But though he was ashamed to admit it and loath to remember, as a young and desperate mercenary, he'd sometimes been a partner to that kind of revenge, delivering wrongdoers into such men's hands, turning a blind eye and walking away while they claimed their payment in flesh and no doubt secured their place in Hell.

Thus Rand had learned that all men were fallible. Honor was fragile. Loyalty was fleeting. With the right motivation, heroes could be turned to outlaws in the wink of an eye.

Was avarice enough motivation for a man to hire a robber like The Shadow to terrorize the countryside?

Most certainly. And 'twas up to men like Rand to stop them.

The Mochrie men had finally settled the damsels' petty bickering by awarding The Shadow's knife to the young lad who traveled with them, much to the ladies' dismay. But as soon as Rand bent to retrieve his broadsword from the forest floor, the maids found something new to pique their interest.

"What's that?" One of the damsels pointed to a shiny object winking up from the ground beside him.

"'Tis mine," one lady claimed.

"I saw it first!"

"Nay, you didn't. I—"

"Ladies!" Rand's irritation was only exceeded by his curiosity. He snapped up the object himself before they could engage in a wrestling bout for the thing.

'Twas a silver coin.

One of the maids gasped. "Is that what The Shadow tossed at you?"

He furrowed his brow. It must be. But why?

"It must be a token of honor," one of the men-at-arms guessed. "He paid you for giving him a good fight."

"How romantic," one of the women sighed.

"I *knew* he was a man of chivalry," another declared.

"Perchance we'll see him again one—"

"I'll take my leave now." Rand's patience was at an end. He flipped the coin once and slipped it into his purse, out of the envious view of the Mochrie maids. Then, sheathing his sword, he nodded farewell.

He planned to spar in the tiltyard again today, to immerse himself in the ranks of the men of Rivenloch, earn their camaraderie, gain their trust. Tonight he'd join in the wagering, keeping a close watch on the players. And he'd try not to get distracted by the breathtaking lass who kept creeping into his thoughts.

Chapter 11

Miriel was finishing up the accounts at her desk when Sung Li came up behind her with a late breakfast of oatcakes and butter.

"It seems your suitor is much more... talented than he led you to believe."

Miriel tensed, but kept her eyes on her ledgers. It made her edgy when Sung Li spoke of Sir Rand. 'Twas obvious he detested the man and would do anything to get rid of him. But Miriel didn't want to get rid of him yet, not before she discovered his intentions. "Talented?"

"He is quite skilled with the sword."

Miriel swallowed hard. Sung Li was right. "Is he?" She shrugged, dipping her quill into ink to scrawl the last figure on the page. "Mayhap his skills are improving because Pagan has been sparring with him. Pagan's a good teacher."

"Those kinds of skills a man does not learn in two

days," Sung Li said, setting the basket of oatcakes at the edge of Miriel's books. "He is born with them."

"So why would he underplay his skills?" She asked the question as much to herself as to Sung Li. "Why would he pretend incompetence?"

"Why would you?" Sung Li asked.

She frowned thoughtfully. "The greatest weapon is the one no one knows you possess."

"Exactly. The element of surprise."

"Hm." Miriel blew on the last entry in the ledger to dry it, then closed the book, sliding it aside. "What makes you so interested in his swordsmanship anyway? Swordsman or not, you know I could knock him on his arse."

"Pah! Sometimes you are overconfident," Sung Li warned, "like a duckling who thinks it can fly because it can swim."

Miriel broke an oatcake and spread a thick layer of butter over it. "If I'm overconfident," she said, giving Sung Li an obsequious grin, "'tis only because I have the best teacher in the world."

"Hmph." Sung Li never fell victim to Miriel's fawning. He was a wise old man who saw through everything, *almost* everything.

"Besides," Miriel said, pausing to nibble on the edge of the oatcake, "I should think you'd be pleased that I have a suitor adept with a blade."

He lowered his brows and intoned, "Those who practice deception have something to hide."

Miriel stared at the old man.

Sometimes his words sounded terribly deep and mysterious.

Other times it seemed he only stated the obvious.

This was one of those times. She opened her mouth to argue with him, to tell him, of *course* they have something to hide, then thought better of it. One never argued with Sung Li. At least not if one wanted to avoid an hour-long diatribe on the wisdom of the Orient.

"You should go to the lists," Sung Li said. "Watch him. Study him."

Miriel took another bite, mostly to delay answering. She supposed there would be no harm in watching Rand fight today. Indeed, 'twas always a pleasure to watch a handsome knight wielding his sword—lunging, thrusting. Gasping. Sweating.

But she suspected Sung Li knew more than he was telling her. His directive was less of a suggestion, more of a command. And she sensed a wary warning in his voice.

"All right, *xiansheng*," she conceded, "if you insist."

In the end, she was glad she had taken an hour out of her day to observe from the practice field fence while Pagan put Rand through his paces. She suspected Rand's congeniality as he sparred with the men was as carefully manufactured as his inability with a blade. But he was damned good at it, nearly as good as she. She had to admire his talent.

He feigned great interest in Pagan's advice, mimicked to perfection the moves that Rauve taught him, and even listened to Deirdre's recommendations regarding his grip on the sword.

His swordsmanship showed marked improvement, which Miriel knew was just as calculated. After all, naught flattered and ingratiated one to a man so well as steadily improving under his instruction.

Miriel took note of his checked swings, the slashes that went wide of their mark, the delayed blocks that resulted in close misses.

He was intentionally minimizing his ability. He was certainly capable of greater strength and speed. He only withheld them because he had no call to use them here.

Deirdre came up beside her. "He's improving."

"You think so?" Miriel affected a small pout. "Helena said he fought like a wee lass."

"Coming from Helena, 'tis a compliment. You should have seen her fight when she was a wee lass."

"What's this?"

Naught could keep Helena from the tiltyard long, even lying abed with her bridegroom on her wedding morn. She arrived in a breathless rush, wrapping a companionable arm around each of her sisters.

Miriel sighed. "Do you think he'll ever fight well enough to protect me?"

Helena gave her a sly smile. "Do you like the handsome lad then?"

Miriel gazed out across the field again, where Rand was crossing swords with Rauve. He *was* a comely man, even if he might be a lying varlet. His shoulders were wide and powerful. His chest was broad, narrowing below his waist where his belt rested. His dark hair hung in damp locks about his face, down which rivulets of sweat ran as he wheeled and lunged with seemingly endless energy. When Rauve called an end to the fight, Rand's face lit up with the most brilliant smile full of flashing teeth.

Miriel's heart fluttered as desire surged through her, unbidden. Lord, the knave was more handsome than any man should be allowed. Still, she tried to keep her tone even as she admitted hoarsely, "He *is* attractive."

"And kind," Deirdre said.

"Aye." He *acted* kind anyway, helping the servants, speaking patiently to her father.

"And generous," Helena added.

"Hm." Generous? He'd given Miriel his silver coin. But 'twas probably to buy her affections. He'd also offered escort to the Mochrie maids this morn, and that was definitely not motivated by generosity. What man *wouldn't* offer escort to a bevy of fawning women?

"Brave," Deirdre suggested.

Miriel glanced at her. "Brave?"

"Did you not hear, Miri?" Deirdre's eyes glittered with sudden delight, and she straightened to her full height to impart the news. "Your suitor, Sir Rand of Morbroch, this very morn challenged none other than The Shadow."

Miriel clapped a hand to her bosom. "What?"

Helena didn't believe her. "Nay."

"Aye. All the keep's a-buzz." Deirdre wrinkled her forehead. "Did no one tell you, Miri?"

Miriel crumpled the neckline of her surcoat. "Was he ... was he hurt?"

"Oh, nay, nay," Deirdre rushed to assure her. "You know The Shadow. Just a few scratches and a bit of bruised pride. But here's the interesting thing." She drew closer to whisper to both of them. "The Shadow left him a tribute."

"One of his knives?" Miriel guessed.

"Nay. A silver coin. A tribute to Rand's worthy battle."

Helena smirked. "Pah! A tribute?"

Miriel frowned. "A tribute? Is that what he said?"

Deirdre nodded. "He apparently had quite a battle with the outlaw."

"Or so he claims," Helena said dubiously.

"I doubt he'd exaggerate," Deirdre argued. "After all, there were a dozen witnesses."

"A tribute?" Miriel asked again.

Helena chuckled. "Perchance 'twas his very ineptitude that made him a unique challenge to The Shadow."

"Ineptitude?" Miriel arched a brow.

Helena ignored her, jesting with Deirdre, "Mayhap we should send children from now on to battle the robber if he's so easily—"

"Hel!" Deirdre gave her a chiding punch in the shoulder and nodded meaningfully toward Miriel.

But Miriel was not offended.

She was irate.

Rand had managed to turn his morn's frolic into a deed of heroic proportions, using the opportunity to garner instant glory among the castle folk and ingratiate himself into the ranks of the knights. Even her oldest sister was convinced he was a champion. How the bloody hell had the varlet done it?

"I didn't mean it, Miri," Helena apologized. "It doesn't matter if he can fight or not. You'll always have us to protect you."

Deirdre frowned. "What Hel means to say is all that matters is that you love him. You love him, don't you?"

Miriel narrowed her eyes at the man grinning victoriously on the field. She'd wipe that smug smile off his face if she had to use every weapon in her arsenal. Molding her own mouth into a tight smile, she bit out, "Oh, aye. I love him very much."

Rand felt Miriel's eyes on him as he spun and dodged and deflected some of Kenneth's blows. He almost wished the beautiful lass would leave. 'Twas difficult enough concentrating on his sparring—fighting well, but not too well, blocking some blows, but not all—without the weight of her adoring gaze upon him.

Part of him itched to show off to her, to display the full measure of his skill, for most maids who beheld his speed and power were left with their mouths hanging open in awe. Most maids except for the maids of Mochrie, he supposed, who'd witnessed his sound beating at the hands of The Shadow this morn.

He hadn't intended to tell anyone about his altercation. But the bruises on his arms couldn't be easily explained away, especially when Pagan eyed him with an accusing glare. As protective of Miriel as they all were, the man likely wondered if she'd given Rand those injuries, fighting off his advances.

So he'd sheepishly confessed what had happened, figuring they'd hear the tale sooner or later from the Mochries anyway.

'Twas a surprise to him that instead of jesting about his lopsided battle, the men of Rivenloch were amazed. They demanded to hear about the fight, blow by blow. Apparently, no one had sparred for quite so long a time with The Shadow. And when he told them the outlaw had left a silver coin to pay him for the pleasure, they were utterly astounded.

'Twas embarrassing to Rand. Forsooth, he got the impression that leaving the coin had been a gesture of mockery, not a tribute. But he wasn't about to argue with the castle folk. If they wanted to make a hero of him, who was he to deny them?

Besides, the story served to earn him instant respect among the knights, respect that would doubtless get him a prominent place at the wagering table this eve.

Over Kenneth's head, he glimpsed Miriel again at the fence. She was waving her hand, trying to garner his attention. He waved back, and Kenneth, thinking he meant to strike, shoved Rand's arm away with his shield. Without thought, Rand responded at once. He spun away, then came around with the haft of his sword, punching Kenneth hard in the shoulder.

Kenneth fell back, gripping his injured arm, his face pale with surprise.

"Oh! Kenneth. Are you all right?" Rand silently cursed himself. He'd been so preoccupied with that smiling beauty at the fence that he'd completely lost his head. Bloody hell. He could have hurt Kenneth seriously.

"F-fine."

"I don't know what happened," Rand said, only half-lying.

Kenneth gave him a feeble smile. "You've got a mean clout anyway," he said by way of encouragement.

Rand winced. Kenneth didn't know the half of it. With a muttered apology, he clumsily fumbled his sword back into its sheath and excused himself to confront the damsel who was causing all this distraction.

"You're improving," Miriel gushed, when he came up to the fence.

Lord, she was breathtaking. This morn she wore a woad surcoat that perfectly matched her merry blue eyes. Her hair was pulled into a neat braid, threaded through with a matching ribbon, a ribbon he longed to untie so those dark auburn waves would tumble down her shoulders.

She stepped up onto the lower wattle rung of the fence so their heads were level. "You'll be able to best Pagan in no time," she cooed.

He chuckled, then used his teeth to tug off his leather gauntlet. He could best Pagan now if he wished to. He shook his head with affected modesty. "Hardly."

"Nay," she insisted. "Even my sisters are impressed."

"Your sisters." That made him laugh again. He still found it hard to believe they were allowed to wield swords at all. "And what about you?" He pulled off his second glove.

She shyly dipped her eyes. "I was always impressed."

When she lifted her eyes again, they'd grown dark with longing. His own desires rose with astonishing speed, as her gaze touched him like flame touched to kindling. A lusty fire flared up inside him, a blaze that threatened to burn quickly out of control.

He forced his voice to a steadiness he didn't feel. "I thought you disapproved of fighting."

She leaned forward until she was inches away, then whispered, " 'Tis not the fighting that impressed me."

"Indeed?"

She slowly lowered her gaze to his mouth, then tucked her lower lip coyly beneath her teeth, leaving no doubt as to what impressed her about him.

"Lady, you play with flame."

One corner of her cherry red lip drifted up in a knowing smile.

'Twas a good thing he was wearing chain mail, else his lust would have been displayed for all the world to see. Lord, he'd never wanted to kiss a maid so badly. Kiss her and caress her, lay her down in the grass and...

"Come with me?" she beckoned.

He barely found the strength to nod.

Vaulting over the tiltyard fence was another matter.

Rand figured he'd done what he'd set out to do this morn—met The Shadow and endeared himself to the Rivenloch knights. Tonight he'd play at the gaming table and do more investigation. In the meantime, there was plenty of time to engage in more rewarding pursuits.

Miriel laced her fingers through his. She must be a wanton wench indeed, he decided, to overlook the fact that he was hot and filthy from the lists and probably reeked of leather and sweat. She tugged him along nonetheless, smiling in conspiracy as they passed the stables.

"Where are you taking me?"

"To a place no one will hear us."

He grinned.

She stopped in front of the dovecote, announcing to any who might chance to hear, "Allow me to show you the fine doves the Cameliards brought with them, Sir Rand."

Rand's mouth twitched with amusement. He wondered if she was fooling anyone. "By all means, my lady. There's naught I appreciate more than a fine dove." As they entered through the oak door, he added softly, "And you, my love, are the finest dove I've ever seen."

The door closed behind them, leaving the interior

dimly lit in stripes of sunlight where the vertical boards of the dovecote didn't quite match. A ripple of coos rolled through the ranks of doves, and the sweet scent of fresh straw diminished the usually pungent dovecote odors.

Miriel wasted no time. She ran her hands over the front of his tabard, pushing him gently back against the closed door to gaze lovingly up into his eyes.

"I've never kissed a . . . a hero before," she breathed.

"A hero?"

"Aye," she said, moving her fingers over the tops of his shoulders as if to judge their width. "I heard what you did."

"That? 'Twas naught."

"Oh, nay. 'Twas amazing." She slid her palm up the side of his neck. "All the castle's a-buzz."

He wrapped his arms around her, locking his fingers above the curve of her buttocks.

He could tell her the truth—that he'd humiliated himself battling with The Shadow. That the outlaw had outwitted and outmaneuvered him at every turn. That the accounts of his heroics were greatly exaggerated.

But 'twas rather pleasant enduring Miriel's adoration. If she wanted to believe he was a hero, who was he to disappoint her?

"Tell me what happened," she pleaded, turning about in his embrace so that her head rested against his chest and her backside snuggled against his loins. "Everything. Leave out naught."

He grinned, propping his chin on the top of her head.

"As you wish, my lady." He slipped his chin down then until he was murmuring against her hair, so she could feel his breath stir her ear. "The woods were dark and sinister," he began in a whisper, "as quiet as death."

"As quiet as death? I thought you were there with the Mochrie maids."

"True." He decided, "But they were chattering in very soft voices...when all of a sudden, in the midst of the forest, I began to feel," he said, disengaging his hands, "a prickling at the back of my neck." He let one hand steal up her back, then fluttered his fingers along her nape. She shivered.

"Naturally, I moved a hand to my hilt."

He clasped his hands again above her waist. She covered them with her own. Her palms felt smooth and delicate on his battered knuckles.

"I glanced through the trees, searching for an intruder, watching for the slightest flutter of a leaf or bowing of a limb. But naught moved in the branches."

"Not even sparrows?"

Forsooth there *had* been sparrows. He remembered wondering which flitted and chittered about more, the sparrows or the Mochrie maids. But he shook his head. Sparrows would detract from the drama of the tale. "'Twas too early in the morn for sparrows."

"What about—"

"Or mice. Or squirrels. Or anything else."

"Owls."

"Nay. No owls." He frowned. Was the lass purposely trying to ruin the story?

"Go on."

He cleared his throat, then purred, "I have somewhat of an instinct for danger. And that instinct told me we were being followed. With bated breath, I crept slowly forward, step by step, my knuckles gripped tightly around the haft of my sword until..." He jerked his arms suddenly, startling Miriel into a squeak. "There he was. He'd leaped onto the path out of nowhere. The Shadow."

Miriel turned in his arms again, facing him with eyes full of fright. "You must have been terrified."

He looked down at her with stern stoicism. "A man dares not give in to terror at a time like that."

She sighed reverently. "What did he look like? Was he as they describe? Was he all in black?"

"Oh, aye, as black as a raven's wing, small but fleet, as deadly as the Reaper."

"What did you do?"

"First I made certain the ladies and children were safe."

She frowned curiously. "And did The Shadow wait patiently by while you did that?"

He paused. There was no getting around the fact that The Shadow had managed to cut two purses before Rand could even lay a hand on the villain. "While I was ensuring their safety, the two men of Mochrie were doing valiant battle with the thief."

"So 'twas two fully armed knights against one small thief?"

He scowled. Somehow she was missing the point. "He was an amazingly elusive small thief."

"Ah."

"By the time I'd seen to their safety, the Mochrie men had already been victimized."

Her eyes widened. "Dear God! Were they wounded? Maimed? Killed?"

How Miriel was managing to ruin his heroic tale, Rand

didn't know, but she was doing a fair job of leaching all the glory out of it.

"They were... robbed."

"Oh." Already the admiration in her eyes was dimming.

"Are you sure you want to hear all this prattle?" he asked, letting his gaze rove slowly over her lovely features. "I can think of much more pleasurable things to do with my tongue."

Her eyes glazed for a moment, and he saw her swallow. His words clearly had an effect on her.

"Kiss me," he urged in a whisper.

A wrinkle of distress flitted across her brow. "I... I..."

"Just one kiss," he breathed. "Then I'll finish the story."

She lowered her gaze to his mouth, considering, then gave him an infinitesimal nod. "One."

He cupped her face in his hands and pressed a sweet, chaste kiss upon her mouth.

'Twas well worth all the nicks and bruises he'd earned this morn to feel the healing brush of Miriel's lips. Her mouth was soft and warm, a soothing balm for his damaged pride, nourishment for his hungry body.

As difficult as 'twas to restrain, he meant to keep his word. One kiss.

'Twas Miriel who would not release him. With a faint sigh, she pressed more deeply into his embrace, gathering his tabard in her fists. She nudged his mouth open, sliding her lips over his, even delving the tip of her tongue within.

'Twas like lightning jagged through his veins then, shocking him, paralyzing him. All thought, all reason, all will deserted him. He could no more resist her than he could have pulled away from charged steel. Nor did he wish to.

Only the sudden flap of a swooping dove startled them apart. Miriel staggered back, her stunned expression mirroring his own emotions. What occurred between them seemed a mystery to them both, some strange force of nature that defied explanation.

She regained her composure before he did, blowing out a calming breath and wiping the back of her trembling hand across her wet mouth. "One kiss," she said, as much a reminder to herself as to him.

Rand knew his animal craving would take much longer to subside, but he'd *make* it subside if 'twas her wish. He couldn't afford to lose control here, where the opportunities the dim privacy of the dovecote afforded were so inviting. Now was not the time to be reckless.

"Where were we?" he asked with a weak smile.

She approached more cautiously this time, turning to incline her head back against his chest. He wrapped one arm about her waist, his other about her shoulders, letting his forearm rest lightly upon her bosom, and she reached up to drape her fingers over that arm. Strangely, it seemed the most natural position in the world. Anyone seeing them might have thought they'd been lovers for years.

"You were telling me about The Shadow robbing you."

He hesitated a moment, collecting his thoughts, then shook his head. "Not me. He didn't rob me."

"He didn't? Why not? Have you no coin?"

The mischievous maid knew better. She'd rummaged through his belongings. "I had coin. But after I was done with him, I imagine The Shadow decided 'twas not worth his trouble."

"Done with him?" Her fingers tightened on his forearm. "What did you do?"

'Twas hard for him to remember. Not only because everything had happened so quickly, but because he was completely distracted by the tempting damsel in his arms.

He didn't want to tell stories. He wanted to slide his palm from Miriel's shoulder down to her breast, to cup her tender flesh in his hand and feel her sigh against...

"Rand?"

"Aye?"

"What happened?"

He swallowed hard. Perchance if he told the tale swiftly, they could move on to more pleasant things. "Naught, really. I drew my sword, brandished it at the outlaw. He yelped in terror and ran off into the forest."

"Indeed? And for that he left you the tribute of a silver coin?"

He winced. He'd forgotten about the silver coin. "Nay. I suppose 'twas a more lengthy battle than that." He gave her shoulders a gentle squeeze. "I just didn't want to bore you with all the fighting."

"I'm not bored," she insisted. "I want to hear every last detail."

He sighed. He was afraid of that. He couldn't remember every last detail. Still, he supposed since he wasn't going to tell her the truth of the fight anyway, he could tell her anything.

"As soon as the women and children were safely off the path," he murmured, breathing in the light, clean scent of Miriel's hair, "I turned to face the robber." He let his thumb stroke slowly along the cap of her shoulder. "He was squat and ugly, like a black beetle, fresh from the grave. And he looked out from his ugly face with the beady black eyes of the Devil."

"Ugly?"

"Oh, aye, as ugly as sin."

"I thought The Shadow wore a mask."

His thumb froze midstroke. "Aye. Right." He resumed stroking. "But there are some creatures whose souls are so ugly, the ugliness oozes from every pore of their bodies. I'm certain he was one of those creatures."

She seemed satisfied with his explanation. But he'd have to be more careful. 'Twas challenging to tell a rational story when one's cock was pressed against a young maid's firm buttocks.

He nuzzled her hair and whispered, "Before I could even raise my blade, the villain hurtled forward like a charging boar, his sharp teeth bared."

"The Shadow has sharp teeth?"

"Nay, a boar has sharp teeth."

"What did The Shadow have?"

"What do you mean?"

"A sword? A mace? A flail?" She tightened her grip, bracing for the worst. "A war hammer?"

He scowled. "I think he might have had one of his knives."

"You mean one of those tiny black daggers?"

"They're not tiny. They're . . . they're . . . quite sharp."

"Hm. Go on."

Disconcerted, he tried to resume control of the story. "Whatever weapons he did or did not have—and 'twas

impossible to tell what was stashed in his Devil's garb—
he moved as fast as the wind." To demonstrate, he quickly
spun her around in his arms, gripping her by the shoulders
and pinning her with a stare. "Like that."

Her eyes were wide. "Were you...frightened?" Her
gaze, seemingly of its own free will, slowly drifted down
to his mouth then. And gradually, beneath the sultry dip of
her eyelids, he saw her hunger grow.

His body answered with a surge of need that rose as
relentlessly as a bubble in boiling oil. He gazed upon her
succulent lips with longing. How he yearned to kiss that
delicious, warm, nurturing mouth.

"What's there to be frightened of?" he whispered,
his thoughts straying far from The Shadow. "'Tis only
a harmless..."

How their mouths met, Rand didn't know. Like a lode-
stone to iron, they were simply drawn together. And once
the kiss was begun, he never wanted it to end.

Miriel knew she was drowning. She felt the whirlpool
of desire sucking her down into the depths and the waters
of passion closing over her head. Yet she couldn't do
a bloody thing to stop them.

Nor did she want to.

This was the balance her body craved, the equilibrium
of her *chi*. Though the sensation was as dizzying as the
first time Sung Li had made her hang upside down from a
tree limb, 'twas somehow *right*.

Suddenly it didn't matter what Rand was, what skills
he concealed, what lies he told, what threat he posed. The
way the blood was singing through her veins, the way her
flesh felt afire with lust, the way her heart pounded against

her ribs, she knew that this man was the completion of her circle, the *yang* for her *yin*.

Somehow her arms found their way about his damp neck, pulling him closer. The smell of sweat and leather and chain mail lingered on him. The scent was undeniably male, foreign, and intoxicating.

He tasted mildly of ale, but mostly of passion, and she drank deep from the font of his yearning to quench her own. Their tongues flirted and mated and danced together like courting butterflies. Their mouths feasted as if they fed on ambrosia.

With one hand, he found and untied the ribbon of her braid, loosening the weave until she felt the waves tumble down her back. Then, growling in soft approval, he delved his fingers into the mass, cradling the back of her head, his fingertips rubbing gently until her scalp tingled.

His armored chest was like a stone wall against her breasts, and she longed to tear away his tabard and strip off his chain mail to get to the supple man beneath.

She felt his fingers teasing at the back of her surcoat, descending over the ridges of her spine, while his other hand ventured over her hip. When it settled with a possessive grasp on her buttock, she gasped, but had no urge to pull away. Rather, she angled her hips more fully against him, melting into his embrace.

He groaned against her lips, and the sound sent a shiver of need through her already awakened womanhood. When his hand eased around to the front of her neckline, his fingers dancing along her collarbone, her nipples began to prickle with anticipation. Atop her surcoat his palm slipped, lower, lower, until he cupped her breast, hefting its weight tenderly in his hand.

Her emotions gone wild, she moaned at the sensation, relishing the ecstasy of his touch, yearning to tear away the fabric between them, thirsting for more.

He gave her more. As if he read her mind, he spread the laces of her surcoat and loosened the top, then, while she suffered in breathless expectation, he let his fingers venture beneath her garments, trailing gently over her burning flesh.

When he touched a fingertip to the sensitive crest of her breast, she gasped at the intensity of heat. And when the hand upon her buttocks curved down to intrude into the crevice between, 'twas all she could do to keep standing upright.

All else but desire vanished. The doves. The dovecote. Her inhibitions.

Rand was her meditation. He was her focus. She wanted to join with him, meld with him, climb inside of him until their souls tangled inextricably.

But Fate intervened.

Just as she was about to collapse in sensual surrender, the dovecote was abruptly flooded with an explosion of sunlight, harsh and blinding, that tore them violently apart.

"Hello?" 'Twas Sir Rauve.

With practiced ease, Rand quickly slipped Miriel's surcoat back into place and set her protectively behind him. "Sir Rauve." His voice had the rough edge of unrequited desire.

"Sir Rand?" Rauve ventured.

Miriel, shaken and confused, hid behind Rand, trying to bring a semblance of order to her hair and surcoat.

Before Rand could answer, Rauve continued in a low growl, "Lucy? Is that you?"

" 'Tisn't Lucy, Rauve," Rand answered quickly.

"Oh." After an awkward silence, he added, "I was supposed to meet Lucy here."

"She's not here."

"All right then. Sorry."

Another long silence ensued before finally Rand said, "Good-bye, Rauve."

"Oh. Aye."

By the time Rauve left, Miriel's heart had almost recovered from the shock of his intrusion. But the abrupt slap of sunlight had done more than just startle her. It had shed light upon her own foolishness.

She'd lost her mind. Her control. Her balance. How Rand had tricked her into believing he was the completion of her spirit, she didn't know. But now, by the clear light of day, despite the deep pool of seduction she'd fallen into, she realized it had all been an illusion.

Quivering with humiliation and self-disgust, she knotted the laces of her surcoat, smacked the dust from her skirts, and prepared to bid him a curt farewell.

She expected a smug grin from him when he turned around, a knowing arch of his brow, a self-satisfied smirk. After all, he must believe he had her at his mercy now.

Naught prepared her for the truth of his mood when their gazes met. His eyes shone as softly as candlelight, smoky with longing, tender with regret. His nostrils flared with residual ardor, and his lips were parted and swollen with kissing. But the gentle understanding in his regard caught her completely off guard.

She'd feigned attraction from the time she was a little girl.

Whenever she wanted a favor from the men of Rivenloch, she coyly dipped her eyes, bit her lip, smiled demurely. But the look on his face wasn't feigned. She was sure of it. And 'twas more than mere lust.

A sparkle of wonder lit his eyes, wonder and a curious affection, an affection impossible to falsify.

Rand might have left her helpless with desire.

But she'd shot him straight through the heart.

Chapter 12

THE EVENING FIRE CRACKLED AND SNAPPED on the hearth. Miriel gazed into the flames, running a lazy finger around and around the rim of her flagon. Beyond her, servants tossed the bones from supper to the growling hounds, while upon the walls, shadows leaped in the flickering firelight, as if they danced to the soft strains of Boniface's lute. But Miriel's thoughts were miles away.

What if she was wrong about Rand? What if he *did* have feelings for her?

Aye, he'd invented the tale about meeting her at the tournament and returning to court her. But what if his deceptions had begun to take on a life of their own?

Mayhap he *was* falling in love with her.

'Twas enough to confound her wits.

Usually she could read a man in an instant. She could spot insincerity in the eyes, hear dishonesty in the voice, detect the slightest departure from the truth just from the way a man carried himself.

But Rand was an enigma. Either he was exceptionally good at deception, or he wasn't deceiving her. 'Twas impossible to tell. Ever since that earth-tilting, soul-shaking kiss in the dovecote, she'd begun to doubt her own judgment.

She couldn't forget the look on his face as they'd parted, the strange mixture of longing and vulnerability in his eyes, an expression too open and honest, too uncertain, too sincere, to be anything but genuine. An opportunity had been lost with Rauve's interruption, and the regret in Rand's gaze was more than simple disappointment.

If he meant what his eyes revealed, if he truly cared for her, if his courtship turned out to be real, Miriel sensed her world would never be the same. 'Twould be set a-tilt, like a spinning toy wobbling wildly off its axis. 'Twas a thought both terrifying and exhilarating.

Boniface's tuneful virelai was drowned suddenly as a roar of protest went up at the gaming table. Miriel glanced up. One of the two Herdclay brothers, stragglers from Helena's wedding, had won yet again.

She sighed. She was glad they were leaving on the morrow. The Herdclays had a nasty habit of draining their flagons every time either of them won, which they were doing frequently this eve, and so the drunken pair was becoming increasingly rude and obnoxious as the evening progressed.

At least Rand was a polite participant. He played beside her father, neither gloating at his wins nor cursing at his losses. The Rivenloch men seemed to have welcomed him into the fold, chuckling with him, elbowing him, coaching him as he wagered against Lord Gellir.

Even her sisters had taken a liking to Sir Rand. Deirdre seemed to believe there was hope for him as a suitor, though perchance 'twas only that in her condition, her heart had grown tender. Helena, far less confident in his warrior skills, still appeared to consider him a decent man, one worthy of friendship, if not her complete respect.

Only Miriel had doubts, and even those were diminished every time she glanced at Rand this eve, at his laughing eyes and his bright smile, his unruly hair and his tempting mouth.

Why could she not trust him?

Perchance because he was too much like her.

Miriel kept secrets. Secrets about what she was capable of, what she knew, and what she did. Secrets about her strength and her nature and her *xiansheng,* Sung Li. She wielded secret authority over castle affairs. She even maintained a secret passageway from the keep.

What secrets did Rand harbor? Were his secrets merely innocent stretches of the truth or the fabrications of a master of deception?

She watched him as he surrendered two more silver coins to Lord Gellir. Rand shrugged modestly, taking his loss in stride, while his fellow players clapped him on the back in consolation. Then, as if summoned by her gaze, he glanced toward Miriel, giving her a fond wink before returning to the game.

Sweet Mary, even that small gesture hastened her pulse. Images of the dovecote flashed through her mind with breathless speed and in sharp relief, piercing through more rational thoughts.

Remembering his kiss, her lips tingled. Recalling the warmth of his breath, her ears hummed with desire. Her breasts, as if feeling again the gentle touch of his hands, tightened and strained at her gown. She shivered. Low in her belly, desire reared its hungry head.

Hoping to wash away the lusty memories, she tossed back a generous swig of ale. 'Twas unwise to let pleasure interfere with reason.

Gathering her wits, she regarded Rand again, this time with cool, calm, collected calculation.

She mentally listed his attributes. He was kind. Good-natured. Respectful. Honorable. Generous. Patient. His manner at table was polite. He was a courteous listener. He was gentle with animals. And children.

And her.

She sighed. How could he *not* be sincere? 'Twas nigh impossible to believe such an innocent and comely face could conceal such a devious trickster.

Yet the same might be said for Miriel.

Miriel wasn't malicious. Or conniving. Or cruel. But she *was* devious in her way. Despite her sense of discipline, she knew there was always the possibility she could choose *not* to exercise discretion. Which would make her dangerous indeed.

Was Rand dangerous? Did he have powers he might misuse? Or was he, as she wanted to believe with all her heart, pure in his motives?

Coming up behind Miriel, as silent as a cat, Sung Li observed, "He wagers as skillfully as he fights."

Miriel smirked. "He's losing almost every round."

"Is he?"

Miriel frowned at Sung Li. Was that sarcasm in the old man's voice, or was he only being mysterious again?

"Or," Sung Li added with a meaningful lift of his brows, "is he sacrificing his coin only to win something more valuable?"

"What do you mean?"

"He is losing intentionally."

Miriel didn't want to admit it, but watching him over the last hour, playing with the men of Rivenloch and the Herdclay brothers, she'd suspected that as well. It seemed like every wager Rand made where he won three shillings, in the next round, he'd lose four.

"By losing," Sung Li explained, "he has won the friendship of your father."

Sung Li was right. Lord Gellir was treating Rand with almost fatherly affection, ruffling his hair, patting his forearm. "Perchance he's only being charitable."

"Perchance *you* are being charitable," Sung Li replied. "You have a weakness for this boy that is blinding you."

"He's not a boy. And I'm not blind."

"Hmph."

Rand tossed a glance her way again, accompanied by a lopsided grin that showed off one of his adorable dimples, and 'twas all Miriel could do not to melt on the spot.

Sung Li shook his head in disgust. "Blinded by a pretty face."

"He's not pretty. He's…" He was splendid. Magnificent. Heart-stoppingly beautiful. Like a dark angel. Or a Roman god. But she wouldn't say that to Sung Li. "Adequate."

"Adequate enough to lead you into danger."

Miriel's cheeks pinkened. Her adventure with Rand in the dovecote had felt dangerous indeed. But she was a woman of strong control. Rand might be able to stir her senses and touch her heart, but when and if it came to true danger, she was more than capable of defending herself.

A sudden cackle of triumph arose from the gaming

table, accompanied by grumbles from the losers. The Herdclays had managed to move a good portion of the silver to their side of the table, and they had no qualms about gloating over their win. Rand laid a consoling hand atop Lord Gellir's sleeve, but Miriel's father was already drifting off to sleep at the table.

Miriel sighed. After she had one of the servants put Lord Gellir to bed, she'd add up his losses. She'd leave sorting out the accounts for the morrow.

Sung Li slitted his eyes, scrutinizing the Herdclay brothers. "They are like young cocks, crowing over a tiny patch of ground."

" 'Tisn't a 'tiny patch of ground.' It looks like they've won close to twenty shillings off my father."

Sung Li scowled. "I am glad the vermin are leaving."

"Aye." She allowed herself a mischievous smile. "Though they'd certainly better be careful with their coin on the road. 'Twould make a nice prize for The Shadow."

"Do you think The Shadow would risk another robbery so soon, now that he has a challenger?"

"A challenger? You mean Rand?" She smirked. "The Shadow was amusing himself with Sir Rand. No one's ever challenged The Shadow and won."

Sung Li grew silent then, and Miriel could only guess at his thoughts. With his belief in *karma,* he probably half hoped the Herdclays would somehow meet with misfortune, whether at the hands of The Shadow or someone else.

Miriel had to agree. They were a vexing pair. The fact that they would gleefully gloat over snatching the last bit of silver from an ailing old man whose only joy in life was gaming made them deserving of whatever ill befell them.

* * *

The sun was not yet awake. But Rand had already positioned himself behind a mossy oak near the entrance to the woods. The Herdclays would be passing this way soon.

Three Rivenloch lads at the gaming table last night had been of a similar build to The Shadow. If one of them was indeed the outlaw, he'd know the Herdclay brothers' winnings had been substantial. He'd also know that they'd be traveling through the forest this morn, just the pair of them.

This time Rand planned to follow the travelers secretly and at a distance. First of all, he suspected the brothers wouldn't appreciate his escort, taking it as an insult. Second, Rand knew that two men were a much more tempting target than three. And third, though he was loath to admit it, he needed every advantage to battle The Shadow, including the advantage of surprise.

Waiting was the hardest part. He allowed himself a yawn, only to have it cut off abruptly as an owl swooped past his head, close enough to ruffle his hair.

He abruptly froze. Perchance the owl had been frightened from its perch by an outlaw in black. For several long moments, he heard his own pulse in his ears as they strained at every rustle of leaves, every whisper of branches. But no robber sprang from the trees.

'Twas a full hour later when the sun and the Herdclays at last made their appearance. The brothers tromped noisily down the path, still boasting about their success of the night before. 'Twould be easy to follow them. They were so preoccupied, listening to the sound of their own voices, that they'd never hear him. Forsooth, the loud varlets made such an easy target, he was almost tempted to rob them himself.

When they neared the place where he'd encountered The Shadow before, Rand silently drew his sword and scanned the trees, ready this time to catch the outlaw unawares. But The Shadow didn't strike.

Nor did he strike at the next curve in the path. Nor where the trail dipped as it passed by a spring. Nor in the dense thicket of hazel where a robber could easily hide.

Rand had decided The Shadow must have overslept, missing a prime opportunity for profit, when he heard an indignant yelp from one of the men.

He stole forward, keeping out of sight, until he glimpsed a black wraith slip between the brothers on the path ahead.

The Shadow.

His heart pounding with the thrill of the chase, Rand nonetheless forced himself to patience. He ducked behind a pine, peering through the branches, as the outlaw proceeded to confront the Herdclays.

Rand had thought The Shadow impressive yesterday, but he was even more astonishing today. The brothers put up an admirable fight for their winnings, attacking with their swords in a coordinated effort from both sides of the robber. But they were no match for The Shadow's quick maneuvering, his uncanny balance, his unusual attacks and defenses, the way he seemed to bound off trees and dance on air.

Rand saw now why the Mochrie maids had been so smitten by the outlaw. And why the folk of Rivenloch were in no hurry to capture the thief. He was truly amazing to behold.

Forsooth, so caught up was Rand, watching the brothers try in vain to prevent The Shadow's attack, that he almost missed his chance to catch the villain.

Within moments, The Shadow tossed one brother into the shrubs and laid the other out flat on his belly, both without suffering a scratch. He tucked their cut purses into some secret fold of his garb as he came down the path toward Rand.

Rand needed to act now. Taking a silent breath, tightening his grip on his sword, he prepared to waylay the thief.

Just as he flexed his knees to spring, a thunk sounded in the trunk beside him, distracting his eye for an instant. But that instant was everything.

In the moment he glanced at the slim black knife, something hit his wrist hard, loosening his grip on his sword. He managed to hold on to the weapon, but a second impact caught the back of his legs, and he fell to his knees on the forest floor while a flash of black passed before his eyes.

He dared not slash blindly forward with his sword. He meant to capture The Shadow, not slay him. Instead, he swung his left fist round, intent on striking whatever part of the robber was within reach. Incredibly, he swung at empty air.

The nimble thief had leaped up to grab hold of a branch overhead, lifting his legs to dodge Rand's blow. Now he swung backward, with the clear intent of kicking Rand on his forward swing.

Rand perceived the attack in time. He threw himself to the right, dropping his sword, and turned swiftly to catch the robber about the legs. Then he gave a hard yank, loosening the man's grip on the branch.

The Shadow fell forward into the brush with Rand's arms still clamped around his legs. For one victorious moment, Rand thought he'd done it. He'd single-handedly captured the notoriously elusive outlaw.

But the cursed thief was as slippery as a trout. Despite Rand's steely grip, The Shadow managed to squirm and twist and wriggle free, his parting insult a swift kick to Rand's chin.

Though the impact was sudden, rocking Rand's head back, 'twas not a disabling blow. Forsooth, Rand got the impression, as the castle folk had said, that the outlaw wouldn't truly injure anyone.

But that didn't mean he wasn't still a menace.

Rand snapped up his discarded sword and prepared to engage the man again.

Undaunted by his near capture, The Shadow sprang to his feet, standing on the path with his legs flexed and his arms raised, ready for combat.

Rand, torn between accomplishing his mission in the most expedient manner or following the rules of chivalry, opted for chivalry. The Shadow was unarmed. In all fairness, Rand couldn't use his blade against him. He cast aside the weapon and made fists of his hands instead.

"Come on, monkey," he goaded. "Fight like a man."

"Get him!" one of the Herdclay brothers prodded.

"Aye, make him pay!" the other chimed in.

Rand gave them a cursory glance. 'Twas not chivalry that kept them from helping him, he was sure. 'Twas a lack of courage.

He looked back at The Shadow. As if he was enjoying himself immensely, the outlaw cocked his head and beckoned Rand with his finger.

Rand prided himself on being a quick study. Though he had limited experience battling The Shadow, already he'd begun to note the man's fighting style. He was crafty and swift, using clever dodges and inflicting blows with the accuracy of a well-fired arrow. And he used his feet. His *feet*. 'Twas a curious way to spar indeed.

But Rand had the definite advantage of size and strength. If he could manage to land just one powerful blow, he'd send the outlaw to oblivion long enough to shackle him.

With that in mind, Rand lunged forward and threw a hefty punch at the man's head.

But where his head was one moment, 'twas not the next. Worse, as his fist flew past The Shadow's head, the man somehow seized Rand's arm and shoved him even farther, using his own momentum to push him off-balance.

By the time he staggered around, The Shadow stood braced for action again.

"Come on, man!" one of the Herdclays yelled. "Show him what you're made of."

"Send that black Devil back to Hell!"

Rand ground his teeth. When he was done with The Shadow, he'd enjoy taking on the cowardly brothers as well.

Rand eyed his opponent, trying to discern the best approach. Growing up a bastard in a noble household had taught him skills beyond those learned by most knights. He knew how to fight with his fists, how to wrestle, how to use crude weapons no honorable knight would touch.

With a menacing growl, he hurtled forward, intending to tackle the robber. Half-expecting the man to step aside at the last instant, he spread his arms wide, like a fisherman casting a broad net.

To his surprise, The Shadow didn't step aside. Instead,

he took the initial impact of Rand's tackle, then rolled suddenly backward upon the ground, taking Rand with him. The man planted his feet in Rand's stomach as they tumbled together, and Rand felt his legs fly up in the air and his head dive toward the earth. In self-defense, he curled into a ball. When he hit the ground, instead of breaking his neck, he landed with a bone-jarring roll along his spine.

He thought The Shadow would escape through the woods then, just as he had the day before. Mayhap the outlaw would even toss another silver coin to him, thanks for the bout. For one ludicrous moment, Rand wondered if he could retire from his mercenary work and make a living sparring with The Shadow every few days. Then he rattled the thought out of his head and rose to reevaluate the situation.

The Shadow had stood his ground rather than flee. He must be enjoying the skirmish.

But for Rand, 'twas a serious matter. His livelihood depended upon his reputation. He couldn't afford to fail in this endeavor. Too many lords knew of his mission. If he succeeded, he might be called upon again for his services. But if he failed...

He thrust the idea straight out of his head. He couldn't afford to fail.

It seemed The Shadow's greatest skill was using Rand's own strength against him. So he'd give him none of that strength. Indeed, he'd prod the outlaw into attacking him first this time.

He weaved his head about and threw a few light punches, luring The Shadow close.

When the robber's attack at last came, 'twas not from

his fist, but from his cursed foot. Rand reared back his head in time to dodge the full impact, but The Shadow had already seized the advantage, advancing on him, backing him up along the path.

Rand blocked a few blows from his attacker, blows that were not made with his fists, but with his open hands. Curiously, they were just as driving and powerful.

Finally, the robber repeated his kick again, and this time Rand was ready for it. He jerked his head out of range, but using both hands, he seized The Shadow's foot, trapping him in midkick.

He might have been able to simply lift the outlaw up at that point, he was so light, dangle the man from his ankle while he used his other hand to retrieve the shackles from his belt.

But The Shadow had another strategy in mind. The moment Rand lifted, the thief's other leg scissored up and over, flipping him backward in the air and giving Rand a solid whack on the jaw as he tore free of his grip.

Rand, acting on blind instinct, lunged forward to make a last desperate grab at his prey. Whatever his arm contacted, it knocked the thief off-balance in midflip. When The Shadow came down, his knee struck the edge of a sharp rock on the trail.

Rand winced in empathy. 'Twould make a nasty bruise if it hadn't cracked the fellow's kneecap. But Rand wasn't about to lose his advantage. He dove forward, trying to catch the injured varlet in a restraining embrace.

But the instant Rand's fingertips brushed black cloth, the thief, as if his wound was of no consequence, bounded up into the trees again, clambering from limb to limb until he disappeared in the woods.

"Oh, fine," one of the brothers complained.

"No thanks to you," the other muttered at Rand.

" 'Twasn't *your* coin, after all."

On his hands and knees on the trail, within a hair-breadth of catching his prey, only to lose him in the wink of an eye, Rand had little temper and less patience.

He narrowed grim eyes at the brothers, and growled, "I suggest you leave before I knock your empty heads together."

He was right. They were cowards. With indignant haste, they turned tail and hied down the path.

When they'd gone, Rand rocked back onto his heels. But just as he was about to lever himself to his feet, something caught his eye.

A fresh drop of bright blood adorned the rock where the outlaw had struck his knee.

He reached forward to touch it with a fingertip, then rubbed the slick substance between his finger and thumb.

The Shadow *had* been injured in his fall, despite his spry departure. That meant his identity should be easy to uncover. All Rand had to do was find out which of the men at the gaming table currently suffered from a limp.

❧

Chapter 13

W HY SUNG LI HAD BEEN HOBBLING about the castle all day, Miriel didn't know. He refused to tell her what ailed him. 'Twas strange that he should be afflicted at all. Indeed, 'twas her *xiansheng* who had taught her the herbs and meditations and pressure points to stave off pain. Miriel used the knowledge extensively whenever she suffered sparring injuries, thus her tolerance for pain was high. Otherwise, she'd be limping about the keep herself.

But there was no point in asking Sung Li about his discomfort. He disliked being reminded of his own frailty.

'Twas admittedly easy to put Sung Li's troubles out of her mind anyway, since her head spun wildly with thoughts of Sir Rand of Morbroch.

Who the Devil was he?

Certainly not the mild-mannered, kindhearted, sentimental suitor he pretended to be.

The fool had gone after The Shadow again this morn,

only this time he'd returned with more than a few scrapes and bruises. Which was why she was now perusing the storeroom shelves for her jars of healing herbs.

Surely the varlet hadn't been hurt *that* badly. He'd broken no bones, only lost a little blood and bruised a bit more than his pride. But he was insisting on playing the wounded soldier, which meant she was obliged to play the healing maid.

She sighed, tapping her finger on a vial of carmine thistle extract, then thoughtfully bit her lip. Perchance 'twould not be so bad a thing to tend to Rand's injuries after all. 'Twas said that men sometimes made bedside confessions to a nurse they'd never utter to a priest. Mayhap when he was under her tender care, she'd find out who the real Rand of Morbroch was.

Satisfied with her harvest of medicines, she tucked in an extra bottle of colchicum for Sung Li. The stubborn old man might not want to admit his joints troubled him, but surely he'd avail himself of a cure left in his reach.

She found Rand in the armory, talking with Colin and Pagan.

"Forsooth, I didn't expect to run into the outlaw at all," Rand was telling them as she stood outside, listening. "I only followed the Herdclays to make sure they did no mischief."

"*They* were a pair of overblown ballocks, weren't they?" Colin said.

"The worst sort," Pagan agreed.

"I'm almost glad they got robbed," Colin added.

"But you shouldn't have tangled with The Shadow alone," Pagan told Rand. "You might have come back with worse injuries than these."

"And for what?" Colin scoffed. "A bit of silver that didn't belong to the louts in the first place."

"I guess I wasn't raised to run away from a fight," Rand murmured.

"Even when you're...overpowered?" Pagan asked as diplomatically as possible.

Rand replied with a humorless bark of laughter. "In my household, I was always overpowered."

Miriel frowned. What did he mean by that? In his household? Wasn't he raised in the household of Morbroch? And overpowered? The knights of Morbroch were fine fighters, but Rivenloch had defeated them soundly at the tournament. Rand couldn't have been overpowered by them.

A hundred questions suddenly clamored in her head.

She swept through the doorway, unprepared for the fact that Rand was standing there, bare from the waist up. With a tiny gasp that almost made her drop her vials, she quickly averted her eyes, but not before the image of his broad, bronze chest burned itself indelibly into her brain.

"Lady Miriel," Pagan said with a nod.

Colin smirked, tossing Rand his shirt. "Hello, Miri."

"Ah, my angel of mercy, come at last." Rand sighed, bunching the shirt before him in a manner that only half-covered that glorious expanse of golden skin.

She tightened her jaw. She mustn't give in to the foolish flutterings of her heart. She'd seen men's chests before. Rand's was no different.

Mayhap a little more muscled. A little wider. A little more sculpted, indeed rather like the flawlessly formed body of Adonis. But...

Tossing her head impatiently, she forced her feet

forward. She was here to treat his injuries and collect information, no more. With single-minded purpose, she pushed down on his rock-hard shoulder, pressing him onto a bench so she could take a look at his wounds.

"Where does it hurt?"

One side of Rand's mouth curved upward in a slow grin. Behind her, Colin stifled a laugh.

Pagan cleared his throat. "Perchance we should return to the lists, Colin." He added sternly, "Behave, Rand, or I'll never hear the end of it from my wife."

Rand gave him a salute, and Miriel resisted the urge to roll her eyes. Sweet Mary, even when they weren't present, her sisters posted guard over her.

When Pagan and Colin had gone, Rand brushed a finger across his lower lip. "Here, my love," he whispered.

Despite her best intentions, Miriel's heart skipped a beat. Lord, the varlet was wasting no time. Her gaze drifted down to his tempting mouth, parted in invitation, and she bit the corner of her lip.

"I think it's split," he said.

For a moment she only stared at him. Then she gave a quick shake of her head. "Of course." She rummaged through her containers, finding the fenugreek balm. She dabbed a bit on her fingertip and smoothed it across his lip.

"Got a good whack on the chin," Rand admitted, "though naught seems cracked."

She pressed gently over the area. He winced as she found a tender spot. "Just a bruise."

"You know, I was thinking on the way back to the keep," he said as she applied rosemary ointment along his jaw, "you're lucky you didn't run into The Shadow yourself that day you met me in the woods."

Her finger slipped in the salve, and she jabbed him in the cheek. "Oh. Sorry." Bloody hell, she had to be more careful. She dabbed away the excess ointment. "Why do you say that?"

"You both seem to have a curious penchant for hiding in the trees."

Rand studied Miriel closely from the corner of his eye. Aside from a subtle twitch of her lip, she exhibited no noticeable reaction to his comment.

Not that he expected one. But it *had* occurred to him as he'd come limping back from his encounter with the agile outlaw that The Shadow wasn't the only person he'd met among the branches of the Rivenloch wood.

'Twas an absurd idea, he knew. There was no way Miriel could be The Shadow. Miriel was sweet, delicate, helpless. She disliked combat. 'Twas impossible to imagine that the tenderhearted maid treating his injuries with such gentle hands could have inflicted them upon him. Nay, she was not The Shadow.

Still, he would have liked to take a peek at her knee.

"I wasn't hiding in the trees," Miriel told him, swabbing some oily substance on a scrape atop his shoulder. "I was rescuing a kitten stuck on a branch."

He smiled. She was good. She hadn't even stumbled over the lie. But he knew better. A kitten stuck on a branch would have been meowing as relentlessly as a Mochrie maid. "Rescuing a kitten?"

"Aye." She shrugged. "You're a knight. I'm sure you've come to the rescue of helpless creatures before."

An unpleasant recollection suddenly popped into his head, making a crease betwixt his brows. "I saved a cat once when I was a lad. The poor thing had been kicked half to death by my father."

She stiffened, and suddenly he wondered if he'd said too much. But she soon resumed her ministrations, circling behind him to examine his bruised backbone. "Your father must have been a cruel man."

He shrugged. "No worse than most, I suppose." He hoped he lied as smoothly as she did. Forsooth his father had been a drunken brute, an evil, conniving, selfish boor who had terrorized his childhood.

"And your mother?"

Rand's memories of his mother were bittersweet. She'd never mistreated Rand. Indeed, she'd seen that he was raised in his father's noble household. But she'd been blind to her lover's abuses and, in the end, too weakhearted to be faithful. "My mother died when I was fourteen."

"Ah. Do you have brothers? Sisters?"

He frowned over his shoulder. "What an inquisitive maid you are today."

She shrugged. "You know everything about my family. I know naught of yours."

"Ah. Well, I have four brothers."

"Is that all?"

"Isn't that enough?"

"I mean, tell me about them. What are they like? Are they overbearing like my sisters, or do they worship the ground you walk upon?" He winced as she slathered some stinging paste on the back of his shoulder. "Would I like them?"

"Nay!" he said more forcefully than he intended. "Nay." The thought of one of his depraved half brothers meeting innocent Miriel was unspeakable.

"Indeed?" She ran a finger lightly down his arm. "Are they more handsome than you?"

He caught her wrist before he realized she was only teasing him. At her gasp, he lightened his grip and raised her hand, pressing a kiss to the back of it. He clucked his tongue. "Handsome? Is that all you care about? I thought you loved me for my wit."

Miriel *did* love his wit. But she wasn't about to admit it. She was learning some very revealing things about Sir Rand, who might or might not be of Morbroch, and she didn't want him to wander too far from their current conversation.

She affected an air of innocence. "Your wit? Oh, nay. 'Twas always about your appearance. Your languid eyes and your noble nose. Your toothsome smile and..."

"Go on. Say it."

"What?"

"My dimples."

"Your what?"

"My dimples. The ladies love my dimples."

She knitted her brows. "Do you have dimples?"

He grinned and shook his head, displaying those very notorious assets. Lord, they *were* adorable.

"Tell me more," she pleaded, spotting a scratch on his ear and dabbing a tiny bit of dill salve on it. "What were you like as a lad?"

He sighed. Rand apparently didn't like to speak much about his youth, which meant it must have been unpleasant. In fact, she'd begun to doubt very much that he'd come from the Morbroch household at all. The Morbrochs were a jovial, well-meaning lot. Any man who'd kick a cat half to death would have been strung up by his thumbs.

"I suppose I was like any lad. Picked up a sword when I was two. Got my first horse at three. Stuck my nose where it didn't belong a few times and earned a few scars. Kissed a lass when I was ten. Bedded my first wench—"

She whacked him on the back of the head.

"Ow!" He chuckled.

She popped a cork back into the vial. "You're finished."

"Finished?"

She arched a brow. "Unless you've got a hangnail that needs surgery."

He grinned.

She gathered her jars, casting a sidelong glance at him as he donned his linen shirt, watching the splendid flex of his muscles. She might appreciate his wit, but the sight of his naked torso did something to her insides.

At long last she thought she'd untangled the mystery of Sir Rand of Morbroch. Indeed, he wasn't who he claimed to be. But she knew now why he'd lied about his identity. And the moving truth of that lie left her with a soft, warm glow that threatened to melt her very soul.

As she headed toward the door, she paused to give him a fond smile and a subtle warning. "Don't challenge The Shadow again. No man can best him. You'll only hurt yourself trying."

With that, she made a smug exit, secure in the knowledge that Rand was as harmless as he was charming.

He was no spy, no criminal, no foreign sapper scheming to undermine the castle. He was but a lost little lad looking for a home. Wherever he'd come from, his life had been miserable. He'd had a cruel father, an absent mother, and brothers of whom he preferred not to speak. 'Twas clear to her now why he'd come to Rivenloch.

He needed to belong.

He'd likely heard that the illustrious knights of Cameliard had allied with the men of Rivenloch. For a warrior with talent, there was no force more desirable to join. But he could hardly ride up to the gates, a freelancer with no title or commendation and expect to be welcomed into the army. So Rand had journeyed here, arriving in the tabard of a trusted neighbor, to ingratiate himself into the fold of Rivenloch.

He'd lied about everything.

And he continued to lie.

But they were harmless lies.

He lied when, winning excessively at dice, he feigned fatigue and excused himself from the table.

He lied when, hearing her father's tale about the Battle of Burnbaugh for the fourth time, he pretended great interest.

And he lied when he claimed he was no great fighter. Miriel knew better. Oh, aye, he'd appeared to improve until he was currently qualified to spar against Rivenloch's best, Lord Pagan himself. But now she knew his apparent ineptitude had been a matter of courtesy. He'd intentionally downplayed his abilities in order to endear himself to the men.

It made perfect sense. If he'd arrived at Rivenloch, a gifted warrior, capable of subduing the best knights, he would have made fast foes. By underplaying his talents, most of the men were only too eager to give him advice, help him better his skills, and ultimately take pride in witnessing his improvement.

'Twas genius. Yet 'twas hardly malicious, just as his apparent interest in capturing the scourge of Rivenloch, The Shadow, was benign. He seemed truly to wish to please

Pagan and Colin, and he presumed that apprehending the local outlaw would secure a place for him among the knights.

What he didn't know was that he'd already been accepted by her family. Her father treated him like a son. Colin and Pagan jested with him as if he were their brother. And her sisters no longer shot threatening glares at him every time he took Miriel's hand. Forsooth, they'd given him leave to take her to the fair unescorted at week's end.

He'd charmed his way into their lives, and he was rapidly winning his way into Miriel's heart.

❧

Chapter 14

For rand, the next few days proved unbearably frustrating. As much progress as he felt he was making in earning the trust of the folk of Rivenloch, he was getting no closer to identifying the outlaw.

If a lad seemed the right size, he was inevitably as hale as a horse. If Rand spotted someone favoring an injured leg, the person was inevitably too tall or fat or old or female to be The Shadow.

Not that he'd completely discounted the notion that the thief might be a woman. Dwelling among the Warrior Maids of Rivenloch, he'd learned to keep an open mind.

But the one woman he'd definitely crossed off the list of possibilities was Lady Miriel.

Rand smiled as he watched Lord Gellir toss the dice once again, eliciting a loud outcry from the men crowded about the gaming table, followed by a shuffling of coin from loser to winner.

Lady Miriel had certainly made Rand's trip to Rivenloch worth every penny of his reward. Now that Helena's wedding was past, she seemed to have more time to spend with him.

She'd invited him on a pleasant walk around the lake two days ago. The air had been cool and still, with water striders skating along the surface of the deep green lake and, here and there, a trout splashing, breaching the waves to nip at an insect. Firs had hunched like washerwomen at the water's edge, and slender reeds had shifted as frogs wriggled among them, startled by the passage of the strolling lovers. They'd supped on wine and cheese and pandemain in the shade of a tall pine . . . and the shadow of Sung Li, who'd insisted on accompanying them, despite complaining of her aching bones.

Yesterday, the three sisters had awakened Rand at dawn to take him fishing at the river. Despite a friendly rivalry that turned into a splashing fight among the four of them, they still managed to catch a few dozen trout, enough to grace the table at supper last night.

This morn, Miriel had challenged him to draughts. He'd chivalrously let her win, and when she discovered that, she'd made him play again. This time she'd defeated him on her own.

He grinned at the memory.

"What are you smiling about?" Colin asked, nudging him from his thoughts. "You just lost."

Rand glanced down at the dice and shook his head. "Looks like I'm done for the night."

'Twas just as well. So distracted was he by thoughts of Miriel that if The Shadow was sitting beside him in his black garb, Rand would never notice.

* * *

Sitting at her desk by candlelight, poring over the ledgers, Miriel found it difficult to make sense of the figures swimming before her.

How it had happened, she didn't know. Mayhap 'twas the carefree stroll by the lake. Or the battle of splashes at the river. Or the silly games of draughts. Mayhap 'twas Miriel's instinctive desire to heal the wounds of a young lad with a miserable childhood. But in the last two days she'd fallen in love with Sir Rand.

The problem was, he was falling in love with her as well. And he didn't have the slightest idea who she was.

He'd been attracted to the woman who flirted coyly with him, blushed easily, and wouldn't harm a spider. If he ever discovered the truth…

She closed her eyes. She couldn't tell him the truth. And yet she couldn't hide forever.

Opening her eyes again, she reviewed the column of numbers for the tenth time, trying to make sense out of them.

Finally, exasperated with how long the accounts were taking this eve, she gave her head a stern shake and muttered, "Concentrate, you foolish mop. The sooner you finish, the sooner you can go upstairs."

Rand was upstairs, likely losing more silver to her father. She smiled, thinking 'twas a good thing The Shadow had tossed him that coin after all. The poor man might need it before long. Especially if, as he'd done with her in draughts earlier today, he was losing intentionally.

She focused on the ledger before her, softly murmuring the numbers aloud, scrawling figures onto the parchment by the candles' flicker.

Indeed, so riveted was her attention upon the page that she didn't hear the intruder entering the room.

"So this is your office," he called softly.

She started so abruptly that she knocked over the vial of ink. She'd stood, spun halfway round, and raised her arms into the ready stance, when she realized who 'twas. Hastily, she lowered her arms, then clapped a hand to her bosom.

"Shite," she said under her breath.

"Sorry." With a grimace of apology, he rushed forward to tip the ink vial upright again. Ink had spilled over the linen tablecloth but thankfully not onto the ledger.

Regardless of her startle, 'twas more than fright that made the blood gallop through her veins as she eased back down onto her chair. 'Twas the sight of Rand—tall, powerful, handsome Rand—his dark hair curling seductively about his ears, his skin golden in the candlelight, his eyes shining with amusement and adoration—that set her pulse racing.

And the fact that they were alone together in the private sanctum of her workroom, where she need only close the door to ensure complete seclusion...

Sweet Mary, the thought made her mind stray with wanton abandon.

"You work too hard," he remarked.

For a moment she could only stare at him in wonder. He was the first person to notice. The rest of the castle folk, her sisters included, seemed to think she came down here to dawdle or nap. They didn't understand how demanding her work was.

Rand came up behind her, placed his hands upon her

shoulders, and began massaging at her tense muscles. "'Tis nigh midnight, my love."

"Is it?" Her voice cracked, unsettled by the perilous pleasure that sang through her body at the touch of his hands. His soothing ministrations quickly began to seduce away her caution. She closed her eyes, and a soft moan escaped her, unbidden.

He chuckled. "Do you like that?"

Aye, she liked it. His hands were strong, and his fingertips quickly found the places where she was most tight. He rubbed persistently at them, as if forcing them into submission, and yet she felt neither the will nor the desire to resist.

With a final caress down her back, he said, "I'm afraid I've made *more* work for you with my gaming."

When she spoke, her voice sounded almost like it belonged to another woman, one more languorously mellow than her. "Did you unbalance my books, you irksome knave? Have you robbed my father of all his coin?"

"Nay, he won a good bit of mine."

"He won?" She smiled. "My father never wins."

"He did this eve, beat me soundly."

"Play him again tomorrow eve, and I'm certain you'll win it all back."

"Indeed? And how will you account for that?"

She shrugged. "I always find a way to balance it."

"It looks difficult." He pointed to the ledger. "What are all these scratchings?"

She gave him a lazy grin. There was another first. Nobody took much interest in her accounting, as long as the castle was running smoothly. No one ever even looked in her ledgers. But she had a great respect for the amazing system of numbers, and the thought of showing Rand her work was exciting.

"Can you read?" she asked.

He hesitated.

"That's all right," she hastened to assure him. "Most knights I know cannot."

His forehead took on a troubled wrinkle. "I can read my name. Not much else."

"Come, pull up a stool, and I'll show you."

Miriel had one moment of misgiving, where she wondered if his interest, too, was a polite lie, if he only feigned fascination to please her. But soon they were hunched together over the ledgers, thigh to thigh, his brow furrowed in deep concentration, while she pointed enthusiastically to the entries she'd just made.

"'Tis almost what Sung Li would call *karmic*," she explained. "The figures in the right column must always balance those in the left."

"What does it say?"

"This is a record of what we've spent. Here is the wine we purchased from the abbey for Helena's wedding. And here is the amount for the spices." She ran a finger down the listings. "The priest's compensation. A new cook pot. Silk sheets."

"Silk sheets?"

Miriel chuckled. The sheets had been a wedding gift, a jest on Deirdre's part, mocking Helena's complaints about her spoiled Norman husband. "A gift for the bride and bridegroom."

"And what are these figures?" He pointed to the numbers on the right.

"This column records the coin that increases the coffers."

He scowled. "There is much less on this side."

For a man who couldn't read, he was quite observant. "Aye, fewer listings, but the amounts are greater. Here are the earnings from selling wool to the abbey. Here is the collection of rents. And here are the winnings from the wagering after the wedding feast."

"I see." His arm went around her shoulders as he pointed to the page. "And where do you record the losses?"

Miriel froze. "The losses?"

"Aye."

No one had ever asked her that. Most of the castle folk couldn't read or do sums, so they took no interest in Miriel's books. "Well," she hedged, "as you know, the men of Rivenloch always return their winnings to the coffers."

"But what about the Mochries, the Herdclays?"

Miriel licked her lips. Since Rand couldn't read, she supposed she could make up anything, and he'd believe it. She pointed to an entry recording the purchase of tallow candles and said, "The losses go here, in the left column."

"Hm."

Miriel hated lying to him, but Rand was getting too inquisitive. After all, she could hardly explain to him that she never bothered recording Rivenloch's losses. Nor why.

"By the Saints," she said lightly, "all this must be dreadfully boring for you."

With that, she snapped the ledger shut.

"Not at all, my love," Rand assured her. Indeed, Miriel's bold deception was anything but boring. He was glad he'd made the detour into her office. This manipulative accounting was very suspicious indeed. "How could I be bored when you're here beside me?" He gave her an unctuous grin.

The wily wench had lied to him about the ledger.

Of course, he'd lied to her about not being able to read.

He knew why he'd deceived *her*. But what was *she* hiding? Why were there no entries for the silver that her father wagered away? Were his losses an embarrassment to Miriel that she didn't wish to record? Or something more devious? Something having to do with a certain woodland outlaw?

He hoped 'twas the former. It pained him to imagine that the lovely maid beside him with the wide blue eyes and the guileless smile somehow contrived insidious accounting plots from the confines of her humble office.

It troubled him even more deeply to imagine that Miriel might be in league with The Shadow.

But he had to get to the truth. And to do that, he'd have to employ more deception.

Rand had long ago discovered that a coaxing voice and a gentle touch brought out the honesty in women. He supposed it softened their resolve to lie to him. As much as he hated using such knavish manipulation on a woman for whom he truly cared, 'twas far more effective than threats.

Besides, he consoled himself, 'twas not as if Miriel hadn't employed the same kind of trickery herself. 'Twas she, after all, who had seized him by the tabard and forced a kiss upon him that first day.

Rand coiled his fingers in the delicate curls at the nape

of her neck, and murmured, "Would it be too wicked to admit I was pleased to find you alone here?" He saw her skin shiver deliciously under his touch, and his own flesh tightened in response. "Forsooth, I feared that meddling maidservant of yours would chase me away."

"Sung Li?" Miriel's voice was rough and low. She was definitely savoring his caresses.

He dragged his fingertip up along the side of her neck to trace the rim of her ear, delighting at the shuddering sigh he elicited.

"Aye." He bent close to nuzzle the lobe of her ear. Lord, she smelled as luscious as sun-drenched roses. "What ails the wench anyway? She's been limping about the keep like a lame hound."

He felt foolish asking the question. The notion that Sung Li might be the one he'd injured, that Miriel's doddering maid was in sooth an agile outlaw with the reflexes of a cat, was absurd. But Rand had earned his reputation for thoroughness by following every lead, even absurd ones. He wasn't ready to rule out any possibility.

"She's an old woman," Miriel said on a sigh, "with old bones."

"Ah." He pressed a kiss against Miriel's throat, reveling in the fragrance of her skin, in the rapid pulse that beat there. "Do you not keep a store of medicines to relieve such suffering?" he murmured, knowing full well she did. She'd treated him with them only a few days ago.

"Medicines?" she said weakly. "Mm, aye."

He slipped his fingers beneath her neckline and slowly caressed the tender flesh above her bosom, idly asking, "Do you list all of them in your ledger as well?"

"Hm?"

"The medicines. You're responsible for them?"

"Aye."

God, she was beautiful, sitting there in the candlelight, her face flushed with desire, her eyes half-lidded, her nostrils quivering. He wanted to swive her. Now.

He clenched his jaw against the urge.

"By the Rood, my lady," he breathed, "you must have a brilliant mind indeed." He moved his fingers down, inch by tortuous inch, until they brushed dangerously close to her nipples. "However do you keep the accounts straight? Do you write down the name of everyone who comes for medicines?"

She answered with a throaty sigh that sent a frisson of lust straight into his loins.

He forced his voice to a ragged whisper. "The salves you used on me the other morn, did you record them in the book?"

"Aye."

"With my name beside?"

"Aye."

He nodded. 'Twas all he needed to know. With this knowledge, he could sneak into Miriel's workroom when she was gone and peruse the ledgers, find out which one recorded the castle supplies, discover who had come for medicines in the last few days, and compile a list of suspects.

He had what he required now. At least what his mind required. His loins were another matter.

For the last few days, Rand had suffered, playing the courteous suitor, when what he truly longed to do was ravish Miriel in the nearest dark corner. His mouth hungered for hers. His nostrils flared with her scent. His body ached for the press of her soft breasts.

He'd fought the yearning. The incident in the dovecote had awakened him abruptly to the fact that he had a serious vulnerability where the bewitching lass was concerned. Sung Li was right. When he touched Miriel, 'twas more than sparks that ignited between them, more than flame.

Even now he felt fire lapping at his veins as Miriel turned her head to gaze at his mouth, her eyes dark with longing.

But he dared not indulge his needs. Not yet. Not when he could be so easily led into carelessness. Despite the aching betwixt his legs, he planned to carry the damsel gallantly upstairs to her chamber door and bid her a chaste good night.

At least, 'twas his intent when he withdrew his fingers from her bosom. Until the damsel burned into the deepest recesses of his soul with her beckoning eyes, and murmured, "Kiss me."

He swallowed hard, and his gaze lowered of its own accord to her cherry red lips. Ah, God, they were tempting. Soft and succulent and delicious.

He supposed one kiss wouldn't hurt. Especially since 'twas her idea. 'Twas the least he could do, considering how cruelly he'd abused her trust. Besides, he was certain he could control his animal instincts for one kiss.

He was wrong.

Miriel knew she was making a mistake, but that didn't stop her from making it. The sizzle of her hot blood muted the voice of reason. Her skin felt afire, and she burned for the quenching ambrosia of his kiss.

'Twould only be one kiss, after all.

The fact that 'twas nigh midnight, that they were alone in the privacy of her workroom, that none would come to disturb them, would not affect her judgment. She only wanted to slake her thirst with a sip of his affection.

The first touch of his lips assured her 'twould be no easy task to cease. Their mouths met with a searing heat that melted them together like ores in a crucible. As their tongues entwined, so did their limbs. Her fists clenched in his tabard while his fingers plunged through her hair. Again and again, she strove forward against his mouth, searching for a greater closeness, a more complete intimacy.

Her heart beat against her ribs like a caged sparrow as he pulled her closer. She leaned forward, slanting her mouth over his, possessively wrapping her arms about his neck, hauling herself into his embrace so ardently that she knocked over her chair and the pile of ledgers.

But none of that mattered. All that mattered was the man into whose soul she was delving.

Suddenly, with shocking familiarity, he reached down to cup her buttocks and hefted her onto his lap. She gasped at the heat of his muscular thighs beneath her, a heat that penetrated the layers of wool and linen between them. She threaded her fingers through his thick hair, angling his head to better access the warm, wet, delicious hollows of his mouth.

But as her blood began to simmer with desire, as her fingers began to scrabble desperately for purchase in the roiling sea of lust, she felt him withdraw. 'Twas subtle at first, a slowing of their kisses, a lightening of his embrace. But soon he clasped his hands about her jaw and pulled gently away, panting heavily against her mouth.

"Miriel... my love... we mustn't..."

Despite the smoldering passion in his eyes, the sincere regret in his breathless words, 'twas like a sobering slap. She knew he was right. If they didn't stop now, they would *never* stop. Their ardor was like a wildfire, blazing uncontrolled across the heath.

Licking her kiss-swollen lips, she closed her eyes, gave him a rueful nod, and withdrew trembling fingers from his hair. He cradled her then, holding her close against his shoulder, while they caught their breath.

When she lifted her desire-weighted eyelids toward the wall, what she saw made her eyes go wide.

Sweet Jesu! When they'd knocked the stack of ledgers over, the tapestry had been dislodged as well. It now hung askew, and from this angle, it clearly revealed the ragged edge of rock and the darkness beyond that comprised Miriel's secret passageway.

The breath caught in her throat. Dear God, what could she do? At any moment, he would turn his head and see it. She couldn't let that happen.

Her brain raced through several possibilities.

She could pretend to be sick. Nay, more tasteful, she could burst into tears. She was good at that. Perchance in his concern for her, he'd overlook the gaping hole in the side of her office.

Nay, 'twas too uncertain.

She could topple all the candles, in the hopes of instantly extinguishing the light in the room. But if they didn't gutter out, they might set something on fire.

She could knock him unconscious. She knew strategic pressure points that would slump him over in an instant, giving her time to straighten the tapestry. But 'twould be impossible to explain his faint later.

Nay, she had to distract him somehow.

What was the best way to distract a man?

That was easy to answer. Doing it was another matter.

Wincing against the impropriety of such wanton behavior, she brazenly slipped her hand over the bulge between Rand's legs and gently squeezed.

Chapter 15

Lass!" Rand gasped, jolting with the shock of her touch. But his shock turned rapidly to lust, and a groan of pleasure was wrung from him as she continued to clasp him with bold possession.

Lord, the wench was wicked. And she didn't play fair. 'Twas difficult enough to curb his passions without her taunting him thus.

"Aye?" she sighed into his ear.

He shuddered. Her palm was stroking along the length of him now with sensual leisure. The cursed woman knew exactly what she was doing. She had him at her mercy.

But two could play at that game.

He eased one hand up the side of her surcoat and brazenly cupped her breast.

'Twas her turn to gasp, yet she made no move to halt him. Instead, with startled surprise in her eyes, she leaned forward, trying to deflect him by reengaging him in a kiss.

This time he pulled back, pinning her with a purposely seductive stare while he brushed his thumb over the spot where he knew her nipple to be.

She groaned, and her lids dipped as he felt her nipple awaken to his touch, even beneath her surcoat. Then, as if in reprisal for his aggression, she reached lower to cradle his ballocks.

He growled as his legs eased apart of their own will, welcoming her caress. The little imp truly knew her power, and he saw by the spark of rivalry in her eyes that she wasn't about to cede that power, not if she could help it.

He'd have to make sure she couldn't. He dragged his hand to her other breast, plucking at its peak until she bit at her bottom lip in ecstasy.

But he hadn't won yet. She nuzzled at his neck, working her way up to his ear, then the sly wench slipped the tip of her tongue into the sensitive recesses there, and a wave of overwhelming desire seemed to melt his very bones.

He held naught back then, plunging his hand betwixt the two of them with pointed precision, pressing at the soft juncture of her thighs where he knew she ached for him.

She drew in a ragged breath, and he chuckled in heady triumph. But when she began to scrabble beneath his tabard at the lacing of his braies, his humor vanished.

Sweet Mary, was she going to...

His question was answered an instant later when she loosened the ties and began rooting inside his braies. His mutinous hips angled upward, guiding her hands.

Yet even in the midst of intense pleasure, he managed

to launch his own counterattack. He threw back her skirts with lusty vengeance and delved his hand into the soft hair guarding her womanhood.

She cried out in astonishment, and in the next amazing instant, her passion took an almost violent turn. Her free arm snagged him about the neck, and she crushed demanding lips to his. He moaned against her teeth as her hand found the naked flesh of his cock, releasing it from its confines.

Scarcely able to think, he nonetheless managed to slide his fingers farther into her nest of downy curls, parting her nether lips to locate the straining bud between them.

She squeaked, jerking back as if he'd burned her, then quickly recovered, thrusting her hips forward against his palm again as she kissed him even more fervently.

She became an animal, lunging at him, growling and snarling and devouring him with her mouth, while she relentlessly stroked his swollen staff. Ill prepared for such unmitigated aggression, he reared back in surrender beneath her onslaught, enough to make the three-legged stool list dangerously.

It tilted and careened, and just before it tipped over, he tried to cast her away, to save her, but she clung to him with the tenacity of a dog with a bone. As the stool toppled backward, he fell, she followed, and they hit the ground together.

Fortunately, a few sacks of grain absorbed most of the impact, though Rand doubted he'd have felt much pain, not with so much pleasure counteracting it. At least he had the foresight to break from the kiss before they struck, so their teeth remained intact.

He thought the fall would jar Miriel back to her senses and destroy the mood.

He was wrong.

As if she hadn't just been thrown to the ground, she continued to assail him, raining kisses over his jaw, his neck, his ears, his mouth. She'd never let go of his cock, and now she explored his every inch, milking him with shameless daring. Her very boldness drove him to utter abandon.

His hand found its unerring way to that sweet spot betwixt her thighs. She'd grown moist with his fondling, and his fingers slipped easily over the slick folds. She moaned and surged forward, as if she might impale herself upon his hand.

Lord, she wanted more. And he wanted to give it to her.

With a whimper of frustration, she snagged her free fist in the front of his tabard. Then she hauled him with her as she rolled onto her back in the rushes, away from the bags of grain and her desk, leaving him looming over her like a ravishing barbarian.

He *felt* barbaric. He was wild-eyed and breathless and as rigid as a poleaxe.

But Miriel was no cowering maid. Eagerly accepting the burden of his body atop hers, she wrapped her stockinged legs around his buttocks and writhed in delicious torment beneath him.

Miriel gasped as Rand's fingers again invaded her most secret place, strumming her like an expert lutist, till her body vibrated with the most amazing music.

She'd never felt anything so wonderful, so intoxicating, so... disabling.

Rand's touch upon her there was more paralyzing than any pressure point. He had her at his mercy now. She was in peril of losing command of the situation. And her wits.

Part of her wanted to break away in panic. The other part wanted to silence the first part and surrender to the exquisite sensations. But she couldn't, not yet.

She opened her eyes a crack and peered at the back wall. They were almost out of sight of the tunnel now. One more sideways tumble, and his view would be completely obstructed.

She caught her breath as Rand's cock pulsed again in her hand. 'Twas a miraculous thing, really, much different than she'd imagined, warm and smooth and responsive, and the way it nestled in her palm, as if it belonged there, inexplicably excited her. Forsooth, the throbbing staff seemed almost as sensitive as her own nether parts. Best of all, 'twas a point of vulnerability and an effective source of distraction.

If she could only keep *herself* from being distracted.

With a soft, lusty growl, she released him and wriggled her arms up between them to tug impatiently at the shoulders of his tabard.

He immediately sensed her intent. When he withdrew his hands from her to pull the garment off over his head, she had a small span of time where she could think clearly.

At least, she'd *assumed* she could think clearly. But once she glimpsed his naked chest, broad and sun-kissed and firmly muscled, her sense of logic fled, and she couldn't resist reaching out to touch him.

He held himself up on his arms, letting her explore. A fine sheen of sweat dampened his skin, allowing her fingers to slide easily over the supple flesh. His nipples were dark and flat, but when she rubbed a thumb across one of them, it instantly hardened, lending her a curious thrill of power. A jagged diagonal scar crossed his breast, and she traced the puckered mark, then let her fingertip follow the fine line of dark hair that started above his navel and led downward.

'Twas the sudden surge of his cock against her belly that jarred her from her exploration, reminding her they were not yet out of sight of the passageway.

With a husky sigh, she pushed at his chest, urging him sideways. He rolled over willingly, and she wound up astride him, blushing to discover that when their hips aligned, she could feel the swelling of his cock between her legs.

He closed his eyes, grimacing as if she tortured him, and 'twas a heady feeling, knowing she could control him with the mere shift of her thighs.

But *he* shifted to press more fully against her, and when his heated flesh contacted hers, 'twas like a bolt of hot fire shot through her loins.

She arched back, and his hands captured her breasts, holding her there for a blissful moment before he untied her surcoat and dragged the garment down over her shoulders.

The linen of her underdress rasped across her nipples as he slowly pulled her surcoat down. When her breasts at last sprang free of the garment, she squirmed loose from the sleeves as well, letting the fabric gather about her waist.

His palms slipped up her stomach to cup her bare breasts. She sighed. His knight's calluses felt foreign and rough and forbidden, yet 'twas as if his hands belonged there, fitting her perfectly.

Suddenly he moved one hand up to catch the back of her neck, pulling her down for a kiss. Naught could prepare her for the ecstasy of their melded flesh. His chest felt heavenly against her breasts, like the most warming, healing bath.

When their lips made contact, she relaxed against him, sinking into the soothing waters of seduction, reveling in the waves of desire lapping against her skin. Their tongues mated with sensual leisure, a leisure that belied the rapid beating of her heart.

In the end, she didn't have to nudge him over the last few inches. He took the initiative, cradling her, rolling them over together with practiced grace so that he could take command.

Of course, now she could end the whole pretense. She no longer needed to distract him. The gaping hole was out of sight. She was safe.

She'd resume the air of a shy maiden now. She'd blush over her indiscretion and cover her bosom with her arms. Perchance she'd even squeeze out a few tears.

Right after Rand finished this next kiss.

Or two.

Or five.

Lord, his mouth was irresistible, gentle yet demanding all at once. She wondered wickedly how his lips would feel upon her breast.

As if he divined her mind, he let his mouth slip from

hers, kissing her cheek, her neck, her shoulder, descending inexorably toward her straining nipple while she waited in breathless anticipation.

One kiss upon her breast, just to see what 'twould feel like, then she'd stop him.

When his lips closed around the taut bud, she arched her head back, astonished by the current that streaked through her body, seeming to connect all the most sensitive places. Her mouth dropped open in wonder as he suckled with tender care for a long while, finally finishing with a lazy lap of his tongue.

Of course, she couldn't let him leave her unbalanced. Biting her lip, and promising herself she'd make him cease in another moment, she offered her other breast.

With a low chuckle, he obliged her, circling the nipple with light, teasing kisses until she forcefully thrust her breast between his lips. This time he drew hard on her nipple, and it felt as if the suction reached all the way to that spot between her legs, for there she began to quiver with need as well.

He finally released her with a soft, wet smack, then blew gently on her nipple, making her gasp with chill.

Now, she thought. Now she'd make him stop.

But in the next moment his fingers began to smooth the curls at the juncture of her thighs, and she instinctively tilted her hips up to increase the pressure of his touch. His hand felt so right upon her, comforting and arousing at the same time.

She was treading on treacherous ground, but she couldn't seem to step back.

When his fingers separated her moist folds, delving

with delicate insistence into the slick, secret hollows, her emotions swelled like a rushing river, hurtling toward a precipice over which she couldn't help but fall.

She had to do something to make him stop, no matter how much she longed to have him continue. And in the rising turmoil of her feelings, she could think of only one way to regain her advantage and control, one way to make him vulnerable and win the upper hand.

While he continued to pleasure her, she snaked one arm down below his waist and grabbed hold of his cock again. To her satisfaction, he sucked a hard breath between his teeth.

Now she had him, she thought. Just as in effective sparring, she'd quickly learned her opponent's weakness and seized upon it.

For one fleeting moment, caught off guard, he stiffened, unable to continue assailing her, and she enjoyed the dominance, stroking his velvety staff like a favorite pet.

Too soon he recovered. This time he attacked her with a vengeance, holding naught back. His fingers danced with frantic virtuosity between her legs until she felt her advantage slipping away as inevitably as the ocean tide.

Yet even while he coaxed her body to betray her, he thrust himself within her hand, sliding along her belly, making tortuous friction between them, to effect his own demise.

Without warning, a curious tension rose within her, like a bubbling spring trapped inside the earth. Her skin seemed to grow more and more taut, too tight for the exquisite fount that longed to burst from its fleshly prison.

Within her palm, his cock, slippery with sweat, hardened even more as he strove boldly against her.

Suddenly, a pleasure so intense 'twas almost pain made her arch upward. For a long moment, the world seemed to still while her ecstasy grew and grew, until she was tossed with the abrupt violence of a boulder from a catapult.

Her bones shuddered. Her muscles contracted. She moaned and cried out and sighed all at once as her body seemed to fly at breakneck speed on a course toward the heavens.

She was vaguely aware that he'd come along with her. Groaning with an animal passion that sent shivers along her spine, he, too, bucked wildly in the throes of desire, until her hands and belly grew slick with the proof of his release.

Afterward, Miriel lay limp beneath Rand, as limp as if he'd pinched the pressure point along her shoulder. She couldn't move a joint. She could scarcely keep her eyes open. Indeed, the only proof she was yet living was the pulse hammering at her temples and the rapid breath rasping through her mouth.

Rand inclined his head to tenderly kiss her brow. She felt his shaky breath, heard his wordless murmur of affection against her forehead. But she had no strength to acknowledge him with anything except a weak smile that seemed permanently affixed to her face.

A curious apathy enveloped her as she drifted along in a pleasant fog. She didn't care that she was lying naked on the floor of her office. She didn't care that Rand loomed over her like a conquering hero. She didn't even care that she'd probably behaved like a wanton.

She felt beautiful. And womanly. And powerful. And cherished.

'Twas just as her sisters had boasted. Being with a man who cared for you was wonderful. Lying with a man you loved was divine. Aye, she might grow to relish this lovemaking.

With her last ounce of will, she opened her eyes and gazed up at him. His face was so full of wonder, so grateful, so content, the sight of it filled her heart. Rand *did* care for her. She saw it in the adoring glow of his eyes. And that knowledge made her feel reckless and impulsive.

"I love you," she breathed.

Rand's heart stilled. No one had ever said that to him before. Not his mother. Certainly not his father. Not his motley assortment of half siblings. Not even the wenches from whom he occasionally purchased favors.

The words were strange to his ears. But whether 'twas from the memory of his wretched childhood or his current vulnerability in passion's aftermath or simply the sincere affection in Miriel's eyes, his heart grasped at the words as if they were a lifesaving timber in a stormy sea.

His throat thickened painfully, and his eyes threatened to well with tears.

Did he love her as well? Was it possible? He'd been prepared for her to cast him away when she was through with him. He'd never in a thousand years expected her to say she loved him. And now the idea of forging a permanent alliance with her presented an amazing possibility.

He might find a home here.

A real home with an adoring wife and children, castle folk who respected him, brotherhood in an elite fighting force, and no more cause to lead the life of a bastard vagabond, selling his services to the highest bidder.

'Twas almost too incredible to imagine.

Yet he'd lose it all if he couldn't find the strength to answer the lass.

His voice cracked over the unfamiliar words. "I love you, Miriel."

Chapter 16

RAND THOUGHT HE'D NEVER FELT more alive as he sparred with Pagan and Colin in the tiltyard. He held back naught, spinning and lunging and charging with unmitigated exuberance, barely able to keep up with the clever swordsmen.

But one glance at the lovely lass standing at the fence, and he knew he was wrong about the sparring. 'Twas Miriel who made him feel most alive.

Grinning hugely at her, he almost got his head lopped off as Pagan came round with his blade.

"Pay heed!" Pagan yelled at him. "And you!" he commanded, pointing the tip of his sword at Miriel. "Stop distracting my man."

My man. Rand liked the sound of that. He'd never been anyone's man. He'd only belonged for a short while to whoever paid the price for his services.

"Do you mind, my lord?" Rand asked Pagan, nodding toward Miriel.

Pagan rolled his eyes and shook his head, sheathing his sword and turning away to seek out someone else to badger.

Rand put away his own weapon and loped up to the fence.

"I was looking for you earlier," he called out.

"I've been doing the accounts."

He cocked his head quizzically. "I went to your office. 'Twas locked."

Forsooth he'd been trying to steal into her office for four days now to take a look at those ledgers. If the room wasn't sealed up like a tomb, then Sung Li was standing guard at the doorway. One would think there was a king's treasure stored inside. Miriel was definitely hiding something.

"I lock the door sometimes when I need to concentrate," she said. As he drew near, her clear blue eyes took on an unmistakable smoky hue. She wanted him. "Otherwise I might get . . . distracted."

The lass wore a simple brown kirtle today, but the plain garment didn't diminish her beauty in the least, especially when Rand could so vividly remember what she looked like beneath it.

His loins responded at once, and he gave her a rueful laugh. The damsel was insatiable. They'd stolen kisses and caresses in every secluded corner of the keep. But this was not the time or place for trysting.

He hooked one foot on the lowest wattle crossbar of the fence.

She grasped the back of his neck, pulling him forward to give him a sound kiss.

As they rested their brows together, he murmured, "I'm sweaty. I haven't shaved. And I stink."

"Love is blind," she whispered.

He grinned. "And apparently unable to smell as well."

She licked her lips. "Perchance a roll in sweet-smelling hay would—"

He chuckled deep in his throat. "The stables?"

She shrugged.

"Little imp," he chided, but already his cock was rising at the promise of feminine attention. He made a cursory surveillance for witnesses, then nodded to her. "You go first."

With a devilish twinkle in her eyes, she strolled casually away from the tiltyard. Rand turned his back on her, pretending sudden interest in the sword battle going on between Rauve and Kenneth. Then, after a reasonable span of time, he walked purposefully toward the stables, as if he intended to check on his horse.

When he arrived, she peered out at him from beneath a pile of straw in an empty stall, looking coy and wanton and adorable.

"Miriel, you naughty wench," he chided, "what have you done with your clothes?"

She wasn't completely naked. She still wore her thigh-high woolen stockings, which actually made her look even more wicked. They were no deterrent. He found plenty of exposed skin to touch and lick and devour.

As for him, when she began to pleasure him beneath his chain mail with her adoring hands, he had to bite his knuckles to keep from bellowing in rapture.

So intense was his climax that he feared he might frighten the horses and set the straw afire. Only her soothing caresses afterward brought him back to normalcy.

As she knelt before him, slipping her kirtle over her

head, she murmured, "Forsooth, I came to tell you I've an abundance of work today."

He smiled, easing up on his elbows to look at her. "You have a most interesting way of telling me. I wish you'd do so every day."

She clucked her tongue, but he could tell his words pleased her. "'Tis just that I won't be able to go riding after all." She'd promised to take him riding today along the boundaries of Rivenloch.

He wiggled his brows lasciviously. "Oh, I think we already went riding."

Her eyes widened in feigned shock. "Sirrah!"

He gave her a wink, then began to lace up his braies. He forced a serious furrow to his brow. "Very well. We'll go on the morrow then."

"On the morrow?"

She studied him for a moment, and though he tried to keep his expression stern, she divined the gleam of mischief in his gaze at once.

"Oh, nay, we won't, you varlet." She gave him a light shove. "You know very well 'tis the fair on the morrow, and you are honor-bound to take me."

He affected a sigh. "No riding on the morrow?" He rocked his hips back and forth suggestively.

She smacked him on the shoulder, fighting back laughter.

Then he rose, dusted off his tabard, and helped her to her feet.

"I'll go first," she decided, her mind already shifting to her work. "I have to speak to the cook. One of the lads seems to be stealing provender from the kitchen."

"Wait." Amused, he snagged her arm before she could

rush off, then clucked his tongue. "You've obviously never trysted in a stable before."

She frowned.

He turned her around backward. Her hair was strewn with incriminating straw. He carefully picked out the pale stems, then kissed her on the top of the head and gave her a dismissive swat toward the door.

She tried to send him a withering glare as she left, but failed. He shook his head. She might have no straw left in her tresses, but by the lusty glow of her countenance there was no mistaking what she'd been doing. He hoped she wouldn't run into that meddling guardian of hers before her telltale flush faded.

Apparently she narrowly missed Sung Li. When Rand emerged several moments later, he spied the old woman hobbling along the practice field. Her joints must still trouble her, though she wasn't limping as heavily now as a few days ago.

Seeing the shriveled old maidservant reminded Rand that, as ludicrous as it might be, he needed to follow up on the possibility that Sung Li was The Shadow.

He might not be able to get to the ledgers, but now was the perfect opportunity to search Sung Li's quarters. While she toddled around the practice field, and Miriel was busy with household affairs, Rand could steal into their chamber and look for evidence.

Aside from Miriel's office and rooms containing precious stores, the doors of Rivenloch stood unbarred, which was an amazement to Rand. As a child, he'd had to sleep curled up around his belongings, lest his greedy siblings steal them. As a mercenary, he never dozed without one hand on his purse and the other on his sword. Yet here, no one lived in fear of losing their things, unless one included the provender the kitchen lad had filched. Thus when Rand casually loped up the steps and along the passage to Miriel's chamber, he knew he'd find it open.

He'd imagined her room would be a reflection of the maid herself, neat, pretty, adorned in soft colors, with subtle feminine touches. Flowers painted on the plaster walls perchance. Or bottles of scent lined up on a table. Butterflies embroidered along the edge of her coverlet. Or hair ribbons hung on pegs.

But when he stole through the door, swiftly closing it behind him, he thought he'd found the wrong chamber.

There *were* ribbons in several colors hung on pegs on the wall. And a few bottles sat atop an oak table. The room was definitely tidy. But it looked naught like the bedchamber of a lord's daughter.

Indeed, it looked like an armory.

Upon two walls hung an array of weapons the like Rand had never seen. Several wide-bladed short swords and long poles with notched heads flanked one end of the display. Beside them hung jointed sticks, flails, and daggers of all sizes with blades, both toothed and smooth, some as broad as an axe, some no wider than a nail. Against the second wall were propped what appeared to be a sharpened shovel, a scythe, a forked staff, and a pole with a large crescent blade atop it. Small plates of steel forged into shapes resembling stars and forks and circles formed a ring around a bronze shield depicting the face of some grimacing beast. And finishing off the display was a collection of metal-spined silk fans, painted not with flowers, but with snarling, curve-clawed, sharp-toothed dragons.

After Rand snapped his jaws shut again, he glanced

around the rest of the chamber. 'Twas definitely Miriel's room. Those were her hair ribbons. There, draped across the chest at the foot of the bed, was the green surcoat he'd slipped off her shoulders yesterday. And the two lower corners of the deep red swag above the bed were embroidered in gold with the letter M.

For a moment, all he could do was stare at the room's furnishings and the jarring juxtaposition of her sheer white linen underskirt hung on one wall beside what looked like Neptune's vicious trident.

What the Devil was going on here?

And mayhap just as intriguing, he thought, his gaze drifting longingly toward the keen edge of one of the short swords, how effective would that weapon be?

He eyed it speculatively. 'Twas a handsome piece, sleek and smooth, its blade broad and flat with subtle carvings near the haft, the grip featuring a steel loop that enclosed the hand. He wondered how light 'twas. It certainly hadn't the reach of a broadsword, but mayhap its speed compensated for its lack of length.

There was only one way to find out.

The sword *was* light, much lighter than his own, and he found that because of its reduced size, he could wield it with more control. 'Twould be useless against a longer blade, but for close combat...

Of course, that pole with the crescent at its end could finish off a foe before he got within sword's reach. Rand hung the short sword back on the wall and hefted the peculiar spear. He tested the edge with his thumb. God's bones, 'twas sharp enough to slice a man in half.

He was carefully replacing the piece when two short-handled forks caught his eye. He took the forearm-length weapons off the wall, testing their balance. They were likely intended for use as a pair, but curiously, the tips were blunted. They couldn't be much of a stabbing weapon.

He returned them to their place, then studied the curious metal stars. These were sharp, their points honed to an almost transparent edge. But there was no handle, no grip. How were they used? Surely holding such a weapon was only inviting it to be embedded in one's palm.

And the segmented spear farther along the wall, seven pieces of wood connected with links of chain, how was that employed? Was it used like a flail, swung over one's head?

He took the piece off its hook. 'Twas a heavy thing and quite long. Perchance 'twas a weapon to be used on horseback. If a rider swung the thing in a great circle, none could draw near enough to attack. He took hold of the last segment, held it over his head, and began swinging it slowly so it circled about his feet. Gradually he increased the speed until 'twas twirling about him at knee level, then higher. 'Twould make an excellent weapon, for the impact of that last chunk of wood at high speed would be heavy indeed.

An instant later, he found out just how heavy.

The chamber door swung open suddenly, startling him. When his arm jerked back, the whirling device wobbled off course and struck the post of Miriel's bed with a loud thunk, making a dent in the oak.

Rand didn't believe he'd ever blushed in his life, but he did now as Miriel and Sung Li stepped in, and he was caught, not only trespassing, but making a fool of himself and damaging the furnishings.

For a long moment, Miriel stared at him, stunned, and

he stared back, mortified, as the weapon, dangling from his guilty hand, snaked about him, finally coiling lifelessly on the floor. Then Sung Li charged forward.

"*You zhi!*" she spit, snatching the weapon from his hand. "Have you no courtesy?" The old woman glared at him and raised the linked spear. For one moment, he thought she might use it on him. If she did, he supposed 'twas no more than he deserved.

"I'm... I'm sorry." He *was* sorry. He knew better than to touch another's weapons. 'Twas only that for a warrior like himself they were so irresistibly unusual and intriguing. He'd lost his head.

"These are *mine*," Sung Li snarled in no uncertain terms. "You do not touch them. Ever."

He blinked. The weapons belonged to Sung Li? What would an old maidservant need with weapons like these? Unless she liked to disguise herself as a woodland outlaw...

Sung Li hung the segmented spear back up on the wall and answered his unasked question. "They belonged to my ancestors. They are sacred. Nobody touches them."

He nodded. Of course.

Sometimes Rand let his imagination get the better of him. Withered old Sung Li didn't cavort through the forest, wielding the bloody things. They simply hung on the wall. He supposed he should have guessed they belonged to the Oriental maid by the strange markings on them, marks that looked like the scratchings of a hen.

It seemed a waste to leave such glorious weapons hanging unused on a wall.

"They're quite magnificent," he said.

"Do you think so?" Miriel asked.

"Oh, aye, most magnificent."

His response pleased Miriel.

When she'd first entered the chamber, she'd naturally been shocked to find Rand within, horrified to find him wielding her *chut gieh*. But to think he might be genuinely interested in her weapons...

She'd begun collecting Chinese arms from the time she'd brought Sung Li home. As far as anyone knew, they were simply pieces of art Miriel liked to hang upon her wall, chosen in part to appease Lord Gellir, who had never understood her dislike for combat. That was the tale she'd told everyone. Not even her sisters suspected Miriel actually knew how to use them.

The fact that Rand seemed interested in them relieved and delighted her. Did she dare to hope he shared the same fascination with such things? Perchance she could teach him how they were used.

Then Sung Li had interrupted, claiming the weapons were his, and Miriel suddenly realized the truth of her situation. She could hardly admit to owning a grisly collection of Chinese weapons herself. How could she possibly explain that the docile lady Rand had fallen in love with was an imposter? That the real Miriel was neither meek nor mild? That she could pick up that *kwan do* and kill a man in a single blow?

Not that she had, of course. One of the important philosophies of Chinese warfare was that violence was always a last resort. Deadly force and lethal skill were paramount, but the preferable choice was having to use neither.

"What are you doing here?" Sung Li demanded, facing Rand with his arms crossed imperiously over his chest.

Miriel wondered that, too. But her curiosity was tempered by pity. Rand was trying desperately to fit in, and he was obviously discomfited by what he'd done. There was no need to make him more uncomfortable.

"I asked him to meet me here," she lied.

There was a flicker of surprise in Rand's eyes, but he was quick to pick up on her ploy. "Aye."

Sung Li narrowed his eyes. "Indeed? In your bed-chamber?"

Miriel shrugged. "I didn't want to go down to the lists." She wrinkled her nose. " 'Tis far too dusty."

"Oh, aye," Rand agreed. "Couldn't have her soiling her pretty skirts."

"Hmph." Sung Li could see Miriel was hardly wearing pretty skirts. Forsooth, 'twas only her drab brown work kirtle. And if he'd known that Miriel had been rolling in the hay in it earlier, he'd have been even more disgusted. "And what were you meeting *for?*"

"Er . . ." Rand glanced at Miriel, at a loss.

"Rand and I," she said, crossing the room to take him by the hand, "are going riding."

From the corner of her eye, she saw Rand's mouth twitch. She prayed he wouldn't laugh, for if he did, so would she, then their perfidy would be discovered.

Sung Li looked from one to the other, clearly displeased, but there was naught he could do. Though he was Miriel's *xiansheng* when they sparred, he was not her master. Forsooth, in front of Rand, he was little more than a servant. He could not dictate where Miriel might and might not go.

Sung Li raised his chin smugly and said, "But what

about the physician, my lady? Did you not promise to accompany him to the monastery today?"

God's eyes! She'd forgotten. She'd offered to help treat an ailing monk. 'Twas the reason she'd canceled her riding trip in the first place. 'Twas also why she'd come to her chamber, to fetch a cloak and a few of her own medicines.

But instead of conceding defeat, thinking quickly, she flashed Sung Li her sweetest smile. "Oh, Sung Li, you'd do that for me? Go in my place? How kind. I'd be so grateful." She turned to ask Rand, "Is Sung Li not the most wonderful maidservant?"

"Wonderful," Rand agreed.

The frown between Sung Li's brows deepened, and his eyes darkened with fury. He might not be able to issue orders to Miriel at the moment or even refuse her requests, but he could make her life miserable when they sparred on the morrow. She could almost see him dreaming up harrowing exercises for her.

Still, 'twas worth saving Rand's pride. Besides, with one of the day's most time-consuming duties delegated to Sung Li, Miriel would have time to spend with her suitor.

"You'd better hurry then," she urged the maid, snapping up two vials from her table and handing them to Sung Li. "Here are the medicines. The monastery may keep them. I'll purchase more on the morrow at the fair."

When she placed the bottles near Sung Li's hand, he grasped her wrist in a subtle but sharp pinch, pinning her with a gaze as pointed as the *shuriken* on the wall.

She refused to cry out or flinch. She understood Sung Li was communicating his intense disapproval. But two could play at that game.

Miriel reached out her other hand, ostensibly to press the vials into his palm, but instead grasped the meaty flesh between his thumb and finger between her short nails and squeezed.

For a long moment, the two of them stared stoically at each other, neither one willing to admit pain or defeat.

"Give the father my best wishes," Miriel said with a taut smile.

"Enjoy your ride," Sung Li replied, returning her smile.

"Tell Brother Thomas I shall pray for his recovery."

"Watch out for slippery ground."

"Don't forget your cloak."

"Don't be late for supper."

'Twas Rand who ended the stand-off. "I'll go find a carpenter to repair your bed."

Miriel released Sung Li and whirled about. "That won't be necessary." Then, with her warmest smile, she crossed the room to open the door for Sung Li, bidding him a deceptively fond farewell. "Have a safe journey, Sung Li."

As Sung Li passed by her, Miriel felt the anger shimmering off him, almost like the heat off a forge. As he walked through the doorway, he turned to have the last word, probably a reprimand for entertaining men alone in one's bedchamber. But before he could speak, she shut the door in his face. Whirling about, she leaned back against the closed door and offered Rand a lazy grin.

Rand clucked his tongue. "What a pair of liars we are."

"Liars? I don't know what you're talking about." Feeling rather self-assured, having challenged Sung Li and won, she ambled up to Rand and coyly walked her fingers up his tabard. "It seems I do have time for a ride after all."

Her own daring excited her, and 'twas only magnified by the gleam of pleasure that flared in Rand's gaze.

"Indeed?" His voice was rough with desire, and there was no doubt when their gazes met just what kind of ride they intended.

She smiled at the way his eyes shone, dark and inviting and full of affection, and suddenly she knew she'd made the right decision.

She had to lose her maidenhood sometime, after all. And there was no one she'd rather give it to than Rand.

He caught her straying fingers, raised them to his lips, and gave her knuckles a slow, suggestive lick that sent a shiver through every nerve in her body. "Your steed is ready and waiting, my lady."

Chapter 17

RAND DECIDED HE MUST BE the luckiest man alive. Miriel was a gift from God, a woman who would lie for him and *with* him.

At the moment, he wanted naught more. It didn't matter that they'd trysted in the stables an hour ago. Nor did he care that she was distracting him from his duties. He'd even lost his interest in Sung Li's exotic weapons.

The temptation of stretching out on a real pallet with his ladylove by the light of day, joining with her in complete union—body, heart, and soul—was impossible to resist.

Somehow they managed to make it to the bed, despite the little wanton's impatient caresses and gasping kisses and frantic clawing at his tabard. He was determined to be gentle with her, no matter how insistent her need. He might be a savage warrior when it served him, but he was also capable of great tenderness, especially when he was making love to the woman he intended to make his bride.

'Twas a most challenging task, for everywhere she touched him, she left desire burning like a brand upon his skin, and in every fiber of his body, he longed to douse that flame.

But he used the utmost restraint, refusing to let her rush him, no matter how her fingers pulled at his clothes, no matter how many kisses she showered upon him. Of course, his withdrawal only incited her further. Soon she had slung her leg possessively over him and was trying to climb atop him on the pallet.

"Ah, lady," he groaned, chuckling ruefully, "if you start at a gallop, the ride will be over before it's begun."

Her eyes looked as hazy and blue as distant pines as she said, "Perchance we shall go on more than one ride."

He grinned. "Indeed? You are a woman of ambition."

Another time he'd let her ride him like a destrier, steering him to her will. Another time he'd let her spur him on and rein him back, give her complete control. But for her first time, he needed to take charge.

He rolled her over forcefully, trapping her legs between his own and seizing her straying hands to still their seduction. She gave a whimper of irritation. The headstrong vixen clearly didn't like yielding to his whims.

"Let me ride you, my wild little mare," he coaxed her. "I promise your day will come."

She frowned, displeased at her unseating, but she wasn't displeased for long. When he loosened her kirtle, dragging it down with his teeth to suckle at her succulent breasts, she sighed in gratification. When he plucked off her shoes, then pushed her skirts up to roll down her stockings slowly, she shivered with delight.

"I want to see all of you," he whispered, "by the full light of day."

Miriel was not a shy creature where her body was concerned, and while the trait seemed at odds with her meek nature, he was grateful for her brazenness. She was like a butterfly, squirming eagerly out of her cocoon, emerging naked and new and beautiful. The sight of her sprawled shamelessly atop the coverlet, her skin the color of honey-eyed cream in the sunlight, her hair tumbling across the pallet in dark disarray, her breasts small and perfect and inviting, left him breathless.

For a moment he only stared down at her, drinking in every aspect of her lovely form—the delicate bones below her throat, the smooth hollow of her belly, the gentle curve of her hips, the soft triangle of chestnut-colored curls at the juncture of her thighs.

Then his eye caught on a recently healed gash with a dark purple bruise marring one of her knees. Shock froze the breath in his lungs. For a moment, he could only stare at the damning mark while astonishing thoughts swirled through his mind.

Nay. It could not be. Miriel could not be The Shadow. The injury was coincidence, no more.

He ran a fingertip lightly over the healing wound. "How came you by this, my love?"

She jerked her knee back reflexively. "That? 'Tis naught. Just an old bruise."

He told hold of her ankle, straightening her leg with gentle but insistent force, to study her knee. "'Tis considerably more than a bruise, I'd say."

"I slipped. On the stairs."

He peered into her eyes. Her gaze was wide and innocent. Surely she was telling the truth.

Then her brow furrowed, and she bit her lower lip. "You find me ugly," she murmured.

Rand blinked, startled. "Ugly?" Was that what she thought? Naught could be further from the truth. "Oh, my lady, I find you beautiful beyond compare. Every scratch, every nick, every bruise." To prove it, he placed a feather-light kiss atop her knee. "They're all a part of you."

Jesu, how could he have ever imagined the sensitive lass offering herself to him so sweetly was a hardened outlaw?

Miriel blushed prettily even as she was screaming a silent curse. Bloody hell! How could she have been so careless?

The injury on her knee was only one of the myriad minor wounds she inevitably earned from combat on a weekly basis. But she could hardly explain that to Rand.

One day she would. One day she'd admit that the weapons belonged to her. One day she'd confess that she was a master of Chinese warfare. But not now. Not while he was gazing down at her as if she were the most precious fragile flower.

Fortunately, he seemed to believe her lie about the stairs. 'Twas a lame excuse at best. But considering she was lying naked before a man she'd met less than a fortnight ago, her blood simmering with desire, prepared to give him the most precious thing she had to offer, 'twas a wonder she could think up an excuse at all.

Unfortunately, he wasn't finished examining her scars.

He spotted the one on her thigh, the slash she'd earned from the swipe of Sung Li's *do* two years ago.

"What about this one?" he asked.

She sighed. Why couldn't he return to seducing her? 'Twas a far more intriguing pastime than cataloging her injuries. "A kitchen knife," she lied.

He kissed her there, too, and she shivered as his lush locks softly brushed her thighs.

"And here?" He touched the scar high on her other thigh where she'd missed a block and been gouged by the *fu pa*.

Still quivering deliciously from the sensuous tickle of his hair, she found it mentally challenging to come up with new lies. "A . . . a cow."

"A cow?"

"A cow's horn. She . . . she didn't like the way I was milking her."

'Twas a ridiculous explanation, she knew, but rational thought had become too demanding. And the fact that he was moving farther and farther upward with his kisses, toward the spot where she most longed to feel his warm tongue and hungry mouth, made her care little if what she said made sense at all.

He brushed a thumb across the fading bruise that ran along the inner ridge of her hipbone. "And what happened here?"

"I . . . I . . ." She'd suffered a hard kick there that she hadn't dodged in time. "I can't remember."

He ran the tip of his tongue lightly over the spot. "Can't remember?"

"Sung Li says I'm . . . clumsy. I probably . . . ran into a table."

He sucked gently at the bruise. Then his mouth followed the curve of her pelvis until it teased the edge of curls guarding her womanhood.

"You know, do you not," he murmured, "that in coupling, I must inflict injury upon you as well?"

Miriel was hardly afraid. The blade in his trews wasn't sharp. Naught he could do to her could hurt as much as the sting of a *shuriken* or a *foa huen's* slash. Indeed, she looked forward to being impaled by his firm, sleek, velvety weapon. Why was he tormenting her with speech?

Once, twice, he moved his head down, parted her downy nether lips, and let his tongue slip between them, touching upon the burning hot bud of her need, making her feel as if she burst into bloom at the contact.

Then, when impatience nearly compelled her to seize his head and force him to devour her wholly, he moved away from her, further frustrating her wants.

While she lay panting in thwarted need, he sat back on the pallet to pull the tabard over his head. Stifling a groan of dismay, she perused the layers of armor he wore. Bloody hell, 'twould take an eternity to undress him. Surely he didn't mean to make her wait so long.

"Come to me now," she bade him, her voice more rough and demanding than she intended.

He gave her a lopsided smile, making one of his adorable dimples appear. "Patience, my sweet."

Why was the varlet making her wait? 'Twas clear by the smoldering in his eyes that he wanted this as much as she did. She intended to remedy his delay at once. When he began to haul the coat of chain mail off his shoulders, she reached beneath it to press her palm possessively against the bulge in his trews.

He groaned, and the sound sent a surge of power through her soul. Now she would make him bow to her will.

To her surprise, he resisted even that, gently but firmly pushing her hand away, though his voice was shaky with restraint. "God's bones," he groaned. "Allow me to at least disarm, my lady."

She scowled in dismay. She cared not. She would make love to him in full armor on the back of a horse if 'twould hurry her fulfillment.

While she waited with ill-concealed impatience, he threw off his coat of mail, then removed the padded gambeson beneath. He painstakingly unfastened his sabotons and poleyns, then unbuckled the belt that held up his chausses, letting them shiver to the ground in a silvery pool. Finally, he removed his linen undershirt and trews, until he stood before her, naked as a newborn babe.

But he looked naught like a babe. Nay, he was all man.

If she thought she'd desired him before, 'twas naught compared to the way she felt when she beheld his glorious body bathed in golden sunlight.

God's blood, he was magnificent. His shoulders were wide and capable, his arms well muscled, his hands broad. His chest should have seemed menacing in its breadth and strength. Yet she found herself longing to burrow into the firm-yet-yielding refuge of his embrace. His flat stomach was lightly furred, and the faint hair glistened in the afternoon sun. His hips were lean, and the curve of his buttock made her want to run her hand along its slope. She let her gaze rove down the strong pillars of his legs, the powerful thighs, the contoured calves. Sweet Mary, even his feet were beautiful.

But naught compared to the dark mystery of the staff that jutted proudly from its nest of deceptively soft curls, and 'twas there her gaze was riveted.

"My lady," he breathed, a smile hovering about his lips, "I believe you're ravishing me with your eyes."

She ruefully quirked up one corner of her mouth. "'Tis all you'll allow, it seems."

"Are you ready for me?"

'Twas an absurd question. Her mouth had gone dry with thirst for him, and her heart fluttered madly against her ribs. "You know I am," she whispered.

"I don't want to hurt you, my love," he said, coming near, reaching out for her ankle and sliding his hand slowly upward, making heavenly friction against her leg. "Make me a vow. Promise me you'll let me take the reins this once."

She closed her eyes in bliss and nodded, willing to promise him anything if he'd continue touching her like that.

Rand swallowed hard. Despite his considerate words, the wolf within him longed to give Miriel what she thought she desired, to throw caution aside, to dive atop her delectable body and sink into her welcoming softness.

As he stretched out beside her on the pallet, though they didn't touch, he felt the heat flowing between their naked bodies like liquid lightning.

Though he'd bedded his share of wenches—innkeepers' lusty daughters, saucy harlots, curious noblewomen— Rand had never lain with a virgin before, nor had he lain with a woman for whom he cared so much. He didn't want to make a single mistake.

He wove his fingers through her hair and pulled her close enough to kiss her. But the mischievous lass wasn't content with a simple kiss. She slung her arm about his neck and insinuated herself into his embrace.

Where they touched, a delicious warmth spread, and when she pressed the soft pillows of her breasts against him, 'twas as if their flesh melted together. 'Twas an utterly blissful sensation, one in which he mustn't lose himself if he was to remain gentle.

He rocked them both over until he loomed above her. He could see by the lusty glaze of her eyes 'twould not take long to ready her for his penetration. Already her pulse throbbed, and her breath came rapidly. Already her nipples awakened under the light rasping of his chest. Already her plump lips grew moist with yearning.

He reached down between them, parting the dewy petals of her woman's flower, to ease the way for his passage.

In spite of her promise, Miriel clutched at his shoulders, thrusting upward with her hips, trying to speed his trespass.

"Aye," she groaned, her voice throaty with longing.

"Not yet," he whispered.

He began to rub slowly at the swollen bud of her need, his fingers made slick by the juices of her desire, and she arched up in invitation.

Sweet Lord, 'twas an invitation he longed to answer. Soon, he promised himself, soon.

Gradually, he increased the speed of his fondling, relentlessly urging her to higher and higher planes of passion, until she began to take the shallow, expectant breaths of impending release.

Only then did Rand finally place his aching staff against her yielding flesh, nudging inward against her maidenhead.

She was on the verge of climax when Rand breathed into her ear. "Forgive me."

The moment she shuddered under the distraction of the initial spasms of release, he plunged into her all at once. She stiffened, but never cried out, still caught up in the throes of climax.

'Twas a mercy to take her thus, and yet Rand couldn't help but regret tearing her frail flesh. While he shivered at the sheer bliss of being surrounded by all that softness, he was careful to remain still to let her body adjust to his invasion. 'Twas not an easy thing, when every instinct told him to strive against the slick, warm sheath of her enveloping womb.

In the end, despite vowing to let him lead her in the dance of love, 'twas Miriel who instinctively initiated the slow withdrawal and penetration that began the most joyous coupling of Rand's life.

Never had he felt so tender, yet so fierce. He surrendered to Miriel's rhythm, though she was like a novice rider, not yet used to walking, but determined to take off at a gallop across the undiscovered landscape.

There would be time later to teach her the leisure of lovemaking. For now, he would knot his fingers in the mane of that wild mount called lust and hold on for the ride.

Their passions rose so swiftly and with such force that their mating soon began to take on an animal ferocity. The pallet groaned with every thrust of their hips, as if echoing their savage cries. And when they began to ascend together the last steep hill of their sensuous journey, Rand felt the world around him fade and disappear. Now there were only his sharpening thirst, demanding to be slaked, and sweet Miriel, the beautiful woman who could quench the fire raging inside him.

When the lass spontaneously threw her legs around him, digging her heels into his buttocks, his loins tightened in reaction, and for one desperate moment, he feared his passions might bolt, that he might leave her behind.

But in the next magical instant, she arched upward, gasping in wonder, and the two of them crested desire's peak as one.

An intense bolt of lightning seemed to sear Miriel's body as she found her pinnacle. Her body shook with thunderous tremors of release. She cried out with the sheer ecstasy of requited desire, while Rand's bellow echoed her own satisfaction.

She collapsed then—boneless, spent, and completely vulnerable. She couldn't even muster the strength to lift her eyelids. Yet despite the weakness that afflicted her every muscle, she felt curiously safe in Rand's arms, protected and precious. He might dominate her physically, looming over her with superior strength and weight; but he, too, had surrendered in her embrace.

As she lay panting afterward, her nerves still buzzing with sexual energy, she realized she'd never felt more alive, more vital. This was perfect balance, perfect *yin* and *yang*. Not only of her body, but of her soul as well. Where they were joined, she still throbbed with the thrill of his invasion. Pressed chest to chest and hip to hip, it almost seemed they were one being.

"Did I hurt you?" he breathed against her ear.

"Nay." It had been only a small sting, like the nick of a *woo diep do*. Forsooth, 'twas the unfamiliar intrusion into her most private place that shocked her more. She'd not expected to feel so... possessed.

He pulled away slightly, easing out a fraction of an inch. But now that she was accustomed to the feel of him, she was reluctant to have him leave. With the little strength she had left, she hooked her heel over his backside and held him close.

"Stay," she bade him softly, and he complied.

When she lazily opened her eyes, he was staring down at her with some inexplicable expression. Wonder. Or joy. Or surprise. Whatever 'twas, it pleased her, and she smiled up at him.

His face slowly bloomed into a grin, and Miriel, suddenly in a playful mood, reached up to touch one of his dimples.

He must have been in a playful mood as well, for he furrowed his brow in mock seriousness, and told her, "I got that in a knife fight with the Devil."

"Oh, aye?" Her lips twitched as she moved her finger to the other dimple. "And this one?"

"He's very fast, the Devil is."

"And fond of symmetry, 'twould seem." There was a real scar, a small notch, along his jaw. She touched it with a fingertip. "What about this one?" Then she added, "The truth."

"The truth?"

"Aye."

"I fell off a horse and hit a fence."

"You fell off a horse?"

"I was three winters old," he explained.

She nodded. Now that she'd shared her battle scars with him, it seemed only right that she learn his as well. As he'd done, she lifted her head and placed a kiss upon the healed wound.

High on the opposite brow, just beneath the hairline, was a thin white mark. "And here?"

"A robber split my brow."

She winced, bending his head down to kiss the scar. Then she searched his face with her fingers, pushing back his hair, rubbing over his lightly stubbled chin, while he patiently suffered her attentions. She found a long, shallow slash at the side of his neck.

"This?"

His eyes turned grave, and she almost wished she hadn't asked him.

"My ... father."

"Your father?"

He seemed suddenly uncomfortable, and again she wished she'd bitten her tongue. The last thing she wanted to do was spoil the carefree mood. But he answered her anyway.

"'Twas an accident. He ... he slipped with his sword when we were sparring."

She sensed there was more to the story than that, but perchance 'twas for another time. Hoping to distract him from his solemnity, she nuzzled his neck, tickling him with her hair, and planted a kiss on the old injury.

Lying back, she let her fingers spread across the lovely expanse of his chest, searching for flaws. There were none. But the cap of his shoulder bore a jagged scar a few inches long. "Here?"

"Arrow wound."

She frowned. That seemed unlikely. A blade wound might be thus gnarled if 'twas inflicted with a cruel twist of the wrist, but arrow wounds were generally clean.

As if he perceived her thoughts, he added, "The point had to be dug out."

A strange unexpected surge of protectiveness rose in her as she imagined someone gouging into Rand's flesh. She muttered, "The physician must have been a butcher."

He gave her a rueful smile. "I was the physician."

She looked into his beautiful brown eyes. Surely he wasn't serious. But as she stared at him, he gave her a sheepish shrug.

She shook her head in amazement. What a remarkable man he was. Miriel prided herself on having a high threshold of pain, but she couldn't imagine digging an arrow point out of her own shoulder. With renewed respect, she pressed a reverent kiss upon his damaged skin.

He lifted himself higher on his arms, allowing her access to his belly. At his lowermost rib was a dark bruise. She slid her thumb lightly across the place. "This is new."

"Ah," he said, glancing down at it. "That's from my battle with The Shadow. 'Tis naught."

A secret smile curved her lips. Naturally he'd say that. He'd never admit The Shadow had bested him.

She glanced again at the black bruise. She wasn't about to disengage from her enjoyable position to kiss him there. His loins were warm upon her, and every time he shifted, his prickly hair brushed tantalizingly against her sensitive woman's mound, arousing her. Instead, she pressed a kiss to her fingertips and touched the bruise.

Before she could withdraw her hand, he took hold of it,

guiding her down his belly. There was smoky mischief in his eyes as he pressed her fingers against the verge of his curly thatch where his inner thigh met his loins. She was surprised to discover a small ridged scar there.

She didn't hear his convoluted explanation for that injury, for she was too distracted by what lay just a few inches away, the place where their two bodies converged. Joined together there, they seemed one creature, and the sight excited her. Her muscles tensed around him as she began, incredibly, to crave him once again.

Ignoring his chatter, she boldly moved her hand inward until she touched the place where they were united, the velvety flesh of his cock and her own soft, womanly folds. He shivered once at her touch, and she felt his staff stir inside her.

"Lady, you sore tempt me," he whispered, "to embark on another ride."

"Mm. This time, I'll hold the reins."

And so she did. She rolled him over and rode astride him, slowly at first, languorously rising and falling upon the saddle of his hips, enjoying the delicious tug of his flesh within hers. But her slow ride soon turned into a rollicking, rocking gallop. Her eager movements jostled her breasts and tangled her hair as she tossed her head in rapture.

Rand's eyes were closed tight, his jaw clenched, his brow beaded with sweat. He seemed to suffer an agony of pleasure. Watching his beautiful, tortured face increased the intensity of her passions, and very soon she found herself riding toward that cliff's edge, leaping off into the deep chasm of release.

He followed her, furrowing his brow as if in anguish

while every muscle tightened with amazing power. When he found his own climax, he cried out like a wounded man, pumping deeply into her still-contracting womb. When he was spent, he relaxed beneath her, trembling like a weary palfrey after a hard day's ride.

Her heart swelled then, both with the heady thrill of controlling the wild steed of their desire and with the affection she felt when she looked down at Rand. He lay quiet now, as limp as a shipwrecked sailor washed up on the shore. Yet there was no mistaking his bridled strength. A moment ago, he'd raged like a thunderstorm. Yet now he seemed as vulnerable as a child.

Overwhelmed by a flood of tenderness and weary from lovemaking, she sank onto his chest, resting her head in the hollow of his shoulder, and closed her eyes.

His arms enfolded her, and the sound of his heartbeat, her complete satiation, and the warmth of the sunlight streaming in the window combined to make a lullaby that sent her drifting off to a pleasant oblivion. There she dreamed of wet kisses and sparkling brown eyes and marrying Sir Rand.

Rand had no bones left in his body. He was sure Miriel had melted every one. Never had he felt such fierce joy, such utter completion. By the Saints, 'twas almost as if *he* had been a virgin till this moment.

Miriel had taken him to a place he'd never been before, to a safe harbor of love and acceptance. And he didn't want to sail away from that harbor. Forsooth, making love to her felt so right that he didn't want to lie with another woman the rest of his life.

'Twas a startling realization, yet he'd known for several days now that if she was willing, and if her family approved, he intended to make Miriel his bride. He'd have never been able to accept the gift of her virginity otherwise. He'd grown to appreciate Rivenloch—the lush landscape, the engaging castle folk, the magnificent fighting force. But his love for Lady Miriel exceeded everything else.

He cradled the lovely lass against his shoulder while she dozed. The sound of her slow breathing was comforting, like the soft patter of rain on thatch, and her breath warmed the place over his heart. He rested his chin atop her head and idly rubbed a lock of her hair between his thumb and finger, marveling at its silky texture.

She was an amazing woman. On the surface, she seemed as fragile as a rose. But the more time he spent with her, the more he realized that the frail flower had a stem made of steel.

Mayhap other men would be repelled by such a maid. They preferred their wives docile, mild, and compliant. But Rand admired women of strength and wit, courage and conviction. Though he was still only beginning to graze the surface of Miriel's character, and though she seemed to take great pains to hide her brave and independent nature, he sensed she was such a woman.

He saw it in the mischievous twinkle of her innocent eyes, heard it in the clever lies she told without blinking, felt it in her brazen, passionate lovemaking.

Miriel was a singular woman. Mayhap, he dared to hope, she was unconventional enough to look past his bastard birth and forgive his past sins as a common mercenary. He was half noble, after all. His father might be a drunken monster, but he was a lord. And as for Rand's occupation, he would gladly give it up for a place in Rivenloch's army.

Mayhap he could prove worthy of Miriel's love.

The precious damsel sighed in her sleep, and her hand curled upon his chest as if laying claim to him.

He didn't mind. Not at all. There was naught he wanted more than to belong to Miriel of Rivenloch.

❦

Chapter 18

Miriel was accustomed to getting her way. No matter how submissive she appeared, she could manipulate her way into almost anything. So while she mimicked Sung Li's *taijiquan* postures by the light of the rising sun, her mind was a thousand miles away, musing over the ways she could entice Sir Rand to ask for her hand.

It had to be soon. Miriel was not naive. She knew there was a slim possibility he'd planted a babe in her womb yesterday. Forsooth, the idea that she might already carry his child was curiously pleasing.

"Do not smile," Sung Li intoned over his shoulder. How the old man could tell she was smiling, Miriel didn't know. Perchance he had eyes at the back of his head.

She tried to comply, but all she could think about was the soul-shaking intensity of coupling with Rand the day before and the heart-melting pleasure of lying in his arms afterward. She never wanted to lose that bliss.

Sung Li lunged slowly to the right, and Miriel mirrored

the movement, though her legs quivered from the exertions of yesterday's lovemaking.

She couldn't tell anyone what she'd done, of course. Not her sisters. Or Sung Li. Especially Sung Li. They would call her careless and irresponsible for surrendering her maidenhead to a man not yet wedded to her.

But she intended to remedy that. Very soon.

Sung Li swept his arm out in a broad arc. She shadowed him. At least, she thought she shadowed him. But when he whipped his head around, and snapped, "Pay heed!", she realized she was using the opposite arm.

He scowled in disgust. "You are not worthy of your master today."

She gulped. He was right. She wasn't concentrating. "I am sorry, *xiansheng*."

"We are finished," he said with solemn finality.

Her face fell. "Aye, *xiansheng*." She wanted to counter him, to apologize, to somehow make amends for the insult. But 'twas useless to argue with Sung Li once he'd made a decree.

The fact that he'd cut their exercises short was a serious chastisement for Miriel. From the very first moment he'd come home with her, he'd explained that his life from that day forward would be dedicated to her, that he would train her in the ancient and sacred ways of his people. He made her realize 'twas a precious gift he gave her, a secret knowledge few were privileged to learn. 'Twas a great affront to Sung Li for her to give less than her complete attention to his instruction.

Perchance he would forgive her on the morrow, but for now he was clearly finished with her. He snatched his maidservant's garb from the hook on the wall and shook out the skirts with a sharp snap before donning them over his linen trews.

Miriel bowed respectfully to him, then sat forlornly on the bed, letting guilt seep into her bones.

"The Night will swallow The Shadow soon," Sung Li said, so faintly that Miriel hardly heard him.

"What?"

"You must be ready."

"What do you mean?"

But whether for spite or to be enigmatic, Sung Li apparently didn't intend to explain his cryptic remark. With a grave expression that sent a chill of foreboding up Miriel's spine, he turned and left her chamber.

Miriel tried to cheer herself with the fact that Rand was taking her to the fair today. As she wriggled into her favorite rose red surcoat and chose a matching ribbon for her hair, she couldn't help but smile as she thought about seeing Rand again. Had it been only half a day since she'd beheld those endearing dimples, gazed into those twinkling eyes, kissed that tempting mouth? It seemed an eternity.

She hurried into her soft leather slippers and whirled her cloak around her shoulders, then eagerly rushed down the stairs, unable to keep the grin from her face.

When Rand looked up from his breakfast to see the delicate rose petal floating down the great hall's steps, he almost choked on his oatcake. Angels in heaven, she was more beautiful than he remembered, even with her clothes on. What would it be like to have her run downstairs to greet him every morn?

Nay, he corrected, smiling slyly, if Miriel agreed to be his wife, he meant to keep her abed till afternoon.

"Good morn!" she called, her face shining.

Like a hound wagging its tail when its master came into the room, Rand's cock roused at once, instinctively responding to her presence. He supposed 'twas pitiful to be so easily manipulated, but he didn't care. He would gladly play the slave to Miriel.

Of course, he could never let her know the power she wielded over him.

He swallowed the oatcake, gallantly bowed, then let his eyes glaze over with feigned nonchalance. "My lady, what brings you downstairs so early? And why are you so gaily attired? Have you plans to clean out the stables today?"

She narrowed her eyes wickedly at him and gave him a chiding shove in the middle of his chest. To his surprise, he was pushed backward several inches. The wee wench was more powerful than she looked.

He grinned, rubbing at the spot.

"I hope you've brought lots of silver," she taunted, arching a brow.

"Enough to buy the moon and the stars."

She cocked her head at him. "What about the sun?"

"The sun?" He pretended to consider the idea, then frowned. "I don't think a lass like yourself should be playing with fire."

She stepped closer and murmured, "But I *like* to play with fire." She lowered her gaze pointedly to his rapidly swelling staff.

"Oh, aye, my wicked lass," he whispered, "that you certainly do."

"Where are my sisters?" she mumbled, glancing about the hall.

He lifted the corner of his mouth. "In the tiltyard."

"Then kiss me," she breathed.

At that most inopportune time, Rand spied, just over the top of Miriel's head, at the entrance of the buttery, that infernal maidservant, glaring directly at him. Instead of the soul-searing kiss he intended, he bent forward and placed a chaste peck upon Miriel's brow.

Miriel scowled, obviously disappointed.

"Sung Li!" he called out, giving the glowering old maid a cheery wave. "Good morn!"

Miriel's eyes widened in surprise, and she took a prudent step away from him.

Sung Li still scowled at him, but he ignored her irascible manner and spoke to her in warm invitation. "Will you be joining us at the fair?"

Dismay flitted across Miriel's features, but Rand knew 'twas a harmless invitation. Sung Li had proclaimed only two days ago that fairs were meant for *you zhi,* children.

Sung Li sent him an undeserved withering glance as she scurried near, and for one instant, Rand wondered if the addled crone intended to poke his eyes or curse him in her tongue for issuing such an audacious invitation.

But at the last moment, she took hold of Miriel's arm. "Be sure you return before supper."

"Of course," Miriel replied.

Sung Li didn't release her. She pulled Miriel even closer by the arm, and said distinctly, "The Night will come very soon. Very soon."

Some secret communication must have passed between

the two of them in the next instant, for Miriel solemnly nodded, then murmured, "I'll be watchful."

Her reply apparently satisfied Sung Li, for without another word, the old woman hurried off as she'd come, silently as a cat.

Rand would have much preferred to continue where they'd left off, with Miriel begging for his kiss and his loins awakening at her urging. But if they did, one kiss would lead to another, kissing would lead to fondling, fondling would lead them up to Miriel's bedchamber, and they'd never make it out the front gates.

Rand had promised to take her to the fair. He'd also promised her a lover's token.

Late last night, after much reflection and consideration, he'd decided what that token would be. And now that he'd made up his mind, he was anxious to make his way to the fair to find the right craftsman from whom he might purchase such a treasure.

He offered her his arm. "Shall we, my lady?"

She looped her arm through his and smiled engagingly. What followed was the most enjoyable day Rand had ever spent at a fair.

Miriel had always loved fairs, but this was the first time she'd been to one with a suitor and without a chaperone. Strolling down the winding rows upon the arm of a man she adored made it a completely new experience.

Naturally she brought a list of necessities to purchase for the castle—beeswax candles and earthen vessels, medicines to replace those she'd given to the monastery, cinnamon from Burma and pepper from India—but for once, at Rand's prodding, she dawdled at booths selling more frivolous wares.

She examined a table full of silver cloak pins, worked into fantastical shapes of dragons and harts, lions and wild boars. Another booth featured a bright array of ribbons in every color of the rainbow. A *femme sole* from Normandy offered bottled scents of lavender and rose. Down another row, a leatherworker sold soft purses of all shapes and sizes, fastened with buttons made of cow's horn. And one merchant offered tiny corked vials of dust, which he claimed was earth from Christ's tomb.

Strolling down the armorers' row, Rand stopped to inspect a display of blades from Toledo, but decided the merchant was overcharging for his wares. 'Twould be cheaper, he muttered to Miriel, to pay for passage to Spain himself and purchase a weapon there.

At another booth, he found daggers of reasonable price, but inferior quality, something only a cautious purchaser would recognize.

He took particular interest in a handsome blade at a third shop, until the vendor told him 'twas the actual sword of King Arthur, at which point he steered Miriel away with all haste, rolling his eyes in disbelief.

Miriel's admiration for him increased with their every transaction. Rand might not be able to read, but he had a sharp mind when it came to commerce. He might not be as wealthy as a lord, but she could be certain he'd never squander her dowry. 'Twas a comforting thought.

They'd almost reached the end of armorers' row when Miriel's eyes lit upon a motley array of used weapons from all over the world. There were curved sabers and short Roman swords, a couple of broad Viking blades and a great Saxon battle-axe. But what made her catch her breath was the weapon propped against the corner pole of the merchant's pavilion. 'Twas a perfect *shang chi*, a Chinese double halberd. The long black handle was painted with a red dragon whose tail spiraled down its length, ending at the red tassel that hung from its end. The twin openwork blades looked like the wings of a silver butterfly.

Completely forgetting Rand, she reached for the beautiful weapon, hefting it in one hand. The craftsmanship was superb, the balance was incredible, and someone had taken very good care of the blades, for as she ran a thumb over one of the edges, she cut through the first layer of skin. 'Twas rare to find a piece of such exceptional quality, and her pulse raced at the idea of acquiring it.

"How much for this?" she asked, trying to keep from sounding too eager.

The merchant blinked at her, aghast, then looked askance at Rand.

Rand's brows drew together in puzzlement. "Are you interested in this?"

Miriel glanced between the two men. God's hooks! In her excitement over the *shang chi,* she'd forgotten that today she was only a maid of Rivenloch, not a master of Chinese warfare.

"Aye," she bluffed. "For Sung Li." She addressed the merchant, pretending ignorance. "'Tis Chinese, is it not?"

The merchant nodded. "Mayhap the gentleman would like to try it." He practically pried it out of her possessive grip and handed the weapon to Rand.

She bit her lip in frustration as Rand turned the blade this way and that.

"How much?" she repeated.

Rand scowled. "It could not be much of a weapon, not with open blades like that. They would break off on impact."

She shook her head. "'Tis made for slicing, not chopping," she told him. "And the steel is very strong, folded and fired up to a dozen times."

Both men stared at her.

"Or so I've heard," she finished lamely.

"If I may?" the merchant asked, gesturing for the weapon.

Rand handed it to him so he could demonstrate its use.

"The *shang fu* is an ancient weapon from China," he intoned.

"*Shang chi*," Miriel corrected.

"What?"

"*Shang chi.* 'Tis called a *shang chi.*" She assured Rand, "Sung Li told me so."

The merchant gave her a disapproving frown. But when she glanced at Rand, she saw subtle amusement dancing in his eyes.

"The *fu* has a closed blade, like a halberd," she said softly. "This is an open blade, a *shang chi.*"

The merchant disliked being corrected, particularly by a woman, Miriel supposed. But he continued his demonstration for Rand, hefting a rotten apple from a basket on his table. "I suppose it doesn't matter what you call it as long as it does the damage, eh, sir?"

Making sure no one was in range, he rested the pole

on his shoulder and tossed the apple onto the path. Then, using both hands, he swung the blade up over his head with the intent of bringing it straight down like an axe to split the apple.

Miriel's heart lodged in her throat. Jesu! The impact of the ground would dull the sharp blade. She had to stop him.

She acted on instinct. As the blade started its descent, she stepped toward the merchant. She grabbed the handle of the *shang chi* with one hand. With the heel of her other hand, she struck his elbow, not hard enough to break it, just enough to make him release the weapon.

With a yelp of pain, he let go, and she managed to deflect the blow enough that the blade only grazed the dirt.

She'd saved the weapon.

But now she'd thrown herself from the kettle into the fire.

There she stood with the incriminating *shang chi* in her grip. The merchant staggered back, cradling his cracked elbow. Rand stared at her in awe. And a small, curious crowd was beginning to gather.

With as much feminine helplessness as she could manage, she shrugged an apology and handed the weapon back to the merchant. "I'm so sorry. I must have... slipped." Then she realized she might use that to her advantage. "I feel so wretched. Please, let me pay you for the blade."

The merchant looked at her with doleful eyes, but clearly he wasn't about to pass up a sale. "That's eight shillings. Nay, ten shillings."

She was tempted to haggle with the cheat, but she supposed she owed him something for the damage to his arm. Besides, that piece was likely worth more than he knew. She counted out the pieces of silver from her purse.

Then the merchant made the mistake of trying to ally with Rand against her. "Naught more dangerous than a wench with a sharp blade, eh?"

Rand grinned back. "Only a knave with a sharp wit." He sidled up to the man, smiling companionably, and spoke loudly enough for the bystanders to hear. "Since my lady saved you from chopping off your own toes, my good man, I'd think you'd be more than happy to shave a little off the price."

"What?" He blinked rapidly.

Miriel raised her brows.

The crowd began whispering among themselves.

"Is that true?" a toothless old man asked Rand. "Is that why the wee lass jumped in front of the blade?"

"Oh, aye," he said soberly, "heedless of her own safety."

"He would have chopped his toes clean off with that Devil's blade," an apple-cheeked woman agreed. "I saw the whole thing."

"Indeed?" A scrawny, bearded man popped his head through the gathering crowd. "And he's going to make her pay?"

"'Tisn't right."

"You'd think the wretch would be grateful."

The onlookers' speculations grew more and more wild, and Miriel began to be embarrassed as the story grew all out of proportion.

"Who saved his life?"

"The wee lass. He might have killed himself with that nasty blade if she hadn't..."

"...snatched it right from his hand."

"...saved his ungrateful hide."

"...swept in like a guardian angel and knocked the Reaper flat on his arse."

"That merchant's a thankless cur, that's what he is."

"I won't be buying my weapons from the varlet."

"All right! All right!" the merchant cried, then told Rand, "Eight shillings."

The toothless old man chimed in. "*You* should pay *her* for saving your life."

As the mayhem grew around her, Miriel stole a glance at Rand. His eyes sparkled with devilry as he stood with his arms crossed smugly over his chest. The wicked lad appeared to be thoroughly enjoying the chaos he'd created.

"You are a knave," she murmured.

"And you are a liar," he said affectionately, carrying the *shang chi* for her.

As quietly as possible, Miriel pressed eight shillings into the merchant's palm and slipped through the crowd. When they left, the bystanders were still arguing about what had happened, who had saved whom, and where they would or would not buy their weapons. Miriel couldn't help but wonder what a toothless old peasant wanted with an ancient sword anyway.

Miriel should have realized she couldn't escape from the altercation completely unscathed. Rand had questions.

"So how did you come to know so much about Chinese weaponry?"

She shrugged. "Sung Li."

"And how did a wee old maidservant come to know so much?"

"She . . . her father was a warrior." Miriel bit her lip. It might be true, but she didn't actually know. Sung Li never spoke of his parents, only of his teachers.

"But surely he didn't teach her to wield such weapons."

He was treading on dangerous ground. She had to be careful. "Sung Li has always been very observant."

"And are you?"

"What?"

"Are you observant? How did *you* learn to wield such weapons?"

She choked on a forced laugh. "Me?" she squeaked. "Wield weapons? Oh, Rand, you know I can't abide fighting."

God's wounds! She couldn't tell him the truth, not when she was trying to get him to ask for her hand. Eventually she'd confess. But 'twould be in her own time, little by little, so he could adjust gradually to her revelations—that the weapons on her chamber wall were hers, that Sung Li was in sooth her teacher, that Miriel was highly trained in the Chinese art of war. And that, if she desired, she could snatch that *shang chi* from him and slit his throat in the blink of an eye.

Miriel furrowed her brow. She wondered if she'd ever be able to tell him the entire truth. 'Twas a huge secret she kept from him. Perchance if he knew the truth about her, he wouldn't care for her anymore.

Then she frowned at her destructive thoughts. 'Twas foolish to feed her fears.

The fact was she'd slept with Rand. Twice. There was no going back, no undoing what she'd done. She'd wooed him to her bed. Now she had to woo him to the chapel before he could unravel too many of her secrets. She intended to succeed...if she could distract him long enough from his dogged pursuit of the truth.

Chapter 19

Rand couldn't help but smile in wonder as he walked beside Miriel, carrying her prize purchase. The clever lass might be able to fool everyone else, but Rand was beginning to recognize when she was making up tales.

He'd seen the way her eyes lit up when she'd spied the magnificent blade. He didn't believe for one moment that Miriel intended to give the thing to Sung Li. In fact, he'd wager half his coin that that entire collection of weapons on Miriel's wall belonged not to her servant but to the saucy lass herself.

The wench claimed she didn't approve of fighting, but 'twas as clear as the shine in her eyes that she adored weapons of war. Not only that, but he'd begun to suspect she was capable of doing more than admiring them from afar.

The way she'd blocked the vendor's blow had been no accident. And now Rand couldn't avoid the recurring suspicion that, as unbelievable as it seemed, Miriel bore a disturbing resemblance to the agile outlaw he sought.

"Look, Rand!" Miriel suddenly cried, looking not at all like a dangerous thief but a beguiled child as she pointed at a tiny monkey with a jeweled collar that was scampering up onto its owner's shoulder. Her giggle was contagious as she watched the little beast's antics.

Yet only moments later, the carefree child turned into a shrewd barterer as she haggled with a cloth merchant who was trying to pass off nubby linen as rare cotton from Egypt.

In one moment she was licking the sticky juice of a cherry coffyn from her fingers.

In the next she was whispering a warning to Rand that the pottery merchant was selling cracked wares.

Miriel bounced constantly between woman and child, and he never knew which would emerge. But perchance that was the thing that attracted him to her. He loved surprises, and Miriel was full of them.

Was one of her surprises a habit of lurking in the woods of Rivenloch, preying on passing strangers with full purses? How could he find out for certain?

While Miriel was applauding at the conclusion of a lute player's performance, Rand spied a game of skill farther down the lane. Perfect, he thought. Grabbing her hand, he pulled her along. "Come on."

She went willingly until she saw where he was going. Then she hesitated. "Knife throwing?"

" 'Twill be fun," he coaxed her.

"You know how I feel about warfare."

He chuckled. " 'Tisn't warfare. 'Tis only a contest."

"But I've never—"

"I can teach you."

"Teach me?"

"Aye," he told her proudly. "I've a keen eye with a blade."

"Mm."

He leaned Miriel's weapon against the corner pole of the booth, then pressed a coin into the proprietor's palm and selected three knives.

"I'll show you how it's done, then you throw the next three."

He eyed the straw target five yards away, then flexed his fingers and picked up the first knife. He took a steadying breath, then, with a flick of his wrist, fired the weapon forward. The blade sank into the straw not an inch from the center of the target.

Miriel clapped and gave a little cheer, but he knew he could do better than that.

He wiped his hand on his tabard, drying his fingers to help improve his grip, then picked up the second knife. This time when he hurled the weapon, it landed beside the first, a blade width's closer to the center.

"You're very good," Miriel gushed.

But not good enough. He had to waken the competitive spirit in her. To do that, he needed to hit the mark in the dead center.

Taking a deep breath and concentrating hard on the target, he flipped the knife off the end of his fingers once more. This time it landed on the opposite side, just shy of the center.

He grumbled and shook his head.

Miriel hurried to assuage his humiliation. "You were so close. By the Saints, if that had been an attacker, you would have saved my life."

"Here," he said, selecting three knives for her while the proprietor pulled out the three Rand had fired.

"Are you sure..." Miriel began, moving reluctantly to the throwing line.

"I'll help you." He placed the first knife in Miriel's hand, then stood behind her, wrapping his arms about her to guide her. 'Twas an intimate position. The soft, fragrant cloud of her hair brushed his cheek, and her backside nestled against his loins. He was sorely tempted to spend the rest of the day teaching her to throw knives.

"Like this?" she asked, stiffening her wrist.

"Nay, like this."

He loosened her taut grip with a gentle shake, then guided her through a couple of practice flings before he told her to let go of the blade. Her arm wobbled, and the knife sailed toward the target, lodging in the outermost ring.

She might have missed intentionally. *He* would have if he was trying to hide his talents. But to his amusement, Miriel seemed absolutely delighted with her performance.

"I did it!" she exclaimed. "I hit the target!"

His worries that she might be an expert marksman vanished. She was truly awful, and bless her heart, the poor lass didn't even know it. Lord, she was precious, Rand thought, particularly when she spun in his arms to give him a victorious kiss on the cheek.

"Try again," he said. "This time keep your eyes on the center of the target."

Their arms moved as one again, and he helped her flick the blade forward. The knife landed one ring closer to the center, but by Miriel's proud grin, one would have thought she'd thrown three bull's-eyes.

Chuckling, he handed her the third knife. "Would you like to try it on your own now?"

"Aye," she said, her eyes alight.

He watched as her face grew very serious and she blew out a few breaths, focusing hard on the straw. Then, after two false starts, she cast the blade forward. It missed the target altogether, landing in the back wall of the pavilion.

"Oh!" She clapped her hands in embarrassment over her mouth.

"That's all right," he assured her, digging in his purse again. "Shall we go another round?"

She whispered, "I don't wish to damage the poor man's pavilion."

He laughed. "I'm certain my coin will cover the repairs. But this time, let's make it more interesting. How about a wager?"

"A wager?"

"Aye. I have a fierce hunger again. If I win, we'll go purchase eel pie." She wrinkled her nose. "If you win, we'll have chicken pasties."

She considered the wager for a moment, her eyes gleaming in speculation. Then she nodded, meeting his challenge. "Done."

To his satisfaction, his first two casts landed in the inner circle, and he made a bull's-eye on the last throw.

Miriel shook her head, sure she'd already lost their contest. She picked up the first knife, biting her bottom lip in concentration. She stood with the wrong foot forward, and Rand stopped her to correct her form. She nodded, studied the target, then squeezed her eyes shut and fired the knife. It stuck at the edge of the straw, missing the target altogether.

At her frown of disappointment, Rand handed her the second knife. "This time, keep your eyes open," he suggested with a grin.

She'd still walk away victorious. He'd give her the prize for his bull's-eye, a ribbon for her hair. But he couldn't deny that his mouth was watering as if he already tasted that eel pie.

Then something amazing happened. With a rapid twist of her wrist, Miriel flung the blade forward, and somehow, miraculously, it landed in the dead center of the target.

She let out a whoop of triumph, and even the proprietor stared at her, doubtless grateful that the blade hadn't lodged in any part of his body.

The man leaned over the booth toward Rand. "Novice's luck," he assured him.

Rand presumed as much, too, until she threw the last knife. It flew to the bull's-eye with such deadly speed and aim, knocking the first blade askew, that it took Rand's breath away. That blade might have been thrown by a hired assassin, so true was its flight.

"Did you see it?" she cried, clapping her hands together in glee. "Oh, I wish my father could have seen it."

"'Twas remarkable," Rand agreed, feeling slightly queasy. "You're certain you've never thrown a knife before?"

"Me?" She laughed.

The proprietor of the booth shook his head. "Never seen a novice throw *two* bull's-eyes."

"I was greatly motivated," she said.

"You like ribbons, m'lady?" the man asked, holding out the selection to let her choose her prize.

"Nay," she confided with a wink, "I truly despise eel pie."

True to his word, Rand bought them chicken pasties, though he hadn't much appetite. There was no denying now that Miriel possessed skills that a woman professing to detest warfare definitely should not have. The question was what to do about it.

He tried to keep a calm head as they sat together under an oak tree, sharing their supper. Perchance he was leaping to conclusions. Just because she could throw knives didn't mean she was The Shadow. Her talent might be a family trait. After all, Miriel's sisters were expert swordswomen. It stood to reason that Miriel might have inherited some of her father's skills as well.

He wondered what would happen if he bluffed, told her he knew who The Shadow was? Would a glimmer of telltale fear enter her eyes?

He swallowed his last bite of pasty and brushed the crumbs from his lap, then caught Miriel's hand in his. "My lady, I have something to confess."

"Aye?"

He watched her eyes carefully. "I know something about . . . The Shadow."

She blinked once, but her gaze revealed naught. But as he continued to stare at her in silence, horror dawned slowly in her eyes. Her mouth formed an "O" of surprise, and she withdrew her hand.

Jesu, Rand thought, he was right. Miriel *was* The Shadow. 'Twas written all over her face.

"Are you ... are you ..." she began, breathless.

He mentally finished her sentence for her. Going to tell my family? Going to turn me in? Going to see that I hang for my crimes?

"Are *you* The Shadow?" she whispered.

"Me?"

Her eyes were wide with fear as she nodded.

"*Me?*" How she'd twisted his intent around so quickly, he didn't know, but the absurdity of her assumption made him laugh out loud. "Of course not!"

"Are you sure?"

"I'm *not* The Shadow, Miriel."

She looked at him with wary eyes. "Then what do you have to confess?"

Lord, she was either genuinely puzzled or brilliantly dissembling. He couldn't tell which.

"Wait!" she said suddenly, placing her hand upon his forearm. "Don't tell me. I know."

He waited. Perchance she was going to reveal herself now. Outlaws often blurted out confessions when their perfidy was discovered.

She shyly lowered her eyes. "You wish to confess that your recent encounter with The Shadow, your close brush with death, has made you realize how valuable life is."

Rand furrowed his brows. What was the maid going on about? 'Twas not at all what he wished to confess.

She leaned in closer and looked coyly up at him. "You've learned that what's precious to a man can be swept away..." She snapped her fingers. "In the blink of an eye."

He smiled uneasily. Where was she going with this?

She returned his smile, then inclined her head against his with an affectionate sigh. "I know, my dearest Rand. You wish to confess that you cannot bear the thought of living the rest of your years apart from the woman you love."

Rand almost choked on astonishment. He was still reeling in speechless surprise when Miriel circled her arms about his neck and planted a deliberate kiss upon his mouth.

Now what the bloody hell was he supposed to do? The conniving little imp had deliberately cornered him.

Not that 'twas an uncomfortable corner. Indeed, her arms felt wonderfully right about him, her lips sweet and warm, her soft, adoring gaze most flattering.

But, damn the wench, she'd backed him into a spot where he couldn't budge. She might have used mere words to do it, but she was no less deft than The Shadow when it came to rendering a man helpless.

"Miriel."

"Rand?" She lowered her gaze to his mouth and hungrily licked her lips.

He sighed. "That's exactly what I wished to confess."

Miriel decided she must share her father's penchant for gambling. She'd taken a huge risk, using her feminine wiles, wagering everything to pull Rand away from the subject of The Shadow and steer him toward the subject of marriage.

Thankfully, the wager had paid off.

And as Rand obliged her with a deep, soul-melting kiss, the reality of what she'd won began to sink in.

"Marry me, my lady," he murmured against her lips.

She flashed him a mischievous grin. "I'll have to think about it."

He lifted a menacing brow. "Think quickly, else I shall withdraw my offer."

Before she could gush out a reply, he began to rain kisses all over her face.

"Well?" he said between feverish pecks. "What say you?"

So intense and overwhelming was his assault that she could scarcely gasp for breath betwixt his kisses.

"No word, wench?" he demanded. "Will you say me aye?"

"Aye!" she managed to cry at last, laughing in delight as he nuzzled at her ear. Her heart felt as if it danced for joy, and her body felt lighter than air.

Finally, he paused in his attack long enough to clasp her face between his palms. His expression was very serious, but his gaze was soft and adoring, and as he continued to stare deeply into her eyes, his mouth slowly widened into a brilliant smile, complete with irresistible dimples.

Then, as impulsive as she, he grabbed her wrist, hopped to his feet, and tugged her up. "Come on."

"Where are we going?"

"I believe I owe you a love token, my lady."

Pausing just long enough to grab her *shang chi,* she trailed gladly after him toward jewelers' row.

His gift was a wedding ring, a beautiful entwined silver piece that the jeweler said was a lover's knot. It looked curiously foreign on her hand, but knowing what it meant, that she belonged to Rand and that he belonged to her, made it seem perfect encircling her finger.

Of course, Rand wouldn't let her wear it. Not yet. On

the day they were wed, he told her, when they made their marriage vows before the people of Rivenloch and the priest, then he'd slip it on her finger and promise his everlasting love.

She could wait. After all, once he placed it on the finger leading straight to her heart, once they became man and wife before God, she knew she could no longer harbor secrets from him.

The grin wouldn't fade from Rand's face as he held Miriel's hand. What was happening between the brightly painted players on the stage before him, he didn't know. He was preoccupied with the lovely damsel sitting beside him, who watched the performance with rapt fascination.

'Twas the most amazing day. A fortnight ago, he'd never imagined that the Lord of Morbroch's mission would earn him such a priceless reward.

That Miriel had coerced him into asking for her hand seemed somehow appropriate. The lass was completely unpredictable and impulsive, just as when she'd seized him that first day and demanded a kiss. Marriage to her would be an endless series of adventures and surprises, he was sure.

'Twould also be a serious responsibility. He'd never been responsible for another person. On his own, he'd always made his bed where he lay, found supper where he could, lived each day at the whim of the wind. He was unaccustomed to the rigors of castle life, where one kept regular hours and followed strict codes of conduct.

But he looked forward to the discipline. Perchance 'twas what had been missing in his life—a sense of purpose, a sense of belonging. He belonged now—to the lovely damsel clinging to his hand with childlike trust. And he intended to become worthy of that trust.

His heart swelled with a reckless longing to please Miriel. He wanted to bring light to her eyes, to make her world safe and blessed and bright. Was that what love felt like? If so, he could see why men did foolish things in the name of love. For at the moment, he'd gladly do anything to bring a smile to her face.

The first thing he'd do was befriend Sung Li. For reasons known only to her, the old maid seemed to detest Rand. Ordinarily he wouldn't care. She was only a servant, after all. But the grumpy old woman was obviously beloved by Miriel. 'Twas important that Rand learn to care for her, even if she never warmed to him.

Second, he'd settle his doubts concerning The Shadow once and for all. He needed to catch the outlaw, to uncover his identity, to complete his mission.

And one day, he'd reveal his secrets to Miriel. But for now, did it matter he was a bastard? Did it matter he was a mercenary, not Sir Rand of Morbroch, but Rand la Nuit? Did it matter he'd come to Rivenloch, not to court her, but to catch an outlaw?

Nay, he decided. All that mattered was that he loved Miriel, and he wanted to make her his wife. The rest he'd tell her soon enough.

He raised Miriel's clasped hand to his lips for what must have been the fiftieth time. She giggled over something the players were doing, and he turned his attention to the stage.

The two ruffians were having some sort of mock quarrel involving a huge fish, slapping each other with the thing. Rand thought their play looked familiar. Aye, he'd seen the men before, shared ale with them, in fact. In Stirling mayhap. Or Carlisle. As he continued to watch the humorous spectacle, grinning as the players punched and dodged, leaped and collided in a well-practiced dance, the most brilliant idea began to worm its way through his brain.

Chapter 20

WHEN MIRIEL RETURNED to the now-deserted stage with the pair of ales she'd fetched for herself and Rand, she was surprised to find him chatting with the gaudily dressed players. Curious, she held back, watching their interaction at a distance. The three of them seemed to be conducting some serious surreptitious transaction, made ludicrous by the fact that two of them had faces painted in as many colors as a bastard's coat of arms.

While she watched, Rand slipped something into their palms, gave them a nod farewell, then glanced up to see her approach. He beamed at the sight of her, and the instant she beheld those enchanting dimples, all her suspicions vanished.

She handed him his ale, deciding she was too cynical by far. Rand wasn't up to mischief. He'd probably given the players a few coins for their entertainment, no more.

She didn't give the matter another thought.

They spent the rest of the afternoon in bargaining and

feasting, watching wrestlers and pipers and mummers, strolling hand in hand down the winding lanes of leatherworkers and jewelers, swordsmiths and chandlers, spice merchants and vendors of holy relics. After a delightfully exhausting day, they sauntered home to Rivenloch, as Sung Li wished, before nightfall.

Rand announced their wedding plans at supper. With perfect chivalry, he first formally asked her father's permission for her hand. Unfortunately, Lord Gellir, his wits more rattled tonight than usual, seemed highly confused by the whole affair, unclear as to who was to wed whom. But where Lord Gellir faltered, Pagan, Colin, Deirdre, and Helena intervened. They gave Rand and Miriel their enthusiastic blessing and hearty cheers.

Sung Li, too, offered quiet congratulations, but Miriel could tell his words were empty. He was displeased. And that angered Miriel immensely.

She silently cursed the peevish old man for his rudeness to Rand. After all, Rand was making a great effort to be kind this eve. He'd helped Sung Li to his seat. He'd assured Sung Li that Miriel would still require the maid's services after they were wed. He'd even told the surly old worm that if he truly disapproved of their marriage, Rand would gladly listen to his grievances.

Still Sung Li offered him a cold reception, and by the end of supper, Miriel was becoming sorely tempted to use her new *shang chi* on the rude old fool.

After supper, Rand disappeared briefly. When he returned to the hall, he was accompanied by none other than the two players from the fair, their faces still garish with paint.

Miriel frowned. What the Devil were they doing here?

With a wink at Miriel, Rand directed the kitchen lads to move some of the tables to make space for a pleasant diversion. Then he introduced the players to the folk of Rivenloch.

The entertainers, Hob-Nob and Wat-Wat, with a flamboyant flourish of their arms, saluted the high table and took to the makeshift stage. Within moments, their unbridled antics had the hall erupting in uncontrollable laughter. Soon even her father was chortling in delight.

When Rand returned to the table, Miriel leaned toward him, astounded. "You hired them? But how did you...? What...?"

He smiled and whispered, "'Twas insurance, in the event your father refused me your hand. What man can say nay when his belly is rolling with laughter?"

Miriel grinned. He was clever, her bridegroom. And eager to please. Chivalrous. And kind. And handsome. And utterly irresistible.

But she supposed she'd have to resist him for the moment. After all, 'twould be inappropriate to seize her beloved Rand by the tabard, throw him onto one of the trestle tables, tear off his trews, and have her way with him with all the folk of Rivenloch for witness. No matter how tempting the thought.

She settled for holding tight to his arm, resting her cheek fondly against his shoulder, and listening to the wonderful rumble of his laughter as he chuckled over the playful fighting of Hob-Nob and Wat-Wat.

At the end of their long performance, Lord Gellir naturally invited the players to join him at dice. They enthusiastically agreed, and soon the wagering turned fiercely comic as Wat-Wat began stealing silver from Hob-Nob's pile and Hob-Nob kept thumping him on the back of the head.

Miriel knew her father would suffer great losses tonight at the hands of the two sly knaves. They were not only experts at sleight of hand, but they talked circles of logic around the men at the table, leaving them scratching their heads and handing over their coin.

But she hadn't seen her father so happy in weeks, and she didn't want anything to dim that happiness. Perchance 'twas worth the loss of a few coins for the joy that blossomed in Lord Gellir's eyes as Wat-Wat and Hob-Nob battled over the single piece of silver they'd just won off him.

As if he'd read her mind, Rand squeezed her hand in reassurance, and murmured, "I'll try to make sure he doesn't lose too badly." Then with a sweet kiss to her brow, he bade her good night and moved to the gaming table to join in the wagering.

Miriel would have preferred that he carry her up to her bedchamber, toss her onto the pallet, throw up her skirts, and give her a proper good night. But he was a man of conscience and good heart, and there was much to be said for prudence, particularly when she seemed to have so little of late.

Besides, as soon as she rose from the table and headed for the stairs, Sung Li followed her.

"Miriel." He snapped like a hound at her heels. "Miriel."

Miriel didn't bother to acknowledge the pesky servant. She was still irritated with him.

"*Miriel.*"

Miriel opened her chamber door, tempted to turn about and slam it in his face.

Then Sung Li reached out to grab her arm, muttering one of his inscrutable declarations. "He is not who you think he is."

She could have pretended she didn't know who Sung Li meant, but 'twould have been useless. Instead, she bit out, "And you are not who I thought you were." She stood nose to nose with Sung Li. "I thought you were my faithful servant, my respected *xiansheng*, my friend." She jerked her arm out of Sung Li's grasp. "But you've been naught but rude to my bridegroom ever since he arrived."

Sung Li raised his chin proudly. "What I do, I do for your protection."

"Protection?" She rolled her eyes, then pulled Sung Li through the doorway into her bedchamber, closing the door against those who might overhear. "Sung Li, you are ever telling me that I am a child. How do you expect me to grow up if you insist on protecting me?"

Sung Li listened in silence.

"I don't know why you hate Rand so," she continued. "But I know he is a good man. He will make me a fine husband. He has been patient with my father and kind to my sisters. And as horrid as you've been to him, he's even been civil to *you*."

Sung Li stared at her a long while, his black gaze intent and probing, his mind probably a thousand miles away, until Miriel was forced to look away in discomfort.

Finally, he spoke. "You are right. It is time that you make your own future."

Miriel blinked in astonishment. 'Twas the last thing she expected from Sung Li. The stubborn old master never admitted he was wrong.

"But there are things I must reveal to you," he said, "very important things that will help you to steer your destiny."

Miriel nodded mutely, still reeling from his concession.

"The two fools are not as foolish as they seem," he intoned.

"Hob-Nob and Wat-Wat?"

"They are strong and agile and clever."

"What do the players have to do with Rand?"

"He hired them, did he not?"

"Aye, but—"

"And they are winning much coin this night."

"As does everyone who wagers against my father."

"Which by now Rand of Morbroch knows."

"What are you saying?"

"Your betrothed hired the players to rob your father of his silver this eve. On the morrow, he will leave with them, and they will split their winnings."

"What?" She was tempted to laugh, so preposterous was Sung Li's accusation.

"He will not return again."

"That's the most absurd thing I've ever—"

"You do not remember him from before," Sung Li reminded her, "when he claims to have fallen in love with you."

Miriel bit her lip. She wanted to gainsay Sung Li, but what he said was right. Forsooth, no one at the tournament remembered Sir Rand of Morbroch. Indeed, he'd fabricated the entire tale. Suddenly her chest felt weighted, as if a heavy lump of lead congealed there.

"He did not come for you, Miriel."

"What are you saying?" Her lungs constricted, making

it hard to breathe. "That he came to Rivenloch to rob my father?"

Sung Li's silence was telling.

"That cannot be true." But in her mind, she knew 'twas possible. He could have used the pretense of courting her simply to gain access to the gaming table. And he could have freely promised her marriage if he planned to escape with his winnings, knowing full well 'twas a promise he'd never be compelled to keep. The possibility sickened her.

Yet why would such a man resort to thievery? He clearly was well funded enough to own a fine blade and a magnificent horse, to suffer gambling losses over the past sennight, to purchase a ring for her at the fair.

"He's a noble knight," she insisted, though she knew 'twas likely a lie.

"Are you certain of that?"

She couldn't meet Sung Li's eyes. "He introduced himself as Sir Rand of Morbroch."

"And Hob-Nob introduced himself as the King of the Faeries."

Miriel felt as if she scrabbled for purchase on a rapidly crumbling wall. "Who but a noble knight could wield a sword so well?"

Sung Li narrowed his wise eyes. "Certainly not the meek daughter of a Scots lord," he said pointedly. "Nor her aging maidservant."

Miriel had to concede—Sung Li was right. One couldn't judge by appearances. But neither could one make rash assumptions.

She shook her head. "I don't believe it. I know Rand. He is a man of honor. And he loves me." To her dismay, despite the conviction of her statement, her voice cracked over the last words.

Sung Li's face looked suddenly old and weary, as if he'd aged ten years in the span of a few moments. "I tell you, he will betray you."

That wasn't what Miriel's heart told her. Her heart said that Rand cherished her, that their souls were inextricably intertwined, that he would never do anything to hurt her.

"You'll see," she told Sung Li. "Come morn, the players will take their leave, and all of this will be remedied. Rand will still be here. He wouldn't leave me."

For a long while her words hung in the air, sounding more hollow and desperate with each passing moment.

Sung Li at last acknowledged her with a nod, then turned and reached for the door. Though his back was to her, she could hear the command in his voice. "'Twould be a foolish thing if The Shadow tried to steal the players' silver in the morn."

The thought had never occurred to Miriel. She supposed she was too caught up in the horrifying possibility that Rand might betray her to think of The Shadow and what might become of the players' winnings. "Foolish?"

"The three of them together make a formidable foe."

"There will be only two," she insisted. "Rand won't go with them."

"Yet on the morrow it will happen. The Night will swallow The Shadow."

Miriel gulped. "What do you mean?" This time the prophecy chilled her blood.

His explanation was as obtuse as his prediction. "Swallowed by the night, the shadow disappears."

'Twas true, she supposed, from a standpoint of pure

logic. But Sung Li's soothsaying was never that simplistic. As she reconsidered the symbolism, a startling possibility invaded her thoughts. God's eyes, by Night did Sung Li mean death? Would The Shadow die on the morrow?

'Twas impossible to imagine. The Shadow was untouchable. He escaped every encounter, unscathed. No one could catch the elusive thief, much less deal him a killing blow. The Shadow was indestructible.

Yet Sung Li seemed very serious about his prediction, and he was never wrong. Miriel had to pay heed to his words. "I'm certain the outlaw won't do anything foolish."

Sung Li hesitated, as if he wished to say something else, then decided against it. Without another word, he opened the door.

"Where are you going?"

"You are right," he said with a slight bow of his head. "You are no longer a child. You do not need an old man to guard your sleep."

With that, Sung Li bade her good night and left her chamber.

Miriel should have felt a heady rush of independence. At last Sung Li had recognized her for what she was—a grown woman. But instead, her heart suffered a twinge of sorrow.

Something had forever changed between the two of them. Miriel was no longer the student. Sung Li was no longer the master. They had come to a crossroads where they had to take separate paths.

But if Miriel had known at that moment that because of her insistence on Rand's innocence, she might never set eyes upon her beloved *xiansheng* again, she would have chased after Sung Li and insisted he spend this fateful night by her side.

Unfortunately, love had made her blind.

Meanwhile, Miriel tossed and turned in her bed, unable to sleep for the troubles tormenting her wakeful brain.

Damn it all! 'Twas unfair.

She adored Rand. He was everything she could hope for in a husband. He was perfect for her. Witty and kind, intelligent and attentive, brave and deliciously wicked, he was just the sort of man who understood her free spirit. He made her feel alive and respected and cherished. She sensed he was a man who could eventually accept her for the warrior maid she was.

Now Sung Li had planted an ugly seed of doubt in her mind, a seed that might grow and bloom into utter betrayal.

She hoped for once her *xiansheng* was wrong. She prayed that there was naught to fret over, that 'twas only a foolish fear on Sung Li's part, that on the morrow she'd wake to find Rand breaking his fast by the morning hearth, his face lighting up at the sight of her.

She prayed 'twas so. For if 'twas not...

God save her, she'd trysted with the man.

Chapter 21

THE SUN'S FACE was fully above the horizon now. Miriel had lain abed as long as she could. Despite a fitful night of little sleep, her bones grew restless along with her thoughts, insisting she rise.

She supposed Sung Li wasn't going to come to her chamber for *taijiquan* this morn. Mayhap he expected her to do the exercises alone from now on. Whatever his intentions, she'd already waited too long to begin. Her family would wonder what had become of her if she was further delayed.

Still, her step was reluctant as she descended the stairs, and her heart fluttered, whether with anticipation or dread, she wasn't sure. Would Rand be in the great hall as she'd imagined, with a cup of ale and an oatcake, greeting her with a wide grin? Or would Sung Li's prediction come true—would he have left the keep, never to return?

'Twas far easier to wonder than to face the truth.

Summoning up her courage, she took the last step into

the great hall and glanced toward the hearth. Several castle folk were gathered there—her sisters and their husbands, Sir Rauve and Lucy Campbell, a few Rivenloch men, half a dozen knights of Cameliard—sharing a light repast and talking in the soft voices of morn.

But Rand was nowhere to be seen.

The breath froze in her throat, chilling her hopes like winter frost settling upon a rose.

"Miri!" Deirdre called. "Finally up and about?" She winked. "Not even wed yet, and already you're lying abed till noon."

Miriel couldn't even summon the smallest of smiles in response. She perused the small gathering again, praying she'd somehow overlooked Rand's presence. But he wasn't there.

A tiny lump of misgiving hardened in her throat.

"Is something wrong?" Colin asked.

She bit her lip. 'Twas foolish to make rash assumptions, she knew. The castle was large. Rand could be anywhere. Still, dread drained the blood from her face.

Pagan frowned in concern. "Are you all right?"

Miriel glanced up, at Pagan, at Colin, at all of them. She couldn't tell them the worst of her fears, that Sir Rand of Morbroch, her betrothed, had betrayed her.

Besides, she had no real evidence he'd left with the players, only Sung Li's prediction and a nagging fear in the deep recesses of her mind.

She managed a shaky smile. "Have you seen Rand?"

Helena, as usual, assumed the worst. She placed one hand on the hilt of her sword. "What's he done?"

"Naught."

"Are you sure?" Helena would fight at the drop of a

gauntlet. No doubt she'd enjoy pummeling Rand if she believed he'd hurt Miriel. 'Twas comforting, though unnecessary.

"Aye," she said with a forced shrug. "I just wondered where he was."

Sir Rauve, one arm around Lucy's shoulders, volunteered, "I think he went to see the players off this morn."

He'd said it so offhandedly that at first Miriel didn't feel the impact of his words. When they finally sank in, her smile faltered, and she felt nausea slowly build in her throat.

Deirdre furrowed her brow. "Do you feel well, Miri? Do you want an oatcake or—?"

"Nay."

"You look ill," Helena said frankly. "Could you be with child?"

Miriel glanced sharply at her. 'Twas a terribly personal thing to ask, and the others scolded Helena for her meddling, saving Miriel from having to answer.

But what if she *was* with child, God help her? Would she bear a bastard?

Somehow she found the strength to ask Rauve, "Did he say when he'd return?"

Rauve chuckled. "I expect he went to seek a rematch with The Shadow."

Colin shook his head in amusement. "Ever since the outlaw gave him that silver coin, I think he's been craving another chance at him."

Pagan muttered into his ale. "I hope he doesn't get too badly hurt."

"The Shadow has never hurt anyone," Helena said.

Deirdre smirked. "Though he may deal a bruising blow to Sir Rand's pride."

A feeble hope sprouted in Miriel's breast. Could that be why Rand had gone with the players? Was he only hoping to meet up with The Shadow again? Sweet Mary, of course! It made perfect sense.

A wry smile of irony curved her lips. Today he'd be disappointed. But as long as he returned faithfully to her, she'd gladly console him for his lost chance at glory.

Forsooth, her blood quickened as she thought of what form that consolation might take.

Her fears soothed somewhat, she managed to stomach a bit of oatcake and busied herself about the great hall, mentally planning her wedding feast. Doubt still lurked like a thief in the corners of her mind, but she swept past, ignoring its presence.

The deception worked for a while as the morn wore on. But when the sun drew high overhead, and still Rand did not return, Miriel found that the lurking thief had begun to whisper taunts from the shadows.

He's left for good.

You'll never see him again.

He's betrayed you.

You were a fool to trust him.

And when by afternoon, still there was no sign of him, the doubts began to be murmured aloud throughout the keep by the castle folk.

"You don't suppose something has happened to him?"

"The Shadow never hurt anybody. Not seriously."

"Perchance he lost his way back."

"Mayhap the players rolled him."

"Aye, the two wily lads probably knocked him on the skull and cut his purse."

"Should we send someone out to look for him?"

"Nay. He's a grown man. He'll come back. You'll see."

Miriel was determined to hold on to hope, no matter by how fine a thread, but her heart told her they were all wrong.

Rand had not encountered The Shadow. He'd not been robbed by the players. Nor had he lost his way.

By the sinking in her gut, she knew Sung Li had been right. Rand had betrayed her. He'd betrayed them all.

Rand walked along the path through the Rivenloch woods with the faith and courage that came from the love of a wonderful woman and the knowledge that he was going to prove her innocence today.

He'd set an ingenious trap, one into which The Shadow was sure to fall.

Rand had funded the players well enough last night to ensure they could wager high and win considerable coin from Lord Gellir. The pair of apparent fools, their purses heavy with silver, would prove an irresistible target for the outlaw.

But what The Shadow didn't know was that the players were quite skilled in combat. Watching them yesterday, Rand realized that the interplay between Hob-Nob and Wat-Wat, though farcical, required a high level of coordination, speed, and agility, the same strengths The Shadow possessed.

If they could catch the thief off his guard, startle him with their antics, match him, move for move, dazzle him with their nimble sparring, Rand could move in while he was distracted and capture the outlaw once and for all.

He'd naturally offered the players a generous reward, the remainder of the advance that the Lord of Morbroch had collected for him. He didn't care about the coin anymore. What he did, he did to exonerate Miriel.

As he'd instructed the players, they traveled jauntily down the path, quibbling loudly, pretending inattention, while Rand followed distantly behind, scouring the trees for signs of the familiar figure all in black.

He didn't have long to wait. But when The Shadow made his appearance, he didn't so much arrive as materialize. Rand would have sworn he'd been staring at a shade-darkened patch in the crotch of a tree when he suddenly realized 'twas more than a shadow. 'Twas *The* Shadow.

The players had sauntered past the outlaw already. Rand gave a quick sharp whistle to attract their attention and drew his sword. As he'd warned them, they'd have to be quick.

While the thief watched with mild interest from his perch, Hob-Nob shoved Wat-Wat, and Wat-Wat's fist came round with a wide swing that missed his opponent's nose by a scant inch. Using the same rapid lunges and feints, punches and kicks, spins and rolls that they had at the fair, the players engaged each other in a mock fight that was so perfectly coordinated and so convincing, Rand himself was distracted for a moment.

In that moment, The Shadow bounded to the ground. When Rand next looked up, the robber was already making his stealthy way toward the players.

Rand narrowed his eyes. Could the thief in black be Miriel? He didn't see how. 'Twas impossible to reconcile the sweet damsel giggling in his arms yesterday with the silently efficient outlaw.

Rand anticipated an entertaining exchange of blows. The players would use their wily moves to confound The

Shadow, and The Shadow would employ his acrobatics to dodge their attack. While they were engaged, Rand would steal up behind the outlaw and take him at sword point.

'Twas not what happened at all.

When Hob-Nob wheeled about, his arms flailing, strewing silver coins all over the path, The Shadow took one calm step toward him. The robber reached out to Hob-Nob, as if affectionately clapping an old friend alongside the neck, then gave a sharp squeeze.

The player's bones seemed to turn to custard. His eyes rolled up, and he collapsed like a pile of laundry. In fact, if The Shadow hadn't reached out to soften his fall, lowering him carefully to the ground, the poor wretch might have knocked himself witless on a rock or a tree trunk.

Wat-Wat hesitated an instant, stunned by the suddenness of his friend's demise. But he quickly recovered and began goading The Shadow with words and blows, allowing Rand to approach slowly from the rear.

"You scrawny black Devil!" Wat-Wat dodged left and right, forward and back, his fists raised before him. "Come fight a real man!"

The Shadow simply stood watching while Wat-Wat danced about, as if patiently waiting for the player to tire himself.

Rand was but eight yards distant. If the player could keep him occupied, and if the outlaw didn't make some sort of swift, impossible leap into the trees, in another few moments he'd be near enough to take him.

"You motherless cur! You demon's spawn!" Wat-Wat danced about, bobbing his head this way and that. "Show me your claws!"

Just four more yards, and The Shadow would be within

sword's reach. Rand didn't intend to use his blade. Unless the outlaw was devoid of common sense, he'd realize when the sword point touched his back he'd have no choice but to surrender.

Then Wat-Wat, convinced The Shadow wasn't going to attack him at all, simply hopped from one foot to the other and spread his arms in askance. "What's wrong with you, you Lucifer's whelp? Are you afraid I might—"

His words were cut off as The Shadow's arm shot out with lightning speed, the heel of his hand striking the point of Wat-Wat's chin and driving his head backward.

Wat-Wat, his arms still extended like branches, continued his backward fall, crashing into the thick brush lining the path, like a tree downed in a storm.

Then The Shadow whipped around toward Rand.

Bloody hell! He was still two yards out of range.

In that instant, the outlaw could have simply turned and fled, making one of his acrobatic escapes into the wood.

But he didn't.

And in that crucial sliver of time, The Shadow's curious inaction gave Rand the advantage.

Rand seized that advantage. He hurtled forward the last few yards, sweeping his blade up and lodging it against the villain's black-swathed throat.

He'd done it. He'd captured The Shadow.

Rand was not the kind of man to gloat. He'd hunted down enough fugitives to know 'twas miserable for them to be caught, so he always spared them the humiliation of crowing over their capture. 'Twas satisfaction enough to know the robber was at his mercy.

Still, he should have been filled with the thrill of victory. He'd caught the outlaw no other man could touch.

Rivenloch would rejoice. He'd collect his reward. And Miriel would look up at him with shining eyes of admiration.

He should have felt victorious, but his triumph was strangely hollow. The Shadow wasn't moving a muscle, wasn't showing the least bit of resistance. Forsooth, Rand got the distinct impression that he hadn't so much conquered the thief as simply accepted his surrender. 'Twas almost as if The Shadow wanted to be captured.

Still, Rand was wise enough to be wary. The man was clever. There was no telling what weapons he might wear up his sleeve or hidden in the folds of his odd black garb.

Keeping the sword at The Shadow's throat, he slipped the shackles from his belt, then bade the robber slowly extend his arms. The Shadow complied, and 'twas the work of a moment to lock the shackles about his wrists, even with one hand. After all, he'd had much practice taking outlaws into custody.

Then Rand was able to lower his sword.

Still he was not content. It had been too easy. Criminal apprehension never went this smoothly. Outlaws fought capture with every last ounce of their strength, some with their dying breath.

Unsettled, he half expected The Shadow to lash out suddenly with one of his powerful feet and send Rand flying ten yards down the path. At the moment, Rand felt about as safe as a mouse scampering across the floor of a mews. He couldn't afford to let down his guard.

There was one more thing he needed to do before he returned to Rivenloch with his quarry. He had to make sure the players were unharmed. Indeed, 'twas surprising that The Shadow had treated them to such violence. All the castle folk insisted that the outlaw had never seriously hurt anyone. But whatever he'd done this time, it had rendered his poor victims as still as death.

"Sit," he told The Shadow, pressing upon the man's small shoulder to force him down.

Then he placed the point of his sword just below the thief's ear. One thrust forward, and they both knew he could sever the artery there, leaving The Shadow to bleed to death.

The Shadow sat, unmoving, while Rand checked for the pulses of the fallen men. They were thankfully strong. Whatever the thief had done to the players, at least he'd left them alive.

Rand was secretly glad. Whether the Lord of Morbroch would ultimately hang The Shadow for his thievery, Rand didn't know. But it seemed the thief had shown a certain restraint in his attack. 'Twas a relief not to have to add murder to the miserable wretch's list of crimes.

Almost at once, Hob-Nob groaned as he began a groggy ascent to wakefulness. Wat-Wat followed shortly thereafter, struggling to sit up while cradling his injured chin.

"You got him?" Wat-Wat asked, trying to smile through the pain.

Rand nodded. "Keep the extra silver for your trouble." Their winnings, currently strewn across the path, he'd originally intended to return to Rivenloch's coffers, to keep Miriel's accounts balanced. Now he would reimburse Lord Gellir with a portion of the reward from Morbroch.

"Happy to be of service," Hob-Nob said cheerily, despite the foggy glaze of his eyes.

With that, the players collected their wits and their winnings and gladly resumed their travel through the

Rivenloch forest, back to the fair, where they could earn their keep for much less demanding labor.

The Shadow remained quiet, which was not surprising. In Rand's experience, cornered criminals behaved like cornered animals. They either put up a desperate fight, howling and whimpering and bellowing with rage, or they fumed in silence, perchance recognizing the futility of resistance, perchance planning for the opportunity to escape.

Still, there was a curious peace about The Shadow's demeanor. He seemed neither fearful nor angry. Which made Rand uneasy.

He'd feel better if he could see the robber's face.

Cautiously sheathing his sword, he drew his dagger instead and crouched beside the captive. Slipping the point beneath the black fabric enshrouding The Shadow's head, he sliced carefully upward until the cloth fell away.

Shock sucked the air from his lungs.

There, sitting stone-faced before him, was Sung Li.

Chapter 22

THE NIGHT HAS SWALLOWED THE SHADOW.

The parchment dropped from Miriel's trembling fingers. Her heart plummeted. One hand still gripping the lid of the empty pine chest, she slowly sank to her knees.

She still didn't completely understand. But gradually, pieces of the mystery were roiling into place, like sinister black clouds swirling together in the portent of a storm. With each passing moment, that storm looked more menacing, more dangerous.

Miriel needed to find out exactly what had happened and act before 'twas too late.

The stark, damning words on the parchment stared up at her from the floor of her workroom as she reviewed what she knew.

Sung Li was nowhere to be found. No one had seen him all day. Yet no one had seen him leave the castle.

Rand had departed with the players hours ago and had never returned. Sir Rauve was convinced he traveled with them in the hopes of reengaging The Shadow. But now 'twas feared that some foul play might have ensued.

Sung Li had warned her that Rand was not who he said he was, that he'd come to Rivenloch, not for Miriel, but for reasons of his own. He believed Rand had conspired with the players to rob Lord Gellir. He'd also told Miriel that The Shadow would be foolish to pursue and engage such skilled fighters.

And now, as Miriel peered again into the empty chest, her heart thumping woodenly against her ribs, she feared Sung Li had acted against his own advice.

The Shadow's disguise was missing.

And so was Sung Li.

Miriel supposed she should have known Lucy Campbell couldn't keep her mouth closed about the black cloth she'd been sent to fetch. Indeed, a few hours later, Deirdre and Helena came barging into Miriel's workroom, demanding answers.

"Miriel!" Deirdre barked. "What the Devil are you..."

Helena gasped. "Bloody hell."

The sisters froze as Miriel whirled toward them, clad from head to toe in black. For a moment, no one said anything. The only movement in the room was the flickering flame of the candle.

"Miri?" Deirdre finally whispered.

Helena's mouth curved slowly into a delighted grin. "I knew it. I *knew* it! You're The Shadow, aren't you?" She couldn't have looked prouder as she beamed at Deirdre. "She's The Shadow."

"I don't care *who* she is. I don't care *who* you are,"

Deirdre hissed in no uncertain terms. "You're not leaving the keep tonight, so don't even think about it."

Miriel frowned, admittedly disappointed by their reaction. Weren't they utterly shocked to discover that their little sister was The Shadow? She thrust out her chin. "I'm not asking for your permission."

Helena crossed her arms over her chest. "At least wait till morn, Miri."

"By then it may be too late." Miriel drew on the pair of black leather gloves Lucy had brought her.

"Too late for what?" Deirdre asked, eyeing the weapons laid out on the desk before Miriel. "God's blood, what are you plotting?"

" 'Tis not your concern."

Deirdre reached out to snag her by the front of her garb. "Do not tell me my sister is not my concern."

Miriel, moved by guilt, acquiesced. After all, Deirdre and Helena were only worried about her. "I'm going to get Father's silver back."

'Twas half-true, but Deirdre wasn't fooled for a moment. "I don't recall The Shadow ever needing such an array of weapons simply to cut a man's purse."

A silent standoff ensued between them until Helena broke the tension. "We'll go with you," she decided.

"Nay," Miriel said. "I work alone."

"Not this time you don't," Deirdre said.

"I *always* work alone," Miriel insisted. She grumbled under her breath as she tied the sash about her surcoat. 'Twas bad enough that they seemed indifferent to the startling revelation that their little sister was the elusive scourge of Rivenloch, but now they refused to give her the respect afforded a notorious outlaw. "God's blood, aren't you even the least bit impressed by the fact that I'm The Shadow?" she muttered.

Deirdre and Helena exchanged glances. Then Deirdre said, "We've had our suspicions for a while now."

"The way The Shadow *accidentally* left food for us in the crofter's cottage," Helena said, referring to Miriel's visit during her abduction of Colin.

"The explosion of the trebuchet," Deirdre added, recalling Miriel's destruction of the English war machine.

"After all," Helena said with a sly grin, "Rivenloch blood runs through your veins."

"But I still won't allow you to leave the keep," Deirdre warned.

Miriel arched a brow. "And how do you propose to prevent me?"

Deirdre gave her a grave stare as she fondled the hilt of her sword. She might be a bit round with child, but that didn't prevent her from wearing a blade, and apparently she'd not hesitate to use it if Miriel defied her.

Of course, she'd never get the chance. Miriel wouldn't let her. "Deirdre, I'm The Shadow," she gently reminded her. "The *Shadow*?"

Helena drew her sword. "Mayhap. But there are two of us."

Miriel sighed. The last thing she wanted to do was fight her own sisters. But time was a-wasting. And if she had to prove herself capable before they'd let her go, she supposed she'd better do it now, quickly.

With an arcing kick, she struck Helena's wrist, dislodging the sword. Then, before the weapon even clattered to the floor, she stepped close and pressed two fingers into the hollow at the base of Helena's throat.

While doing no real damage, the move caused discomfort and induced retreat. Helena staggered back, tripping over a stool to land on her hindquarters.

By then, Deirdre had her blade halfway out of its sheath. Miriel wheeled about, seizing Deirdre by her sword arm and the front of her surcoat. Then, hooking Deirdre's heel with her toe, she swept her off her feet and carefully lowered her to the ground.

When Miriel released Deirdre, the stunned silence was thick enough to cut.

"Any more objections?" Miriel asked.

She glanced from one sister to the other. Now they looked properly shocked, their eyes wide, their mouths agape.

Helena was the first to speak. "Bloody hell."

"How did you... what did you..." Deirdre asked in awe, propping herself up on her elbows. "Where did you learn..."

Miriel didn't have time to answer. 'Twould only upset them anyway. How could she explain that everything she knew, she'd learned from her maidservant? They still didn't realize that Sung Li was a man. "Later."

She began caching the weapons she'd chosen earlier— *sais, shan bay sow, woo diep do,* and *shuriken*—in the folds of her surcoat, while Helena came to her feet and lent Deirdre a hand.

"I don't know when I'll be back," Miriel told them. "But you needn't fear for me. You know there's not a man born who can best The Shadow." Then she added with a smug smile, "A man *or* a woman."

Helena and Deirdre, still staring at her in mild awe, gave her fierce hugs of farewell. Then Miriel escaped through the tunnel and into the woods, moving through the trees with silent stealth and blending into the night as invisibly as wind.

"She *is* good," Helena admitted when Miriel was gone.

"Aye."

"How much of a lead shall we give her?"

"Two hours. Mayhap three."

Once Rand recovered from his shock, finally accepting the incredible fact that The Shadow was Sung Li, he realized he had a dilemma of the worst kind on his hands.

He'd vowed to catch the outlaw.

He'd also sworn to protect Miriel.

Never had he imagined those two goals would conflict.

He could see now that Sung Li had betrayed Rivenloch, but more significantly, she'd betrayed Miriel. The maid-servant had ingratiated herself to the trusting lass, befriending her, charming her, bowing and scraping and playing at obsequiousness, using that trust to gain access and knowledge.

Then, like an ill-bred hound, she'd turned on Miriel, biting the hand that provided for her.

Rand paced before the glowering maid, rubbing the back of his neck, wondering what to do with her. 'Twas still difficult to believe an old, withered crone could move with such speed and grace. But he'd seen her with his own eyes. She'd laid Hob-Nob and Wat-Wat out flat in the space of a heartbeat.

Perchance she was bewitched. Perchance she was the spawn of the Devil, as Wat-Wat had said. Or mayhap she was but the daughter of a great warrior who'd passed on his talents. Whatever else she was, she was clearly a threat.

And now, with her identity discovered, she'd be even more of a menace. She could hardly return to her comfortable life at Rivenloch. And if she had no place for shelter, no source of sustenance, she would grow more and more desperate.

Rand had turned in a hundred such outlaws, men who'd once been decent folk but had turned to thievery and mayhem and even murder out of necessity.

Rand couldn't just let her go. She might not have killed anyone yet, but she certainly had the skills. When circumstances grew dire enough, she'd resort to violence. And then no one—strangers, Rivenloch folk, not even Miriel—would be safe from her lethal talents.

He had no choice but to spirit her away to Morbroch. He dared not even return to Rivenloch first, for Miriel would surely weep and wring her hands and beg him to set the old maid free. She wouldn't understand the peril. And she'd never forgive him.

"Do you not realize what you've done?" he muttered in frustration. "The position you've put me in? Curse you, wench!"

Sung Li answered him with an inscrutable smile. "For a hired hunter, you are hopelessly blind."

Rand stiffened. How did the maid know he was a hired hunter?

"Oh, aye," Sung Li said. "I know who you are, Rand la Nuit."

Rand clenched his jaw. Did Sung Li recognize him? If she knew his name, knew he was a mercenary, knew his reputation, had she told Miriel?

"I know why you have come," Sung Li continued. Then her shriveled mouth curved into a smirk. "But you still do not know who I am."

Rand had had enough of her disrespect. He straightened to his full height and sneered down his nose at her. "I know you are my captive, wench."

"I am no wench."

"What?"

"I am no wench." Sung Li continued to stare at him with that smug grin.

Rand frowned in disbelief. Surely the maid was lying. "Nay," he whispered, studying Sung Li's wrinkled face.

"Aye."

The possibility that Sung Li might indeed be a man, that, unbeknownst to Miriel, the maid who'd shared her bedchamber all these years, helping her dress, tucking her in at night, was in sooth a man, ignited Rand's anger faster than flame to dry grass.

He seized the front of Sung Li's clothing and wrenched the maid to her feet. Then, with a violent jerk, he tore open the top of the black garment, exposing the pale flesh beneath.

Nausea and rage rose in his gorge, making his arms shake as he beheld Sung Li's flat, withered chest.

'Twas true then. This conniving knave was a villain of the worst kind. And innocent, trusting Miriel had been his victim. The miserable worm had deceived her. He'd deceived them all.

Rand's hands trembled with the urge to take out his dagger and render Sung Li a woman once and for all. But he resisted the ugly temptation.

Instead, he shoved Sung Li forward along the path, drawing his sword to prod the old man along.

There was no question now. He'd march the lecher straight to Morbroch and let the lords do with him what they willed. In Rand's mind, the gallows wasn't enough punishment for The Shadow's crimes against his beloved Miriel.

The fair was eerie at night. The booths, their bright colors muted now in the starlight, seemed like ghostly memories. A gentle breeze stirred, making odd music of clanking iron pots and rustling silk veils, rattling glass beads and flapping canvas walls.

But the sound served Miriel well, for she could slip along the lanes and in and out of the pavilions unnoticed.

The players were easy to find. They slept behind the platform that served as their stage, nestled like spoons for warmth. But there was no sign of Rand or Sung Li.

As silent as death, she stole up behind them, drew her *shan bay sow*, and pressed one against each of their throats.

"Hist!" she whispered.

They jerked awake.

"Don't move!" she hissed. "And don't make a sound. Give me what I want, and I won't hurt you."

Wat-Wat whispered, "The silver's in my purse."

Hob-Nob hissed back, "Don't tell her where the silver is."

"Am I the only one with a blade at my throat?"

"She said she wouldn't hurt us."

"Shh!" Miriel glanced about the clearing. Hopefully nobody had heard the chattering players. "I'm not interested in your silver. I want information. Where is Rand of Morbroch?"

"Who?"

"Rand of Morbroch," she said, "the man who left Rivenloch with you this morn."

"She means Rand la Nuit."

"You mean Rand la Nuit?"

Miriel frowned. Why did that name sound familiar? "Is that what he said his name was?"

"Aye. Rand la Nuit, the mercenary."

Miriel's memory was suddenly jarred. Rand la Nuit was indeed a mercenary, a well-known hunter of miscreants and outlaws, a man that unscrupulous nobles sometimes hired to do their ugly deeds. But surely Rand, *her* Rand, wasn't such a man.

"Where is he?"

They hesitated, and she prodded them with the points of her blades.

"Gone," they both replied.

"Gone where?"

"He didn't say."

"He just took that thief and—"

"What?" she asked, her heart tripping. "What thief?"

"The Shade he called him."

"Nay, The Shadow."

"Nay, nay, I'm sure 'twas The Shade."

"The Shadow sounds better."

"It doesn't matter if it sounds better."

"If I were a thief, I wouldn't call myself The Shade."

Miriel's heart was beating louder than their bickering, and dark thoughts began to swirl around her head, pulling her down like a deadly whirlpool.

If Rand of Morbroch was in sooth Rand la Nuit, the mercenary...

If he'd captured The Shadow, or the one he *thought* was The Shadow...

Sweet Jesu!

Rand la Nuit. La Nuit. The Night.

The Night has swallowed The Shadow.

Miriel couldn't breathe.

Rand had betrayed her.

Sung Li had sacrificed himself.

And Miriel had been a fool.

The players were still quarreling when she slipped off into the forest.

For a long while she walked woodenly along the path, not sure where she was going, too stunned to do more than put one foot in front of the other.

How could she have been so blind?

How could she have not seen that Rand was a scoundrel?

He'd not come to Rivenloch to join Cameliard's fighting force at all. He'd come to collect the reward for capturing The Shadow.

Her chest felt as if it were being crushed between the grinding wheels of a mill, squeezing her heart so that it pinched with every knifing pulse, making it nigh impossible to breathe. Not even sobs could escape the tight prison of her aching ribs, though her throat constricted with the urge to weep, and her eyes stung with unshed tears.

Curse his deceiving tongue. She'd entrusted her heart to him. She'd promised herself to him in marriage.

God's wounds! She'd bedded the bastard.

Now she was paying for her folly.

But worse, Sung Li was paying for it.

Somehow, Miriel managed to keep moving. Eventually,

whether by instinct or design, she found herself on the road to Morbroch. Rand la Nuit might not be a proper knight, but he'd likely borrowed his title in the service of the Lord of Morbroch. 'Twas there, no doubt, his reward awaited.

As she trod past moonlit pines and the skeletons of leafless oaks, the hurt of betrayal festered within her breast, curdling like cream in verjuice, to form a hard knot of rage.

All her energy, she focused to a single purpose. All her thoughts centered on vengeance. With every breath she took, she exhaled the last shreds of mercy. With every ounce of her will, she wished him dead.

Miriel had never killed a man.

But she knew how. Sung Li had taught her both how to end a man's life in an instant and how to prolong his dying. He'd also taught her 'twas the act of a coward to kill when 'twas unnecessary.

But for the first time in her life, Miriel felt 'twas not only necessary, 'twas desirable. As ignoble as it might be, as much as Sung Li would bristle at her bloodthirsty lust for revenge, when Miriel imagined thrusting her sharp *woo diep do* through Rand's lying heart or slitting his throat with her *bay sow,* a twisted satisfaction served as a temporary balm for her wounded soul.

'Twas that nagging hunger for retribution that kept her awake all night, kept her trudging purposefully toward Morbroch.

Forsooth, she slept and ate very little over the next few days, for fear she might miss her chance to save Sung Li, and mayhap more significant, lose the opportunity to slay Rand la Nuit.

On the third day, at twilight, she dragged herself up the

hillock that formed part of a circle of small hills surrounding Morbroch Castle.

Now, knowing Rand was within her grasp, knowing she'd get the vengeance she sought, she felt the exhaustion of the past days slip away. Her mind found new focus, and as she gazed at the blue sandstone castle sprawled across the rise in the midst of the valley, she began to formulate a plan.

She'd wait till nightfall. After all, night was the domain of shadows.

Chapter 23

Rand PACED THE DRAFTY BEDCHAMBER his host had lent him, making the candle's flame flicker dangerously. But he didn't care if the thing went out. Mayhap then he'd get the sleep he so desperately needed.

There was no good reason for the burden of guilt weighing so heavily on his shoulders. He'd achieved his mission. He'd collected his reward. The lord was well pleased, so well pleased he'd invited him to stay on at Morbroch. Rand had ridded the world of a troublesome outlaw. Most important of all, he'd saved his precious Miriel from the perfidy of her trusted servant, a debauched old man.

Yet his heart was heavy.

He ran a weary hand over the back of his neck. Mayhap when 'twas all over, when they took Sung Li to be hanged, Rand would receive the absolution he sought.

But he doubted it.

He slumped down onto the pallet and sank his head into his hands.

Miriel would never forgive him.

That was what agonized him.

No matter what he'd try to tell her, how patient and honest and compassionate he was, explaining Sung Li's deception, the old man's devious plotting, his villainy, his betrayal of her and her father and her people, Rand knew Miriel would never forgive him for sending her lifelong maidservant to the gallows.

And if she didn't forgive him, she'd never take him back.

Part of him wished he'd never caught The Shadow at all. Part of him wanted to undo everything he'd done, turn back time, and let the robber run off into the woods to return to Rivenloch and his rampant thieving.

But another part of him, the reasonable part, knew that what he'd done, he'd done to protect Miriel.

God help him, he loved the lass. He'd never loved anyone as fiercely as he did Miriel. He'd do anything to keep her safe. And if keeping her safe meant making her hate him, 'twas a sacrifice he must make, a burden he must bear.

He dared not even torment himself by holding on to a shred of hope that Miriel might one day understand. In her eyes, he'd betrayed her trust as much as Sung Li had. Once she found out who he was, a bastard mercenary who had come to Rivenloch on false pretenses, she probably wouldn't even believe that he'd truly fallen in love with her. Forsooth, she had no reason to believe anything he said.

Eventually, he'd learn to live without her love. He'd take

solace instead in the fact that once the felon in the dungeon was executed, Miriel would be safe from Sung Li's villainy forever.

Misery coiled like a vile serpent about his throat, strangling his need to weep, squeezing the life out of his sorrow, leaving bitter poison in its place.

'Twas probably best if Rand didn't see her again. Perchance 'twas cowardice on his part, but he couldn't bear the thought of Miriel gazing upon him with tears of betrayal flooding her innocent eyes, knowing he was the cause of her hurt.

The Lord of Morbroch had made him a generous offer, a position in his retinue. A sennight ago, Rand might have been glad of such an offer. Weary of wandering from village to village, living by the edge of his sword and the seat of his trews, finally glimpsing a beautiful possibility for permanence and stability with a woman whom he loved and who loved him in return, Rand had dreamed that he might make such a life for himself at Rivenloch.

But now that dream seemed a thousand miles away, from another lifetime.

Now all he wanted was to slouch off into the familiar shadows of the woods, lie in the arms of his always welcoming mistress, loneliness, and hide himself from the condemning eyes of the world.

Lost in self-pity, his head buried in his hands, Rand almost ignored the faint prickling at the back of his neck, the prickling that told him he was not alone.

By the time he lifted his head, something slammed into the back of it, shooting bright stars across his vision and catapulting him forward, off the bed and onto his knees.

Dazed, he was unable to do more than curl into a protective ball and crawl out of range.

At least, he'd thought he was out of range. But when a second impact knocked his head sideways, sending him sprawling across the planks, he quickly drew his dagger and scanned the room. Between the dim candlelight and the stunning blows to his head, he was nigh blind. But a good hunter could always rely on his ears.

Unfortunately, his attacker made very little sound.

Rand thought he saw, from the corner of his eye, a dark movement, like a shadow shifting in the flickering flame. Then something flashed like lightning through the air, striking the side of his neck, searing his skin as it passed and smacking into the wall behind him.

There was no time to look at what had hit him, no time to fret over the blood welling from the glancing wound. He scrambled back against the wall, using it to lever himself to his feet.

Tossing his head to clear the blur, he searched the corners of the room, but saw naught. The only sound was his own labored breath.

He tossed the dagger to his left hand and drew his sword with his right, then slowly edged away from the wall. Before he'd taken two steps, his eye caught a movement just above the far edge of the pallet.

A glint of silver warned him a blade sailed directly for his chest. He turned, catching the knife in his right shoulder instead. He grunted as the thin blade bit deep. With his dagger hand, he yanked the knife out, ignoring the pain and blood.

Then, with a snarl of fury, he took one great step onto

the pallet and lunged forward, intending to crash down on top of the invader on the other side.

But his boots slammed down on empty floor. The attacker had vanished.

Rand whipped his head about. Where could he have gone?

His answer came in the next instant. As he stood, casting about, a dark shadow swept out from beneath the pallet, catching him forcefully behind the heels.

Knocked off-balance, his hands full of weapons, Rand fell backward, hitting hard against the wall. Scraping his head down the plaster, he landed on his hindquarters with a bruising thud.

Through the fluttering slits of his eyes, he saw the silhouette beneath the bed, skittering away like a great black spider.

The Shadow.

Nay, it couldn't be. Sung Li was locked up in the dungeon.

Before Rand could guess what other enemy might have found him, the attacker's cowled head edged up over the pallet, and he snapped his wrist forward.

Rand jerked his head aside just in time to see a sharpened silver star lodge in the plaster beside him.

It must be The Shadow. That star was one of the strange weapons he'd seen on Miriel's chamber wall.

But how had he escaped the dungeon?

There was no time to wonder. However he'd done it, Sung Li could just as easily have escaped the castle. But he hadn't. He'd lingered behind to finish off his captor.

There would be no holding back then. This was a fight to the death.

* * *

Though Miriel tried to train her mind to the serenity and purpose required for cold-blooded killing, within her breast, her heart hammered relentlessly.

She'd hoped 'twould be over by now, that Rand la Nuit would be dead. Forsooth, she'd been surprised to find him awake. The rest of the castle slumbered, including the two guards whom she'd interrogated. Before she'd sent them to sleep with a well-placed punch, they'd told her that The Shadow was to be executed in the morn, then pointed her in the direction of Rand's chamber.

She'd come directly to his room. She knew if she went to Sung Li first, he'd talk her out of killing Rand. He wouldn't understand. He didn't know that she'd given Rand everything—her heart, her body, her soul. He wouldn't understand the unbearable hurt that drove her to murder.

But she'd expected 'twould be a simple thing. She'd creep into the room, find the wretched, conniving, deceptive bastard of a mercenary asleep in his bed, and quickly slit his throat. Indeed, 'twas a mercy that she'd planned for him a swift and painless death, for he deserved far worse.

Instead, not only was he fully awake and prepared to defend himself, but her own deadly calm seemed to fail her. That last *shuriken* should have struck him in the throat. Instead, it slipped off her nervous fingers. Likewise, her *bay sow* had strayed off course. Even the sweep of her legs and his subsequent collision with the wall only rattled his brain where it should have knocked him cold.

Her heart wasn't completely invested in killing him.

But an instant later, all that changed, for 'twas clear that Rand had become fully determined to kill her. He stealthily edged around the end of the pallet, armed with his dagger and his sword. He might not see her perfectly, but 'twas obvious by his movements that he knew where she was.

Scowling in determination, she pulled out her *sais,* hunkered with her knees bent, and prepared to engage him at close range.

Before he could get near enough to strike, she lunged forward with the blunt *sais,* missing his sword with one, but catching the blade of his dagger with the other and, with a twist of her forearm, snapping it off.

Now he had only his broadsword.

But he was unbelievably fast with it. Before she could leap away, he swung forward, slicing through her garments and grazing her belly with the sharp point.

The sting made her suck air between her teeth. But she couldn't afford the luxury of pain. She was fighting for her life.

Snagging his wrist between the tines of one of her *sais,* she thrust his sword arm away and ducked past him to slide beneath the pallet again for refuge.

He wasted no time. While she huddled there, he jumped atop the mattress and stabbed his sword down through it.

The first thrust missed her hip by inches. The second landed short of her shoulder. The third carved a sliver of flesh out of her thigh. She gasped in pain, then rolled out from her haven before he could land another.

As he made the fourth downward thrust, she came up beside the mattress and jabbed her *sais* forward to catch his ankles, sweeping him off his feet. He landed first on his hindquarters, then tumbled backward off the pallet onto the floor. Best of all, he was left weaponless. His sword yet lodged in the mattress.

She quickly pulled her second *bay sow* from her arsenal and prepared to fire it at him. But just before the blade left her fingers, something knocked her hand askew, and the weapon landed harmlessly on the ground beside him.

When she glanced down at her stinging knuckles, she found she'd been struck by her own *shuriken*. He must have retrieved it from the wall. She picked it up from the floor with the intent of sending it back into his throat. But he was no longer there.

Her heart tripped.

Where was he?

A quick glance told her he'd not reclaimed his sword. It still protruded from the mattress like a holy cross.

She scoured the chamber quickly, looking for a flutter of movement. Then it came. A scrabbling in the corner. On instinct, she hurled one of her *sais* toward the sound.

As it clattered heavily upon the floor, she saw, by the faint moonlight, a startled mouse race across the planks.

The next thing she saw was the planks rushing up toward her. Her head hit the hard wood as her feet flew up behind her, and she dropped her remaining *sai*.

For one stunned moment, she lay there, blinded by a veil of stars, felled as surely as a tree by a woodsman's axe. Only desperation, and the knowledge that she would die if she remained, moved her to slither away with all haste.

She heard him grunt, heard the scrape of his broadsword as he pulled it free of the pallet's stuffing. But she could see naught. Praying for invisibility, she scrambled back against a wall, making herself as small a target as possible.

Suddenly she was seized by the front of her clothing and hauled upright. Her vision cleared, and she saw him draw back his sword with the intent of plunging it through her belly.

Before he could thrust forward, she kicked him as hard as she could in the ballocks. As he sank, moaning in pain, she poked her fingers hard into the spot above his breastbone, making him reflexively pull his head back and drop her.

She scrambled a hasty retreat. Her eyes watered, blurring her vision. Her head swam. Her thigh was bleeding. She had cuts across her belly and her knuckles. But she dared not succumb. 'Twas a matter of life and death.

Her gloves slick with sweat, her heart thundering, the breath rasping through her lungs, she somehow managed to struggle to her feet. Rand staggered toward the window, reaching for the support of the sill, his sword dragging along the floor.

He was a clear target now. The moonlight illuminated him. With a trembling hand, she unsheathed her *woo diep do*. She didn't dare throw it, for she couldn't afford to lose her last weapon. Instead, she feinted to the left, throwing her empty arm wide, at the same time diving forward with her right.

She thought he wouldn't have time to lift his heavy blade.

She was wrong.

He knocked the dagger from her hand with a hard blow of his pommel, then returned with a wide slash meant to lop off her head.

Only her quick reflexes saved her. When she drew her head back, the blade whistled across her throat, but cut only deep enough to slice away the fabric of her hood.

Still, the attack left her at a disadvantage. The folds of the slashed hood fell over her eyes, blinding her. Panicked, she clawed at the hampering remnants of cloth.

His hand clutched the front of her garb, and he hauled her up close just as she tossed her head free of the stifling hood.

Chapter 24

Rand froze. 'Twas as if he'd been struck in the belly by a catapult missile. He couldn't move. He couldn't breathe.

Nay. 'Twasn't possible.

Sung Li was The Shadow, not...

Miriel.

Nevertheless, he couldn't deny 'twas his beloved who stood before him. There was no mistaking her glittering blue eyes, her flaring nostrils, her trembling lips.

"What...? How...?"

He felt like he might lose his supper at any moment.

She took advantage of his confusion, wrenching from his loose grasp and giving him two sharp jabs just below the ribs, then beating a hasty retreat.

While he stood with gaping jaw, cradling his aching, nauseous stomach, she bumped into the pallet, scampered backward across it, then half fell, half dove to the floor.

How could this be? How could Miriel be The Shadow? Where had she learned to fight like that? And why the bloody hell was she fighting *him?*

As he stood there, staring at the far side of the pallet, where she undoubtedly crouched, waiting for his attack, he began to tremble with the reality of what he'd done.

Jesu, he'd tried to kill her.

He'd sliced her belly, slashed her knuckles, nearly cut off her head. The idea left a bitter taste at the back of his throat.

He glanced down at his sword, its edge marked with her blood, and suddenly the weapon seemed a vile, white-hot serpent. He dropped it, and it clanged heavily on the floor.

His voice quaking, he whispered across the darkness. "Miriel."

There was no reply, only a silence, impossible to decipher. Was she surrendering or stalking him?

"Miriel," he breathed, taking a step toward the bed, "come out. I won't hurt you."

Still she didn't respond.

He took another step. "I'm unarmed. Come to me, Miriel."

She was quiet so long, he feared she might have hurt herself, hurtling over the pallet. Or mayhap his blade had cut deeper than he knew. The possibility sickened him.

"Miriel," he rasped, slowly stepping around the end of the pallet.

No sooner did he note that Miriel had disappeared under the pallet than he felt an incredibly sharp sting at the back of his ankle, like an unruly hound nipping at his heel.

He staggered back to discover one of those devilish stars stuck in the back of his leg. When he reached down to pull it out, her fist whipped out from beneath the pallet, coming down hard atop his hand. The blow drove his hand down onto the sharp point of the star, and he groaned in agony.

Sick with the reality that his lovely Miriel had done this, that she'd intentionally caused him such excruciating pain, he crawled into the corner to extract the miserable weapon from his flesh, dizzied by the spurt of blood that issued forth from his hand.

Able to see the entire room from his vantage point, he took a moment to tear a piece from his undershirt and bind the bleeding wound. As he wrapped the cloth around his burning palm, he glimpsed Miriel's arm reaching out from under the bed like a stealthy wraith toward his broadsword.

He should have dove forward, claimed the weapon, held it to her throat, and forced her to surrender. Then he might have made her listen. Then he might have found out why she was trying to slay him.

But he had neither the heart nor the will. He hurt, inside and out, from the wounds of her hatred.

Instead, he let her claim his blade while he tied off his makeshift bandage with his teeth, then watched her as she jumped nimbly to her feet, holding the weapon in two hands before her.

"Miriel?"

But she wouldn't speak to him. And neither, did he suspect, would she listen. There was too much anger, too much fear, too much desperation in her eyes. She was beyond reason.

When he stood to face her, she took a swing at him, close enough to make him flinch. On her return swing, he ducked under the blade and charged her, bowling her over onto the floor. The thought of inflicting harm upon her was distasteful, but he had to do what he needed to survive.

The weapons Miriel wielded were deadly, and 'twas clear she had every intention of using them.

Even flat on her back, she had remarkable defenses. She drove her knee up hard, catching the point of his chin. When he reeled back, she plowed her fist into his belly, stealing the breath from him.

When she started across with his blade again, intent on beheading him, he had no choice but to strike her forearm with full force, causing her to drop the sword. Even so, he winced as her bones gave beneath his blow.

"Yield," he gasped, hoping she would surrender then.

But she seemed bent on killing him, with or without his sword.

She skittered away beneath the pallet, and he picked up his fallen blade, struggling to his feet. Someone had to put an end to this. He didn't want to hurt Miriel, but neither did he want to die.

Miriel quivered beneath the pallet, cradling her bruised forearm. This was not going well at all.

What had started as a simple assassination was now mortal combat. Now she had to kill or be killed. And unless she could recover them somehow, she'd exhausted her supply of weapons.

"Come out, Miriel," Rand's voice rasped.

She steeled her jaw. Of course he wanted her to come

out. She made a much better target when she wasn't huddled beneath the pallet.

She watched the silhouette of his boots as he strode past once, twice, like a restless cat standing guard at a mouse's hole. Then he retreated, and she heard the squeak of a stool.

"I'm sitting down," he told her. "My sword is on the floor before me. I just want to talk, Miriel."

She didn't trust him for a moment. Talk? Everything he'd ever told her was a lie, from *my name is Sir Rand of Morbroch* to *I love you.*

She no longer believed anything he said, including *I won't hurt you.*

He intended to kill The Shadow. For the reward.

She scowled, shutting out painful memories, concentrating on the dilemma at hand.

She had no weapons.

He knew exactly where she was.

His sword might be lying on the floor, but if she came out of hiding, he could snap it up in one instant and run her through in the next.

What could she do?

Sung Li had taught her that the most lethal weapon was the mind. Even a more powerful, more seasoned, more expert opponent could be outwitted. Miriel wondered if she could outwit Rand la Nuit.

What would take away his killer instincts? What would bring him to his knees? What would make him forget all about murdering The Shadow? What would leave him most vulnerable?

She narrowed her eyes. Of course.

She began with a light sniffling, just enough to make

him lean forward on the stool. Then she progressed to soft sobs, muffled in her hands.

"Miriel?"

She smiled grimly. He was like a coney, sniffing at a snare. There was something about a woman's weeping that could reduce the most heartless man to a quivering lump.

She wept harder, more pathetically, and she heard him rise from the stool.

"Miriel, are you all right?"

With one last, long, piteous wail, she drew back her legs and watched as he crouched down to look under the bed.

"Miriel, don't cry. I'm not going to—"

She cut off his words with a hard kick to his face. Then, before she could see the results of her violence, she rolled out from under the pallet and onto her feet.

Searching for a weapon, any weapon, she found a crockery pitcher and cracked it down hard along the edge of the table, making sharp shards of the rim. Armed again, she turned to Rand.

He lay silent on the ground. His face was bloody. His body was splayed across the planks, unmoving.

The only sound in the chamber was the rasp of her breathing, though it seemed her heart pounded like a drum as she stood ready with the broken crockery.

Gradually, she lowered the pitcher. Had she kicked him so hard? Was he unconscious? Was he dead?

The possibility, as desirable as it had been a moment ago, horrified her now, sinking into the pit of her stomach like a ball of lead.

Dear God, what had she done? Had she truly killed a man? Had she killed... her betrothed?

She took one cautious step nearer. Fresh blood glistened upon his lip. His jaw sagged sideways. And naught indicated he was alive. No flutter of eyelashes. No rise and fall of his chest. No pulse visible in his throat. No whisper of breath from between his lips.

She swallowed hard and stepped closer.

Jesu, had she slain him?

It seemed impossible. Yet that had been her intent. 'Twas why she'd come into his chamber, to seek out the man who had lied to her, betrayed her, then turned in her beloved *xiansheng* to be executed, all for money. She'd meant to kill him.

And now it appeared she had.

She should feel victorious. Instead, she trembled as the weight of his lost soul settled upon her shoulders and uninvited tears welled in her eyes.

God help her, she'd adored him. As foolish as 'twas, she *had*. And now she'd killed the only man she'd ever loved.

Swallowing down the thick lump in her throat, she forced herself to forget what she had done, steeled herself for what was to come.

Sung Li would be disappointed in her. It didn't matter that she'd done it for her *xiansheng,* that she meant to save Sung Li's life. He would never forgive Miriel for taking vengeance in his name.

Revenge is a fool's weapon, he always said, *a weapon born not of reason, but of passion.*

She couldn't tell him what she'd done in the name of passion. Not at first. Somehow, she'd find a way to rescue him from the dungeon and make sure they were well away from Morbroch before she confessed that she'd killed his captor.

Taking a steadying breath and wiping a stray tear from her cheek, Miriel inched closer, bending down to make sure he was dead.

Rand waited in agony, resisting the urge to breathe, resisting the need to assess his damaged face, resisting the instinct to curl into a protective ball as his attacker neared.

He'd been a fool. She'd drawn him into her trap, feigning tears, only to betray him. But two could play that game.

He supposed he deserved a bloodied nose for falling prey to such an obvious ruse, but love had blinded him. He'd made the mistake of believing Miriel would react like a woman when in sooth she reasoned like a warrior. He wouldn't let it happen again.

The moment he sensed Miriel draw near, felt her breath upon his cheek, he sprang into action. Encircling her ankles with his arms, he jerked her feet out from under her, sending her tumbling against the foot of the pallet. Then he struggled to a crouch, spitting the blood from his cut lip, edging one hand behind him to locate his sword.

But just as his fingers discovered the blade, she crashed something against the side of his head, and he lurched sideways from the impact.

Blinking back the black clouds that wanted to overwhelm his vision, he caught her by the throat in one desperate fist and found his sword with the other.

She punched and kicked at him while he lifted her with one arm, half-strangling her in his grasp. But with all the other injuries she'd dealt him, he scarcely felt her pummeling.

He tossed her onto the bed, and she immediately scrabbled backward until she came up against the plaster wall. With a snarl of rage and frustration, he swept his weapon up to her throat, pinning her at sword point.

For a long while they only stared at each other, their eyes flashing fire, their breath wheezing in the quiet night, neither one backing down, neither one blinking.

There was no fear in her gaze, only hatred and bloodlust.

He knew now why she wanted him dead. She'd discovered who he was. She'd learned of his lies, his false pretenses, his deception. She'd trusted him, and he'd betrayed her. And there was no storm more violent than a woman betrayed.

'Twas his fault. He couldn't blame her. He was a fool to have believed that when she learned the truth about him, learned that he was not Sir Rand of Morbroch, but Rand la Nuit, a bastard mercenary, learned that he'd come, not for Miriel, but to hunt The Shadow, somehow love would conquer all.

But Rand could see by the blaze in her eyes that not only did she no longer love him. She despised him. Enough to want him dead. And if he didn't kill her now, she would surely slay him at the first opportunity. Bloody hell, she already thought she *had* killed him.

He'd been in such predicaments before. Men he'd had no quarrel with he was sometimes forced to kill, else they would hunt him down and deliver him into the Reaper's hands.

But he'd never killed a woman. He'd never killed anyone undeserving. God's eyes, he'd never killed anyone he loved.

He didn't think he could.

It didn't matter that his body was covered with slashes from her weapons.

It didn't matter that his back throbbed and his hand stung and his nose felt like it was naught but a mass of splinters.

It didn't matter that she'd turned on him like a rogue hound, snarling and snapping at the hand that had once offered her loving caresses.

It didn't even matter that the instant he dropped his sword, she'd sweep it up to slay him.

Gazing into her smoldering eyes, he remembered they had once looked upon him with love. In her company, he'd known delight. In her arms, he'd known affection. In her bed, he'd known acceptance.

He couldn't destroy those memories, even if memories were all they were, with a slash of his blade.

Though he held his own assassin cornered, at his mercy, a whisper away from death, his fingers trembled upon the hilt of his sword.

"Nay," he whispered. "I cannot." He lowered his sword, then carefully placed it between them on the pallet.

As he'd predicted, she instantly took advantage of his weakness. She seized the blade in both hands and turned it on him.

He lowered his eyes then, wanting to remember the once sweet adoration of her gaze, unable to face the bloodthirsty gloating that doubtless resided there now.

He made no resistance as she prodded his throat with the point of the sword. It hurt no worse than her hatred.

But as the moment dragged on, as the silence lengthened,

and she did naught, keeping him in agonizing suspense, his melancholy curdled slowly into anger.

Had the wench no kindness left in her heart to grant him a swift and merciful death?

"Be done with it!" he muttered.

The sword point jerked against his throat. "Do not order me about!"

"If you would slay me, slay me!"

"I'll not be...rushed."

He wasn't about to submit to slow torture for her pleasure. He'd send his soul to hell by impaling himself first. "What do you want?" he growled.

She hesitated.

He sniffed once through his battered nose, and the pain made his eyes water. "Bloody hell, wench! What do you want?"

"I...I want to know what you did to Sung Li." She raised the blade beneath his chin. "And for once, see if you can tell no lies."

"Lies?" He gave a humorless chuckle. "You are a strange one to speak of lies," he said, raising his eyes to pin her with his gaze, "Lady Shadow."

A flicker of guilt flashed through her eyes like lightning, there one instant, gone the next, and the sword point jumped in her startled hand, nicking him.

She lifted her chin with false bravado, but her eyes she lowered. Her voice trembled, and he almost felt sorry for her. Almost. "What did you do to him?"

Rand blinked. Him? Did Miriel *know* that her maidservant was a man? Was this yet another of her deceptions? "Who?"

"Sung Li!" she said impatiently.

"Sung Li?" He scowled. "Sung Li?" So outraged was he that Miriel had known all along, that he'd worried for her for naught, that in his vehemence, he almost stabbed himself on the blade. "You mean your *maid*servant?"

He could tell she was blushing, even if he couldn't see the pink hue of her cheeks.

"You wouldn't understand," she said lamely.

"Aye," he retorted, his anger fully engaged now. "I *wouldn't* understand how an innocent maiden would willingly sleep with an old man disguised as a wench!"

"I never slept with him!"

He didn't bother to guard his words, snarling nastily, "No doubt you were too busy swiving to sleep."

He wouldn't have been surprised if she'd run him through then, but instead she withdrew the blade and slapped him across the cheek with her open hand.

He moaned as the blow jarred his injured face, wondering if impalement might be less painful.

Her voice was a harsh whisper. "You know better, you son of a—"

"Aye." Already he regretted his rash words. After all, she'd come to him a virgin. "I do." He dabbed at his bloody lip with the back of his hand. "Unless you lied about that as well."

She gasped and raised her hand to strike him again. This time he caught her wrist.

"Listen, my lady," he ground out, "I've had enough of your pummeling and enough of your lies."

"My lies? What about *your* lies?" she hissed. "What about, 'I am Sir Rand of Morbroch'? What about, 'I've come to court Miriel'? What about, 'I was knocked

witless in the melee'? What about, 'Miriel, I love—'"
She choked on her words.

He narrowed his eyes. "That wasn't a lie, Miriel.
I swear it." She tried to pull her hand out of his grasp,
but he wouldn't let her go. "I swear it. I loved you." He
swallowed hard, glimpsing the hurt in her eyes, manifesting now as real tears. "God help me, I still do."

Chapter 25

MIRIEL'S THROAT SWELLED. She tried everything to stop the tears.

She forced her brow into a fierce scowl.

She steeled her jaw.

She tightened her fist around the hilt of the sword.

Using the skills of concentration that Sung Li had taught her, she repeated over and over in her mind that Rand's words were only manipulation. Manipulation. Manipulation.

But her chin began to tremble, her hand grew limp around the weapon, and against her will, hot tears started to spill over her lashes.

"Why should I believe you?" she whispered.

"Look at me," he murmured back. "Look into my eyes."

Against her better judgment, she did. It sickened her to see the mess she'd made of his face, evidence of the violence of which she was capable, but she forced herself to meet his gaze.

"'Tis true I deceived you about many things," he said. "My name. My title. The tournament. My purpose for coming to Rivenloch. My skill with a blade." His gaze turned fierce with emotion. "But I never deceived you about this. I love you, Miriel, with all my heart. What I did, I did to protect you. I thought Sung Li was a true threat." His jaw tensed. "I knew if I saved your life, you'd never take me back. But I couldn't bear to leave you in danger."

She averted her eyes. Was he playing her for a fool again? How could she trust the adoration in his gaze when she, too, was able to feign emotions she didn't feel?

As if he was privy to her thoughts, his fingers loosened around her wrist in chilling realization as he breathed in wonder, "My God. Did you never love *me*?"

She paused. Admitting her love would leave her vulnerable to betrayal again.

He took her long hesitation as assent. "I see." With a bark of self-mockery, he let go of her hand. "Then you are a better liar than I am, my lady."

She frowned. She couldn't let him believe that. Aye, she had a talent for deception, but not about this. She *had* loved him. She *had*.

At her lack of response, he murmured bleakly, "Sung Li is in the dungeon. I didn't hurt him." With a rueful smile, he added, "He might be a master of Chinese warfare, but he's still a wee old man."

Miriel felt a tear spill down her cheek, and before she could stop herself, she blurted out, "I did love you." Then, mortified by her rash confession, she added, "Before."

He stared at her, wavering between belief and disbelief, as mistrustful as she was. "Did you?"

Sweet Jesu, how had it come to this? How had she become a slave to her emotions? 'Twas not at all what Sung Li had taught her. He'd taught her to be strong, indifferent, unflinching, focused, a perfect warrior.

At the moment, she was none of these. Her energies were scattered like chaff in a whirlwind, her thoughts ran rampant, and her *chi*...

She felt so unaligned, so out of balance, that she feared she'd never center herself again.

She brusquely wiped away the tear and adjusted her grip on the sword, determined to pull herself together.

What would Sung Li do? How she longed for his wisdom at this moment.

"Prithee do not torment me with waiting, my lady." Rand let out a ragged sigh. "Kiss me or kill me. But make me wait no more."

Miriel knew then she had no will to murder Rand. Varlet he might be. And knave. And cad. Deceiver. And cheat. And liar.

But he was the man she loved.

And in all fairness, who was she to judge him?

Had she not told just as many lies, deceived him just as surely, misled and manipulated and coerced him? She had no right to fault him for his sins, for she was just as guilty.

She lifted her chin, took a deep, steadying breath, and studied his face.

Did Rand la Nuit love her? Truly?

For Miriel, there was but one way to find out.

She cast aside the sword, letting it rattle upon the floor. Then, careful not to injure him further, she moved close, cradling his damaged face between her hands, and lifted her head to bestow upon him a kiss.

His mouth was swollen, his lip was split, and the scent of his blood was heavy in her nostrils. But there was no mistaking his tenderness as he responded to her tentative caress.

She carefully tilted his head, weaving her fingers into his mane, and pressed light kisses along his lips in soft apology for each cut, each bruise.

His arms came slowly up between hers to cup her face. With his thumb, he gently coaxed her jaw wider, opening her mouth so she could receive the full measure of his affection. His tongue ventured within to taste her more intimately, and he seemed to pour the nectar of his soul into her mouth, imbuing the kiss with every ounce of love he felt for her.

Her unguarded heart was no match for such a tender assault. Relief rushed over her, draining the dregs of resistance from her bones. The ambrosia of his soul was pure and delicious, and she sobbed at the sweetness of it, drinking deep and willingly of his passion.

Miriel knew the truth now. Their tongues might lie, but their hearts spoke true. 'Twas not only desire that burned brightly between them. 'Twas love, as pure as white-hot flame.

God help her if she was wrong, for she was well and truly lost in it now.

Rand could no longer think.

'Twas just as well. Even if he'd been able to string together two thoughts, they'd likely have been a contradiction.

Miriel hated him.

Nay, she loved him.

As long as she was pressing her soft lips to his, combing her fingers through his hair, murmuring sweet promises against his mouth, he didn't care which.

Later they could untangle the complex web of lies. Later they could make confession of their sins. And later they could decide whether Miriel loved or hated him.

For now, 'twas good enough that he held her in his arms when he'd despaired of ever seeing her again.

At least, he'd *thought* 'twas good enough. Until the wanton lass gasped out a lusty request.

"Make love to me."

That was when he knew he was definitely a man. For despite his battered body, despite his smashed face, his pierced palm, his wounded shoulder, his cracked head, even his bruised ballocks, all suffered at her hands, there was naught he desired more.

He nodded his assent, and both of them began tearing off their clothes as if the garments were afire.

If 'twas a fool's path he followed, so be it. He'd never known such contentment as that he found in Miriel's embrace. So if Fate planned that he should die in her arms, at least he'd die a happy man.

Having believed that he'd never touch her silken skin again, never taste her luscious mouth, never suckle at her sweet breasts, he now glutted himself on her body. He spread her out on the bed, and there wasn't an inch of her he neglected as he swept his hands carefully over her scraped flesh, damp and warm from battle, and bathed the salty sweat from her with his tongue.

He breathed softly into her ear, relishing her shivers of desire. He taunted her nipples with his lips, drawing them to stiff points. But just as he was about to move lower to taste the dark, moist secrets of her womanhood, she suddenly stiffened.

"Sung Li!"

Rand whipped his head around. Bloody hell, was the old man here? Had he escaped the dungeon? 'Twould be just like Miriel's vigilant guardian to appear now.

But the chamber was empty.

Miriel, her eyes flashing with urgency, sat up on one elbow and raked back her disheveled hair. "I have to save him."

Rand frowned, trying to shake the cobwebs of desire from his brain. "'Tis the middle of the night."

Miriel's mind was no longer on coupling. She slipped from the bed, then cast about, gathering her clothes. "He's going to the gallows in the morn."

His ballocks still aching with need, Rand nodded reluctantly. She was right. They could hardly tryst while Sung Li yet languished below the keep. "But he's locked in the dungeon. How are you going to—"

"I don't know!" she cried in frustration as she began to dress. "But I have to try."

Rand winced from his wounds as he sat up and reached for his own cast-off clothing.

She slipped one of her lovely legs into her black braies. "You needn't come."

He arched a brow in challenge, shoving his arms into the sleeves of his tunic. "'Tis my fault he's there."

She hopped on her first foot, wiggling the second into the leg of her braies. "I do my best work alone."

He glanced pointedly at the bed, saying under his breath, "I'd have to disagree."

She pulled up the braies and tied them about her waist.

"I'm serious. I have much more experience slinking about the shadows."

He hauled the tunic over his head. "I won't let you go alone."

She scowled, snatching up her own tunic. "*Let* me?" She thrust her arms through the sleeves. "How do you propose to stop me?"

He shrugged, shaking out his braies. "Guilt."

She started to poke her head through the tunic, then lowered the garment again, staring at him askance.

As he sat on the bed, shoving his legs into his braies, he explained. "You would not be so cruel as to deprive a man of righting the wrong he has done, would you?"

Cursing under her breath, she burrowed her head through the tunic, then jabbed a finger toward him. "You had better not get in my way."

"Believe me," he said, gingerly pressing at his bloodied nose, "I won't."

Moments later, against Rand's better judgment, they were creeping through the dark halls of the keep. Miriel had reclaimed her weapons, though how she'd managed to cache them all in the folds of her garments he couldn't begin to guess. He kept his broadsword drawn as they stole past slumbering servants and hounds softly yipping in their sleep.

When they found the steps leading under the keep to the dungeon, Rand took the lead, whispering, "Stay close behind me."

But the impertinent lass ignored his command, slipping past him like a shadow, hurrying down the torchlit stairs before he could snatch her back, and he had no choice but to follow.

He'd wanted to warn her there was likely a guard manning

the door. If she wasn't careful, she'd barrel into him and trap herself. Then Rand would have to come to her rescue.

But by the time he rounded the last curve of the stairs, she'd already met up with the guard. To his astonishment, the poor wretch lay crumpled at her feet, unconscious. Rand's jaw dropped. "How did you...?"

Mistaking his awe for horror, she tried to explain. "He's not dead. 'Twas only a pressure point."

He shook his head and whistled low. "By the Saints, you must teach me that."

Miriel gave him a ghost of a smile, then dropped to the lowest part of the door, pressing her cheek against the oak. "Sung Li," she hissed. "Are you there?" She rapped softly. "Sung Li!"

"Miriel?" came Sung Li's voice beneath the door.

"Are you all right, *xiansheng*?"

"What are you doing here? You must go," Sung Li said. "It is not safe for you."

"I'm not leaving you."

"You must. Listen to me, Miriel. Your bridegroom is not who you think he is. He is not a knight. He is a... mercenary." He muttered the word like an oath, as if a mercenary was someone who drowned kittens for a living. "A man whose whose loyalties shift with the wind," he continued, "who hires out to the highest bidder, who preys upon the misfortunes of—"

"I do not prey on anyone's misfortunes," Rand said with a scowl, having heard enough. "I lend my sword to those who cannot fight for themselves. I hunt down outlaws. I right wrongs."

"You brought him with you?" Sung Li hissed, incredulous.

" 'Tis all right, Sung Li," Miriel assured him. "He's here to help."

Rand, still irked, muttered under his breath, "Unless you *wish* to hang on the morrow."

"Miriel, you foolish child!" Sung Li scolded. "You cannot trust him!"

Miriel's eyes narrowed dangerously. "I am *not* a child."

"You are acting like one."

"And *you* are acting like—"

"Cease, the two of you," Rand bit out, "unless you would summon all of Morbroch down on our heads." They complied, and he blew out an impatient breath. "Now, we need to find the key."

"You cannot," Sung Li said smugly.

"Why?" Miriel asked.

"The Lord of Morbroch wears it about his neck."

Miriel chewed at her lip. "Then I'll steal into his chamber and—"

"You'll do naught of the sort," Rand told her.

She lifted her chin. "I will do as I please."

"Not while I'm here to protect you."

"Listen to him, Miriel," Sung Li said.

Rand's brows lifted. Was Sung Li actually allying with him now?

"He is right," Sung Li said. "You must not endanger yourself."

"Endanger *my*self? Was it not you who pretended to be The Shadow so you would be caught in my place?"

"Shh," Rand interjected.

"Would you make my sacrifice in vain then?" Sung Li asked her.

"There will be no sacrifice," Miriel insisted.

"Hist!" If the two of them didn't stop their quarreling...

"I knew what it would cost," Sung Li said, "but I am an old man. Better I should die—"

"Shh, damn you!"

But 'twas too late. Footsteps approached. In another moment, they would be discovered.

Chapter 26

H IDE!" Rand urged, pushing Miriel toward the shadows.
Then he slumped against the wall, propping up the unconscious guard beside him, and putting a companionable arm
around the poor wretch.

By the time the Morbroch man came down the stairs
to see what all the noise was about, Rand was engaged in
drunken singing.

"Hey, what's all this?" the man demanded.

"Jus' havin' a bit o' fun," Rand slurred. He hiccoughed,
then giggled.

"You're drunk."

"Shhhhhh," he whispered loudly, mashing a finger
against his lips. "My friend here is sleepin'."

The man frowned. "Drinking when he's supposed to be
on guard?"

"S'all right," Rand said, tapping his temple. "I got my
eye on the pris'ner. B'sides, he's locked up tight." He
banged on the door for emphasis.

The man hesitated, unsure whether 'twas safe to leave.

"Hey, y'haven't got a wee drink with you, have you?" Rand asked. "I've run dry."

The man shook his head in disgust. "You've had enough." He turned to go, then muttered over his shoulder, "Keep it down. Some of us are trying to sleep."

"Shhhhhh," Rand whispered. "I'll be quiet as a mouse."

Once the guard was gone, Miriel crept out from the shadows. "That was quite convincing."

He cocked a brow at her. "As convincing as your, 'Oh, Rand, you know I can't abide fighting'?"

Her eyes twinkled.

"Now," he said, "we've got to find a way to get Sung Li out. I say we use force. Break down the door or collapse part of the wall."

Miriel shook her head. "Nay, the noise will draw too much attention. Stealth is better. I still say we should slip the key from about Morbroch's neck."

"'Tis too perilous."

"And breaking into the dungeon is not?"

"There is another way," Sung Li said, "a way of stealth *and* force, *yin* and *yang*."

Rand had no idea what the old man was talking about, but Miriel furrowed her brows, deep in thought.

Finally, she straightened, a look of wonder on her face. "Of course. *Huo yao,*" she whispered. She rapped lightly on the dungeon door. "Sung Li, on the morrow, you will let them take you to the hanging tree."

"Nay!" Rand barked. Was she mad?

But by the time Miriel explained her strategy, her eyes were alight with the thrill of hope. Though Rand didn't fully understand the methods of her desperate plan, he couldn't prevent the grin of anticipation that came to his face every time *huo yao* was mentioned.

That was the word Sung Li had used to describe the strong sparks of fire between Miriel and him. He hadn't been able to define it clearly for Rand then, nor could he now. But Miriel assured him 'twas a powerful force.

There was much work to be done and little time to do it.

Miriel prowled the keep's chapel, seeking out Morbroch's precious illuminated Bible. She used her thin dagger to pick the lock chaining the book to the pulpit, no doubt murmuring prayers of contrition as she did so.

Meanwhile, Rand raided the kitchen for the elements Miriel required—a large iron pot, a spoon, twine, an armful of kindling twigs, charcoal, sulfur, and saltpeter—filching a wineskin as well to plant on the still-unconscious guard. Between that evidence and the witness of the second guard, no one would believe his claim that he'd been felled, not by drinking, but by a mysterious woman in black.

When they met up again in Rand's bedchamber, Miriel cleared off the table, lining up the powders, the pot, the twigs, and the ball of twine. Then, flinching as she did so, she cut several pages from the Bible, one by one, littering the pallet with the colorfully decorated vellum. When she was finished, the room resembled an alchemist's workshop.

With meticulous care, she measured out the powders, mixing them together in the iron pot. Then she cut a dozen pieces of twine, dredging them in the mixture and setting them aside.

'Twas Rand's task to lay a twig and a piece of coated twine along one edge of a Bible page so that it protruded at one end. Miriel would sprinkle a generous spoonful of the black powder in the midst of the page. Rand would then roll the page tightly around the stick, folding the tube closed halfway through. The last edge of vellum would then be sealed with a drop of candle wax.

The process was a painstaking one, but before long, it became routine, and soon they were working together as flawlessly as guildsman and apprentice. In an hour, they'd assembled nigh a hundred of the devices.

"You know," Rand said, laying out a piece of twine with fingers that were now stained black, "Sung Li told me once that you and I are like *huo yao*."

"Indeed?"

"He said what passed between us was more than sparks, more than flame, but he couldn't describe it."

She smiled. "I think he's right. You'll see." She sprinkled powder over a page of Genesis.

He rolled up the vellum. "So Sung Li is the one who trained you?"

"From the time I was three and ten."

"And no one suspected? Not even your sisters?"

"Sung Li always said the greatest weapon is the one no one knows you possess." She held the candle aloft and let a drop of wax drip onto the page betwixt his anchoring thumbs.

"True." He blew on the wax, hardening it. "But what of the weapons they knew about? The weapons on your wall?"

"They believed I only collected them. They never suspected I knew how to use them."

He set the finished piece aside. "And no one found out your maidservant was a man?"

"Nay."

He frowned, irritated at the petty jealousy that began to needle him. "The two of you shared a chamber. Did he... dress you? Tuck you into bed?"

She glared at him in response, then decided, "Enough about me. What about you? Why did you become a... you know... a mercenary?" She said the word under her breath, echoing Sung Li's prejudice.

He scowled as he reached for another page, this one featuring the Serpent in the Garden. "'Tis an honorable profession. I never slew a man who didn't deserve it. I never took coin from men seeking selfish vengeance. And I'm bloody good with a blade."

"Hmm." She drizzled powder over the verse. "You did not seem so skilled when you first came to Rivenloch."

"Ah," he said, breaking one twig, then casting it aside for another. "That's because the greatest weapon *is* the one no one knows you possess."

She chuckled. "Did you learn to fight from your father?"

His father. He winced in spite of the age of that particular wound. He sighed, rolling up the vellum. He might as well make a full confession now. God alone knew if he'd even survive the day. After the way they were desecrating the Holy Bible, 'twould not surprise him if lightning struck him down before dawn.

"I'm a bastard." He held out the rolled page for a drop of wax. "My father was a drunken Norman lord, my mother his Scots mistress." He paused to blow on the seal. "When I was fourteen, he found out my mother had another lover. He murdered her and tried to slay me." He touched the scar on his neck.

She set the candle down. "But you escaped?"

"I killed him." He smiled grimly. "And thus began my illustrious life as a mercenary."

There was a long quiet in the chamber, and Rand wondered if Miriel was too appalled to speak. Finally she tucked her hand into his and murmured, "I'm sorry." And as odd as it seemed, those two simple words did much to assuage the pain of that memory.

"What about you?" he asked. "Why did you choose a life of crime?"

"Oh, 'tisn't crime," she said, picking up the spoon to stir idly at the powder. "Not really."

He arched a brow. "Stealing silver from strangers' purses? I'm fairly certain 'tis a crime."

"But 'tisn't their silver in the first place."

"Nay?"

"'Tis coin won off my father at the gaming table. So you see, I'm not really committing thievery. I'm..." She hesitated.

"Aye?"

"Balancing the accounts."

"Balancing the accounts," he echoed.

"Mm. 'Tis what Sung Li calls *yin* and *yang*. You wouldn't understand."

He spread out another page. 'Twas the most inventive excuse for robbery he'd ever heard, and he'd heard a lot of them. "I don't believe Lord Morbroch understands either."

A tiny frown creased her brow. "He's the one who hired you."

"Aye, along with half a dozen other...affronted victims."

She didn't look up from her stirring when she asked him, "And how much did you collect for turning in The Shadow?"

The air grew taut between them as she awaited his reply. He realized then the full measure of what he'd done, the pain she must have felt at his betrayal. He'd come to Rivenloch, not to court her, but to capture her. For profit.

And now she wanted to know the price of that betrayal.

Of course, now that he was going to help The Shadow escape, he didn't deserve the reward.

"A shilling?" she guessed. "Two?"

Forsooth, all told, they'd paid him fifty, but that didn't matter now. He intended to leave it behind. He answered softly, "Not nearly as much as she's worth."

The sky had lightened from ebony to indigo by the time they exhausted their supply of black powder.

Miriel glanced at the arsenal of devices, lined up like ranks of soldiers upon the pallet. She couldn't help but grin, thinking of the havoc they were about to wreak.

Rand, seeing her smile, smiled back. "What?"

She glanced at him. His face was covered with smudges where he'd inadvertently rubbed black powder. Using the corner of her sleeve, she wiped carefully at the marks. "You're going to enjoy this."

He shrugged. "I've been in battle before. I've seen all manner of war machines—catapults, trebuchets—"

"'Tis much better than a trebuchet."

"Flaming arrows?"

"Child's play."

"Greek fire."

"Naught is quite like *huo yao*."

There was still much to do. Miriel was intent on returning as much of the Bible intact as possible. And there had to be no evidence of their mischief. The elements had to be returned to the kitchen, the pot to its hook, the spoon to its place, the ball of twine from whence it had come. No one must ever discover what they'd wrought.

And one other assurance remained.

"You must make me a promise," she said to Rand.

"Anything."

"The secret of *huo yao* is a sacred one. 'Tis not to be used except in the most dire of circumstances, or its mystery will be lost." She gazed into his eyes, intent on making her message clear. "You must tell no one. You must keep this knowledge as a secret of your heart. Do you understand?"

He frowned. No doubt a hundred tempting uses for *huo yao* rushed through his mind, but she couldn't let him waste the sacred knowledge in that way. 'Twas a destructive and dangerous tool in the hands of fools.

"You must promise me," she said again.

He nodded, and she was glad she'd secured his vow here, before he witnessed how spectacular and thrilling and breathtaking *huo yao* really was.

By the time the morning clouds had begun to blush at the imminent arrival of the sun, their tasks within the keep were complete. Because the guards were on watch for intruders, not those *leaving* the castle, Rand simply told them he'd decided to depart before the execution and directed them to give Lord Morbroch his regrets. They assumed that Miriel, bundled in a cloak, was his consort.

That had been an hour ago. Now, from Miriel's vantage

point, she could see Rand with his torch, half-hidden beneath the trees at the rim of the hill overlooking Morbroch. Standing vigil along the edge like the front line of an army were the nigh two hundred devices they'd assembled, though from where she perched, Miriel couldn't see the sticks among the tall weeds. Which was perfect. If she couldn't see them, then neither could the people of Morbroch.

Her eyes stung from lack of sleep, but though she already half reclined along the high branches of the hanging tree, she was far from dozing off. Her nerves were stretched taut with anticipation. 'Twas a brazen thing they attempted, the three of them, pitting their wits against all the castle folk. If this didn't work...

She steeled her jaw, adjusting the obscuring cloth over her face again. It *had* to work.

She focused on a single leaf of the tree, centering her mind for the task ahead. But she never realized how difficult 'twould be to maintain her calm when the portcullis grated slowly open and the blackened felons' cart rolled out through the gates.

It seemed an eternity passed as the creaking cart made its way up the hill, followed by frowning men, jeering children, and women who looked like they'd rather be snug in their beds. Miriel, peering through what remained of the tree's leaves, glimpsed Sung Li, his hands bound, riding in the bed of the cart. Though he held his head proudly, when Miriel saw how small and helpless he appeared, her heart lurched.

At last the execution party arrived beneath the hanging tree. Nobody noticed the dark figure lurking silently in the branches. They were preoccupied with gawking and spitting curses at the prisoner. Even the executioner himself, who tossed the hanging rope over the thickest branch, never saw Miriel there. Of course, invisibility was her talent. 'Twas how she'd earned the name, The Shadow.

What accusations were made by Lord Morbroch, what vicious epithets the crowd sneered, what last prayer the executioner murmured, Miriel didn't know. As they spoke, Miriel stole with infinite patience and stealth from branch to branch until she perched directly above the rope. Then she drew her *woo diep do* and waited.

She swallowed hard when the executioner placed the rope around Sung Li's neck, as if she herself was about to be strangled. Then she took a deep and silent breath. Her timing had to be perfect. So did Rand's.

Rand watched the proceedings with the eyes of a falcon, not daring to blink. The torch stood ready in his hand. But though he'd never admit it to Miriel, he had little faith in the long row of sticks set along the crest of the hill. How could a few powders from the kitchen rolled up in the pages of a desecrated Bible do more than incite the wrath of a vengeful God?

Yet he did as Miriel wished, for what other choice did he have? They were three against many, and in his heart, Rand knew she was right. Even if he'd been able to convince Lord Morbroch 'twas not The Shadow he'd caught after all, 'twould have changed naught. The man was eager for a scapegoat, mostly to appease his fellow lords. And the fact that the outlaw was a strange-looking old man from a far-off land no doubt made his execution all the more palatable.

Still, Rand hated the fact that he'd left Miriel alone down there to battle the whole of Morbroch while he played Prometheus upon the hill.

Rand narrowed his eyes. The rope was about Sung Li's neck now. The executioner stepped back. In another moment...

The man gave a shout, the driver cracked his whip, and the cart bolted forward.

Sung Li's feet were dangling only an instant when a black figure descended the hanging rope, slicing through the bonds around his wrists. With amazing agility for his age, Sung Li swung his freed arms up, seizing the rope above his head before it could strangle him and scrambling up it until he disappeared into the tree.

That was Rand's signal. Walking slowly along the row, he touched the burning brand to the pieces of coated twine, one by one.

The first sharp hiss almost startled him out of his braies. When he cast a glance over his shoulder, he saw a bright flash of flame, and the stick shot up with as much force as if 'twas fired by an archer, then sailed down like a falling star.

An instant later, the second shot up as well. This time, he watched as it arced high into the air. Sparks and flame and smoke made a trail across the morning sky.

As he paused to watch, the third followed closely thereafter in a burst of fire, then the fourth, with a fierce sizzle, causing the castle folk to start shouting in panic. When the fifth almost exploded upon his foot, Rand realized he shouldn't have stopped walking. The small beasts were closing in on him, nipping at his heels with their fiery teeth.

He increased his pace, lighting the sticks in a steady rhythm that kept the sky full of the most incredible explosions and crackles and puffs of smoke, as if some horrific dragon swooped over Morbroch, raining fire upon the countryside.

The horse spooked and bolted, dragging the cart, rumbling and skittering over the rocky road, all the way back to the castle. The crowd scattered like mice before a cat, screaming and shrieking, racing, tripping, half-tumbling down the hillside as they ran in terror from the smoke and flames. Like bats from hell, the projectiles streaked in every direction, popping and whistling and spitting flame, filling the air with noxious fumes.

Rand couldn't help but grin at the glorious chaos he'd wrought. And for one mad moment, he didn't care what he'd promised Miriel. These amazing weapons, like lightning and thunder all in one, were too magnificent to keep a secret.

"What the bloody hell was that?" Helena asked Deirdre, stopping in her tracks on the forest trail.

Deirdre frowned, one hand on the hilt of her sword. "It sounded like..."

Before she could finish, another unearthly whistle rent the air. Then another. And another.

Helena drew her blade. "'Tis coming from Morbroch."

The two sisters exchanged grave looks, then bolted forward along the path. 'Twasn't for naught they'd stolen away from Rivenloch under the noses of their husbands, tracked Miriel for three days, and now charged onward, fully armed and ready for battle. No matter what Miriel called herself, no matter how expert a warrior she was, they had always come to the defense of their little sister, and they weren't about to stop now.

But when they reached the place where the trees

thinned and the trail emerged on the hill above Morbroch, they could do little more than stand with their mouths agape and stare in awe.

People were tearing across the field toward the castle, howling as if their hair were on fire. The sky looked like a vision of Hades, filled with toxic smoke and some strange sort of devilish locusts that buzzed and spit fire as they dove this way and that in pursuit of the fleeing castle folk.

Not fifty yards to their right, Deirdre and Helena discovered the source of the monstrous swarm of insects. Rand, his face lit up with diabolical glee, was setting fire to a row of sticks that sizzled and shot up into the air at the touch of flame, like bolts from a bow.

"What the Devil...?" Helena said.

Then Deirdre elbowed her and nodded to the pair of wretches scrambling up the hill toward them. "Miriel," she breathed.

"Lucifer's ballocks, is that Sung Li?"

Chapter 27

Rand crowed with triumph as Miriel and Sung Li came racing up the rise, looking none the worse for wear. It had worked. Their plan had worked. The folk of Morbroch, thinking they were being assailed by some unholy plague, had fled like sinners for their lives.

"Miriel!" came a feminine shout from behind him.

He whipped his head about. "Helena?" He scowled in surprise. "Deirdre? What the bloody hell...?"

Rand stood, flummoxed, still holding the burning brand, while the three sisters collided in victorious reunion, hugging and grinning and all talking at once. He shook his head. He supposed the Warrior Maids of Rivenloch were going to take credit for Miriel's rescue now.

"All this," Deirdre was asking Miriel as she gestured to the smoky sky, "just to recover Father's silver?"

Miriel shrugged. "I couldn't leave Sung Li behind."

"By the Saints," Helena breathed in wonder. "Sung Li's a man."

Miriel attempted to level a stern frown at Deirdre. "But what are you doing here? I told you I didn't need your help."

"Oh, we didn't come to help," Deirdre assured her. "We came to watch."

"Deirdre," Helena whispered, tugging on her sister's sleeve, "Sung Li's a man."

Rand cleared his throat. "Well, now you've watched. I suggest we resume our escape."

No one was paying the least bit of attention to him.

"After all," Deirdre said, "I've never actually seen The Shadow in action."

"Aside from my knocking you on your arse," Miriel teased.

"Oh, aye, aside from that."

"Miriel," Helena hissed. "Miriel. Your maidservant—"

"Aye," Sung Li bit out impatiently. "We all know Sung Li is a man."

"Ladies," Rand tried again.

Deirdre finally noted the bruises on Miriel's face. "Oh, Miri, what happened to you?"

"'Tis naught. Just a few scratches I—"

"Scratches?" Rand burst out, finally garnering their attention. "'Tis more than scratches. I was fighting for my . . ." He trailed off, suddenly realizing 'twould be a grave mistake to let the two sword-wielding sisters know that he was the one who'd inflicted those injuries upon their darling Miriel.

But their suspicions had already been roused. Helena's weapon was halfway out of its sheath.

"Did you do this to my sister?"

Miriel pushed Helena's hand back down. "Helena, you don't know the whole—"

Now Deirdre was skewering him with a glare. "If you touched one hair on her head—"

"Deirdre, do not," Miriel pleaded. "I'll explain everything."

Rand cast a glance down the hill again.

The knights of Morbroch were no longer terrified by the unearthly assault. The bravest men had armed themselves and were now ascending the hill, prepared to challenge whatever hellish beast threatened Morbroch.

"Run!" Rand yelled at the women.

They stopped their chatter and looked at him as if he were addled.

"Run!" he shouted again.

Still they stood their ground. What the Devil was wrong with them?

Of course, he realized. He'd made a poor choice of words. Saying "run" to a warrior woman was like saying "surrender" to a knight.

"Hurry!" he amended. "They're coming. Take Sung Li to safety."

With a verifying glance down the hill, they complied, bolting into the woods.

Then, with a final headlong rush, Rand lit the rest of the *huo yao*. The sound was incredible, like a whole row of trebuchets firing rocks upon a castle wall in rapid succession. As if Hephaestus were forging armor upon his great anvil over Morbroch, sparks flew everywhere, their brilliance rivaling the sun.

There was no time to see what effect this climactic series of explosions had upon the knights. Rand had to join the other fugitives. He lit the final stick, tossed down the torch, which guttered out upon the damp heath, and made his escape into the forest through the concealing veil of smoke.

Why he imagined he'd get a word in between the excited palavering of the sisters, he didn't know. They were clearly too busy untangling years of secrets to pay heed to what he was saying.

"So in all this time," Deirdre said, "Father hasn't lost a penny?"

"Not a penny."

Helena murmured, "And Sung Li. Has he been a man all along?"

"Of course," Miriel said with a laugh.

"He was your teacher, wasn't he?" Deirdre guessed.

"Aye."

"I wish you'd told us," Helena said with a pout.

"Amazing," Deirdre marveled. "Sir Rand kept tracking The Shadow, never realizing he was on the trail of his own ladylove."

Helena laughed and clapped Miriel on the shoulder. "And she had the ballocks to leave him a silver coin."

"What about your collection of weapons?" Deirdre asked. "Do you actually know how to use them?"

Miriel nodded.

Helena's eyes lit up. "You must show us, Miri. Promise."

Sung Li didn't bother trying to interject any words of wisdom as they hurried along. Nearly an hour into the journey, he finally remarked upon Rand's injuries. "So what happened to you?"

"The Shadow happened to me," he replied.

"Hmph." Then a smile of pride mixed with something wicked slowly curved Sung Li's lips. "You are lucky you are still alive."

Rand nodded. He knew just what Sung Li meant. If Miriel hadn't had one tiny sliver of love left for him, he might lie dead now.

But so might Sung Li.

"You are lucky as well."

Sung Li raised his head proudly, like a man speaking of his daughter. "Miriel has a strong heart."

"And a big one," Rand said, placing a hand on the smaller man's shoulder. "Big enough for the both of us."

So began the peace between Sung Li and Rand. Indeed, while the sisters chatted on and on, marveling over Miriel's hidden talents, the two men spoke of more practical matters.

By the end of the fugitives' long journey, when they drew close to Rivenloch, they'd come to at least a tentative agreement as to what would and would not be revealed about their grand adventure. Rand's true identity would be uncovered, but Sung Li would remain Miriel's maid-servant. As for The Shadow, his disappearance would remain a mystery, and, of course, there would be no mention of *huo yao*.

A hundred beeswax candles filled the great hall of Rivenloch with golden light and scented the air with a summery warmth that belied the November fog lurking beyond the stone walls. Miriel, dressed in the ruby sur-coat Sung Li had insisted she wear for luck, sat beside her new husband at their wedding feast, gazing fondly now and then at the silver knot encircling her finger, as pleased as a knight with a new sword.

Course after course of delectable fare arrived from the kitchen—broiled venison, trout with galentyne, civey of hare, mushroom pasties, roast leeks and onions, flaky apple coffyns, fig and raisin cream, pokerounce dripping with honey. But of course, everything was apportioned and accounted for by Miriel herself.

Merry music filled the hall, the notes of harp and gittern and psaltery following after the pipe and tabor like noisy sparrows making chase in a spring forest. Boniface sang roundelays of tender romance and lusty adventure, and several wee children, more excited than hungry, abandoned their places at the table to dance and twirl before the consort.

Forsooth, Miriel might have been tempted to join them in their carefree celebration if she hadn't been indulging in some clandestine revelry of her own beneath the table.

She fought back a startled gasp as Rand's fingers dragged up another inch of her gown, dangerously close to revealing her thigh.

Not to be outdone, she repaid him in kind, working his surcoat slowly upward until her fingertips tapped idly on his bare kneecap.

His mouth twitched, but with his free hand, he lifted his flagon of honey mead as if naught untoward was going on. "A salute to my lovely new bride. Without her, I would dwell," he announced, "in shadow."

Miriel's eyes widened at his risky choice of words. But none seemed to notice. Everyone raised their cups in accord, echoing his sentiments.

Miriel almost spit mead when Rand's palm slipped brazenly up over her knee to settle on her naked thigh.

Recovering quickly, she gave him a wicked glance and

proposed a toast of her own. "And here's to my worthy bridegroom. As the Chinese say, *Wo xiang gen ni shang chuang.*"

At the next table, Sung Li choked on his supper, initiating a fit of coughing. Miriel beamed at Rand, raising her cup with one hand and venturing boldly up his naked leg with the other.

While the crowd cheered, Rand leaned close and whispered, "Dare I ask what that means, my sweet?"

When she breathed the suggestive translation into his ear, he made a curious strangling sound. Determined not to lose his composure, he somehow managed to swallow a calming draught of mead. But there was no hiding the desire glazing his eyes at her blatant invitation.

Like well-matched warriors at an impasse, each held the other at bay now, their fingers mere inches away from rendering their opponent helpless.

Meanwhile, the castle folk continued in their celebration, unaware of the silent battle raging beneath their noses. Sung Li shot Miriel a severe glare for her vulgar toast. Lord Gellir supped blithely on, likely unaware that he witnessed the marriage of the last of his daughters, yet enjoying the festive atmosphere. Lucy, newly wed herself, clung to her beloved Rauve like dew to a thistle. Deirdre and Helena gave Miriel sly glances, as if they knew that the hot Rivenloch blood flowing through her veins wouldn't keep her at the table much longer.

Forsooth, the lust between Miriel and Rand *was* simmering, dangerously close to boiling, mostly because of their promise to Sung Li. The old man had insisted upon their chastity for the last fortnight, babbling some nonsense about abstinence increasing the power of their offspring. Given the circumstances of Sung Li's sacrifice and his long and loyal service to Miriel, they'd honored his request. But now that they were wed, and Rand's wounds had healed, Miriel could scarcely wait to climb beneath the linens with her new husband.

Rand's thoughts were apparently aligned with hers. He raised his flagon again in her honor. "My dear bride, may this tiny bud of love..." With unerring stealth, his fingers slipped through her woman's curls, parting her nether lips to light upon the very bud of which he spoke. "... bloom into a perfect flower of marriage."

She couldn't speak. She couldn't breathe. She could hardly think while his fingers rested upon her, unmoving, as if daring her to writhe beneath his touch. Her cheeks flushed hot, and she prayed the guests would think it simply a maiden's blush.

Somehow she managed to swallow a bracing gulp of mead. Then, her heart set on delicious revenge, she returned his favor, lifting her cup. "Dearest husband, my love for you grows by the moment so that my heart..." She stared pointedly into his wary eyes as she let her hand slip beneath his surcoat to boldly invade his trews, capturing the engorged treasure within. "... my heart swells nigh to bursting."

His shudder was so slight as to be invisible, his quiet groan imperceptible to all except Miriel, who secretly reveled in her victory.

Yet that victory came with a price. When she saw the smoky longing in his eyes, the subtle flare of his nostrils, the quickened breath between his parted lips, it increased her own craving. 'Twas all she could do to resist diving beneath the table at once and having her way with him.

"My love..." he croaked beneath the ongoing chatter of the castle folk, "take care you do not—"

Suddenly, the door to the great hall swung violently open, throwing a wedge of harsh gray light into the chamber and banging hard against the stone wall. Even before the fog had a chance to swirl into the room, Miriel and Rand had abandoned their mischief and, along with most of the knights of Rivenloch, sprung to their feet, weapons drawn.

"What is the meaning of this?" the invader bellowed.

The breath froze in Miriel's throat, as if the chill mist had crystallized it there. 'Twas the Lord of Morbroch. He'd come with his men.

Bloody hell.

Was their marriage to be ruined before it had yet begun? Had the Lord of Morbroch discovered the trickery played upon him? Did he realize that Rand had deceived him? Had he returned for Sung Li? Had he come for *her*?

Rand, his protective instincts in play, hauled her behind him, out of sight.

Miriel, her instincts just as strong, stepped out from behind him again, wrapping a ready hand around the hilt of the *bay sow* hidden up her sleeve.

"Morbroch!" Lord Gellir called out cheerily, unaware of the tension in the room. "Welcome!"

Morbroch entered the hall, his men close behind him, while the Rivenloch knights waited in wary silence. The candles flickered as if in fear, and even the hounds whimpered uneasily.

Miriel glanced quickly at Sung Li. What if Morbroch saw him? Would he be fooled by the maidservant guise? Sweet Mary, if he recognized Sung Li, if he revealed him as The Shadow...

But to Miriel's surprise, when Sung Li looked back at her, his face was as calm as a winter pond.

"You *do* remember me!" Morbroch thundered back at Lord Gellir.

"Of course I—"

"And yet you do not invite me to the wedding?"

Miriel blinked. Had she heard him rightly? She exchanged fleet glances with her sisters, who looked as baffled as she was.

Morbroch sniffed, highly offended. He brushed the moisture from his cloak as he strode forward. "You realize, do you not, 'twas by my design, this alliance between your daughter and Rand la Nuit."

She briefly caught Rand's eye. A tiny furrow creased his brow.

"Rand la Nuit?" Lord Gellir paused, his cup of honey mead halfway to his mouth. His white brows shot up, then knitted in perplexity. "Rand la Nuit? Isn't he that mercenary?"

"Not anymore, Father," Deirdre assured him, patting him on the arm. "He's Miriel's husband and one of Rivenloch's knights now."

"That's right, my lord," Pagan said firmly, more to Morbroch than to Lord Gellir. "He's one of us."

The Lord of Morbroch, undaunted by the less-than-hospitable welcome, elbowed his way through the crowd. "Fear not," he grumbled irritably. "I've not come to... disrupt your celebration." He stopped before Rand. "I've only come to deliver a wedding gift. It seems you left Morbroch in such haste to return to your bride, Sir Rand, that you left something behind."

Beside her, Rand stiffened.

Morbroch reached beneath his cloak and tossed a bag of coins onto the table before Rand. "Your reward?"

Rand had to choose his words carefully. Everyone knew that he'd been paid to capture The Shadow. But those involved had agreed to omit the details of the outlaw's escape. "You owe me naught. I heard The Shadow slipped the hangman's noose."

Morbroch's laugh was a bark. "The hangman's noose mayhap, but..." Then he frowned. "Did his sister not tell you?"

"His sister?" Miriel asked.

"The Shadow's sister," Morbroch said impatiently. "You know, the..." He scoured the room. Then his gaze settled, and he nodded toward Sung Li. "Her."

"The Shadow's *sister*," Miriel repeated, giving her *xiansheng* an accusatory glance. Sung Li had apparently been up to something devious.

"Did she not tell you?" Morbroch asked.

"Tell us?" Rand echoed, looking expectantly at Sung Li.

"Nay?" Morbroch brought his hands abruptly together with a loud clap, startling everyone, then began to rub them together with glee. "Then I've quite an amazing tale for you, lords and ladies."

Miriel, her guard relaxing for the moment, unclasped her knife. All around her, weapons found their sheaths again.

"Of course," Morbroch said with a sigh, "the tale would be much better told had I an ale to wet my tongue."

The castle folk crowded along the benches to make room for the knights of Morbroch. Fortunately, Miriel had planned for an abundance of provender, so Rivenloch was able to offer hospitality to the unexpected guests.

When all were seated, they were treated to Morbroch's account of The Shadow's escape, a story so greatly exaggerated that it left Miriel squirming.

"I wouldn't call it an escape," Morbroch said, shaking his head. "Nay, not at all. That black creature that slithered out of the tree was one of Satan's serpents, come to retrieve a minion of Lucifer himself."

Miriel skewered Sung Li with a glare, but her *xiansheng* seemed completely unperturbed. Forsooth, if she didn't know better, she'd swear he was smiling.

As the story continued, it became more and more obvious what that cunning Sung Li had done. He must have traveled back to Morbroch on his own, dressed as a maidservant, on the pretense of finding out what had become of his "brother," The Shadow.

When the story was related to him by the people of Morbroch, Sung Li had simply filled in the gaps of understanding regarding the curious aftermath. Morbroch and the other lords, unable to explain the strange occurrence, embraced Sung Li's explanation as the truth.

"The outlaw roused the wrath of the great Dragon of China," Morbroch said, widening his eyes dramatically. "The beast swooped down upon the hanging tree, snarling and spitting fire, and snatched up The Shadow in his horrible claws to deliver him back to Hell. The sky was filled with thunder and lightning, moon and sun all at once, and the light of a thousand stars as the great Dragon raged and shrieked and roared across the heavens. At last, in a cloud of poisonous smoke and with a mighty swish of his terrible tail, he ascended into the clouds with the doomed Shadow, never to be seen again."

A long silence ensued. Miriel had pressed her fingers

to her lips, pretending astonishment when she felt laughter bubbling in her mouth. From the corner of her eye, she saw her sisters struggled with their amusement as well. Sung Li gazed on with smug satisfaction, as if her imaginary wicked brother had deserved no less. As for Rand, his eyes gleamed dangerously at the fanciful account. No doubt he was reliving his role as the great Dragon.

Again and again the tale was told. After the tables were cleared, and everyone had their fill of dancing, when all had gathered around the great hearth in the midst of the hall, still the story circulated. All of the Morbroch knights had been there, and each had his own unique version of the incident. The people of Rivenloch listened in rapt awe, marveling at the heretofore unknown magnificence of their outlaw. Boniface even composed a verse on the spot to honor the event.

But while she should have been grateful for Sung Li's stroke of genius, Miriel found herself growing more and more glum and troubled as the night wore on.

When Rand left her for a moment to visit the garderobe, Sung Li joined her. "It is your wedding night," he scolded. "You should be happy."

Miriel frowned. "You killed The Shadow."

Sung Li shrugged. "It was time for him to die."

"But now how will I balance the accounts? You know how my father wagers. The coffers will run dry if—"

"As long as your *yin* and *yang* are in balance as husband and wife, the accounts will remain so as well."

Not in a mood for Sung Li's indecipherable advice, Miriel snatched him by the front of his kirtle, and bit out, "What the bloody hell is that supposed to—"

Sung Li reached up calmly and pinched hard at the flesh between her thumb and finger, making her yelp and release him. "The reward your husband earned for catching The Shadow will greatly *un*balance the accounts. It may take years of losing at the gaming tables for your father to put them right again."

It took a moment for Miriel to understand. When the truth finally penetrated, that Rand had been paid handsomely for The Shadow, she raised her brows in wonder.

"However," Sung Li added as Rand entered the great hall again, "if the accounts should become unbalanced again..." He gave her a sly smile. "There is always my *second* brother."

"Second brother?"

"The Ghost."

Miriel smiled conspiratorially. Somehow she suspected there would be no need for The Ghost. Still, 'twas good to know if times became desperate, if she was forced to turn to a life of crime...

"It is time," Sung Li said.

"Time?"

"You will make your babe now."

Miriel's jaw dropped. "Sung Li!" She furrowed her brow. "Do not deign to tell me when I will and will not..."

But when Rand swept up, grinning wide enough to show off his twinkling eyes and irresistible dimples, and wrapped an arm around her shoulders, she had to admit that the prospect of making a babe was indeed tempting.

* * *

Rand kissed his bride's damp forehead as they lay in the sweet afterglow of coupling. He wondered if Sung Li's prophecy was right, if they would make a babe this night.

It didn't matter. If not this night, then the next. They had a whole lifetime of lovemaking ahead of them.

Miriel nuzzled his shoulder, murmuring, "Sung Li was wrong, you know."

"Wrong?"

Where he still nestled within her, she tightened around him, whispering, "'Tis The Shadow that has swallowed The Night."

He drew a lusty breath between his teeth as his cock awakened yet again to her coaxing. Soon the warm coals of their desire were stirred to life, igniting and exploding into searing flames of passion.

When they finally fell back to earth, like spent fragments of falling stars, Rand realized there was one thing Sung Li had been right about. Their joining was as fiery and magical as *huo yao*.

Surely the child forged from such a union would be likewise unique—as strong and fearless as his father, as brave and clever as his mother. Sung Li had promised to take the babe under his wing, to teach him, or her, the Chinese arts of war, just as he had Miriel.

Miriel burrowed affectionately against Rand's shoulder, and he buried his nose in her silken tresses, breathing in the soft, unforgettable scent.

Miriel was a sweet prize indeed. She was beautiful and wise, headstrong and brilliant, kind and coy and charming. And, he thought as his gaze caught on the gentle flicker of candlelight reflected in the array of silver blades on the wall, as fierce a warrior as he'd ever met.

He grinned. Just as he'd needlessly feared that Miriel would scorn his mercenary past, she'd assumed he'd be appalled to learn she was capable of wielding those weapons.

Naught could be further from the truth.

She'd forgiven him for hunting her down.

He'd forgiven her for attempting to slay him.

And once he recovered from the shock of being viciously attacked by his own betrothed, his surprise turned quickly to respect and admiration. He'd learned something from Miriel and her sisters. Never again would he scoff at a woman with a blade.

Miriel sighed.

"What is it?" he murmured.

"I wish Sung Li hadn't killed The Shadow."

"You liked life as an outlaw?"

She shrugged. "Just once, I would have liked my father to see me."

"I think he knew."

She lifted her head. "What?"

"I think he knew you were The Shadow. He once said to me, 'The Shadow walks among us, under our noses.'" He grinned. "I think he knew all along. Indeed, I suspect 'tis why he lost so often at wagering. He wanted to keep his outlaw daughter in fighting form."

She smiled then in wonder and fell quiet, but he still sensed a melancholy to her silence. Now that The Shadow was dead, he supposed Miriel's talents would go to waste.

As Rand lay there for several moments, admiring the display of exotic weapons on the wall, a spark of a clever idea began to smoke at the back of his brain, burning away like a black powdered fuse.

"Miriel, are you awake?"

"Mm?"

"I've been thinking."

"Aye?"

"I've decided the mystery of *huo yao* is too precious to allow it to disappear in secrecy."

That brought her wide-awake. "What?" She speared him with a threatening glare. "You promised!"

He shrugged. "But do you not see? That knowledge would make Rivenloch an impenetrable fortress." He let a gleam come into his eyes. "Its knights would be undefeatable," he reasoned, "its lands unconquerable. Rivenloch would become the roaring dragon of all Scotland." He shook his head. "Nay, I don't see how, in good conscience, I can hold my tongue."

Whether 'twas the telltale twitch of his lip, the merry sparkle of his gaze, or simply that she knew him too well, Miriel quickly guessed his game.

"I see," she said, feigning a sigh of defeat as she settled back onto the coverlet. "And what would it take to convince you to hold your tongue? A purse full of silver? A new coat of mail? My firstborn?"

"Teach me."

She craned her neck to look at him. "Teach you?"

"Teach me the ways of Chinese warfare."

"You're serious."

"Of course." He grimaced in false regret. "Unless you wish me to reveal the secret of *huo yao*."

She arched a brow. "'Tis extortion, you know."

"Aye."

* * *

Miriel turned her back on Rand and let out a long-suffering sigh. "Very well."

Forsooth, naught thrilled her more than the prospect of sharing her knowledge with Rand. Though she was loath to admit it, being The Shadow had been an enjoyable diversion. Now that Sung Li had seen fit to kill the outlaw, some of the purpose had vanished out of her life. Teaching would give new direction for her talents.

Of course, she wouldn't tell Rand that. She'd pretend 'twas an awful inconvenience. And he'd pretend revealing the secret of *huo yao* was a terrible temptation. They were incurable liars, the two of them.

But despite their lies and trickery and word twisting, despite the coy coaxing and sly manipulation that came to them by nature, one thing between them remained true. They loved each other with purity of heart, clarity of spirit. Their passion might spark and flash and flare like the fleeting flames of *huo yao,* but their love would burn as slowly and sweetly as a steadfast fire on the hearth.

She grinned like a kitten with cream as Rand drew her back into his arms, pressing his loins warmly against her buttocks. Nested beneath the furs as snugly as a pair of bronze *tuns,* Chinese shields, they gazed out the open shutters toward the clear night sky beyond.

Rivenloch didn't need the power of *huo yao,* Miriel realized. Between the skills of the knights of Cameliard and the Warrior Maids of Rivenloch, the renown mercenary—Rand la Nuit, and the infamous outlaw—The Shadow, the keep would be well protected for years.

And if Sung Li was right, if Miriel and Rand spawned

a whole new brood of gifted warriors, Rivenloch would stand for all eternity.

Somewhere against the black sky, a bright star streaked across the heavens, leaving a long dragon tail of sparks.

But the lovers were too engaged to notice. The Shadow had swallowed The Night again. The first of the next generation of Rivenloch warriors had been conceived.

❧

About the Author

Born in Paradise, California, Sarah McKerrigan has embraced her inner Gemini by leading an eclectic life. As a teen, she danced with the Sacramento Ballet, worked in her father's graphic arts studio, and composed music for award-winning science films. She sang arias in college, graduating with a degree in Music, then toured with an all-girl rock band for CBS Records. She once played drums for a Tom Jones video and is currently a voice-over actress with credits including "Star Wars" audio adventures, JumpStart educational CDs, Diablo and Starcraft video games, and the MTV animated series, "The Maxx." She now indulges her lifelong love of towering castles, trusty swords, and knights (and damsels) in shining armor by writing historical romances featuring kick-butt heroines. She is married to a rock star, is the proud guardian of two nerdy kids and a pug named Worf, and lives in a part of Los Angeles where nobody thinks she's weird.

THE DISH

Where authors give you the inside scoop!

♥ ♥ ♥ ♥ ♥ ♥ ♥ ♥ ♥ ♥ ♥ ♥ ♥ ♥

From the desk of Samantha Graves

There are some characters who will haunt a writer until their story is told. Raven Callahan from SIGHT UNSEEN (on sale now) was one such character.

She was born from a One-Page Workshop exercise at my local writing chapter, where she fended off an attacker in an underwater cave. Call it intuition or inspiration, I decided that psychic touch was the edge Raven needed to be a world-class art thief and give her a humanity she didn't always welcome. Fearless, capable, and fiercely independent, I knew I had a character I would never forget. But when the workshop was over, I filed her scene into the "Someday" folder on my desk as other obligations called.

For three years, Raven waited impatiently for me to create a story worthy of her courage and skill, full of high-stakes adventure, danger, and a hero who would challenge her at every turn, yet accept her just the way she was—the one man she couldn't walk away from. Enter David Maddox, an ex-cop surviving on guilt and vengeance. With nothing left to lose, he needed redemption as much as Raven did, even if she would *never* admit it. They would learn the hard way that the only thing they could depend on was each other.

But I have to admit that half the fun of writing this book was the opportunity to research some remarkable locales I have always wanted to visit myself. From the excitement of Miami to the tropical paradise of Key West to the sultry heat of Havana, I made their adventure mine.

So now their story is told in SIGHT UNSEEN, and although my "Someday" file doesn't look much smaller, Raven Callahan can finally rest.

Happy reading!

Samantha Graves

www.samanthagraves.com

❤ ❤ ❤ ❤ ❤ ❤ ❤ ❤ ❤ ❤ ❤ ❤

From the desk of Sarah McKerrigan

In KNIGHT'S PRIZE (on sale now), the final chapter in my Warrior Maids of Rivenloch trilogy, Rand la Nuit, infamous mercenary and expert swordsman, hunts the elusive outlaw known as The Shadow. But who is the mysterious, quick-as-lightning thief? And what is sweet Miriel of Rivenloch hiding from him? The quest draws Rand closer and closer to a shocking truth—that the seemingly innocent woman he's falling hopelessly in love with knows more than she's letting on about The Shadow.

Writing KNIGHT'S PRIZE presented a fascinating challenge for me—intertwining the cultures of East and West in a medieval setting. The Silk Road trade route was established at this time, so I imagined that some martial arts might have been imported along with the silk. Thus was born a very different type of damsel in shining armor—a medieval heroine who kicks butt Chinese-style!

Why martial arts? As a kid, I always thought Kato was way cooler than The Green Hornet. My guilty pleasure is Jackie Chan movies, which I watch with my teenage son. And I could watch that beautifully choreographed foyer fight scene from *The Matrix Reloaded* a hundred times.

The best thing about martial arts is that size doesn't matter. I learned that as a pint-sized girl, studying judo. It's all about momentum, strategy, grace, speed, agility, and surprise, using an attacker's own strength against him. And as you can imagine, martial arts are also the great equalizer of the sexes!

As a reader, I love surprises, so I've packed plenty of them into KNIGHT'S PRIZE. No one is who they seem to be, twists and turns abound, and the story has an explosive ending! The romance and adventure should keep you up all night. Let me know if it did at www.sarahmckerrigan.com.

Sarah McKerrigan

♥ ♥ ♥ ♥ ♥ ♥ ♥ ♥ ♥ ♥ ♥ ♥ ♥ ♥

From the desk of Elizabeth Hoyt

Gentle Reader,

Whilst going through some old papers I found the pamphlet below. Although the author chose to remain anonymous, I have reason to believe that Lady Georgina Maitland, my heroine from THE LEOPARD PRINCE (on sale now), in fact wrote it.

Advice for the Landowning Lady of Means on the Hiring of Land Stewards

by an Anonymous Lady Who Knows

1. When hiring a steward the genteel lady should keep in mind that there are many Aesthetically Pleasing gentlemen who are just as much in need of work as those that are older, surlier, and not nearly as pleasant to look upon. It is your duty to hire them.

2. The Feminine Employer should remember that it is she who is in charge. Do not be afraid to issue orders to your Male Employee, although there are times when it may be to your advantage to permit your steward to issue orders to *you*.

3. Do not under any circumstances enter into an Intimate Relationship with your land steward.

4. However, should you succumb to broad shoulders, a dry tone, and a knowing gaze, do try to be discreet.

5. Whatever you do, do not let your brothers become aware of the liaison.

6. Or your sister.

7. Or your aunt, your family, your friends, your lady's maid, or indeed any of the other servants, passing strangers, and the public in general. *Discretion* should be the watchword for the Genteel Lady desiring Further Acquaintance with her land steward.

8. It is This Author's opinion that it is of Paramount Importance that the land steward be skilled in kissing and other Intimate Arts. She cannot stress this particular point enough.

9. The Lady of Means should try to refrain from mooning about and thinking obsessively of her land steward. This behavior is apt to attract the notice of Other People (see points 5, 6, and 7 above).

10. Finally, the Genteel Lady Landowner must never, *ever*, fall in love with her land steward. That way lies disaster—or at least a very good book.

Yours Most Sincerely,

Elizabeth Hoyt

www.elizabethhoyt.com

Medieval Scotland has never
been more romantic...

Amanda Scott

"A most gifted storyteller."
—*Romantic Times BOOKclub Magazine*

PRINCE OF DANGER
0-446-61668-0

LORD OF THE ISLES
0-446-61461-0

HIGHLAND PRINCESS
0-446-61462-9

Sue-Ellen Welfonder

"A writer on the way to stardom."
—*Romantic Times BOOKclub Magazine*

WEDDING FOR A KNIGHT
0-446-61381-9

MASTER OF THE HIGHLANDS
0-446-61233-2

BRIDE OF THE BEAST
0-446-61232-4

Sarah McKerrigan

"A fresh, exciting voice!"
—*Romantic Times BOOKclub Magazine*

LADY DANGER
0-446-61617-6

CAPTIVE HEART
0-446-61616-8

AVAILABLE AT BOOKSTORES FROM WARNER BOOKS.